DOUBLE CROSSING VAN DINE

Introduction by
Catriona McPherson

Edited by
Donna Andrews, Greg Herren, and Art Taylor

DOUBLE CROSSING VAN DINE

Introduction by
Catriona McPherson

Edited by
Donna Andrews, Greg Herren, and Art Taylor

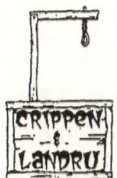

CRIPPEN & LANDRU PUBLISHERS
Cincinnati, Ohio
2025

For information contact:

Crippen & Landru, Publishers
P. O. Box 532057
Cincinnati, OH 45253 USA

Web: www.crippenlandru.com
E-mail: Info@crippenlandru.com

ISBN (softcover): 978-1-936363-96-4
ISBN (clothbound): 978-1-936363-97-1

First Edition: August 2025

10 9 8 7 6 5 4 3 2 1

Contents

S.S. Van Dine, The Introduction by Catriona McPherson

S.S. Van Dine is famous for two things. Or, to be completely honest, when I gratefully accepted the honour of writing the introduction to this anthology, I knew two things about S.S. Van Dine. He created Philo Vance and he handed down twenty rules he liked to think governed detective fiction.

But wait. Was it three things? Certainly from somewhere I had got the impression he was waspish, acerbic, unlikely to pop up on many "dream dinner party (dead or alive)" lists. And, having always been someone who doesn't suffer those who don't suffer fools gladly gladly, I imagined that the more I found out about him the more my feelings towards him would cool.

Wrong. In fact, the more I found out about Willard Huntingdon Wright, art critic, literary editor, literary biographer and philosopher – not to mention his crime-writing alter ego, the more I wished I could host that dinner party and invite him. Failing that, I'd be prepared to take him in and give him some warm milk and a cuddle. He appears to have been a man never at ease with himself, needing the income from commercial writing but despising the craft itself. How I wish I could sit him next to Dorothy L Sayers, hardly a woman who wore her learning lightly, and have her encourage him to enjoy the low-brow end of life, guilt-free.

We've got enough trouble without causing it for ourselves, I'd tell him when he had his mouth full and couldn't argue. Because S.S. was smacked down time after time by viperish critics, especially when he tried to innovate and elevate, and it's painful to any genre writer to see the ways in which he was the most poisonous Van Dine critic of all.

Mind you, he wasn't one for kindness when he levelled his gaze at others either and, if his disdain for detective fiction was sharp, it was nothing to the level of contempt in which he held romance. Certainly if he had a second nom de plume for writing love stories, it has gone with him to his grave.

In his wide-ranging career, Van Dine – or rather Wright – did have triumphs though. He succeeded in raising the profile of avant-garde art in the American consciousness, and he contributed to the patriotic sport of taking England down a peg, with his critique of the Encyclopaedia Britannica. But for every hit, there was a corresponding miss: his attempt to do for Nietzsche what he did for abstract art failed and he had the misfortune to be a devotee of all things German, at one of the two times in the twentieth century when such an attitude was likely to raise eyebrows and hackles.

Would all the bouquets and brickbats, both outgoing and incoming, have troubled him less if he had had a happy home life? Unfortunately, we can't know. He did not enjoy good mental health and relied on alcohol (among other things) for respite from his troubles. I imagine also – without much evidence, but ask a fiction writer to turn her mind to a biography and see what you get – that, in his last years, being married to a painter while he made his living from movie adaptations of the Philo Vance stories, he can't have been at peace. Yet again, I pine for that dream dinner party. For one thing, I'd add Judi Dench to the guest list, to talk to him about Shakespeare and Bond films and contentment. But, besides that, I'd relish the chance to talk to this intriguing individual for myself. It's beyond peculiar that someone can be so open to innovation and experiment in one artistic form and so determined to impose order on another.

Which brings us to yet another misfortune in S.S. Van Dine's varied life. A year after he gave us – for whatever reason – his twenty commandments, along came Ronald Knox and gazumped him with a snappier ten. Ten is always going resonate, commandment-wise.

And now this! Twenty tales that take his rules and break them like kindling. It's not merely the flagrant disobedience, moreover. It's the unashamed fun everyone's having in this collection. Without squeamishness or snobbishness, here are twenty little gems sparkling all over the mystery map, complete with switches, tricks, and stings in the tail.

There's verve and vividness in the meticulously drawn historical settings of a handful of the stories – including more than one butler, for an extra, cruel twist. There's glamour despite everything when Marcia Talley and Alan Orloff write about art and jewel theft. Then there's the grunge of a YMCA conjured up so completely you can smell it, courtesy of Delia Pitts. There's a sweet and soothing love story from Barb Goffman and horror delivered through clinical prose by Vaseem Kahn. Whole worlds in miniature can found among Cheryl Head's genderfluid thespians and J. C. Bernthal's sharp-elbowed journalists. There's also the unsettling realisation that Donna Andrews's world of reptile overlords is so recognisable, but to balance it there's the comfort of discovering that Gigi Pandian couldn't really cheat in a locked-room story if the devil himself was chasing her. And, as a grand finale, here comes Richie Narvaez putting the cherry on top.

That's not what S.S. Van Dine would call the final story of the collection, I'm sure. The tin lid, perhaps? The bitter end? The last straw? Because make no mistake: Double Crossing is a treat for mystery fiction fans, but it is most assuredly not what he would have wanted.

Sweet Poison by Elaine Viets

#

1. The reader must have equal opportunity with the detective for solving the mystery. All clues must be plainly stated and described.

My friend Queenie was a fallen woman, but that didn't mean she'd stoop to murder. No matter what people said.

I'm Eleanor Abramowski and Queenie Isaacs is my best friend. We grew up in the Lower East Side in the early 1900s, when that was the worst slum in New York City. Our families are Ashkenazi Jews from Poland. Everyone looks down on Ashkenazim, even other Jews.

Queenie is a year older than me. She quit school in the fourth grade and went to work in a sweatshop. I made it to the fourth grade a year later and had to quit to work in a pickle factory. My family needed the money and thought girls didn't need an education. I could read, write, and speak English, which made me more educated than my Yiddish-speaking parents.

Queenie got me tangled in a murderous mess when her Wall Street sugar daddy got clipped.

In 1921, I'd been a Florodora Girl for a year, a star chorus girl. I was fifteen. My parents disowned me as a "hoor" when I sang and danced in the Broadway smash-hit musical *Florodora*, even though I'd never been kissed. Still, anything beat being forced to marry Mateusz Metzger, the local butcher.

Queenie is sixteen. She quit the sweatshop when her own father molested her, then she lit out to work at Madame Evangeline's boarding house. "Since I'm 'ruined,'" she said, "I might as well make some money. It's easier on my back."

I wasn't quite sure why she was having back trouble, and I was afraid to ask.

We might seem young to you, but girls brought up in the New York slums get old quickly. We lived in one-room apartments crammed with a dozen family members or more. We knew what it was like to miss meals, and stretch dinner out of a handful of shriveled vegetables and puzzle bones. (Those are beef neck bones, if you've never had them.)

Girls our age quit school to work in factories and sweatshops, or to marry, and most of the married ones wound up as poor and pregnant as their mothers.

Queenie and I had managed to escape that awful fate. Though we were teenagers, our time in the school of hard knocks made us at least ten years older.

Today we were celebrating Queenie's arrangement with Walter Chandler, a former client of Madame Evangeline, in Queenie's new flat. "Walter bought me these digs," she said. "And the furniture."

"It's the berries." It was. She had brand-new walnut suites in the bedroom, dining room, and living room, upholstered in cut velvet, straight from the Sears catalogue.

"Plus he gives me three hundred a month for clothes and expenses."

I whistled. "That's more than a family man makes in a month."

"And I got three years' worth of expenses upfront."

"Walter has a big heart," I said.

"Almost as big as his wallet," Queenie said. "I think he's serious."

We didn't mention marriage. We both knew Walter was already married and would never be free.

"All I have to do is put on my glad rags twice a week and we have lunch here. I'm dessert."

She giggled. "Not bad for twenty minutes of work a week," she said. "If that."

Walter, fat, fifty, and bald, was no sheik. He was a Wall Street big cheese. "Most days he likes to talk about his latest business deals in bed," Queenie said. "I listen, rub his noggin, and make sympathetic noises."

We clinked teacups and toasted Queenie's good fortune. We were drinking gin and tonics out of bone china. Thanks to Prohibition, more booze was drunk out of teacups than that brown British dishwater the drys claimed they loved.

Queenie looked at the mantel clock and said, "Ellie! It's eleven. You better skedaddle. Walter will be here at one o'clock and I have to order his lunch and get dressed. He can't see me in a house dress."

Queenie, with her dark, curly hair and blue eyes, would look good in a burlap sack, but she took her arrangement seriously.

I was slipping into my spring coat when Queenie said, "Would you have time to pop by after your matinee? Walter's going to bring a couple of bottles of real bubbly, imported from Canada. There should be some left."

"You bet. The theater's dark tonight and I'm not turning down the chance to drink real champagne. I can come back about five."

"That's perfect," she said.

I raced back to my shared dressing room at the theater for the matinee. I had to climb into my Florodora outfit, a ruffly pink "walking dress," a style from the time of King Edward.

First, I put on the blasted corset. The whalebone stays stuck me in the ribs. My friend Doris, another Florodora Girl, laced me up, but not too tight. Otherwise I couldn't breathe. We helped each other get into our costumes.

Then I put on a corset cover, a froth of whispery petticoats, and high-button boots. I stepped into my long pink ruffled dress, but didn't pull it up yet. I still had to put on my stage makeup.

I quickly makeup, powdered my face, and added pink lipstick. patted on my Doris buttoned my dress and then I helped Doris with her costume. Next I pinned on my black picture hat, festooned with bows and pounds of black feathers, and finally pulled on my long black gloves.

Whew! I'm glad modern women don't dress like this anymore.

After a few adjustments, we heard the cry of "Places, everyone!"

Soon the curtain rose on the mythical island of Florodora, and the flower farm. For two hours, we Florodora Girls sang, danced, and smiled. When the show was over, I'd worked up quite a sweat. I didn't smell like any flower farm, that's for sure.

Backstage, a note from Queenie was on my dresser. It said: *Please come quick, Ellie. I'm in trouble.*

Doris helped me out of my dress and hung it up. I slathered on cold cream to remove my makeup and was out the door, still wearing my corset. My stays creaked as I ran for a bus to Queenie's flat, and I was out of breath when I climbed the stairs to her place.

Queenie met me at her doorway before I rang her bell, and dragged me inside. She was dressed for a formal dinner in a fringed, black satin dress, long gloves, and a diamond headband. Her face was white as flour. Her eyes were red with weeping.

"What's wrong? What happened?"

"It's Walter. He keeled over after lunch. Here! Look!"

She led me to her bedroom, where Walter was lying on the blue silk spread. His skin was a matching blue. I'd seen skin that color on a corpse before. His teeth were clenched. I leaned in and sniffed his mouth. Sure enough, I caught the odor of bitter almonds.

Walter was dead as a mackerel.

"Oh, Lord," I said. "Walter's been poisoned." I turned to my friend and asked, "Who killed him, Queenie? Was it you?"

Het blue eyes widened in shock. "No! Why would I kill Walter? He was good to me."

"Was it suicide?"

"Of course not. Walter had everything to live for. He was rich and successful. How do you know he was poisoned?" she asked between tears.

"I've seen it before. Where I used to live. Mrs. Jablonski's little boy ate rat poison, thinking it was sugar. His skin turned blue, he had trouble breathing, seizures, and then he passed out and died before we could get the doctor."

"That's exactly what happened to Walter. He just up and died."

"Someone gave him that cyanide," I said. "Tell me what happened, step by step, starting with right after I left."

"I set the table," she said, and pointed at the dining room table set for two, with a pair of massive silver candelabra and fresh roses in a vase. The candles were melted down to almost stubs.

"Walter had those flowers delivered right before he arrived," she said. "He always sends flowers on the days he dines with me.

"I got dressed in this outfit. Walter likes to dine formally."

"That dress is the cat's pajamas," I said.

She managed a lopsided smile, then said, "I ordered dinner from O'Connor's Steakhouse, as usual. I had all Walter's favorites: tenderloin with fried mushrooms, potatoes stewed in cream, and his favorite dessert, apple fritters with powdered sugar. I had the same thing, except I wanted sliced oranges for dessert."

"That lunch cost major mazuma," I said.

"It was two-fifty with tip, and Walter always tipped.

"Just before one o'clock, the food was delivered by Billy, our usual waiter. Walter arrived right after Billy brought the food. He brought two bottles of cold champagne. Dom Perignon. We drank one."

She indicated the bottle neck-down in a silver bucket by the table. Two gold-rimmed coupe glasses were still on the table. The champagne looked like the real deal, not the coffin varnish that passed for alcohol these days.

"Walter uncorked the champagne and we ate in the dining room," she said. "He was in a good mood, and we talked for hours. It was nearly three o'clock when we finished our lunch, except for dessert. Walter was tired, and said he wanted to have his dessert in bed. The apple fritters, that is."

She blushed. I laughed.

"He was feeling fine up to that point?" I asked.

"Hitting on all eight," she said. "I carried the dirty plates into the kitchen and put the coffee on. Then I brought in our coffee on a tray."

The tray was on a bedside table next to the body. "Walter was sitting up in bed. He took a big bite of an apple fritter."

Big bite? Walter demolished most of the powdered-sugared fritter in one go. He probably ate enough cyanide to kill a horse.

"That's when Walter got a funny look on his face and had trouble breathing. I thought he was having a heart attack. He was dead before I could do anything."

I looked at Walter again. He had what looked like powdered sugar on his lips. There was more on the spread.

"The cyanide was on his apple fritter," I said. "Along with the powdered sugar."

"Couldn't he taste it?"

"If he could, it was already too late. Cyanide works fast."

"What am I going to do? What do we do about Walter?" Queenie was wringing her hands.

"Did anyone see Walter come here today?" I asked.

"Billy, the server, probably passed Walter on the stairs after he delivered lunch. Besides, our lunches are charged to Walter's account at the restaurant, and I ordered his favorite foods, so they'll know he was here."

"I'm sure George O'Malley, the beat cop, saw him," Queenie said. "George keeps track of everything on his patch."

She was pacing back and forth like a caged animal. The beaded fringe clicking on her dress was driving me nuts. "Sit down," I said.

She sat on the cut-velvet couch. I poured her a stiff shot of gin from a bottle on the sideboard. "Take this to steady your nerves."

Queenie obediently downed the hooch. I joined her on the couch.

"At least two people saw Walter come in here, so we can't make him disappear," I said. "Thank heaven he died in your bed with his clothes on. You can say he got sick while eating dessert and collapsed on the bed."

"It's the bed that will cause trouble," Queenie said. "What if the newshounds get wind of this? I can see the headlines now: 'Financier Poisoned by Flapper in Ritzy Love Nest.'

"I could wind up in the big house – or do the dance."

I didn't mention that in New York, killers weren't hanged. They were fried in the electric chair.

"Okay, we're in a jam, Queenie," I said. "First, we need to keep your name out of the papers. What's an innocent reason why Walter would be at your place?"

"Well, he's a financier," she said. "What if he was financing a business for me?"

"That's good," I said. "What kind of business?"

"Well, I worked in that dress factory, so I know how to sew. And I've always wanted to open a hat shop. I trim my own hats."

"That has possibilities," I said.

Queenie opened a closet in her bedroom and said, "See? I did all these."

She already had enough hats for her own shop, including daring cloches, brimmed hats, and romantic wide-brimmed capelines for summer frocks.

"That's good," I said. "We can sell the hat shop idea. Now, do you have any cyanide in your flat?"

"No," she said.

"What about ant killer or rat poison? Those both can have cyanide."

"I use arsenic," she said. "It's safer."

"Good. The cyanide must have been on the food from the restaurant. Was anyone at O'Connor's mad enough to kill Walter?"

"No! He was a good tipper and a regular customer. They wouldn't kill a steady source of income."

"All right. We're going to have to notify the police. But first, let's get rid of the candelabra and the booze. That will get us in trouble for sure."

"You aren't going to throw out the champagne, are you?" Queenie sounded horrified.

"No, I want to hide it. Okay if I use the Victrola?"

"Actually, it's an Electrola," Queenie said.

I must have looked puzzled because she said, "An Electrola is a Victrola I don't have to wind because it's electric. The horn is inside the cabinet. There's enough room in the cabinet to hide the booze in the horn opening."

The Victrola, excuse me, Electrola, had two small doors. I slid the booze bottles inside and out of sight.

"Walter did get you the best of everything," I said.

"I'm going to miss him." She glanced sadly at the body on the bed and the tears started again. I had to snap her out of her funk.

"Queenie, you're wasting time. Change into something businesslike while I set up your hat shop display. Hurry up. We can't have Walter getting stiff on us."

"Oh, don't worry," Queenie said. "That almost never happens."

"I meant stiff as in rigor mortis. My Aunt Selma worked for Chernich, the undertaker. She told me dead people start stiffening up anywhere from two to four hours after they die. Walter's been dead at least an hour."

Queenie went to her dressing room to change while I washed the lunch dishes except for the plate with poor Walter's dessert, which I moved to the dining table. Queenie's orange slices were still on the table at her place.

I stashed the candelabra in the back of the coat closet, behind the winter clothes, then put away the freshly washed dishes and champagne glasses. The empty champagne bottle was hidden in the bottom of the trash under a pile of old newspapers and eggshells. I carried the trash to the hall and dropped it down the chute.

Next I set up the hat display, opening the hatboxes and showing each creation to best advantage. Queenie had a flair for design. When I finished, more than twenty hats graced the dining room table, the lamp tables, even the tea table. Just as I finished, Queenie emerged from her dressing room in an outfit suitable for a schoolmistress: a dove gray number with a skirt almost to her ankles and sturdy black lace-up shoes. Queenie didn't bob her hair, and she'd pulled it back into a sedate bun. Her face was makeup-free.

"Well, what do you think?" she said.

"You could have tea at the Plaza in that outfit," I said. "It's perfect. Now, before we get O'Malley, the local flatfoot, how well do you know him?"

Queenie lowered her eyes. "O'Malley passes this building twice an hour, like clockwork, when he's on duty. He warns me if there are any problems in the neighborhood. I think George is carrying a torch for me, but he's always been a perfect gentleman."

"Do you like him?"

Queenie sighed. "He's a lovely man. Black Irish. Big and strong and . . . so virile."

"Would you marry him if you could?"

"I'm not anxious to slip on the gold handcuff, but it might be nice to settle down with a good man. I have this apartment, free and clear, some diamond jewelry I could sell, and some savings. I really could start a little hat shop."

She looked dreamy, and then said, "What am I doing? Poor Walter isn't even cold yet."

"Before we get Officer O'Malley up here, does the copper know about your previous . . . uh, work?"

"You mean at Madame Evangeline's? Yes, he knows I was a pro skirt and he doesn't care. He worked our old neighborhood. He knows I had to survive."

"Okay, that's good. Now, who would want to kill Walter?"

Queenie blinked, then said, "No one. He had business rivals, but

I don't think they'd knock him off. I can't think of anyone who would want to kill Walter."

"What about his wife?" I asked.

"Hermione? She didn't care what Walter did, as long as she could spend his money on the fancy wingdings she loved to throw, with champagne towers and Paul Whiteman's Orchestra. She didn't care if Walter showed up at her blowouts, either. He didn't fit in with her society friends."

"What about you?" I asked.

"Me! Hermione wouldn't kill Walter because he had a girlfriend." Queenie laughed. "I did her a favor. Once she gave Walter an heir and a spare, Hermione decided she'd done her wifely duty and barred her bedroom door. She didn't care how much time Walter spent with me, as long as he was discreet."

"And his sons?" I asked.

"The boys are both at Harvard. As long as Walter sent them their allowance, they didn't care, either."

Queenie paused for a moment, then said, "Poor Walter was just a piggy bank for those people. I'm the only one who cared about him." A single tear trickled down her lovely face. She dabbed at it with a lace-edged handkerchief.

"One last question before we get the copper," I said. "Why didn't you have apple fritters for dessert?"

"Because, well, I'm reducing," she said. "Now that I'm getting three squares a day, I'm putting on a few pounds. I tried La Parle Obesity Soap."

"What's that?" I asked.

"It's supposed to be a miracle soap. The ads said it would reduce fat without dieting or gymnastics. All I had to do was wash with it and the excess fat would come right off."

"Sounds good."

"Except it didn't work," Queenie said. "It was expensive, too. Two dollars for two cakes and I didn't lose an ounce.

"Now, I'm dieting. When I had lunch with Walter, I'd have the steak, skip the potatoes in cream sauce and eat fruit for dessert. Just another five more pounds to lose." Queenie patted her stomach, which looked flat to me.

"Now that we have our story straight," I said, "it's time to go get your copper."

Queenie's couch overlooked the street at the front of the building. "He's walking his beat now," she said. "It won't be too long before he passes by here."

It wasn't. We waited about ten minutes before we heard someone whistling as he walked down the sidewalk.

"That's him!" Queenie was off like a shot, running down the stairs so fast I was afraid she'd break her neck. "Help! Officer O'Malley! Help, please!" she shouted.

I saw a blur of blue and flash of brass buttons as the copper came running toward Queenie. I couldn't hear what she was telling him over the traffic noise, but she was sobbing and wringing her hands while he gently patted her shoulder.

Queenie flew up the stairs to her flat, her blue eyes wide, her long dark hair escaping its severe bun. She looked beautiful in her distress.

Officer O'Malley followed. He stood in the doorway for a moment, and all I could think was "Hubba, hubba! What a hunk of man."

Queenie introduced me as her friend. The copper tipped his hat at me and then asked, "Where is Mr. Chandler?"

"On the bed," Queenie said. "That's where he fell when he got sick."

She twisted her handkerchief and cried while O'Malley examined the body, then sniffed around Walter's mouth.

"He smells like bitter almonds," he said. "Definitely cyanide. Why was he here?"

She fed O'Malley the fairytale we'd concocted about the business lunch. She showed him the hats for her mythical hat store. O'Malley clearly couldn't tell a cloche from a cabbage, but I could see he was definitely stuck on Queenie, and she had feelings for him, too. The air between them positively zinged with animal magnetism.

Queenie told him what they ate and showed him the remains of the apple fritter, dusted with powder. "I'm guessing the cyanide was in the powdered sugar," the copper said. "You both ate the same things?"

"Except for dessert," Queenie said.

"Any idea why someone would kill a powerful man like Walter Chandler?" O'Malley asked.

"Not the slightest," she said. "He was a quiet, generous gentleman."

"I'll have to search your apartment for cyanide." O'Malley sounded embarrassed.

"Help yourself," Queenie said. "I keep all the cleaning products and pesticides in the hall closet. May I fix you some coffee?"

"No, thanks," he said.

O'Malley checked the hall closet and looked in the cabinet near the sink. That was all. This had to be the lightest grilling in police history.

"Just a few more questions," he said. "Tell me about this lunch. Did you cook it yourself?"

"No," she said. "I knew Mr. Chandler liked O'Connor's Steakhouse, and ordered our meal from there. Billy the waiter brought the food here."

A flash hit me. "Queenie, what was the waiter's name?"

Queenie looked at me, wide-eyed. "I just said it. Billy. Billy Butler."

"The waiter is the killer, officer. He poisoned Walter. I'm sure of it. Quick! Get him before he leaves the restaurant for good."

O'Malley ran down the stairs and across the street to the restaurant. A few minutes later, we saw a police wagon pull up. O'Malley loaded Billy into the back and slammed the doors.

Then Queenie and I waited. It felt like hours. We drank cup after cup of coffee until my nerves were jumping like a Harlem jazz club.

The whole time, Queenie talked about O'Malley. I began to think maybe she was ready to march down the aisle with her handsome young copper.

It was dark when O'Malley returned. Queenie greeted him at the top of the steps.

Inside, the copper turned to me and said, "You were right, miss. Billy confessed to poisoning Walter Chandler."

"Why?" Queenie's voice quivered.

"Because of you, Queenie." His voice was soft. He held her hand while he told the story.

"Billy's sister, Irene, worked for Madame Evangeline about the same time as you. Irene liked hooch a little too much. Madame gave her several warnings, but Irene's behavior was soon out of control. Finally, Madame had no choice but to fire Irene. The only job Irene could get was washing dishes at O'Connor's Steakhouse, and she hated it. She was having trouble holding that job.

"When she found out you were living across the street in a fancy apartment, she was crazy with jealousy. Why should you live in the lap of luxury while she was washing greasy pots and plates?

"Irene cracked today, and sprinkled cyanide ant killer on Walter's apple fritters. Billy saw what she did, but agreed to carry the poisoned dessert to your apartment.

"Irene wanted you framed for Walter's murder, Queenie.

"Fortunately, Billy had a guilty conscience and confessed. He and his sister have a date with the electric chair."

Queenie burst into tears again. She was one of those lucky women who looked pretty when they turned on the waterworks. "Oh, Ellie, thank you so much," she said. "You saved my life. You and Officer O'Malley." She gave him a dazzling smile.

"One more thing, miss. " O'Malley turned to me. "How did you know the killer was Billy Butler?"

"Easy," I said. "When it comes to murder, everyone knows the Butler did it."

What Dreams are Made Of by Cheryl Head

#

2. No willful tricks or deceptions may be played on the reader other than those played legitimately by the criminal on the detective himself.

Chapter One

1938

It had been a difficult ten years for our traveling troupe. Prohibition shifted into the Depression and just when things were picking up, that nasty little German nationalist put people on edge again. The Conaghan Bard Players might have dissolved altogether had it not been for the Federal Theater Project.

Our little group had performed in theaters in all but four states—with full costumes, wigs, and set pieces. But now, we were headed back to our home base—Baltimore, booked for a six-week run of The Tempest at the quaint theater owned and operated by my fraternal twin, Percy. He'd also wired to say a personal inquiry case was waiting for me. That's how I actually kept the three-man, three-woman company afloat: doing private investigations for clients who had means, and required discretion.

We were on the final day of train travel on the National Limited, a three-day trek from St. Louis. The trip had almost depleted my savings, and I was tired and irritable. So were the other actors, all except Margaret Staunton, our newest and youngest member. Margaret and I had an agreement that she would contain her morning exuberance until after nine. I looked at my watch. It was almost ten after. I set my coffee cup aside, clasped my hands under my chin and leaned my elbows on the table between us. "Something on your mind?"

In a millisecond she shifted from impatience to enthusiasm. Her spontaneity was an attribute which made her a gifted actor, but it was also her personality.

"I wondered if you'd heard from Percy?"

"Not since we left St. Louis. Have you heard from him?"

Margaret bobbed her head then smiled. "Yes. There was a telegram for me at the last

station in Ohio." Margaret reached into her purse fingering what must have been the cable. I wondered if she intended to show it to me until she reclasped the purse.

"Well, you seem much too serene for it to be bad news."

"Oh, no. It's not what would be considered bad news."

Margaret drifted into a reverie staring out the dining car window. I watched her while a couple of pastures came in and out of view. She and Percy had been miming a courtship for the past two and a half years that would have tested Job's patience. In truth, they seemed opposites in temperament and interests. Except for their devotion to theater.

I sank a spoon into my dippy eggs. "Did you want to discuss something related to Percy?"

"He's asked me to marry him," Margaret said with raised eyebrows. She was spreading apricot jam on a toast slice.

"Are you asking for my permission?"

"No. But if I married Percy the others might be uncomfortable with the new dynamic."

"What dynamic is that?"

"As your sister-in-law you might be inclined to give me better roles."

I signaled for more coffee and the waiter topped off our cups. I admired the silver spoon as I stirred the brew into a golden brown.

"Margaret, my policy is always to cast an actor into the role for which he or she is most suited. I'd intended to tell you this at today's meeting, but I've decided you will play Ariel."

"Oh," Margaret said, her shoulders slumping. "I was hoping I might play Miranda."

"No. Christiana will be our Miranda, but I know you'll be a wonderful Ariel, and you and I will also take on a couple of the other male roles. I'll even ask Percy to fill in. I'm excited for this production. The Tempest is always such a challenge in small theaters, but Percy's large stage is so well suited for the ship scenes. Come. Let's go see our fellow thespians. Thank the heavens we'll be in Baltimore this evening."

# # #

Christiana sat on a trunk, her stockinged legs dangling over the side. Tina, as she preferred to be called, was a seasoned actress. Even with the limitations of the train's tiny mirrors, her hair and makeup were impeccable. Tina was ten years older than Margaret, but what she lacked in coquettish appeal, she made up threefold in her worldliness. John—tall, full-headed, and refined—was handsome enough to play Duke Orsino, but talented enough to bring delicious delight to the villain roles. He would be my Prospero. Hugh, in his mid-twenties and a strong character actor, would be Ferdinand. He could—as was the case in Shakespeare's day—be cast in roles of both sexes. Thomas was the oldest of the troupe. He'd played every one of the Bard's principals in his career. In the last couple of years, I'd had to tame the fight scenes to make up for his lack of agility, and I monitored his drinking, but tipsy or not, he could act circles around the rest of us.

"The Tempest will be easy for us," I said, rallying the team. "I chose it for that reason. It's time to love what we do for a couple of months. Rehearsals will start Monday. Percy will meet us at the station, and you can all head home for a couple of days of well-deserved rest."

# # #

Percy was a respected architect with a slew of wealthy clients who wanted a house or a place of business designed by him. My generous brother had hired a dray for our costumes, trunks, and set pieces, along with three men to help load them, so John, Hugh, and Thomas were off the hook from their usual additional duties. He'd also hired cars to take the tired actors to their homes. Everyone thanked him profusely as one by one they left. Except Margaret. She hung around showing no signs of exhaustion. Percy deposited her into a private car with a promise to see her later.

When Percy and I arrived at the theater, I went straight to his office, poured a sherry, and put my feet up on the desk while he supervised the unloading of the dray. He employed ten people at the Baltimore Builders Theater. It was his avocation, but gave him as much pleasure as his work as an architect. He entered the office out of breath and wiping his hands on a rag.

"If you pay someone to work you shouldn't help them do the work, you know."

"Says you." Percy tossed the oily rag at me and poured himself a sherry. He plunked into the desk chair, pulled out a brown envelope, and slid it across the desk. "Your sleuthing is requested by a colleague of mine. Mr. Roger Collins. His name and address are there, along with a message and instructions on how to contact him."

"You know what the job is?"

"He, uh, believes his wife is having an affair. He wants you to find proof or set his mind at ease."

"Do you know the wife?"

"Only through mutual acquaintances."

"Why do I always get these depressing domestic cases?" I poured another glass of sherry. "Aren't I smart enough to catch an arsonist, or solve the mystery of a missing person?"

"Of course, but you're perfect for this case because you're a woman. Roger would rather you know his shame than a male detective. In some areas of life, women have more agency."

I gave my good-looking brother a dour look. He was a couple of inches taller than me, and mustachioed, but we shared the same tousle of reddish-brown hair and deep-set eyes.

"Plus, Collins said he'd pay a generous price."

"How generous?"

"I believe he wrote a number in his message."

I opened the envelope and unfolded the sheet of paper. I raised an eyebrow.

Percy laughed.

"I need to get home and make a plan. Enjoy your dinner, Brother. Oh, and I understand

congratulations are in order?"

"Congratulations?"

"On your betrothal." Percy looked quizzical. "To Margaret?"

"Oh. I haven't asked her yet."

#
Chapter Two

The offices of Hopkins & Associates on Lombard Street were a sign of the city's rebound from the Depression. Chrysanthemums in neat rows decorated the small patch of green in front of the brick colonial. Its concrete steps gleamed white.

The receptionist had been alerted of my visit, and sounded a bell that brought an apprentice to walk me to Collins's office on the third floor. He waved me to a chair while he penciled in some detail on a set of blueprints. Instead, I admired the framed certificates, degrees, articles, and proclamations. Percy was currently Baltimore's most sought-after architect, but Collins might be the most celebrated.

"Thank you for coming so quickly, Miss Conaghan. I heard you just arrived last evening."

I wondered how he'd heard that.

"Mr. Collins, I received your generous offer of recompense, and I wish to take on your investigation, but I must be clear, I won't be able to devote myself full-time to your case."

"How much time do you expect it will take?"

"I believe I can finish my investigation within two weeks. Maybe sooner."

"That's most satisfactory. Your discretion is more important than speed. And unless you insist otherwise, I prefer to pay you in full for your time. It keeps paperwork to a minimum. Is the amount I've suggested enough?"

"More than enough."

Collins wrote a check on the spot. He placed it at the edge of the desk. The notation was "consulting services."

"Thank you. Now I have a few questions which may take a half-hour, and I'll need a photograph of your wife."

# # #

I'd arranged to meet with the backstage staff before the weekend, and I decided to walk to the theater. Walking helped me think.

Collins's suspicions of his wife were ones I'd heard before in such investigations. His philanthropist wife, Abigail Collins, had been returning home later and later from her many engagements, and always with a minimum of explanation shared over their breakfast the next day. She'd recently traveled, solo, to Chicago for some business with a new charity; and upon her return had displayed uncharacteristic mood swings. Collins's only real evidence of his wife's suspected infidelity was a note he'd found on the floor of her dressing room. I paused to look at the note—handwritten in a dense cursive, and torn from high-quality paper that might be stationery. It read: Thank you, Abby. And was signed X. What was most interesting about the note was the ink. It appeared to have been written with one of those new pens I'd seen in Chicago.

I arrived at the theater in time to watch Inez groom a wig. In addition to a vast inventory of men's and women's costumes from Elizabethan to turn-of-the-century to modern, Percy's wardrobe manager, Inez Cranston, had a separate room where more than a hundred hats and two dozen wigs were displayed on individual mannequin heads.

"You've added costumes and hats since I last saw you, Inez. Where do you find these gems?" I exclaimed, trying on a beaver top hat.

"I've been in the business so long that when a theater closes, they call me to take their collections. And your brother has never refused me when I've asked him to purchase these treasures."

Inez and I bounced around ideas for costumes and hair for a couple of hours before I met with the set designer, the electricians, and the lighting team, and then headed home.

# # #

Both of us single, Percy and I shared a house. Each had our own floor, which included a bathroom, bedroom, and office. We shared the main floor's common spaces. Since Percy was eating out, Cook made me a nice chicken meal and I spread my investigation documents across the table. I had a photo of Roger and Abigail Collins, my notebook, and the handwritten note Roger had found in Abigail's dressing room. My reputation depended on my swift and successful completion of this investigation.

I stared at the photograph, a formal pose. Abigail was certainly a beautiful woman, perhaps one or two years older than Roger. Percy had mentioned that her family had money. She looked unsettled in the photo—even with the sparkling eyes and smile.

My food was excellent, and when I retired to my rooms, I spent the remainder of the evening in bed with a sherry, perusing the Social Register and Percy's stockpile of the Baltimore Sun, for mention of Abigail Collins. When I awakened the next morning, I was still surrounded by newspapers, and began my research anew.

# # #

Chapter Three

On Monday morning I deposited Collins's check into my b ank, holding back one hundred dollars in denominations I could use for tips, information, and other palm greasing, then headed to Ferry's Newsstand.

George Ferry had been blinded in the war, and later worked side by side with his father for more than a dozen years before taking over the newsstand. George was an invaluable informant. People seemed to assume that because he was blind, their conversations around him were private, so over the course of a week he overheard the casual chatter of hundreds of customers and passersby.

"Shelley Conaghan," George said as I approached the stand.

"My cologne?"

George laughed. "Yes, and your footsteps. You've been away for a while."

"We toured the Midwest. Pittsburgh, Chicago, Cleveland, St. Louis. But it's good to be home."

"'If I have ranged, Like him that travels I return again,'" George quoted from Sonnet 109. "You want to buy a paper?"

"No. But I'll take a Collier's and a bit of information. Do you know of any businesses using those new-fangled pens? I think they're called ballpoints?"

George pulled the magazine from a rack and placed it on the counter. I folded two bills-a clue to their denomination-and placed them next to his hand.

"Ah. Two Lincolns . I hope my information is worth it. I've heard the Hopkins Hotel and a tea shop on Chambers use[s] those new writing instruments. The ladies really seem to like them because they don't stain their gloves."

"Your news is always worth it, George. Thank you."

The Belletree Tea Shop was a fussy little place wedged between a flower shop and a fabric store. "Feel free to browse," the proprietor called out to me and returned to her explanation of the benefits of green tea to a lady in a floppy hat. I roamed the shop feigning interest in the dozens of bins and ended up at the counter. There was a catalogue, along with slips of tan paper, a pencil, and a spool of white wrapping paper.

"I need a tea that will help me sleep," I said to the clerk when it was my turn. "Something that will ease a busy mind at bedtime."

The woman smiled. "That would be chamomile."

"Can you spell it for me?" I'd already commandeered the pencil.

"Why, of course," the clerk said grabbing a ballpoint pen from under the counter and writing on a square of the tan paper. "Here you are."

I looked at the ink on the paper. Not at all similar to the Collins note. "Yes. I have heard of this tea. I'll take a quarter pound, please."

# # #

I was at a corner table in the Hopkins Hotel dining area with my Collier's, a glass of port, and an open-faced roast beef sandwich when I saw Margaret walk into the lobby. She joined a woman sitting on one of the sofas. I lifted the magazine to cover my face as they hugged. Her companion was a bit taller and like Margaret, brown-haired and stylishly dressed. They began an animated bantering. I peered from behind the Collier's when the woman signaled for the concierge, who brought over what looked like brochures. After about fifteen minutes the two stood and left. I signaled for my check.

"Excuse me," I said to the concierge. "I was dining over there and one of the women who just left dropped this earring." I presented a bauble I'd selected this morning from my vast collection of inexpensive costume jewelry. The match was in my pocket. The pair was cheap, but didn't look so. "One of the women is an acquaintance—Margaret Staunton, but it was the other woman who dropped it."

"Oh. Mrs. Barrie. She's a regular. I'll see that she gets it." The man placed the earring in an envelope. "May I tell her who came to her aid?"

"Just say it was a friend of Margaret."

When the concierge turned away, I ripped a sheet from the pad of stationery, and pocketed the pen he'd left on the desk.

# # #

Our first rehearsal went well. We ran through the entire play with scripts. Thomas and I worked out several blocking problems, John agreed to contact a couple of actor friends to join us in small parts [as extras], and I discussed makeup with Tina. At the end of the day everyone was extremely comfortable with the material, and I called the next rehearsal for two days later.

I was in my lounging pajamas and smoking one of Percy's Italian cigarillos when he

arrived home at five p.m. He joined me in the den, and poured himself a whiskey.

"Rehearsals go okay?"

"Splendidly. But I still need your acting talents. Rough day?"

"A bit more than usual. I'll be working in my study most of the night."

"So, no dinner with Margaret?"

"Afraid not. I'll ask Cook to make me a tray and eat while I work. And to tell the truth, I need a bit of a break from Margaret. She's a dear girl, but so quickly delves into the dramatic."

I nodded. "She told me you'd asked her to marry you."

"See, that's what I mean. We've joked about me making a decent woman of her. But I've not proposed." Percy paused. "Although, I expect I will."

I pondered that information, tilting my head and blowing a smoke ring. "I thought I saw her today. Downtown."

"What?" Percy's eyebrows and voice rose. "Margaret?"

"Yes. She was walking alone on Chambers Street."

"Oh. She did mention having a lunch appointment today with her mother."

I blew another ring. I didn't tell Percy that it was not Margaret's mother she met with. Nor that the paper and pen from the Hopkins Hotel were a match for the note I had in my pocket. Nor that Margaret, along with Abigail Collins, had been photographed by the Baltimore Sun at a charity event on behalf of The Full Circle—an organization that purchased, refurbished, and operated homes for battered women. Collins was its benefactor.

"Sorry, I need to go to work," Percy said finishing his whiskey. "You'll fend for yourself tonight?"

"Of course. I'll probably go out. Can I borrow the Packard?"

Two hours later, I was in costume. A mousey brown wig covered my pinned-up red hair, and I was dressed in a plain dress and gray coat. I finished off my look with brown shoes and a gray purse.

I'd paid another informant, a desk sergeant at the downtown police precinct, for the two addresses in my purse, and arrived at the first address—a modest two-story house with a fenced- in side yard—just before seven-thirty. I drove past the house and walked back carrying the small suitcase I'd added to my disguise. I watched curtains move and lights come on when I rang the doorbell, and after another peek through the curtains, a middle-aged woman answered the door. A big man in work clothes stood behind her. I understood the precautions necessary for these sanctuaries.

"May I help you?" the woman asked.

"Mrs. Collins asked me to come by to see her."

The woman's shoulders relaxed, and she dismissed the man. She scanned the street over my shoulder and ushered me in.

"I expect to see Mrs. Collins tomorrow, but she isn't here now. Are you okay?" she asked looking at my suitcase.

"Oh, yes. Thank you for your concern. I'm Mrs. Collins's book-keeper. I must have misunderstood her instructions. She's probably waiting for me at her residence."

The downtown address on Charles Street was an unassuming three-story brick home. Not the Collinses' residence. I ditched the suitcase, added eyeglasses to my get-up, and knocked. A buzzer prompted me to open the door, and I stepped into an elegant anteroom. A burly man in a tight-fitting suit waited behind a marble counter. He seemed incongruent with the tasteful wallpaper behind him. There was soft music coming from a darkened area across from the counter, and a velvet rope was draped across the stairs to the upper levels.

"May I help?" he asked, looking down from his six-foot-four perch.

I decided to take a chance. "I'm here at the invitation of Miss Staunton."

He glanced to the sheet at his fingertips. "She hasn't arrived yet. But she should be here shortly. You're welcome to wait. You can get a beverage at the bar, or join the others in the game room. I believe they're just finishing up a bridge tournament."

I wandered to the door of the game room. Six tables of players were in deep concentration. A tournament director was circling the room. A handful of spectators sat in chairs around the perimeter, and in rows near the door. I noticed a few Negro women—unusual in the regimented social strata of Baltimore. I recognized Abigail Collins at one of the tables, and turned toward the bar. Two men in business suits were in deep conversation at a wall table.

I appraised my drab attire. It had been perfect for the first establishment, but not this one. I sat at a stool. A twenty-something bartender walked toward me with a smile. She wore a black dress and heels. "Can I get you something?"

"I'd love a glass of red wine. Something with lots of body."

"Good body is always a plus," the woman said with a wink. Then it hit me. The door buzzer, the guard at the desk, the roped-off stairs, the attractive patrons. I began to pay attention to what I hadn't noticed before—a finger brushing aside an errant hair on [the] someone's forehead; a head tilted back with throaty laughter; eyes locked between the two wearing men's suits in the barroom; and the two smiling, middle-aged women walking hand-in-hand as they descended the steps. This was a lady's club. I'd heard of them in New York, and in Hollywood.

How did Margaret fit into all this?

I didn't have to wait long to find out. At the sound of the buzzer I took my drink to blend into the back row of spectators in the game room. Margaret entered, looked around, and not recognizing any visitor, went straight to a chair near Abigail Collins's foursome. I saw the glance between them before she sat. When the tournament concluded with applause and hugs for the winners, I slipped out of the room. With a quick smile/grimace to the sentry/greeter , I was buzzed out of the building which housed this secret gathering.

# # #

Chapter Four

The next day's rehearsals were uneventful. Two male extras had joined the company and we focused on acts Two and Three. Percy was able to read lines with us for an hour before he had to rush back to his office. Margaret didn't seem any different. But I watched her more closely, as she enthusiastically embraced the Ariel role. She was, obviously, one of the women the tabloids described as "queer birds." Ones that even those of us in the theater spoke of in whispers.

What should I say to Percy?

I stayed in the dressing room after the others left, promising the stage manager that I'd lock up. I strolled up and down the wardrobe aisles until I'd found the perfect garb. Inez's loan system was more stringent than that of the public library, and I placed a white card on the empty hanger, I noticed a few more cards in various aisles, then entered the wig room to borrow a mustache. The soft bowler was my finishing touch.

The house on Charles Street had lights on all three levels. Maybe Abigail didn't attend the house functions every night, but I intended to watch for her. I leaned in close to the side hedges of a home across the street, and hoped no one reported a loiterer to the police.

Women came to and went from the house in twos, threes, and solo. After more than an hour of waiting, I heard two pairs of footsteps approaching. George was right, people do have distinctive steps. I hurriedly crossed the street, turned in the opposite direction, then darted behind a parked car. I poked out my head as Margaret and Mrs. Barrie walked arm-in-arm up the steps of The Full Circle club. I was confused. Was Margaret Abigail's paramour or this woman's? Maybe she was both. I waited another hour without a[nother] sighting of Abigail or Margaret. Finally, tired and discouraged, I walked away from Charles Street and hailed a Yellow Cab.

# # #

I sat alone in the dressing room, knowing I must break my brother's heart. I'd removed the nose extension, sideburns, and eyebrows when I heard a sound in the next room. Turning off the light, I inched open the door. The wardrobe room was dark. As I stepped through the door I was illuminated in a flood of light.

"Shelley! What are you doing here? Why are you dressed like that?"

I covered my eyes from the blinding light. And I had to hold onto a wardrobe pole to steady my knees.

"I might ask you the same question, Brother!"

# # #

Chapter Five

"I am your twin sister. Why have you never told me?"

Percy and I sat side by side in front of the dressing room mirror. Only our sad eyes were familiar.

I still wore the mustache, but Percy's fake one was removed from his lip—his makeup flawless. A soft blouse ballooned under [from the collar of] his gold-and-pink brocade jacket. He looked like me when I played Imogen five years ago.

"Who else knows?" I asked.

"Only Inez. She's known for years."

I covered my face. Overwhelmed by what felt like betrayal. Percy put his arm around me. "I'm sorry, Shelley, I should have been braver. I wanted to tell you, but I knew this investigation would finally bring out the truth."

I pulled myself from his arms. "You mean you already knew about Margaret?"

Percy nodded. "Margaret and Abigail are in love. But Abigail would never hurt Roger's reputation, nor ever leave him—not for a man or a woman. She knew Roger suspected her of infidelity, and would probably hire a detective. We all thought if the truth came from you, Roger might be able to handle it, and see the wisdom of maintaining his marriage just the way it is. And, Margaret and I were sure you'd be the only one to keep the secret of The Full Circle."

"You knew I'd found out?"

"Margaret said someone had come to the house on Charles asking for her. She gave me the description, and I checked with Inez. I knew you were the woman in the gray coat."

I rubbed my fists into my eyes, and shook my head. "So, you're not in love with

Margaret?"

"She's my cover. And I'm hers."

Percy reached for my hand. I tried to pull away, but he held fast. "Shelley, I've always wanted to be a woman. I'm not alone. There are so many of us." His eyes pleaded for understanding. I squeezed his hand.

"If you knew I could keep a secret, why couldn't you trust me with yours?"

We both cried until we'd run out of tears. Then I stood, pulling Percy to the door.

"Come on, let's get into our real clothes," I said. He hesitated. "Oh, these are the clothes you prefer, aren't they?"

Percy nodded. "Sometimes I just want to wear how I feel."

"Well, let's just wear these clothes home!"

# # #

Epilogue

Roger was embarrassed and angry when we talked. I sat across from him at his desk and lied to him about some of the details. He tore my report in half, and I absorbed his profanities. My job was to convince Roger to leave things as they were.

"Abigail loves and respects you, but she can't help who she is. She understands you might want to take a lover, or change the way you live together, but she is very clear, she does not want a divorce, or to jeopardize your reputation."

"Nor hers," Roger replied angrily.

"True. But it's not the point. Who has the most to lose in this world run by men?"

Roger sat back in his chair and didn't speak for a long time. "So, you approve of this...this activity, Miss Conaghan?"

"I approve of people being happy and prosperous and safe."

"And your brother knows nothing of this?" Collins challenged.

I lied again. "No."

"And I can count on your full discretion?"

"You can be assured of that."

# # #

Opening night of The Tempest was a success. All the seats were filled, and the audience was appreciative. Mr. and Mrs. Collins were in attendance and joined in the applause for the spritely performance of Margaret Staunton, and the brief, but brilliant, appearance of Percy Conaghan. The next day's write-up in the Baltimore Sun called the work of the Conaghan Bard Players "a refreshing take on the themes of art, illusion, and dreams."

Baby Love by Barb Goffman

#

3. There must be no love interest in the story. To introduce amour is to clutter up a purely intellectual experience with irrelevant sentiment. The business in hand is to bring a criminal to the bar of justice, not to bring a lovelorn couple to the hymeneal altar.

I wasn't the greatest at math, but even I knew having a savings account balance nearing zero was problematic. Especially when your wife wanted to have a baby.

And not sometime in the future. Hannah wanted that baby now—or at least nine months from now—and she was doing everything she could to make it happen. I was exhausted.

Stretching, I leaned back in my soft leather chair. It was part of the furnishings Hannah's grandmother had left us—along with this Tudor home—when she died a few months ago. Moving in here had been an easy decision. Good school system. Nice neighborhood. But there had been one big drawback—the impact on my work.

Movement outside the casement window caught my eye, fish crows nasally cawing hello as they flew past, their short squared-off tails shining in the early-afternoon light. I wished I could be as carefree as those birds. I had time on my hands like they seemed to, but I was bogged down by my frustration. I wanted—I needed—to pull my own weight, to be a good provider instead of relying on Hannah's family money. But finding new clients had been hard since we moved.

If only I could get one really good case—one to put me on the local radar—I could get my PI business off the ground here. I'd been doing fairly well before moving across the state, but starting over hadn't been so easy. At least we didn't have a mortgage to worry about, and I didn't have to pay rent for an office. Not to mention, it was peaceful working in this town filled with interesting shops, canopy trees, and friendly folks. Though, can you call it work if you do so little of it? I'd joined the Kiwanis Club, hoping to make friends while helping kids, and maybe reeling in some business at the same time. A few friends had come quickly. The work, well, you know.

The phone on my desk rang, a beige-colored landline that came with the house. I immediately felt hopeful but wary. I'd run some local ads using that number, but most of the callers were scammers. Considering that I had a cell phone, the landline was a waste of money. Still, I couldn't bring myself to cut the cord. You could hear a pin drop through that forty-year-old relic. Besides, I liked picking up an actual receiver, feeling like my idols from old black-and-white movies, hoping there might be a dame on the other end, needing my assistance.

"Demsey Investigations," I said. "Dan Demsey speaking."

"Mr. Demsey, this is Catherine Richardson. I live next door. We met when you moved in."

So it was a dame, but this one was short and scrawny and about seventy years old. While she might need my help, it likely would be of the household-chore variety. We might as well be living in the Cotswolds.

"I remember, Mrs. Richardson. It's nice to hear from you."

"Catherine, please."

"All right, Catherine. You can call me Dan. How are you this fine spring day?"

"Not so good. I need your help."

Here it came. A leaky faucet? A loose gutter? I hoped I wouldn't have to climb a ladder.

"It's Brody," she said, her voice breaking. "My dog. He's been stolen."

I sprang up from my chair. "I'll be right over."

# # #

I was grabbing my keys from the ceramic bowl by the front door when Hannah called to me from the top of the stairs.

"Oh, Danny," she said in her most sultry voice.

She was wearing a peek-a-boo nightie, her long brown curls spilling over her shoulders, just barely brushing... I averted my eyes. When we'd started the baby-making process, I had been all in. No pun intended. But after so many...attempts...in such a short period of time, I needed a break to recharge, despite how hot my wife was. She could melt ice by simply glancing its way.

"Sorry, no time," I said. "I have to see a dame about a dog." And I dashed out the door.

When Catherine opened her own door, she seemed even shorter than I remembered. Was she even five feet tall? She held a tissue to her pert nose and looked like she'd been crying. I didn't blame her. I'd grown up with dogs, and thinking one had been stolen would be agony.

"Thank you for coming," she said.

I followed her to a flowered couch in the living room. A laptop lay open on the mahogany coffee table. Its screensaver was of a small black dog. "That's Brody. He's a Scottish terrier. I got him three years ago, shortly after my husband, Warren, passed."

Catherine hit a few keys and a montage of photos began running. Brody had small prick ears and short sturdy legs, but when he smiled, you could tell he had a big personality. "He's adorable."

"He is." She hit another key, and a video began. Brody had a lot of energy and a sharp, high-pitched, raspy bark. A bright blue tag with his name on it hung from the collar around his neck. "He's a very good boy."

I had no doubt. I pulled out my notebook and pen. A lot of PIs record their clients, but taping made some people uncomfortable. Besides, I can find things much faster flipping through my notes than repeatedly starting and stopping a recording, trying to land on the right spot. "Can you tell me what happened?"

"At nine o'clock each Saturday morning I take piano lessons." Catherine nodded toward a baby grand by the picture window, overlooking the front lawn. "Brody loves Myra, my teacher, but he often gets bored and goes into the backyard through the doggie door. He likes to trot along the fence line, smelling things and barking at squirrels. After Myra left, I went out back to check on him, but Brody wasn't there. The gate was open. I was horrified. I hurried to the front of the house, calling for him, searching up and down the street. But he wasn't anywhere. That's when I phoned the police."

I felt terrible. If I'd heard her screaming Brody's name, I would have come out to help. Hannah and I had been trying to conceive little Dahlia or Thor, so I'd been…focused on my task. The name Thor, by the way, was still under discussion. Hannah thought a kid named Thor would get beat up, while I knew he'd be the coolest kid in school. But I digress.

"If the gate was open, why do you think Brody was stolen?" I asked. "Couldn't he just be lost?"

Catherine shook her head vehemently, the ends of her white hair brushing her jawline.

"That's what the officer who came here said. A part of me had hoped Brody was roaming nearby and would come when called, but as soon as I saw that open gate, I knew deep down that someone took him. The gate was closed this morning, when we were playing fetch in the backyard before my lesson, and it has never blown open. Never. Not once in the thirty years we've lived here."

"Now that I think about it, it's not windy today."

"Exactly."

"Have any workers been here since then who could've forgotten to close it? Landscapers, people like that?"

"No." She huffed out a breath. "That policeman treated me like a child, refusing to believe someone must have opened the gate and taken Brody. He told me to post lost-dog signs in the neighborhood and on social media."

"Have you?"

"Yes, but as expected, no one has seen him. I know it's only been a few hours, but I'm afraid..." Her eyes watered. "I'm afraid he's been stolen to be used as a bait dog."

Revulsion slammed through me. The very thought of that poor dog being hurt that way made my stomach roil.

Catherine grabbed my arm, her delicate hand surprisingly strong. "Please, you've got to find him before it's too late. I'll pay anything." Now she was crying full-out.

Normally I would've talked price, gotten a retainer, and had her sign a contract, but she was a neighbor and, as she said, time was of the essence. So I asked Catherine some more questions, assured her I would do my best, and headed out back to inspect the yard.

# # #

Catherine's backyard was similar to ours, except it had a six-foot wooden fence—no way Brody jumped it. As I walked the fence line, searching for holes or loose boards or anything that might suggest what happened to Brody, I dialed the mobile number on the card the cop had left with Catherine. Officer Floyd Jackson answered after three rings. He didn't come across as patronizing to me. Then again, I wasn't a little old lady.

"I understand her concern," he said, "but we can't spend our time searching for lost dogs."

"Could Brody have been grabbed to be used as a bait dog?"

"We haven't had any reports of dogfighting in our area. No rash of missing dogs that could indicate a ring we don't know about. She should keep looking. He could be hiding under a bush, or maybe somebody found him and brought him to the shelter."

"She checked there."

"Well, he could still turn up—at the shelter or in the neighborhood. I hope he does. Good luck to you both."

I finished inspecting the yard. I spotted no holes in the fence. No signs of a scuffle. Nothing indicated someone had come inside and grabbed Brody, though that didn't mean it hadn't happened. I went to examine the gate. It had a black lever-latch handle on both sides. They were stainless steel. Sturdy. Someone would have had to press down on one of the handles for the gate to open. No way it did it on its own or even with a little help from the wind.

"Hey, handsome." Turning around, I found Hannah standing a few feet away in my tan trench coat. It hit me mid-calf. On her, only her feet were visible. "Whatever your case is, it surely can wait awhile," she said. "Why don't you come inside for some fun?"

Slowly she untied the belt, then whipped the coat open. She wore high heels and nothing else. Her legs and…other parts…were so shapely, I became sorely tempted, until I was distracted by her left hand. More specifically, by her diamond engagement ring glinting in the sunlight.

Ring. *I should see if Catherine or any neighbors have a Ring camera. They might have footage showing what happened to Brody.* Hannah smiled triumphantly as I hurried toward her. I gave her a quick peck on the cheek. "Sorry, honey. But I'm on the trail of a missing dog. Gotta go."

"Seriously?" she said as I rushed off.

Babies were important, but first things first.

#

Catherine didn't have a doorbell camera. Nor did any of the immediate neighbors, including me. But Judy Sheluk, who lived across the street and three houses down, did. She and her golden retriever, Enzo, greeted me with friendly smiles, and once she heard why I'd come by, she was eager to help.

I followed her and Enzo to her home office, noticing how Judy's salt-and-pepper hair was more salty in back than in front. She pulled up the footage from the fifty-minute period during which Brody had gone missing, and I sat down to review it. We lived on a quiet side street, so I was able to fast-forward a lot. Not much traffic on the road. There were some walkers and runners. Judy didn't know any of them, and no one appeared suspicious. I couldn't see Catherine's house, so the footage was of limited use. Still, I asked if I could copy it onto a flash drive. I always kept a spare one on my key ring for this type of situation.

"Of course." She clicked a few buttons and copied the whole day onto my drive. "I wish I could be of more help. I simply don't remember anyone hanging around who seemed out of place or hinky."

Hinky? Not a word I typically heard from middle-aged women not living on the mean streets.

"I loved when they used that word in *The Fugitive*," she said. "Do you ever do that, search for wanted criminals, I mean?"

"Not really. That's more of a police matter." People often expected my work to resemble what cops and PIs do on TV or in the movies. But in this town, I probably would have more missing-dog cases in my future than ones involving convicts, especially ones on the run, though hope sprang eternal. "Thanks for your help."

"You're welcome. I pray you find Brody soon. I won't be letting Enzo out of my sight outdoors until you do."

"Good idea." I gave her my card, in case she thought of anything relevant. After patting Enzo's dark-blond head and receiving a kiss in return, I went on my way.

I hadn't reached the sidewalk when my phone buzzed. Hannah's face popped up on the screen. She wore deep red lipstick and heavy mascara.

"Hey, sweetie," I said.

She slowly licked her lips, and when she spoke, her words came out at the same leisurely pace. "Hey, yourself. I'm here all by myself. So lonely. You sure you can't put your job on hold for a little while?" She moved the phone sideways and away from her body. Her nude body. She was standing with her back to the full-length mirror in our bedroom, so I had a complete view of her perfect derriere. So round yet firm. I groaned. Hannah knew I was a butt man.

"Butts," I said, widening my eyes. I'd staked out a lot of folks over the years who had been smokers, and they often stood under streetlamps while puffing away, leaving cigarette butts behind. Occasionally I saw people, mostly dog walkers, smoking beneath the streetlamp under the tall oak tree that shaded the sidewalk between Catherine's house and my own. They left their butts behind, too. Granted, I had no reason to think the person who snatched Brody—at this point, I did believe he had been snatched—was a smoker, but he could be. Or she. And the thief likely had staked out Catherine's house, trying to determine when Brody would be alone in the yard. The hour Catherine sat beside her picture window each Saturday morning learning piano would have offered the perfect opportunity.

"I only have one butt," Hannah said, "and it's spectacular. Why don't you come on home and—"

"No time. You've given me a great idea. Thanks, darling."

"But—"

"Not but. Butts. The solution to this case could be right outside our front door."

"Are you kidding—"

I punched the off button. I shouldn't have hung up in the middle like that—never a good idea to stop in the middle with Hannah—but I was too excited. I'd make it up to her later.

# # #

Five cigarette butts were lying beneath the streetlamp. A couple of them littered the sidewalk. The rest lay in the grass or in the soil beneath the tree. Until this week, I'd found one or two discarded butts each time I wheeled our trash bin to the road on Tuesday evenings. I always cleaned them up, which is why I'd noticed when the number doubled. Now five butts had been discarded here in the last four days. That was interesting, but something also was strange. Three of the cigarettes hadn't been smoked all the way down to the filter—the normal way of things. Instead, about three quarters of each cigarette remained, just like with most of the butts I had picked up on Tuesday. Could this smoker be trying to quit?

I hurried to my car in our driveway and pulled latex gloves and a baggie from the center console. The gloves might have been overkill. But if I found Brody at someone's home, and if the butts had that person's DNA on them, they might help put the baddie behind bars. They'd be proof that the dog snatcher had stood here, watching Catherine's house, waiting for the perfect opportunity to sneak into the backyard.

I returned to the sidewalk to collect all the butts. Other than the length of some of them, there was nothing distinctive about them. They didn't even have lipstick stains, which might have indicated the thief's gender. But now that I crouched close to the ground, I noticed shoe prints in the soil beneath the tree. They didn't have a distinctive pattern or logo, but they were large—larger than my own size twelves, probably a size fourteen. So they likely belonged to a guy who was taller than me, and I stood six-one. You so often hear about the supposed correlation between a man's shoe size and his, um, baby maker, which isn't true. But there is a real correlation between shoe size and height. One of these smokers was a tall guy.

A noise from above caught my attention. Hannah was leering down at me from our bedroom window, fluffing her hair. She was still nude, at least from the waist up, which was all I could see. How I loved her headlights.

Headlights! A memory popped into my mind of a Jeep Wrangler. They have distinctive headlights. I knew this guy from Kiwanis who drove one. What was his name? We'd chatted a couple of months ago while returning to our cars after a meeting. He was taller than me, six-foot-three or maybe six-four. White. Lean. Bald. He didn't smell like smoke, but he had the husky voice of a smoker, and his breath had a metallic odor. He drove an older-model dark-orange Jeep, not a common color.

I couldn't imagine why this dude would have stolen Catherine's dog. It seemed hard to believe anyone who was a member of a charitable organization devoted to helping children would be involved in something horrible like dogfighting. Though, considering what Officer Jackson said, there probably was another reason Brody was taken, no matter who did it. Could there be a market for stolen Scottish terriers? I'd heard about French bulldogs being snatched in big cities, sometimes resold for big bucks. But here in our small town? Besides, Scotties weren't one of those ultra-popular breeds.

Thinking about why the thief snatched Brody wasn't getting me anywhere. I needed to focus on the evidence I'd gathered. Since few people smoked these days, knowing someone local who had a smoker's voice and was even taller than me—someone who could've left some of those cigarette butts and the large shoe prints—was too good a lead to overlook. I had to run it down.

I dashed to my office. I wanted to review Judy Sheluk's doorbell camera footage to see if I spotted an orange Jeep driving by, ideally one slowing down to park or zooming off around the time Brody was taken.

As I plugged the flash drive in, Hannah's sultry voice called from upstairs.

"Danny, where are you? I saw you running into the house. I'm waiting for you. I put your favorite sheets on our big bed—the extra-soft ones."

Too tempting. *Be strong. Be strong for Brody.* "Sorry," I shouted. "Still working."

I super-fast-forwarded until about a half hour before the piano lesson began and then watched carefully. Some sedans drove by, most not adhering to the speed limit. A couple of kids carrying baseball gear walked past. A tuxedo cat chased a squirrel up a tree. And then—*bingo!* I'd been right. Ten minutes before the piano lesson began, a dark-orange Jeep Wrangler crept past, going slow enough that the driver appeared ready to park.

I enlarged the image, trying to get a better look at the driver. Instinct told me it was a man, but I had to be sure—not think it just because it fit my theory. I craned my neck. That was definitely a guy, a white guy. He wore a ball cap that brushed the ceiling. I couldn't see his hair. Did he have hair? I rewound for a few seconds, then let it play again. I still couldn't tell.

Focus on the car. The Jeep had no dents or other distinctive features on the driver's side. I couldn't see the license plates either. I picked up the phone to call the Kiwanis office. Someone there might be able to ID him for me. I hoped they were open now.

The sound of throat-clearing lured my attention to my office doorway. Hannah sauntered in, wearing a red lace teddy and red thigh-high stockings, held up by garters. Hubba-hubba.

"That chair looks awfully comfortable," she said while she approached me, swaying her hips.

My mouth watered as I set down the handset.

She climbed onto my lap. *Brody*, I reminded myself, as she rubbed my cheek, then slipped her hand down my neck and under my shirt. *You have to find Brody.* Her mouth pressed against mine, so soft and warm. *Sorry, Brody.* I pulled her closer, my hand sliding over the back of her teddy—

Teddy! My eyes flew open as I lifted Hannah off my lap and onto my desk.

"On the desk, huh?" she said. "Well, I'm game if—"

"His name is Ted. Ted Mulgrew."

"What?"

"The guy. The one I think stole the dog. I don't know why yet, but I feel it in my gut."

Hannah snuggled toward me. "I think that's something else you're feeling down there."

I kissed her hard but only for a moment. "Honey, I promise, when this job is done, we can get busy making a baby all over this house. But for now, I have work to do."

She let out a deep, defeated sigh. Hannah slid off the desk and left the room as I logged into our state's DMV database. Seconds later, I found him. Ted Mulgrew, thirty-six years old, six-foot-four, two hundred pounds, sandy blond hair. He owned an orange Jeep Wrangler. Definitely the Kiwanis guy, though now he was bald and a bit thinner. He lived a few blocks away. Close enough that he could have walked by, maybe saw Brody through the window. He easily could've driven home with Brody long before the dog was even missed.

I logged out of there and into another database, checking if Ted had a police record. He didn't, at least not in this state. Then I turned to my favorite search engine to see what else I could learn about him. Always best to be prepared.

The first few results weren't useful, but the top one on the second page of results was. A news article. As I read it, the pieces fell into place.

# # #

I parked under the maple tree beside Ted's driveway. His slate-gray colonial had seen better days. One of the second-story black shutters was partially detached. The aluminum siding needed a good power wash. The lawn was mowed, though, and the fence looked solid, so he was keeping up with some things—or at least someone was.

Ted's car wasn't visible. Either he wasn't home or it was in the garage. I retrieved a folding step-stool from my trunk, then wandered around the side of the house toward the backyard. I knew Brody was there. His bark in real life was just as distinctive as it had been on Catherine's video. Sharp, high-pitched, and raspy. Still, I needed to be absolutely certain. So I climbed onto the step-stool and peered over the six-foot-tall fence. A pigtailed blond girl, about eight years old, was playing with a dog that matched Brody's description to a T, though his tag was gone. The girl's happy squeals filled the air. I hated that I would have to break her heart. But this was the job.

I took video of Brody and the girl with my phone, just in case Ted gave me any problems. Then I returned the step-stool to my trunk and made a call. A few minutes later, I rang Ted's bell.

He appeared to recognize me when he opened the door. Worry settled onto his features, his brows forming a V. Then he forced himself to smile. His pale face was thinner than when we'd met two months before. He'd lost fifteen, maybe twenty pounds. He hadn't needed to lose a one of them. His clothes hung so loosely on him, he could've been a scarecrow that lost its stuffing.

"Dan, right?" he asked.

I nodded. "From Kiwanis."

"This is a surprise. What can I do for you?" He didn't welcome me inside, just stood there blocking the entry, like I was a door-to-door salesman and he didn't want my wares but was too polite to shut the door in my face.

"I'm here about Brody." I was certain Ted knew the dog's name, even if he had thrown out his tag. His wince confirmed it. There were a lot of ways I could have approached this, but I hoped straightforward would work. He knew I was a PI, so he would be able to piece things together, just as I had.

His smile fell away, and for a moment, I feared he might fall, too. He let out a deep sigh before he stepped aside. "Come on in."

He lumbered wearily to the kitchen. His lung cancer was killing him, and he seemed far more fragile than when we had first met. Back then, I hadn't realized he was sick. Maybe I wouldn't have guessed now if I hadn't known he'd lost so much weight so quickly—and if I hadn't read about his illness in the newspaper. Last year, some Kiwanis members had participated in a run to raise money for Ted's family. He was drowning in medical bills. His little girl had been quoted in the article, saying she hoped that they would be able to get a new dog. Their old one had recently died.

"Can I offer you something to drink?" he asked, as if this were a social call. "We don't have much right now. Water. Tea. My wife is at the market, but she probably won't be home for at least a half hour."

"You sit," I said. "I'll get it." I took a pitcher of iced tea from the fridge and two glasses from the cabinet Ted directed me to. After I filled our glasses, we sat quietly at his kitchen table, Ted adjusting to the reality that I had found him out, while I took in the room. Crayoned artwork hung on the refrigerator, a smiling girl holding hands with a man and woman, a dog by their side. A nearly full water bowl inscribed with the name LUNA sat in a corner. The sweet vanilla scent of Play-Doh filled the air. I hadn't smelled it in decades, but I recognized it instantly. This was a home filled with happiness and love, despite their sorrows.

Ted stared at me and heaved another sigh. "I assume you know about my situation." I nodded. "I have six months left—a year if I'm lucky. The chemo has delayed the inevitable, but I can't stop it."

"I'm sorry."

"Me too." He laughed, then coughed, a deep hacking, crackling sound. When he finally stopped, he said, "My doc recommended I take regular walks. Said it would be good exercise. Not too strenuous for my condition. That's how I met Brody. He sure is a cute little thing. Quinn—my daughter—has begged for a Scottie for years, ever since my wife read these books to her about one named Angus. After our dachshund died, I looked into getting Quinn a Scottie, but the puppies are so expensive. And they never show up in the county shelter or nearby rescues." He shook his head, seemingly disgusted, though whether by the situation or himself, I couldn't tell. "I just wanted to get my little girl the dog she's dreamed of before I die."

I understood, even if he had gone about it in the wrong way.

"How'd you find me anyway?" he asked.

"Your car is memorable. And you left footprints in the soil under the tree you stood beneath, as well as cigarette butts."

His jaw hung open. "You're good. I used to stop under that tree while walking Luna. She'd sniff to her heart's content, then search for the perfect spot before leaving her calling card. I'd smoke a cigarette while waiting. I got used to stopping there. That's when I figured out that Brody's mom had piano lessons every Saturday morning. Her teacher has bumper stickers on her car. One says BACH OFF! IF YOU CAN READ THIS, YOU'RE TOO CLOSE."

"Clever," I said with a laugh. "No disrespect, but I'm surprised you still smoke."

"I don't. But I miss 'em. Sometimes when I'm outside and have time to kill I light one so I can smell it. It makes me feel like the old me, before everything changed. Then, when the breeze burns it out, I light another. I went through three this morning, waiting to get my nerve up. Last week, I chickened out.... So what now? You calling the cops?"

"I don't think that'll be necessary, considering the circumstances. Brody's mom wants her dog back, of course, but she says Quinn is welcome to come to her house most anytime to play with him."

A sad smile crossed Ted's face. "That's real generous of her."

"There's more. Catherine, the owner, would like to give Quinn a Scottie puppy."

After I'd called Catherine about finding Brody and explained the situation, she'd immediately come up with this idea. She wanted Ted's daughter to have a furry friend to get her through the hard times that were waiting in the wings. It felt fitting, considering that even after Ted knew he was dying, he'd still gone to Kiwanis meetings and activities, giving his time to help other people's children. Catherine and Ted, they both were good at heart.

Still, even good people had pride. As expected, Ted held his hands up in a stop motion. "No, we couldn't accept something like that."

"Listen to your daughter out there, how happy she is." Quinn's giggles and Brody's barks had mixed into a sweet melody. "Catherine can afford this. She wants to do it. Let her."

Ted stared out the window. The light of his life flopped onto her back in the grass. Brody jumped on her chest and licked her face. Quinn couldn't keep Brody, but she could love another dog just as much. I prayed Ted wouldn't let his pride stand in the way of that child's happiness. I vowed to be as mindful when my own child came along. He swallowed hard. "Okay." He rose and knocked on the sliding glass door, then waved the girl inside. Quinn and Brody came running. While Ted introduced Quinn to me, Brody hightailed it to the water bowl, drinking heartily. The dog had adjusted quickly to this family, but I bet he would be as thrilled to get home to his mom as she would be to hold him in her arms.

"Princess," Ted said to Quinn, "you know how I told you I found Angus this morning. Well, it turns out he wasn't homeless. Just lost." Ted glanced my way, and I nodded my approval of his white lie. "He belongs to a lady who lives a few blocks from here. Mr. Demsey has come to bring him home."

The girl's lip wobbled.

I kneeled before her. "Mrs. Richardson says you can come over to her house whenever you like to play with Brody."

Upon hearing his name, the dog barked and scampered over. Quinn petted his wiry coat. "His name's Brody? That's a good name."

"Angus is a good one, too," I said. "Maybe you can save it for your own Scottie puppy."

Her eyes lit up, and she gazed hopefully at her dad. He cupped her chin. "Mrs. Richardson wants to give you a puppy to thank you for taking such good care of Brody today," he said.

She grinned. "Really?"

"Really," he said.

"It may take a few months," I added, "but the puppy will have the same mother as Brody."

"They'll be brothers," she yelled.

I laughed at her exuberance. "They will at that."

Brody wagged his tail like crazy. He definitely approved.

# # #

A little while later, I returned Brody to his mom, and their joy at being reunited was infectious. After he zoomed around the living room several times, we all sat on the couch. Brody crawled into Catherine's lap as I filled her in on the details I'd learned from Ted.

She shook her head. "Cancer is a terrible thing. It's what took Warren from me way too soon. And this poor man, to be dying so young. Sometimes, I don't know what the good Lord is thinking. I have to assume he has his reasons."

I handed her a sheet of paper from my notebook. It had Ted's, his wife's, and Quinn's names on it, as well as their phone numbers. "You're going to love Quinn. She's so excited to get her own Scottie puppy. It was such a kind offer."

"I'm happy to do it. I talked to the breeder, and she has a litter already on the way, due in about three weeks. Once the pup is eight weeks old, it will be ready to leave its furry mama and get a human one."

Thinking about how Hannah couldn't wait to become a mama herself, I rose. "I should be going."

Catherine stood, Brody in her arms. "Don't forget to send me a bill. Whatever the charge is, I'll be adding a nice tip for such fast and wonderful service. And I happen to know a lot of people in this town, so you can expect to find more business heading your way."

I smiled. Now that I'd vowed not to be so focused on building my business, my business prospects were on the upswing. Life sure could be funny sometimes.

# # #

I texted the good news to Judy Sheluk and thanked her again. Then I went inside my house. "Honey, I'm home."

"I'm in the kitchen," Hannah called.

I found her chopping vegetables behind the counter, wearing a halter dress. I finally was ready to resume our baby-making attempts, and she was dressed—and not in lingerie either. She looked up.

"Did you solve your case?"

"I did. It was all thanks to you."

She crooked her neck and set down the knife. "How did I do that exactly?"

Should I tell her how helpful her amorous advances were? That I focused on her diamond ring, and then Ring cameras, instead of her nude body? That her butt led me to think about cigarette butts and her headlights reminded me of a Jeep Wrangler? That her silky teddy helped me remember the name of a living one? Probably not. "Let's just say you pointed me to some clues."

"Does that mean you're ready to give me what I want?"

As if I hadn't done so three times yesterday, once in the middle of last night, and twice this morning. "Ready and willing. But one thing first. Since you're not sold on the name Thor, what do you think of Teddy?"

"Is that the man who stole the dog?"

I'd forgotten I had mentioned that to her. "Yeah, but it turns out he's not a bad guy. Just a guy in a bad situation. I'll tell you the details later. The important thing is he reminded me of the value of putting family first."

"He sounds wise... Teddy. I like it."

He had been wise when he prioritized his daughter over his pride. Sure, he'd made a big mistake taking Brody. But in the grand scheme of things, Ted seemed like a decent guy, worthy of being remembered for the good he had done.

Hannah stepped out from behind the counter, and I realized she wasn't wearing a halter dress. She was wearing a full apron. Only an apron. One I hadn't seen before. It read IS IT HOT IN HERE OR IS IT JUST ME?

The apron fell to the floor, and suddenly I was feeling hot myself. "Baby, it definitely isn't just you."

"Baby." She pressed against me, her kiss long and delicious. "That's the magic word."

I kissed her back. "It most certainly is."

The Devil Himself
by Vaseem Khan

# # #

4. The detective himself, or one of the official investigators, should never turn out to be the culprit. This is bald trickery, on a par with offering some one a bright penny for a five-dollar gold piece. It's false pretenses.

There is a village further down the coast that people pay to visit. The website tells you that the place was once owned by William the Conqueror. The website also tells you that the toll is necessary to pay for cliff maintenance – the village is perched on a three-hundred-foot vertical ridge. Left untended, the cliff will erode several inches each year until the whole thing falls into the sea. They don't really police entry; but I've never heard of anyone just wandering in and not paying the toll.

The hamlet of Krike doesn't charge for entry. No one wants to come to Krike, not by choice. Krike's two hundred or so residents are either sitting around waiting for death or trying to figure out how to leave the place.

I should know. I grew up there.

Earlier this evening, I killed a man.

My name is Harry Foden. I am a detective in the county constabulary, a murder squad veteran of three decades. As a young man I left the coast, worked for many years in London. I've worked more cases than I can remember, seen more corpses than I care to remember. Stabbed, shot, strangled, bludgeoned. I've notified the living of the deaths of loved ones, watched them cry out in anger and disbelief, weep uncontrollably, sink into despair. I've taken cases home with me, and let them live inside my head. No death has left me untouched.

The man that I killed? We'll get to that.

Earlier today, I drove out to Krike in abominable weather. Wet, shiny roads, headlights battling a horizontal torrent in the dark. It took me an hour to get here. For the last thirty minutes, I didn't pass a single car. Krike isn't just isolated. It is determinedly cut off, its collection of spread-apart homes as misanthropic as their residents.

I parked the squad car outside Tom Fincher's home, a single-storey bungalow fashioned from moss-covered grey stone, balanced on the edge of a sheer drop into churning ocean. In summer the views are spectacular: the iron blue of the Celtic Sea, picture-perfect boats hovering on the horizon, island humps in the near distance blanketed in nesting gannets.

I went into Fincher's house.

#

Everyone in Krike knew Tom Fincher. Everyone knew him and no one liked him. Fincher was a hateful old fisherman, retired, inasmuch as a man who lives off nature's bounty can truly retire. Fincher had never married, had no children, no family, no friends, no meaningful relationships. Save for a two-year absence in his early twenties, he had spent his life in Krike, just over five decades. Those two years were shrouded in mystery. No one knew where he had gone. He had taken off days after the death of his mother, not a word to anyone. Fincher had grown up without a father, a former soldier who had come out to the coast running from God knew what. But the sea doesn't suit everyone.

I remember Fincher Senior as a big man, bearded, dangerous-looking, a gaze that looked right through you. At school – or what passed for a school in Krike – someone set loose a rumour that Fincher's dad was on the run from the law. No one had the guts to confront him about it and the law never came to Krike looking for him. He vanished when Tom turned eleven. Four years later, word came back to Krike that his body had been found in a crack den. Whatever he had been running from, he had finally found a way to escape.

A few years ago, just after the Covid epidemic, a local newspaper ran a piece on Tom. The piece, about real-life hermits, was written in the wake of the navel-gazing that followed the national lockdowns. Tom Fincher had been in lockdown mode for close on two decades. He associated with no one, tolerated no visitors. Anyone foolish enough to venture near his property was given short shrift, usually from behind the pointy end of a double-barrelled shotgun. It shocked Krike's other residents that Fincher had allowed a reporter into his home, let alone answered questions. I know this because my grandmother still lives in Krike.

Not that the article revealed much. No deep personal insights. No Thoreau-like sagacity. Fincher talked about his day-to-day existence. The practicalities of living alone on the edge of nowhere. The only titillating morsel had been the revelation that he kept the bleached skulls of his former dogs on a shelf in his bedroom.

No one knew why Fincher had broken his self-imposed solitude. The reporter hinted that Fincher had repeatedly seemed on the verge of revealing something deeply personal, a wild and woolly secret, but had shied away at the last.

'What now?' Clara asked me, staring at Fincher's cooling corpse.

Fincher's body lay in the living room. Blood matted his clothes, the floorboards, and a threadbare carpet.

Clara Decker works the homicide beat with me. She's only been on the job a couple of years, but we gelled instantly. Clara hails from a village much like Krike. Like me she managed to get out, finding her way to university, then moving to a county town, joining the force, and working her way up through the ranks. Clara is on a fast-track programme. I am her mentor. I have two decades on her; sometimes, I feel like a schoolboy in her presence.

'We follow procedure,' I said. 'We get the medical examiner out here. We call in forensics.'

She seemed uncertain, but nodded, then slipped her phone from her pocket.

An hour later, the medical examiner ducked into the house. His name was Kevin Walsh. He was short, fat, and balding. I had known him for years. Walsh was one of those guys who made a virtue of being single at an advanced age. Footloose and fancy-free. Twice divorced, he pretended to himself that both times it had been his own decision. He has a daughter somewhere, but they rarely see each other.

Walsh and I are not so different. My wife left me a year ago. But I don't pretend that I haven't hated every day since.

'Harry. Clara.' Walsh shook off the rain, set down his bag, took off his coat, and then stood there dripping on the wooden floorboards as he looked around. His gaze alighted on the body. 'Christ. Is there a full moon out?'

Clara and I stepped away as he set to work.

When he was done, he walked to the back of the space and opened a door facing out on to the rear of the house where a narrow garden ran down to the cliff edge. Rain fell against his thickset figure; he didn't seem to notice. I watched him fumble a vape from his pocket.

I walked over to stand at his shoulder, looked out into the night. Visibility was reduced to a few metres. I thought I could make out the shape of a well, piping running back towards the house and up to what I presumed was a water tank somewhere above our heads. Beneath the rain, I could hear the steady whine of a generator.

'Someone was very angry with him,' said Walsh, eventually. 'Multiple stab wounds. At least thirty. A crime of passion. Reckon he knew his killer.'

'Are you asking me or telling me?'

Walsh twisted his neck around.

'The door was unlocked,' I said. 'It could have been anyone.'

'No one locks their doors in Krike. Why would they? There's fuck-all to steal.' He stuck the vape back in his mouth, puffed silently for a while. 'No sign of the murder weapon?'

'No.'

'So we have a frenzied killer running around out there with a bloody knife. Perfect.'

'Perhaps he threw it into the ocean.'

'Sure. If he had been thinking straight. Which, given the circumstances, seems unlikely. . . . Who found the body?'

'I did.'

Walsh frowned. 'What were you doing out here?'

'I was visiting my grandmother. She's ninety and on her last legs.'

'I'm sorry to hear that. But how did you end up at Fincher's?'

'My gran said they hadn't seen Fincher at the general store for a few months. He usually turns up there every few weeks to buy supplies.'

'She was worried about him?' Walsh's tone hinted at incredulity.

'My gran worries about everyone and everything. She knew Fincher as a boy. Always had a soft spot for him. After what happened with his father.'

Walsh shrank back as a lightning bolt split the sky. Seconds later, thunder rolled over the cliff. The rain intensified. 'I don't think the crime scene gang are going to be out here anytime soon.'

I had to agree. The forensics unit was based further away than Walsh.

'Christ, I'm getting soaked,' Walsh muttered. He stuffed his vape into his pocket, stepped back into the room, and closed the door behind him. 'Have you searched the place?'

'We've had a preliminary look,' I said. 'Nothing.'

Walsh found a seat, an armchair that looked as if it had been in a wrestling match with a tractor. He pulled a flask from his bag, tilted it to his mouth, then stopped. 'Fancy a drop?'

I shook my head.

'What about you, young lady?'

Clara glanced at me. Her face was ashen. In the dim light her blond hair, pulled back into a ponytail, had taken on an egg-yolk hue. I said nothing.

'What's the matter?' said Walsh. 'You've seen plenty of corpses. This isn't your first rodeo, as our friends across the pond might say.'

I willed her to speak. Walsh had a nose for anything that smelled a little off. Frankly speaking, he would have made a good investigator, if he hadn't been such a dissolute bastard. Clara and I had spoken before the doctor had arrived. I had told her what to say. We had worked together long enough for her to do as I asked. I could see that she was in shock. Discovering the worst about a person you thought you knew can do that.

'Been a bit under the weather. Nothing serious.'

Walsh grunted, then allowed his eyes to wander around the space. There wasn't much to look at. A kitchen area to one side, a small wooden dining table and chairs, a battered sofa arrangement – on which we now sat – a sideboard and a bookcase, largely empty save for a stack of fused-together magazines and ancient hardbacks. No TV or anything approaching modern technology. A radio sat on the sideboard, a relic from the nineties.

Fincher's body lay cooling beside the dining table. Walsh tried to ignore it, but his eyes were drawn back to it. Bodies tend to do that. Doesn't matter how many you've seen, there's something magnetic about a corpse, something that touches us in a way the conscious mind cannot truly comprehend.

Walsh lifted his eyes to mine, returned to our earlier exchange. 'So you came out here to check on old Tom Fincher? On a night like this. You never cease to surprise me, Harry.'

I said nothing.

'And then you called Clara out? Is that right?' He looked at the junior detective.

'Yes,' she said.

Walsh's brow furrowed. 'Why?'

'Why what?' Clara's eyes seemed to glow in the gloomy light.

'Why did Harry bother to call you out here? Knowing you weren't feeling well? Weather like this?'

'Two detectives at a crime scene,' I said. 'Standard operating procedure.'

Walsh looked sceptical. 'SOPs can and often are treated more as guidance notes, Harry. You know that.'

'What exactly is it you're asking, Kevin?'

He blinked, suddenly aware of the undertone in my voice. 'Oh, nothing, nothing. Just trying to pass the time here.' He hid his discomfort by taking another sip from his flask.

A silence enfolded the room.

#

I wonder how long it will be before the truth comes out.

In the UK, the homicide clearance rate is well over fifty percent. And the ones that aren't solved are the randoms, the ones where there is simply no connection to the victim. Perhaps either I or Clara would confess, of our own accord or in an interview room. Perhaps the truth would spill from us unbidden, by gesture, by facial expression.

I have told you two untruths tonight. Both times it was a deliberate misdirection rather than an outright lie. Semantics, as my gran would say. I lied and I will have to explain the first lie if you are to understand the second.

I told you that my wife had left me a year ago. I wanted you to think that we had divorced or separated. My wife died. Cancer. She was diagnosed not long after Clara joined our unit, after I became Clara's mentor. Clara surprised me. She saw that I wasn't coping, saw that I needed help that a man like me would never ask for. And so, she offered it willingly and without comment. She talked to me, words beyond her years, even when I offered nothing in return. She sat with me, shared the unbearable silences as I contemplated life without the only woman I have ever loved. She came to our home, became friends with my wife. We had never had children and suddenly it was as if Anne had found that missing part of our lives. Not that it saved her. But I am certain it made that final year bearable, more than bearable. Clara's presence, her attentiveness, filled Anne with a joy I cannot put into words. Clara was an orphan, had never known real parents. Shuffled between foster homes, she had navigated life on others' terms until finally finding her own place in the world.

My wife fell in love with Clara and so, by extension, did I. Anne had always told me that I would have made a great father. I don't know about that. But standing beside my wife's grave on a freezing cold January morning I had felt Clara's presence by my side and knew that if ever I had had a child I could not have felt more for it than I did for this young woman who had suddenly appeared in our lives.

'I need to use the bathroom.' I stood up and walked towards a door at the back of the living area. I shut the door behind me, walked to the sink, turned on the tap, splashed cold water on my face. I faced my reflection, pale and ghostly beneath the light bulb.

And now to the second lie. I told you that I had killed a man. As my story unfolded, you took it to mean that I had murdered Tom Fincher. You waited for me to explain why. But here is where words can become slippery, can shape-shift and take on new meaning once you change the angle of view. I didn't kill Tom Fincher. The man that I had killed was looking back at me from the mirror. . . . Do you understand? For a man to go against everything he believes in, everything he has ever stood for, he must first kill that version of himself. That's what I had had to do in order to help Clara. That is the decision I made when the moment came.

Clara had called my mobile earlier that evening. Her voice had sounded as if she was calling from another world. She told me, calmly, that she was standing inside Tom Fincher's home in Krike and that she had just murdered him. She explained why.

It took only seconds for me to arrive at my decision. And once it was done, I moved ahead without looking back.

I told her to wait there for me, not to call anyone else.

An hour later, I arrived at Fincher's home. Quickly, I assessed the scene. Clara was sitting on the sofa, the knife still in her hand. A lifetime processing such environments stood me in good stead.

I pulled on gloves, then gently pried the knife from Clara's hands. I walked out of the back of the house, down to the cliff edge, and threw the knife into the ocean.

I went back in and cleaned up evidence of Clara's presence as best I could. Thankfully, there hadn't been a struggle. Clara had simply picked up a kitchen knife and stabbed Tom. Taken him completely by surprise. She had blood on her. Tom's blood. I sent her to the bathroom to clean up as best she could. Then I went to my car and brought back two white crime-scene suits and two sets of blue latex gloves. By the time we were done, Clara simply looked like what she was: a homicide detective attending the home of a murder victim and taking every precaution not to contaminate the scene.

Will it work? I don't know. Homicide detectives are a rare breed. Because the crime of murder is so serious, we don't give up easily. We have a duty to the living not to give up, never to give up. I have tried to control the variables as best I can, but we will have to wait and see what the forensics unit throw up. The only twist here is that, unless the case is assigned elsewhere, we will be investigating ourselves.

I saw Clara looking at me. Something hung in her eyes, a small sense of the horror that I knew was taking root inside her.

She had explained to me what had happened. A moment of fugue that had ended in madness. Clara had always kept her past hidden from me. Now she explained that her mother had been murdered by a man who had come into their lives when Clara had been barely a year old. A twenty-something from the coast calling himself Tom Shaw. That killing sent Clara into the social care system. Her subsequent life had been coloured by that singular event. Nothing had ever been right again.

And then, out of the blue, just a day earlier, she received a phone call. From a man calling himself Tom Fincher. Fincher told her that he was the one who had killed her mother. And now he wanted to atone. To confess.

Clara drove out to Fincher's place, they spoke, and then, the next thing she knew, Fincher was dead on the ground and she was covered in blood.

And then she had called me.

So that is the story, the whole of it.

No more lies.

Confess Your Secret!
by J.C. Bernthal

#

5. The culprit must be determined by logical deductions–not by accident or coincidence or unmotivated confession. To solve a criminal problem in this latter fashion is like sending the reader on a deliberate wild-goose chase, and then telling him, after he has failed, that you had the object of his search up your sleeve all the time. Such an author is no better than a practical joker.

So far, 1930 was not proving a good year for the Star of Suffolk. Our decline had been so obvious by the end of the twenties that we'd reported on it ourselves.

From announcing ourselves as "the source of news for the east of England," we had progressed to "the principal news source for East Anglia," and more recently I'd heard our Editor-in-Chief, Sir Willard, describe the Star as "a pretty well-trusted newspaper."

"All this competition," Sir Willard liked to say. "What's wrong with one paper for each neck of the woods? It's all the same news, after all." Perhaps this reveals the extent of his business acumen.

But don't ask me. I was little more than a secretary. Although, since we made cuts – or, since we made "ahem – changes," as Sir Willard would say – I'd had actual writing work to do. Not quite journalism, but definitely work.

When I joined, in '28, we kept a staff of thirty, not including the printers, and filled the offices, publishing seven days a week, plus evening editions. Now, the five section editors had become the sole reporters, I handled "letters and women's things," and the main part of our building, the shared office, stood largely empty, an army of dust-laced typewriters disturbed by occasional freelancers and mostly, echoingly, silent. We published only on Sundays.

"Letters and Other," as it was properly called, had never had a "team" in the way Politics, Sport, Crime, Literature, and Theatre and Society (a.k.a. gossip) had. But it had struck me as a chance to bring something to the paper that our readers would enjoy and to which they'd return. I had volunteered to keep it going for no extra pay.

Those last three words had encouraged Sir Willard, who'd given me free rein with the section. Reactions had been mixed. "Really, Miss Snape," George Jessup, the Crime reporter, had said, flinging down Tips for Cleaning Your Wax-Blocked Ears as if forced to eat earwax. "This is hardly journalism."

But Handy Household Hints had proven a hit, and soon I'd had to invent a nom de plume. Ideas conjured up by 21-year-old unmarried Dorothy Snape didn't have the same ring as homespun wisdom from the stately, comforting, and entirely imaginary Mrs Miller.

So successful had Mrs Miller become that I'd been forced to give her more featurettes. Far and away my most successful was Confess Your Secret! in which readers were encouraged to write in with a secret – something they had never told and may never tell anyone, but which they would like to see in print. Strictly anonymous at every stage. Perhaps they would get a thrill, reading their own words at the breakfast table and knowing that thousands of others were reading them, too.

By August 1930, it looked unstoppable. We received dozens of write-ins every day. Filtering out the incomprehensible and the disturbing, I was usually left with a pool of six or seven each week to write up for printing on the Saturday. I was working on them that day, while manning the reception desk.

"My husband snores," I typed from the handwritten postcard, "and it drives me to drink. He is a good man but sometimes I long to slap him!"

That exclamation mark struck me as unnecessary. I debated removing it, something Oliver Westwood, our Literature reporter, would have done without hesitation. But, no. Perhaps it softened the tone and dressed up the grievance with a jest.

I was typing the signature, MRS NEVERSLEEPS, when the front door clicked open.

"I am so sorry to intrude...." It was a quiet, twittery voice which didn't sound sorry at all. Its owner seemed to me impossibly old.

I adopted my most professional tone. "Welcome to the Star of Suffolk. How may I help you, Mrs–?"

"Miller," she said. "Miss Mary Miller."

"Oh, my stars!" I chided myself for intoning the exclamation mark. But – Miller!

"Is something the matter, my dear?"

"No, no." I recovered my tone. Miller was not an unusual name. "How may I help you?"

The elderly Miss Miller placed her knitting bag on a chair. I came out from behind the desk to hear her.

"I would like," she said, "to speak to your Mrs Miller."

"Ah. I'm afraid it's not possible."

"It is urgent."

"Mrs Miller is not here," I said. To reveal the lie of her existence could have cost me my job, so this would have to do.

"Please, my dear," said the visitor. "I am her sister."

Quite uncontrollably, I laughed. "She is Mrs Miller," I managed at last. "That is her married name."

"Sister-in-law, if you will." Mary Miller waved aside such matters. "Now that that is all settled, I'm afraid I really must see dear..." Here, she trailed off. I had never bothered to give my alter ego a Christian name. "My dear sister," she concluded.

"And what is this about?"

Before she could answer, the telephone started ringing. Retreating behind my desk, I muttered an apology and lifted the receiver.

"Star of Suffolk. How may I assist you?"

The voice on the other end was faint and coarse, as if the receiver had been smothered. "I need – I need to confess my secret."

When one has answered the telephone enough times, one develops the ability to categorise the parties on the line. I identified this gentleman (almost certainly a man) not as a nuisance caller but as a difficult one. He would have something earnest to tell me. Certainly, it would be something unimportant, but important to him. It would be quite unprintable because it would be so earnest and, most likely, rambling. Whatever his story, I knew he would take a long time telling it.

A little-appreciated thing about secretaries is that people like to talk to, or at least at, us. That is why so many of us have cultivated a stiff, forbidding demeanour. But I never did. I have always tried to be easy to speak to.

"And what secret would you like to confess, sir?" I prompted. My pencil and paper were ready for shorthand.

After what felt like a very long time, he spoke.

"I did something terrible. Many years ago. I want – I need – I must confess."

This sounded slightly more serious than a snoring husband. No words escaped me. I listened.

"I... I killed someone."

The silence that followed felt eternal, but it must have lasted no more than ten seconds. It was broken by an unusual-sounding click, which seemed to spur the man on the line into speech .

"I'm so sorry – it's changed everything about my life – I was almost a kid myself, back then – I didn't know what we were doing – that poor boy – and his sister – I – I don't know why I went along with it – I don't want to be a murderer – please, don't write this up – I just had to tell someone – after all this time – I am so sorry, Dotty – I …"

He called me Dotty. He knew my name, then. More than that, he knew me well enough to shorten it.

The voice was not well disguised. The second he said my name, I knew.

"Charlie," I interrupted. Mr Jessup was right. I do not have a journalist's instincts. A real journalist would have let him talk. But it was a shock. If I was right, this caller was not only known to me, but in the building. A colleague – Charlie Shard, our Sports reporter. "Charlie," I said again. "Is this a joke?"

The line went dead.

# # #

A word on the building. My fiefdom is the threshold, and one door separates it from a large room containing typewriters, once filled with reporters, and now treated largely as an extension of the kitchen. Along each side are private offices for the remaining journalists, and at the back is a staircase leading down to the press and archives. Next to those stairs is Sir Willard's office, overlooking the whole operation.

The old woman was still there, and talking at me. I managed to get some words out – something about an emergency – and raced into the echoing, door-lined hall without looking at her. I wasn't thinking as I darted to Charlie's office. I tapped on the door, and of course no one answered. I hammered on the door. No answer. Then my brain caught up to the fact that he'd just confessed to murder, so I opened the door.

There was nobody in the room. A sheet of paper rested unkeyed in Charlie's typewriter. Beside it lay an empty decanter, a single glass, and an overflowing ashtray. There was nobody there.

Next, I rushed to Sir Willard's office and bang-bang-banged on the door. Most unladylike. The Editor-in-Chief opened it roughly and beckoned me in. He closed the door, which I didn't quite like but it was probably just as well.

What to say was beyond me. In lieu of words, I gave an accurate impression of a fish, freshly dehooked.

"Cat got your tongue?" Our leader was not averse to clichés, nor would he have recognised one had it hit him in the typeface. "Spit it out, gal."

Some inner lens of my mind focussed on those professional women in magazines, who always have a solution and who, between crises, keep the order. The kind of woman who thinks ladders are for climbing, not for darning [stockings]. What would she do? She would report the situation, calmly.

"I'm sorry to disturb you, Sir Willard." And I swear my accent moved up a postcode. "But I'm rather concerned about Mr Shard."

"Charles? What about him?"

You have doubtless heard of newspaper magnates – self-made millionaires with no breeding, overdoing the formality to play the part. In this respect, Sir Willard was the opposite. He was a baronet with old money and vaguely subversive tendencies, which manifested in writing about politics and referring to people by their Christian names.

I continued. "Mr Shard spoke to me on the telephone a few minutes ago."

"Hmm... that is odd. You are in the same building and he has working legs. That's the problem with this generation," the baronet concluded, as if this were an original or logical observation. "They're all work-shy. Well, Dorothy, thank you for telling me."

The women in the magazines would stay composed. I breathed in. "Excuse me, Sir Willard. It's not that. It's more to do with what he said. He said some rather disturbing things and hung up. Now I can't find him. He's not in his office."

"Did you ask the operator to reconnect?"

When he said it, like that, it seemed obvious. I shook my head.

"Well, try that. Or, no, I have a better idea." He grinned like he had just thought of the most ingenious thing. "There is a telephone booth outside. One of those new red whadjamacallums. I'll wager he's calling from there."

I'd forgotten about that abomination. It had caused quite a stir upon its installation. A public telephone cabinet – pay a penny and make a call, just outside our offices. I thanked Sir Willard and hurtled – there is no other word for it – down the steps by his door to the printing press. The lower exit, adjacent to the cabinet, was open, which was unusual. This convinced me I was on the right track.

Stepping outside, what I saw was very red. The brilliant paint on the booth was sharpened by sunlight. The sun was menacing against the glass panes, and I couldn't see into the box until I stepped up to it.

And I saw him. Down in a corner, eyes bulging, almost apologetic for the purple marks around his neck. I'd located Charlie Shard.

# # #

While I had rattled from the Reception to … that place, I walked back as if hypnotised. I have no idea how long it took me to get back to my seat, how many people I ignored along the way, or how and when the receiver ended up in my hand. The next thing I knew, I was asking the operator to connect me to the police.

"Is Mrs Miller ready to see me?"

The old woman was still here. I pasted on that smile I once told myself I'd never adopt. The smile a nanny gives a child she's one transgression away from beating.

"It would be best, madam, if you left," I said, and turned my attention to the device in my hand. Then I told the police station exactly what had happened.

The voice on the other end was very kind. They said Inspector Wright would be along in five minutes. In the meantime, I was to inform Sir Willard and, somehow, ensure nobody entered or left the office, or the scene of the crime.

When I hung up the receiver, Miss Miller resumed loquacity.

"Murdered!" she said, almost enjoying herself. "I bet it was a woman. Women do get jealous, don't they? And this gentleman was young, you say? A spurned lover, mark my words. Feminine intuition never lets me down."

"Miss Miller, he was strangled."

There was a lover in the building, as it happened. A fiancée, no less. But Lottie Carter, couldn't write a gossip column without needing a rest. The idea of her throttling a grown man was comical.

"My feminine intuition is finely attuned, and I am never wrong." Except about your namesake's existence. "Besides, I'm practically a detective. I've read all of Sherlock Holmes," Miss Miller added, proudly. "Well, most of him. The recent ones are a little… tedious, don't you think?"

"I'm sorry, madam. I don't have time for this. I must inform my colleagues."

I made for the door and collided with one of them.

"Dotty! I was looking for you," said Oliver Westwood. "What's the matter?"

"Oliver. Mr Westwood. I ain't got time to tell you."

"You haven't got time," said Oliver, automatically.

That was very like him. Oliver Westwood was in his thirties and technically good-looking. That is the most charitable thing I can say.

He'd worked his way up to Literary editor, first as a kind of office boy who stepped in when George went over to Crime, then as a correspondent, and he stepped into the post in 1928 when the old Literary editor retired. To the extent that he had a personality, it was based entirely around the written word. I suppose that made him a good editor. He never corrected Sir Willard's grammar, but he corrected mine frequently.

"Miss Miller will explain," I said, perhaps cruelly, and I left them together.

The others were gathered in the spacious area among the typewriters. Miss Carter, petite and delicate; Mr Jessup, flecked with dandruff; and Sir Willard, holding court. They seemed to be on an impromptu tea break. I asked to speak to Sir Willard privately, and he simply responded, "Dorothy, something terrible has happened."

"I know, sir," I said, a little stunned.

"You know?" Lottie gasped. "Isn't it horrible?"

"I'm so sorry, Miss Carter. I've telephoned the police."

This seemed to confuse her. She stared, and I noticed that she hadn't been crying. I've never had a fiancé, but I imagine that if mine had been murdered, I might cry. Not to mention, Charlotte Carter cried at everything. She was that sort of person. When Oliver told her the only things worse than her split ends were her split infinitives, she took a week off work, citing emotional distress.

I, too, was confused.

The Crime reporter took over. As he spoke, I felt my attention wandering to the checks on his suit and then to his very strong hands. George Jessup was a man in his forties, and had been here longer than any of us, bar the Editor-in-Chief. He spoke carefully. "Miss Snape, we've run out of tea."

"Tea?"

"Tea. Has something else happened?"

"I'm afraid it has."

That wasn't me. It was Miss Miller, joining the party. Oliver protested mutely in her wake. It was she who broke the news to the assembly of news-breakers.

#

George Jessup and Oliver Westwood stood sentinel around the telephone booth, while I offered Lottie brandy in Sir Willard's office. He was trying, vainly, to get rid of Miss Miller.

The brandy made me think of the empty decanter in Charlie's room. He must have been in quite a state when he telephoned me. Guilt over something many years in the past. Whatever state he'd been in, though, Lottie seemed to be in a worse one.

"My poor Charlie," she managed through sobs. "We've known each other since I was sixteen. Why would anyone do that?"

Our visitor had simply told people that Charles Shard had been strangled. She had not, after all, heard the other side of my telephone conversations. I wasn't sure how much to say before the police arrived.

"It was probably some madman who wanted to use the telephone," said Lottie, in a parody of her usual that's-that-and-let's-not-think-any-more-or-we'll-get-wrinkles custom.

I decided to leave it. The poor woman had been through enough. After all, this wasn't her first brush with death.

The story of Arthur Carter was legendary all over Suffolk. Lottie's little brother, he was only eight when he died. But by the time they found the body, he should have been ten.

His had been the most sensational kidnapping of the early post-war years. It had been an astonishing case, because the Carters were not a wealthy family. Still, they had gathered and paid the ransom, and then – nothing. Until, two years later, the bones were found. The boy had probably died the night he was taken, before the first letter.

What made it worse – the ransom notes, so cruel and taunting, had not been sent to the parents but to the newspaper, where Arthur's big sister was working. The Star of Suffolk. I was roughly the age Arthur would have been had he lived and, on this occasion, holding Lottie's hand, I felt guilty for being alive.

"You're brave," I said at last.

"Please stop talking," said Charlotte Carter.

# # #

Inspector Wright had a Mephistophelean beard which didn't suit him, and looked like a man trying to appear clever. He gathered us all in the big typing room. Once we'd introduced ourselves, none of us spoke until he cleared his throat.

"I hope not to detain you for long," he said. "My men are attending to the – to Mr Shard. They have also looked inside his office and discovered, on his typewriter, a letter."

I spoke up without noticing my own voice. "That's impossible. I checked that room before I found him, and the paper in it was blank."

"I said on the typewriter, not in it, Miss Snape. You're the lass who found the –" He glanced tactfully at the weeping Lottie. "The lass who found him?"

"That's me."

"I am, or, it is I," said Oliver, automatically.

Inspector Wright arched an eyebrow.

"Dammit all, man." This was Sir Willard. "What does the letter say?"

And I realised, but did not say, that in or on the typewriter, I would have noticed the letter had it been there before.

The inspector produced a sheet of Basildon Bond paper, and as he unfolded it I could see large, childish capital letters.

Flatly, he read it out. "YOU COULDN'T CATCH SHARD AND ME. YOU CAN'T CATCH ME ALONE. HA. HA. HA. Signed, FIVE HUNDRED POUNDS RICHER. Does anyone here have any idea what that means?"

The reaction was instantaneous. Only the inspector, Miss Miller, and I seemed unignited. Recognition spread among the other three.

George spoke. "Yes, we all know what that means. It means that bastard – excuse me, ladies – is back."

"Which bastard – excuse me, ladies – would that be, sir?"

"The author of that letter," George sighed, somehow contriving to make this story about himself, "is the reason I became the Crime reporter. It must have been a decade ago."

"Ten years exactly," put in Sir Willard. "I'll never forget it."

"We received some terrible letters."

It took George several minutes, but he described the dreadful kidnapping of Arthur Carter, and the letters the Star had received. Lottie wept quietly on Oliver Westwood's shoulder. "They looked like that," he concluded. "The same sort of paper. Capital letters that looked left-handed. I was a Literary editor at the time," he added, returning to the topic of himself. "But Sir Willard decided we needed someone to lead on crime. There had not really been a cause for it before, but things were getting more violent, so I switched over."

"And I went from letters to books," put in Oliver.

"Please, Mr Westwood. This is not about you," the Crime reporter snapped, amazingly. "The letters referred to 'we' and 'us' and the demand was for one thousand pounds. So, signing the letter 'Five Hundred Pounds Richer' indicates this murderer was someone with half the loot. I mean, half the ransom."

I raised my hand. When nobody paid me attention, I spoke. "Inspector, I'd like to speak to you privately."

Just as Inspector Wright was launching into one of those masculine know-your-place spiels that never fail to bore me, the flutelike voice of Mary Miller broke in.

"I am so sorry to interrupt, but I think you may be heading in the wrong direction," she said. "You see, I know who the murderer is." She placed her knitting on her lap and beamed at the room. "The murderer," she said at last, "is Mrs Miller. If that is her real name; she's certainly not one of the Felixstowe Millers. And I note that Mrs Miller is curiously absent from this room."

The inspector gawped at her. "Mrs Miller, the publicity gimmick from the back pages? 'How to Please Your Husband With Seed Cake.' That Mrs Miller?" What interesting reading habits he had. "Who are you and why are you here?"

"I'm practically a detective," said Mary Miller. "And when I noticed some inconsistencies in Mrs Miller's columns – last week, she said her husband had been in the Boer War, and this week he was turning forty – I came here to raise serious concerns about her character. Now, it appears I was justified."

So, that was the nature of her urgent business.

The inspector flicked through his notebook.

"There is no Mrs Miller working today," he said diplomatically. "And according to my notes, Miss Snape spoke to the deceased on the telephone just minutes before he was – before the incident. It took place outside, by the back entrance to this office, and the murderer must have escaped via this building."

"How do you make that out, eh?" asked Sir Willard, gruffly.

"Oh, that's easy, sir. The note. It was left in Mr Shard's office. And you, Miss Snape, didn't see it when you checked on him before. That means it was delivered while you were speaking with Sir Willard."

I spluttered. "But I never mentioned whether I'd seen it or not."

"You mentioned what was in the typewriter. You'd have mentioned something on it." Not so unobservant after all. "That places the assailant inside this building, and the only way he could have escaped is through the front door."

"Nobody left that way," said the old lady. "I was there the whole time and saw nobody."

"We only have your word for that, Miss—?"

"Mary Miller."

The inspector rolled his eyes. "Of course it's Miller. Lord, if only this were a detective story. No confusingly similar names in those."

Oliver Westwood cleared his throat. "I can vouch for Miss Miller," he said. "I came through to find Miss Snape – I was going to ask if she had seen the tea – and Miss Miller was knitting. She'd clearly been there some time."

"When was this?"

"About five minutes before all this kicked off."

"So, you were making tea in the kitchen during this time?"

"No. I was looking for tea. There isn't any. I thought I'd ask the secretary first. Then I knocked on doors."

"So, you would have seen anyone pass through this room and into Mr Shard's office."

Oliver hesitated. "I wouldn't say that. You see, I rummaged around the kitchen pretty thoroughly, and didn't pay attention to anything out here. It's quite closed off."

The inspector eyed him suspiciously.

"Well," he said. "If nobody else came in or out, it stands to reason that one of you did this. But what does this old case have to do with Mr Shard?"

That was my cue. Haltingly, I told all I knew – the exact nature of the telephone call. The room fell deathly still.

# # #

"It's a bad business," said George Jessup, unoriginally. He was showing Inspector Wright the archive, downstairs. I was with them because I had keys.

"Poor Miss Carter. It was on this day in 1920 that we received the first letter. She was just a girl of sixteen, and it was her first week as an assistant. I cannot believe it. Mr Shard was so kind, so supportive. He more than anyone looked after her. What she must be feeling, I can't imagine."

I unlocked the relevant drawer and he rifled through files of correspondence.

"Please, Miss Snape," he said, "look after Miss Carter. She's been on rather strong sleeping salts for the last few years. To deal with her nerves, you know. And she might do something silly. Here we are."

Letters. August 1920. There were about one hundred letters in the folder. Many of them had been annotated in angry red ink.

"What's all this?" asked Wright.

"Oh, that's just Oliver," I said. "He dealt with letters back then, and liked to correct the grammar."

Wright shrugged. "We all deal with stress in our own ways." He found a sheet of unfolded Basildon Bond paper. This one had presumably shocked Oliver so much he hadn't annotated it. He read: "WE HAVE ARTY CARTY. WE WOULD LIKE ONE THOUSAND POUNDS . IF IT IS NOT LEFT BEHIND THE TREE ON BOURBON AVENUE AT 11 P.M. ON FRIDAY, THE BOY WILL DIE. WHAT FUN. Succinct and to the point."

"They grew more elaborate. More gloating," said George. "By the fourth or fifth letter, it was clear we needed a Crime reporter. I was only too happy to—"

"Quite so. And nobody ever discovered the authors."

"We always suspected there was someone on the inside. The letters used to appear without postmarks."

"Could the fiancée have found out? Perhaps, on this anniversary, overcome with guilt, Mr Shard chose to confess." Well, he had done – clearly – on the telephone to me. "They'd just become engaged to wed. It must have been an emotional time."

George scoffed. "Charlotte Carter is a frail woman. She couldn't have throttled a man. Even an emotional one."

"What about the others?"

This time, George shrugged. "Miss Snape we can let out for the same reason. Sir Willard would hardly kill his Sports correspondent a week before the Stowmarket horse race. Mr Westwood only cares about books. And I – well, I know I didn't do it," he finished, weakly.

"Do you have an alibi, sir?"

"No," said George Jessup. Unsuitably, he grinned.

# # #

Upstairs, silence had evolved to furore. As we entered, Mary Miller was in full force.

"I tell you, this Mrs Miller is a blackguard. She must have come in disguised as a… a waiter. Nobody notices servants."

Sir Willard had grown quite rubicund. "And I tell you, madam, that everybody would have noticed a waiter in a newspaper office. Wait! No! I tell you that this Miller woman does not exist."

"Does not exist?! Certainly, I do!"

"Mrs Miller, Miss Miller."

The old lady turned to us. "Ah, Inspector. Sir Willard has gone mad." Sir Willard exhaled.

"As for the letter," Miss Miller continued, a little more serenely. "It's like that story of Edgar Allan Poe's. It was hidden in plain sight all along. 'The Pearlescent Letter'. You should read it."

"'The Purloined Letter'," said Oliver through his teeth.

"Please, Mr – whatever your name is – I know what I'm talking of."

"You know of what you speak."

"Indeed, I do. I'm glad you agree. And this is just the same. Monsieur Dupin, a great detective but rather indebted, I think, to Sherlock Holmes."

"Dupin came first!" cried Oliver.

"Details, details," said Miss Miller, breezily. "Now, if we examine the letter, we find something quite interesting."

"Inspector, can't you make her shut up?" asked Sir Willard.

But the inspector merely stood there, trying to appear clever.

"I think," said Mary Miller, "that the choice of words is most significant. "You couldn't catch Mr Shard and I..."

"Shard and me..."

"No, Mr Westlake – it was definitely 'Shard and I'."

"It absolutely wasn't."

"That is proper formal grammar, dear sir."

"I know my grammar and it bloody well wasn't."

"If you say so. This letter – this Shard and I..."

"...and me!" Oliver was quite as red in the face as our Editor-in-Chief. "Me! Me! Me! I would rather die than write 'You couldn't catch Shard and I'! I know what I wrote and I wrote 'me'!"

Another moment of stasis.

# # #

Several days passed before we got the full story. His English usage challenged, Oliver had broken down utterly. He told the police everything. How, ten years ago, he'd selected Charlie Shard, his most impressionable colleague, to join him in a murder plot.

Killing for pleasure, they'd called it. Seeing if they could get away with it. That hadn't been his motive, of course – he had wanted to advance his career. With a murder case on their doorstep, or in their letterbox, they'd needed a Crime reporter, and with George Jessup taking that role, a vacancy had opened up for Oliver's ideal position – working with books. He had not accounted for Charlie's growing closeness to the victim's sister.

On the anniversary, exactly as Inspector Wright guessed, Charlie had broken down with guilt. I'd barely acknowledged the click on the 'phone line, but now it was clear that Oliver had been listening in from his office. As soon as he'd established what was happening, he'd gone out, strangled his accomplice, and returned.

Miss Miller had nearly discovered everything. What led him to write that silly note? A murderer's vanity, I suppose, or the comforting ritual of old habits. That was something I should have spotted – even in times of stress, he had time to correct other people's grammar, but those letters had been the only ones he hadn't annotated back in the day – because they were already perfectly written. He'd rather die than commit an error of usage, even writing in disguise.

For whatever reason, he'd written another one this time and, hearing me with Sir Willard, tried to bring it to what he thought was an empty Reception. When he'd found someone there he'd invented a tea break and slipped the note into Charlie's empty study. The tea leaves, incidentally, were found in the kitchen bin.

I should have known something was wrong. A man like that doesn't look for the tea leaves. He waits for someone to find and brew them.

# # #

The Star was closing down. I exchanged appropriate platitudes with Sir Willard and wished Mr Jessup well, but the person I really wanted to see was Lottie. She was packing things up in her office. She was, she said, finally sleeping well – and without her sleeping powders. "Just as well. I ran out the day Charlie died."

"Really?" I felt there was a story here. Perhaps I should be a journalist.

"You know," she said. "I thought so much of the stuff would over-power the taste of brandy, but it didn't. It was all I could think of, when Charlie told me what he'd done. I poured the sachet into the decanter and watched him drink the whole thing, while he told me the story. Just before he stumbled out to telephone you. I think it was enough – or would have been."

She said it like that, very matter-of-factly. Then she caught herself.

"Have I been very wicked, Dotty?"

"I think," I said, taking her hand in mine, "that the case is already closed. No need to get bogged down in details."

I glanced towards Sir Willard's office, where Miss Miller was drumming the door, refusing to accept his silence as proof that he wasn't in. An interesting woman – and she had said this would prove to be a woman's crime. Perhaps there was something in her feminine intuition, after all.

With a Little Help
by Edith Maxwell

#

6. The detective novel must have a detective in it; and a detective is not a detective unless he detects. His function is to gather clues that will eventually lead to the person who did the dirty work in the first chapter; and if the detective does not reach his conclusions through an analysis of those clues, he has no more solved his problem than the schoolboy who gets his answer out of the back of the arithmetic.

Josie Page gazed at the new wing of the Free Hospital for Women and swiped at a tear. The main part of the Brookline institution was decades old and provided health care to all women at no cost. The addition, built only four years ago in 1922, was for well-off ladies who could afford to pay for their private rooms and better treatment. If only her mother could have been treated there, she might still be alive today.

Josie squared her twelve-year-old shoulders. Mother was gone, and that was that. Her satchel was packed with a good haul from today's work near the entrance to the new wing, and the fall light was already dimming at three-thirty. It was time to head home to Father and her little brothers.

She slowed her step as the streetcar clanged to a stop and two ladies stepped down. These were not society matrons in fur coats and heavy gold jewelry. Matrons didn't arrive on the streetcar. These two were both tall and looked under thirty. One had a tousled cap of honey-colored hair unadorned by a hat and didn't carry a handbag. The other, in a navy cloche and open coat over a blue dropped-waist dress, smoked a ciggie. They paused in front of the entrance to the addition.

Josie pretended to fumble in her pockets for streetcar fare until the trolley moved along. The two women were well-dressed. Maybe she could relieve that handbag of a small purse.

"Amelia, we have to get to the bottom of the suspicious death," Cloche said. "And I can't figure out how we're going to do it."

"We must," Amelia said. "But you're the lady PI, Dot. You're supposed to know these things."

Josie tried to hide her interest. Suspicious death? A lady private investigator? This afternoon had just grown a lot more intriguing.

"Let's continue with our plan," Dot said. "We're not going to learn the truth about that patient expiring without any apparent cause if we don't apply some shoe leather to the hallways of the hospital."

Amelia shuddered. "Do you know how much I hate hospitals?"

"Be that as it may. We're a team, remember? It's Wednesday, and you can't fly until the weekend. Come on."

Amelia shrugged and followed Dot through the door.

Fly? Josie thought the tousled hair looked familiar. That woman had to be the daring lady pilot, Amelia Earhart. Josie had read a story about her in the newspaper. She wanted to follow the pair inside, except she needed to get along. Father had no idea she'd quit school. He thought she merely had a job after classes ended where she earned the money she brought home. She would keep her new occupation a secret from him as long as she could.

But Josie was intrigued. She thought she might return here tomorrow afternoon. With any luck, she'd encounter the PI and the aviator again.

* * * * * *

Inside, Dot succeeded at moving them past the gorgon at the front desk. If Dorothy Henderson couldn't talk her way past an obstacle, no one could.

"Remind me how you came to know of this woman's death," Amelia said to Dot.

"Mrs. Ursula Fleming was an acquaintance of Aunt Etta's from some literary salon she frequents. When my aunt asks me to investigate, she always has a sound reason for doing so." Dot steered them past an orderly with a mop who was adding a new layer of acrid-smelling cleaning solution to the tiled hallway.

Amelia sniffed the scent and shuddered but kept going. "Do any of the people in charge think this Ursula's demise was suspicious?" She kept her voice low.

"No. Etta requested the police look into the matter, but she said they didn't investigate at all." Dot matched her soft voice. They didn't need any snoopy eavesdroppers. "They called Ursula a sick old lady who died of natural causes."

"Was she Etta's age?" Amelia asked. "Your aunt isn't particularly old. What is she, fifty?"

"Fifty-five and in excellent physical shape. She devotes herself to staying fit, certainly. I believe Ursula might have been all of sixty, if that. Some people wear that age poorly. Not Ursula, according to Etta."

The two walked on, past doors open to private rooms, past aproned nurses in white, past a closed door marked, "Surgery. No Admittance." Dot had already outlined the bare facts of the case to Amelia and wondered for a moment why she didn't remember. Still, her friend had a busy life in her daytime role as teacher and social worker at the settlement house, and her thoughts were usually on her next gravity-defying flight. Going aloft in a flimsy airplane was not for Dot. She'd been strong-armed into accompanying the aviator once in the name of an urgent crime-fighting inquiry. Her nerves and stomach had barely survived the experience.

"Here we are." Dot pointed to the "Nurses Only" sign on a closed door to their left. "Follow my lead, all right?" She rapped on the door.

Amelia nodded.

A young woman in a crisp white apron who didn't even look twenty opened the door. "Yes, miss?" Her hat was the slouchy cap of a student nurse

Dot pulled up to her full height and spoke with as much authority as she could muster. "I am Miss Dorothy Henderson with the HS Agency. I need to speak with Nurse Madeline Day, if you please."

The girl opened her mouth, closed it, and finally spoke. "I'm sorry miss, she's not in. Perhaps you'd like to talk to Matron?"

"Is Nurse Day in the hospital, or has she left?" Dot asked.

"She's, um, well, I'm not supposed to..." Her voice trailed off as she shot a quick, panicked glance behind her at the large room full of white-clad women. Some attended to paperwork, while others sterilized equipment or measured medicines. The door was open to an office at the back, which also had a large window in the wall, revealing a stern-looking and robustly figured woman in white at the desk.

A nurse bustled up behind Amelia, who stepped to the side. "Is there a problem?"

"Nurse Day, these ladies would like to speak with you." The girl's face and shoulders relaxed.

"Very well," the nurse said. "Back to your tasks, now please."

"Yes, miss." The girl scurried away in relief.

"I'm Nurse Day." The woman clasped her hands in front of her, her starched hat firmly pinned to blond hair in a sleek bun, her eyes an icy blue. "How can I help you?"

Dot introduced Amelia and herself. "We'd like to discuss the circumstances of Mrs. Fleming's passing."

Nurse Day blinked and her shoulders tensed. "If you're with the police, they have come and gone. They agreed with the doctor and the medical examiner and officially declared her death to be uncomplicated." She cocked her head. "You don't look like you're police officers in the least."

"We're not." Amelia smiled with her gap-toothed grin. "But we're close friends of Mrs. Fleming's beloved niece, Winnie, who is distraught with grief. We'd only like to have a look at the room where the deceased went to meet her heavenly Father, if you don't mind, so we can set Winnie's mind at ease."

Dot suppressed a snort. Her friend hadn't exactly followed Dot's lead, but it was a good ruse. She was happy to play along.

"That's fine, then." The nurse's shoulders relaxed. "We haven't yet cleaned out the room. Please follow me."

As they walked, a solemn procession approached. A male orderly pushed a fully draped figure on a stretcher. A different student nurse accompanied him, her eyes reddened.

"What's happened, Student Nurse King?" Nurse Day asked her.

"Doctor couldn't save Victoria Child, ma'am."

"She'd been ill," the nurse said. "I'm not surprised."

Miss King gaped for a moment before closing her mouth and composing her face.

"May she rest in peace," Nurse Day said. "Come along, ladies."

"Were you in charge of Mrs. Child's care?" Dot asked Miss Day as they walked on.

"I was. I supervise half the floor."

# # #

Outside the window to Ursula's former room were the now-bare branches of a stately elm tree. The coverlet on the bed was pulled up but not neatly made. The room had none of Ursula's personal effects in sight. Etta had said her friend had had a successful surgery but then developed complications and had stayed in the wing for several weeks. Wouldn't someone close to her – Etta, even – have brought in a favorite photograph, a cherished book of poetry, a vase for flowers?

"You were quite deft, my friend, by convincing that nurse to leave us alone in here," Amelia said.

"We can't very well snoop for clues with Nurse Day watching us." Dot pulled the door shut and turned the lock.

Amelia plopped into a chintz-covered armchair in the corner. "I need more information. All you told me was that we were on another sleuthing excursion, and that this Mrs. Fleming's death seems odd. Why? Clues to what?"

"I'm not sure. Etta said she hasn't heard a thing about these so-called natural causes. The lady was a widow with no children, so she doesn't have family to prod an investigation. I think we're going to need an informant, and a glance into the medical record."

"The name of the doctor who declared it a natural death would be useful, as well," Amelia said.

"Let's get searching. They're not going to want us in here forever." Dot knelt and peered under the bed.

"Right, you are." Amelia jumped to her feet. She opened the top bureau drawer and ran her hand around the inside.

Dot lifted the bed covers, felt around the edges of the mattress, and lifted it to check underneath. Amelia searched the last drawer and then opened the closet door.

"Empty," she declared before closing it.

As a knock came at the door, Dot slid her hand between the armchair cushion and the side.

"Ladies?" The doorknob rattled.

Dot fished out a slip of paper and pocketed it. "Are we done?" she whispered to Amelia.

Her friend nodded.

"Look sorrowful and pious," Dot murmured. She opened the door to Madeline Day, whose knuckles were raised to rap again. "Thank you for giving us these few minutes with the memories of our dear friend's auntie. We won't take up any more of your time." Dot slid past the nurse.

Amelia nodded her thanks as she followed Dot down the hall.

#

Amelia pulled Dot to a halt outside the entrance. "What does that piece of paper say?" She pulled a crumpled cigarette out of her pocket and smoothed it out.

"Light?" Dot snapped open her silver lighter and lit Amelia's smoke as well as one for herself. She treated herself to a nice long drag, then blew it out as she fished the paper out of her pocket. She read the only word – *Help!* – and frowned, extending the note to Amelia.

"Help?" Amelia handed it back. "She wrote a note asking for help. With what?"

"Maybe someone had threatened her, or she was being poisoned."

"That's horrid." Amelia puffed on her ciggie. "Like that awful man at the Halloween parade, remember? Has he been convicted of his poisonings?"

"Not yet, but he's still behind bars. The legal system can take a while, you know."

"I suppose. But we don't have a while. What if another lady dies? Maybe that Mrs. Child dame was also killed before her time."

Dot gave a slow nod. "Did you see the student nurse's reaction when Nurse Day said the deceased was sick?"

"The girl looked like she was about to object."

"Exactly. We need to get to the bottom of this, and fast." Dot took another puff.

Amelia checked her wristwatch. "Crikey. I have to run along. I have a meeting at Denison House at five o'clock."

"Go ahead. I think I'll head to the library and do some digging for information."

"Shall we return tomorrow and see what we can see?" Amelia asked.

"We shall, my friend."

# # #

Dot made her way to the Boston Public Library. Inside, she hurried between the marble lions guarding the wide steps of the stately, reverent building devoted entirely to books and learning. After she settled into the second floor reading room, Dot's task was to discover the name of the head doctor in the wing. She was curious about the regulations governing the medical examiner and if the hospital had a board of directors. Aunt Etta might be acquainted with one or more of them.

An hour later found Dot striding toward Etta's Beacon Hill home, Dot's temporary residence, nearly stomping in frustration. She hadn't been able to uncover a thing. Not the doctor's name, not the names of the board members, not the regulations governing the medical examiner. By now the street lights were lit and it was too late in the day to make telephone inquiries. A good long walk followed by a stiff drink, thanks to her aunt's stash of excellent hooch, would be just the ticket. Dot would start anew tomorrow.

# # #

Amelia pulled her bright yellow Kissel Speedster to the curb in front of the hospital at a little after one o'clock the next afternoon.

Dot repositioned her cloche on her bob. "Must you drive so fast, Amelia?" She'd clutched the hat in her lap on the way here so it didn't fly away. Amelia never put the auto's top up unless the weather was inclement. Today was sunny, although the November air was chilly.

"I love speed." The aviatrix grinned at Dot. "What more can I say? Now, what's our plan?"

"I've gotten absolutely nowhere in my inquiries. We're going to have to talk our way into the inner workings of the place." Dot pulled out her smoking kit and lit a cigarette to calm her nerves.

"I wonder if we can have a little chat with that student nurse," Amelia said." What was her name, King?"

"Good idea. One of us can make up a female relative who is thinking of coming here for treatment and ask Student Nurse King what she thinks. Or we could pretend one of us needs a stay in a nice private wing of a hospital."

"That's even better. We can say we'd like to meet with the supervising doctor."

"We'll have to avoid Madeline Day, though," Dot said.

"Yes."

A slender schoolboy of perhaps eleven or twelve passing on the sidewalk slowed his pace. Dot thought it was a bit early for school to be out but she shrugged it off. Perhaps the children had a half day on Wednesdays.

"Do you know how your aunt's friend actually died?" Amelia asked.

"No, but Etta thought it was too sudden. Ursula had had surgery to remove her gallbladder or some such thing and was recovering well. And then last weekend, *bam*, she was gone."

The lad knelt to retie his shoe.

"I found it odd when Nurse Day said the police agreed that Ursula's death wasn't suspicious," Dot said. "Do you think she was telling the truth?"

"That's why we're here, isn't it? To discover the truth in all its sometimes sordid glory." Amelia opened her door and sauntered to the sidewalk, where the schoolboy had begun to move on. "Say, young man, can you watch my car for me? There's a coin in it for you."

The lad, in knickers and cap, turned. His face was pretty, with long dark lashes and not a trace of a beard, and he had a satchel slung crosswise across his chest.

"I'd be happy to, miss." He touched the brim of his cap.

"We're just going inside." Amelia gestured toward the hospital. "Be back in an hour or less. That all right?"

"Yes, miss."

"Thanks, kid."

Dot and Amelia made their way along the brick walkway to the entrance of the private wing a few yards away. The door opened before they arrived at it. Student Nurse King pushed through. Her face was flushed and her cap slightly askew. Not wearing a coat, she hurried in their direction but her gaze was focused downward and her arms were wrapped around her chest.

"Miss King," Dot began. "Are you all right?" The poor thing certainly didn't look all right.

Startled, the girl glanced up. "Pardon me?"

"I asked if you were all right." Dot kept her voice low and gentle.

Her eyes filled. "No, I don't suppose I am."

"How can we help, sweetheart?" Amelia asked. "And what's your first name?"

"I'm Harriet, miss. I don't think you can help at all. It's just…" Her voice trailed off.

"Come and sit, Harriet." Dot led her to a nearby bench under a bare-branched maple tree. "I'm Dot Henderson, and this is Amelia. Would you like a smoke, dear?"

"No, thank you, Miss Henderson. The one time I smoked with my girlfriends, it made me sick to my stomach," Harriet said. "Anyway, Nurse Day would have my head. She's very strict with the students."

"Tell us what's troubling you," Amelia urged.

Harriet studied her hands. She gripped one with the other and spoke gazing at her lap. "It's Dr. Ross, you see. He…" Her voice trailed off.

"He what?" Dot prodded. She would light up a cigarette for herself, but she didn't want the girl returning to work reeking of tobacco.

"When he thinks no one is looking, he lets his hands free on the students." She lifted her head and squared her shoulders. "It's horrid. The man is married! He shouldn't be doing that."

Amelia's mouth turned down as she made a growling sound.

"Have you told Nurse Day or the matron?" Dot asked.

"They don't believe us. It's like Doctor is a god or something. And I can't leave. I need to finish my course, or I'll never work as a nurse. My family relies on my pay."

"We understand." Amelia leaned against the tree, crossing her ankles.

"Is Dr. Ross the head doctor?" Dot asked.

"He's the only one for this wing."

"What can you tell us about the deaths of Mrs. Child and Mrs. Fleming?" Amelia asked.

Harriet's eyes went wide.

"It's all right, Harriet," Dot said in her most soothing voice. "It's just that we saw your reaction when Miss Day said Victoria Child had been ill."

"She hadn't been ailing at all," the student said. "She'd had an operation on her knee, but she was to be discharged in two days' time. I have no idea why Nurse Day said that."

"In what way did the lady die?" Dot asked.

"I don't know, exactly. She had vomited overnight, and the odd thing was that several of her teeth fell out."

"Was she old?" Amelia asked.

"Not very. I believe her chart said she was forty-six," Harriet said. "Her teeth had looked healthy during the week I cared for her. And she wasn't one of the rich biddies we usually treat. I mean, Mrs. Child must have had enough money to pay the bill, but she was nice. Some of our patients, well, I don't think they've ever done a lick of actual work in their lives."

"How about Ursula Fleming?" Dot asked.

"She was so kind to me." Harriet swiped at a tear.

"Had she also vomited and lost teeth?" Amelia crossed her arms.

"She'd vomited, but she wore false teeth, so—"

"Student Nurse King!" Madeline Day stormed toward them. "What are you doing out here?"

Harriet jumped to her feet. "I'm sorry, Nurse Day. I'm on my way."

Madeline's nostrils flared. "See to it that you are. We don't want any more of your patients expiring because you neglected them."

Harriet's face paled as she hurried back toward the building.

Dot stood. "It's not her fault, ma'am. I'm afraid we waylaid her. Miss Earhart might need to become a patient here."

Amelia nodded.

The nurse's expression changed from angry to welcoming. "I'd be happy to give you a tour of the facilities, miss."

"Thank you," Amelia said. "We wondered if we might speak with Dr. Ross, however. I'm rather particular about my medical care."

"I'm afraid he's quite busy, miss. As am I. Please telephone our office for an appointment." She walked briskly to the door and disappeared through it.

Dot glanced at the Amelia's car. The boy charged with watching it was staring at them, with the fair skin of his brow knit into a frown.

"Well, now, that's a fine kettle of fish." Amelia, fists on waist, stared at the building. "A doc too busy to talk to his next rich client. A head nurse with no soft corners who might be lying about patient deaths and who changed her mind in a flash about the tour. And a poor girl prey to the doctor's wicked advances and not even allowed a few minutes' break."

"All of that, plus teeth falling out of a dead woman otherwise in the prime of health." Dot turned to Amelia and lowered her voice to a murmur. "Your guard there seems keenly interested in our conversation. I wonder why."

"He may have recognized me. I've never met a boy who wasn't interested in airplanes."

"Very well." Except they hadn't been talking about flying. The kid had some other interest in their conversation, Dot was sure. "Do you think we'll get anywhere if we head inside and try to find this Dr. Ross?"

"If we do, I'll have to invent my fictional malady." Amelia grinned. "What is it that I need treatment for, exactly?"

"I did rather spring that on you, didn't I?" Dot thought for a moment. "Perhaps I should come back in one of my disguises."

"Go undercover, as it were, just like the lady PI you are. Why not? Listen, I should get back to Denison House. I'm coaching a practice this afternoon."

"With the Chinese girls?"

"You bet," Amelia said. "We have a few new ones who're still learning the game of basketball. Want a lift home?"

"Thanks, but I think I'll stick around here. Maybe go for a walk to clear my head. I can always take the trolley home."

Amelia thanked the boy and paid him before driving off.

Dot thought she might make a return visit to the BPL. "What could possibly cause a patient to vomit and then lose teeth?" she asked aloud.

# # #

Josie pocketed the coin and stared at the lady called Dot Henderson as she walked away. She and Miss Earhart seemed to be working together as detectives. Miss Henderson had mentioned donning a disguise. Had she recognized that Josie was doing the same today?

It was the mention of Madeline Day that had truly perked up Josie's ears. Madeline lived in her West End neighborhood. She knew Madeline, at least in passing, even though the nurse was much older than Josie, and she hadn't realized Madeline worked here.

Josie had heard of people vomiting and losing teeth just before or after they died. Her auntie had expired in that way after taking too much of a laxative medicine for being chronically stopped up. Josie thought she remembered hearing a story about Madeline's younger sister, who was in service to an imperious dowager. The sister had complained of being ill, but the lady refused to give her time off or to call a doctor, and the sister died, also losing teeth despite being only seventeen.

Perhaps Josie should have spoken up to these two. Despite Miss Henderson being a PI, she seemed lost as to the cause of the two women's deaths. Josie didn't know where to find either Miss Henderson or Miss Earhart, unless they showed up again here tomorrow. She could still see the back of Miss Henderson far down the sidewalk. Josie could set off running after her, or maybe she should try to find Miss Earhart at the settlement house.

But, no. For today Josie would keep working. She could poke around in the gossip byways near where she lived a bit more after she returned home. Maybe she'd have more to share with the ladies tomorrow.

# # #

The next morning, Dot stepped out of a taxi in front of the private wing of the hospital. Rather than dressing as a stylish but businesslike young woman, today she'd worn her most luxurious day dress, which was several inches longer than her normal hemline. She was decked out with heavy gold jewelry, Aunt Etta's mink coat and black velvet hat, and the all-important non-prescription spectacles. She'd Marcelled her hair into waves and added powder on her cheeks, plus a different shade of lipstick. A pair of staid black shoes completed the look of an older and much more wealthy lady.

She raised her chin and mustered an imperious smile to hide her frustration in not yet making a speck of progress on who'd killed Ursula – or how. She'd once again come up short at the library in her efforts to learn about Dr. Ross or the mysterious malady both Ursula and Victoria had died of. Etta had said she had a contact in the medical examiner's office. With any luck, by the end of day they would learn more about the two deaths.

Today Dot was determined to speak with the doctor face to face. Inside, the gorgon at the front desk had been replaced by a student nurse.

"I must speak with Dr. Ross," Dot said.

"I'm sorry, ma'am, but he's—"

"He'll see me. Tell him Mrs. Elizabeth Rogers is here regarding a sizeable financial contribution I plan to make to this institution."

The girl's eyes widened. "Oh, yes, ma'am. Will you please have a seat? I'll fetch him." She scurried away.

Was the hospital short on funds? The facility looked to be in good repair, although that might be due to the wing being less than a decade old. The student seemed to know Ross would be eager to speak to a rich donor.

A man strode up. The buttons of his vest strained over a well-fed midsection, and the tiny broken veins in his cheeks indicated a fondness for drink. He made a small bow at the waist.

"Mrs. Rogers, I am Dr. Roland Ross. How can I help you?" He led her into an office and gestured to a chair. He sat behind the broad and nearly empty desk.

"I've heard a quite a lot about this new private wing, and I'm considering bestowing some considerable funds toward its operation."

His eyes lit up, and it seemed he barely kept from rubbing his hands together.

"But first," Dot went on, "I must inquire about the recent deaths of my friends Ursula Fleming and Victoria Child. They were both in the prime of health needing only a minor surgical procedure. And they both left here dead. How did that happen?"

His eyes narrowed and his mouth looked like he'd tasted a particularly sour lemon. "The well-being of the ladies unfortunately took a turn for the worse, may they rest in peace. These things happen."

"You must have signed the death certificates. What did you put as the cause of death?"

"Now, now, Mrs. Rogers. You don't need to be worrying your head with sordid details like that."

"But I am." She folded her hands and waited.

He straightened two pencils and a blank pad of paper. He glanced at the door. He checked his watch and pushed up to standing.

"Would you look at the time? I have surgery in ten minutes. You can contact our business office about your donation, ma'am."

"Very well." Dot let herself be ushered out and started for the door.

At the desk, Ross leaned over and murmured to the girl. "Tell Nurse Day I need to speak with her in my office immediately."

Surgery? Somehow Dot didn't think so.

# # #

This morning Josie had dressed as the girl she was. It was only ten o'clock, and she'd already succeeded in lifting a fat money clip from a well-dressed gent and had slipped a loaded purse from a gay young lady's open handbag. Both hauls were secure in her school satchel, their owners none the wiser.

She kept the corner of her eye on the entrance to the private wing of the hospital. She hadn't yet spotted the lady detective or Miss Earhart, but she hoped she would. She'd picked up a couple of pieces of information in her neighborhood she thought they would be interested in.

Instead, a slender, mink-coat garbed lady emerged. Everything about her shouted "rich," from the fancy hat to the jewelry. The lady wore a slight frown under her cheaters, but Josie was mostly interested in the unclasped handbag. She was sure it held something that she could benefit from more than this rich dame, who certainly would have more of the same at home.

Josie gauged the woman's trajectory toward the street and positioned herself accordingly. When her mark reached a few others at the curb, all trying to hail a cab, Josie trudged toward her with her gaze on the sidewalk. As she jostled the lady, she tried to slide her fingers into the handbag.

She gasped when an iron grip on her elbow pulled her away from the curb.

"Not so fast, young miss."

Josie looked up, astonished. "Miss Henderson?" She recognized the voice.

The lady stared into her face. "You're the lad from yesterday. I'd know those eyes anywhere. Good at disguises, are you?"

"Well, I..." Josie didn't know if she should launch into the truth or make something up.

Miss Henderson laughed and slipped off her glasses. "I rather am too, it appears. Come sit with me. Let's have a little chat."

She was still gripping Josie's elbow, so she had no choice but to sit on the bench next to the detective.

"Now, what's your name, and why were you were trying to steal from me?"

Josie swallowed. "I'll tell you, but first I need to give you some information. Madeline Day lives in the West End near my father's house, and she's stepping out with the doctor in there." The words gushed out. "I've heard of others who died after vomiting and then losing teeth, including Madeline's little sister, who worked as a maid for a rich lady. The girl was ill but the lady wouldn't let her see a doctor. Madeline's father is a chemist. I think Madeline is poisoning other rich women to get revenge for her sister's death. You should look into what mercury salts do to a person."

Miss Henderson blinked. "Mercury salts."

"Yes, ma'am."

"You've come up with a lot."

"Thank you," Josie said

"You should come and work for me instead of picking pockets. You didn't tell me your name."

"Josie Page, ma'am, and thank you, but I can't." Josie jumped to her feet and sprinted away.

"Wait!"

Josie raised her hand in a wave but didn't slow her pace. She'd been getting the hang of fingersmithing lately. She was good at it. With Father's illness worsening, she needed the money for her family. Miss Henderson wouldn't be able to match her take, she was sure.

# # #

Dot telephoned Amelia at home that evening and related her encounter with Josie.

"She's good, that kid," Amelia said.

"There's more. Aunt Etta pulled some strings in the medical examiner's office. The fellow who signed off on those fraudulent death certificates has been fired. They're doing autopsies on Ursula and Victoria now, but the new examiner knows about mercury salts and said the vomiting and tooth loss is consistent with that kind of poisoning. No wonder poor Ursula tried to ask for help. She must have known she was being poisoned."

"Can you believe it?" Amelia asked. "Josie solved the whole case for us."

"She did. Amelia, we were bested by a twelve year old girl. We needed a little help, and she provided it."

Amelia laughed. "Good for her. You should give her a job."

"I tried to, but she ran away. Also, I wouldn't be surprised if tomorrow morning's newspapers report the arrests of Nurse Day and Doctor Ross."

"And rightly so. It's a good thing this business is over," Amelia said. "The weather tomorrow looks perfect for flying, and now you won't be pressuring me to skip it in favor of helping you."

Dot laughed. "No, I won't."

A Murder Mystery Without a Body by Elly Griffiths

#

7. There simply must be a corpse in a detective novel, and the deader the corpse the better. No lesser crime than murder will suffice. Three hundred pages is far too much bother for a crime other than murder. After all, the reader's trouble and expenditure of energy must be rewarded. Americans are essentially humane, and therefore a tiptop murder arouses their sense of vengeance and horror. They wish to bring the perpetrator to justice; and when "murder most foul, as in the best it is," has been committed, the chase is on with all the righteous enthusiasm of which the thrice gentle reader is capable.

Of course there was a body. I buried it myself. It was a lovely service. Reverend Julie always does a good funeral. 'A woman vicar and a woman undertaker,' I heard Stephen Longstaff say. 'What's the world coming to?' What indeed, I thought, walking slowly down the aisle, preceding the coffin. I kept my face impassive though. Caring and respectful, that's what it says on my reviews. Yes, undertakers get reviewed, too. Karen Claybourne, Lady Funeral Director, is all five stars.

Stephen Longstaff was the dead woman's oldest son. He got the chief mourner's pew at the front of the church and he inherited the Hall, too. There was something squat and satisfied about him, almost toad-like, as he sat beside Caroline, his second wife, and their ten-year-old son, Sebastian. His grown-up son and daughter, with teenage children of their own, sat in the pews behind. Martin, the younger brother, who did something nebulous in Dubai, sat on the other side of the church. No wife, no children.

But, as I say, it was a nice service. May Longstaff was ninety-three, so there was none of the raw horror of a young person's funeral. She'd been a regular at the church, too, so Julie was able to talk about her with familiarity and warmth. As far I know, neither of May's sons went to church but someone had advised them well on the readings. Romans 8:35 and John 14:1. I have a particular aversion to secular funeral poetry, especially the one that ends, 'I am not there, I did not die.' I always want to stand up and shout, 'In that case, it's a shame I embalmed you and nailed you into a coffin then.' But, in this case, those words would prove surprisingly prescient.

May had left detailed instructions for her funeral, which is always a relief to an undertaker. You'd be surprised how many relatives have no ideas of the deceased's wishes and insist on inserting foibles of their own. I had someone dressed up as a dancing squirrel once, and a woodland funeral when the dead man was obviously a C of E–service-at-the-crem type of chap. May wanted to be buried, which is rare these days. It's a bit of a pain for the undertaker, you have to secure the plot, arrange gravediggers, and be sure that your team are capable of lowering the casket. It's a much harder job that just dumping it on a trestle table at the crematorium.

But May's committal was perfect. The sun was shining, not a given in England in April, and a gentle breeze rippled through the yew trees. When the coffin was in the ground, I handed the tray of soil to Stephen. He threw in a careless handful as if he were scattering birdseed. Caroline was more circumspect, letting the dirt trickle through her fingers onto the mahogany coffin lid (no wicker or cardboard for the Longstaffs). I caught the glint of her diamond engagement ring as the sun slanted through the trees. Freddy, Stephen's elder son, was next, then his twin sister, Iris. I offered the tray to Martin, but he shook his head impatiently. Sebastian backed away as if he were scared. I approve of children attending funerals but Sebastian really did look overwhelmed by the occasion. He was a sensitive-looking boy, nothing like the other Longstaffs.

It was as we were leaving the churchyard that I saw him. I was supervising packing the trestle and planks into the hearse, when I noticed that one mourner, a man, was still at the graveside. Everyone else had gone to the wake, which was at Stephen's house, a modern monstrosity within metres of the beautiful Tudor mansion that he had recently inherited.

I approached the man, who was conventionally dressed in a black suit with matching tie.

'Excuse me?'

The man turned and I backed away in surprise, almost stumbling on the uneven ground. Because this man was Stephen Longstaff's double. He was younger, in his thirties was my guess, but I remember when Stephen had that mop of curly hair. Freddy and Iris don't have it but Sebastian has a blond version. This was a Longstaff. I'd bet my best coffin on it.

'The family have gone to the barn,' I said. 'It's in the grounds of the Hall.'

I wasn't invited to the wake. The vicar always is, but never the undertaker.

'I know it,' said the man. 'I'll be on my way there soon.' His accent was strange, nothing like Stephen's upper-class drawl. This was a mixture of West-country and Australian, with maybe a bit of American Midwest around the vowels.

I didn't want to hurry the man away but Arthur was ready to fill in the grave. I could see him, a slightly sinister figure with his spade, lurking in the church porch.

'Have you come far?' I asked, trying to be pleasant whilst subtly suggesting that he should be on his way.

'You could say that,' said the man. 'I wanted to pay my respects, although I never knew May. I've read her books though.'

In addition to being a wealthy landowner, May Longstaff was a prolific writer of detective fiction. But more of that later.

The man took the hint and walked with me towards the lychgate.

'Nice to meet you,' I said, standing under the shadow of the old stone.

'Oh, you'll see me again,' said the man.

# # #

Things were fairly quiet after the funeral. The gravestone was erected: MAY LONGSTAFF. BELOVED WIFE, MOTHER AND AUTHOR. NEVER FORGOTTEN. I did wonder if May would have preferred these words in a different order. Stephen and Caroline moved into the big house. Iris moved into the barn, along with her husband, Adrian, and their two children. I can't say I would have fancied it. I visited when I discussed the funeral arrangements with Stephen and I thought it was a cheerless place: lots of chrome and glass, vaulted ceilings, the furniture huddled together, as if for safety, in the centre of the vast floor space. Iris was apparently having some building work done but I doubted that she could do anything to make the barn cosy or attractive. But that was the thing about the Longstaffs. They might not have been a very close family — emotionally, anyway — but none of them seemed to want to move far from the ancestral home. Stephen had built his house in the actual grounds. Martin, when he was in England, inhabited the old Lodge Cottage. Freddy lived in the next village and there was even talk of converting an outbuildingfor Sebastian, when he grew up.

The next event was another death. May's cat, Willard, passed away, aged eighteen. Normally I don't have much to do with dead pets. Oh, I'm an animal lover, don't get me wrong. I've got two pugs called Starsky and Hutch. But I don't quite approve of the trend for pet funerals. Our graveyards are full enough with human corpses. Dig your cat a grave under the apple tree in your garden, that's much more seemly. But Willard was different. Firstly, because he was the hero of May's books. Yes, all her murders were solved by a cat. Don't ask me how, it's not my sort of thing, but you see her books everywhere. The covers are usually bright green or pink and have a big black cat on them. He has white markings around his mouth that make him look a bit like Hercule Poirot. That's Willard, the Feline Mastermind.

As I said, May had left detailed instructions about her funeral and burial. This included the request that, when Willard died, his remains should be interred with hers. It took some time to get the exhumation licence, so the Longstaffs had Willard cremated and it was his ashes I prepared to bury on a sweltering morning in July. The only member of the family present was Caroline, Stephen's wife. She had taken Willard in after May's death and seemed genuinely affected by his death.

Arthur had dug up the turf and soil the night before. Two of my strongest team members, Barry and Ned, raised the coffin, and prized open the lid. As tactfully as I could I had told Caroline she might not want to look. 'The body will be covered by a shroud but, even so, after three months…' I took the casket from her and leant forwards, holding my breath.

'Steady on, Karen.' Barry grabbed my arm because I was in danger of falling. I tried to speak but couldn't. Instead, I pointed into the coffin.

It was empty.

Barry swore and, out of force of habit, apologised.

Caroline came to my side and looked down. 'I don't understand,' she said. 'Have you taken Mama's body away?'

'Mama' took me by surprise. May was Stephen's mother, not hers. In fact, I'd heard that May hadn't much liked Stephen's second wife. She'd disapproved of the divorce from Wendy. Besides, who says 'Mama' outside of the Royal Family?

'I don't understand either,' I said. 'We need to call the police.'

#

Body-snatching, although it sounds rather nineteenth-century, is an offence under the Human Tissue Act of 2004. The two detectives, though they both looked about fifteen, treated the case pretty seriously. They put police tape around the graveyard (Julie was furious) and interviewed me, Arthur, Barry, and Ned. I told them that I had no idea what had happened to May's body. I remembered, though, that the grass had started to grow over the grave and so it was my guess that the corpse had been removed shortly after the funeral in April.

'Did you organise the funeral?' asked the woman detective, DS Polly Squires.

'Yes,' I said. 'I've got the details in my ledger.' I showed them.

'Everything paid by Stephen Longstaff,' said the man, DS Sam Noakes. 'Was he the son?'

I filled them in on the Longstaff family. They both took notes, I was pleased to see. I also described the events that led up to the exhumation.

'Oh, I love the Willard books,' said DS Squires. '*A Game of Cat and Mouse*. That's my favourite.'

Willard's remains were still on my mantelpiece. After the shock of the empty grave, Caroline seemed to forget about the animal's ashes. I gave the tiny urn an apologetic look.

'May's instructions were that Willard should be buried with her.'

'What about her husband?' asked Noakes. 'Where's he buried?'

Funnily enough, I'd never thought to ask this. May's parents and grandparents were buried in the churchyard. She was the local girl, the one whose ancestors had built the Hall. Ernest Longstaff, an American millionaire who died in the early nineties, hardly figured in the family stories.

'I couldn't tell you,' I said. 'I don't know the family that well, although I was brought up in the area.'

'I expect they move in different circles,' said Squires, kindly.

You can say that again, I thought. I remembered Stephen when he was a young man, roaring into the village in his red sports car, his wild hair surrounding him like a halo. My dad owned the pub and I used to watch Stephen and his friends as they lounged in the beer garden, surrounded by shiny-looking women who were rumoured to come from London. Sometimes I even collected their empty glasses, but they never noticed me.

'They're far too posh for me,' I said, aiming for a light tone.

But there's one thing that makes us all equal. Death.

# # #

I used Willard as an excuse to visit Caroline the next day. I'd been to the Hall before. I went to an open day with my mum when I was ten, no doubt hoping to get a glimpse of twenty-one-year-old Stephen. Then I had thought it looked like a castle, grey stone with turrets at each corner and crenellations around the roof. But, on this summer morning, it seemed a lot friendlier. The mullioned windows twinkled in the sun and bees buzzed in the formal garden. There was no answer at the front door but I could hear trickling water at the back of the house. I followed the gravel path between the box hedges and found Caroline watering plant pots on the terrace. She gave a little start when she saw me.

'Karen! I didn't hear you knock.'

'Sorry to take you by surprise.' I proffered the urn. 'You left this behind yesterday.'

'Oh, I'm sorry.' Caroline put the watering can down and took the urn from me. She placed it on the patio table, next to a water jug and glasses. I wished she'd pour us a drink. It was a very hot day.

'I'm sorry,' said Caroline again. 'I was just so shocked by...you know...the...the *body*...going missing. You know we had the police round. Stephen is furious.'

Furious. Not shocked, upset, or grief-stricken. Furious. That fitted with my impression of Stephen Longstaff.

Caroline sat down at the table. She obviously wanted to talk so I took the seat opposite and looked encouraging.

'Karen,' she said. 'Did you see a man at the church after the funeral? A stranger. Wearing a black suit. He had dark curly hair.'

'Yes,' I said. 'He stayed at the graveside after everyone else had gone. I told him about the wake. I hope that was okay.'

The wake I wasn't invited to.

'Of course.' Caroline waved this away. 'He came here and he talked to Stephen. In fact, he made a bit of a scene. He said...'

She stopped and absentmindedly deadheaded a flower. I waited.

'It's too mad,' she said, in a rush. 'He said he was Stephen's son. He said Stephen had had an affair with his mother. She worked in a local pub. She moved to Australia when the man — Dylan — was five.'

'Did he have any proof?' I asked.

'He said he did,' said Caroline. 'He said Stephen's name was on his birth certificate. And, I have to say, he did look a bit like Stephen.'

I said nothing, not wanting to add that I'd seen the resemblance at once.

'It's not that I mind,' said Caroline. 'It was before Stephen met me. He was still married to Wendy then. Maybe that's why Freddy and Iris were so cross. They're protective of their mum. I think she had a very difficult time of it.'

'A difficult time being married to Stephen?' I couldn't help asking.

Caroline blushed. 'It wasn't a very happy marriage, I don't think, but there were reasons. Wendy had difficulty conceiving. Then, when the twins came, she was paranoid that something would happen to them. She would hardly even let Stephen near them. Maybe that's why...'

'Why he had an affair?'

'Maybe. I'm not excusing him....' But she was. 'Dylan said he was thirty-four. The twins are forty so Stephen must have had the affair when they were five or six, which is when Wendy was at her most...troubled.

But Stephen stayed with her. They didn't divorce until the twins left home for university. I didn't meet him until much later,' she added hastily.

Everyone in the village knew that Stephen met Caroline, who was an interior decorator employed by one of his friends, when he was fifty and she was thirty. This must have been about seven years after the divorce from Wendy. Caroline and Stephen married when he was fifty-two. They had Sebastian three years later.

'Did Freddy and Iris hear what the man — Dylan — said?' I asked.

'Yes,' said Caroline. 'Dylan asked to speak to Stephen in private but no-where's very private in the barn. They went to Stephen's study but, when Stephen started shouting, we could all hear. Freddy came in and threw Dylan out.'

'Why was Stephen shouting?' I asked, though I thought I could probably guess.

'He thought Dylan was after his money. He said Dylan had only come sniffing around when Stephen had inherited the Hall. Dylan said he just wanted to go to his grandmother's funeral. I felt a bit sorry for him then. He said that his mother had died last year. She couldn't have been very old.'

I thought of the man at the graveside. He definitely had a rather sad look to him. Not always true of mourners.

'What's going to happen now?' I asked.

'I don't know. "You'll see me again." That was the last thing Dylan said.'

'He said something similar to me,' I said.

'I can't help thinking that Dylan turning up is linked to the other thing. May's body disappearing.'

'How could they be connected?' I asked.

'I don't know,' said Caroline again, rather hopelessly, 'but it's a bit of a coincidence, isn't it? Dylan turning up and then May's body going missing. The detectives told us it must have happened quite soon after the funeral.'

'But why...' I started, then stopped. Footsteps were approaching, accompanied by a slashing noise like a stick being dragged through a hedge. Seconds later, Stephen appeared, red-faced and dressed in tennis clothes.

'Beat Fred in straight sets,' he told Caroline. 'I'm sweating like a pig though. Bloody ridiculous that we don't have a pool at the Hall.' Then he seemed to notice me. 'Oh hello, Karen. What are you doing here?'

Not very friendly but I answered pleasantly, 'I brought Willard's ashes back.'

'That bloody cat,' said Stephen. 'All this trouble started with him, if you ask me. Can't stand those books either.'

Again, not very charitable. Particularly when you think that the royalties from the Willard books probably paid for the upkeep of the Hall. Incidentally, the deceased cat was the third incarnation of the feline sleuth. I don't know where the others are buried.

'I've been telling Karen about the young man, Dylan,' said Caroline.

'Well, you shouldn't have,' said Stephen, dumping his racquet on the table and drinking straight from the water jug. 'We should keep these things in the family.'

'Don't worry,' I said. 'Undertakers know how to be discreet.'

Stephen seemed to register my actual existence for the first time. 'Didn't your father used to own the pub?' he said. 'The Bird in Hand?'

'That's right,' I said.

'Do you remember a barmaid there? Leanne, her name was.'

Of course I'd thought of Leanne as soon as Caroline mentioned Dylan's mother. She was blond and good-looking, very popular with the clientele. She'd left rather suddenly and I remembered hearing that she'd emigrated to Australia.

'I remember Leanne,' I said. 'She was nice.'

Stephen grunted. 'Did you ever hear anything about her having a child? I mean, you're local. You hear things.'

The Longstaffs were local, too, of course. But in another way they weren't. Their friends are people they met at boarding school or glamorous creatures 'down from London', like the girls Stephen used to drink with. Iris had a village boyfriend once and, by all accounts, Stephen was furious. Again.

'I never heard anything about a child,' I said. 'But I was probably away at university.' Mortuary science, since you ask.

Stephen made another grunting sound. He likes to boast that he studied at the university of life. I decided that I'd outstayed my welcome, especially as I clearly wasn't going to get offered even a glass of water.

I left them sitting on the terrace. The brass plaque on the urn gleamed in the sun. I wondered if Willard's ashes would ever make their way into May's grave.

# # #

As far as I know, they never did. The grave was filled in eventually but May's body was never found. About three years after she died, Stephen started work on a swimming pool at the Hall. He died of a heart attack almost as soon as the excavations began. I didn't arrange the funeral. In his will Stephen nominated a London firm, which I considered rather a snub, if very much in character. It wasn't in church either, a quick humanist service at the crematorium, ashes scattered on the golf course. The musical chairs started again. Freddy and his family moved into the Hall, Caroline and Sebastian took over the Lodge. Martin now seemed to live permanently in Dubai. He didn't even come home for his brother's funeral.

Freddy continued with the swimming pool but, before they had dug much further, the builders encountered a problem. A dead body. I got the details from Polly, DI Squires now. She'd become quite a friend after I buried her mother. That's how you meet people in my line of work. The body was male, probably between thirty and forty years old. They took samples but his DNA didn't match anyone on the missing persons database. Polly asked for samples from all the adults living in or around the Hall but none of them were a match either. Polly had seen the body, though, and she said it was well preserved because it was tightly wrapped in plastic bin liners. She said you could even see the hair. Curly dark hair.

I thought of Dylan, the young man who had come from Australia for his grandmother's funeral. And I thought of Freddy and Iris, the twins who were born to Wendy after she'd had such a difficult time conceiving. If Dylan was Stephen's son, then where did it leave his heirs? Was it possible that the twins were not his biological children? Wendy could have used a sperm donor without telling him. Maybe this was why she kept Stephen away from his own children, in case he found out? Wendy lived on the Isle of Wight now. Could I write and ask her? But no, there are limits to what even a funeral director can get away with.

I called on Iris after Stephen died. Just a courtesy visit really.

'I remember your father when he was young,' I told her. 'He was very glamorous, dashing around in his sports car.'

'The Alfa Romeo,' said Iris, smiling sadly. 'He loved that car. It's still in one of the outbuildings somewhere.'

It was a cold November day and the rain lashed against the plate glass of the barn. Iris and I sat at a marble edifice that more closely resembled a catafalque than a breakfast bar. Iris seemed embarrassed by my presence, perhaps because I hadn't been asked to do the funeral, so I didn't stay long. As I left, hurrying to my far less glamorous car with my hood up, I thought of the day Dylan had appeared from nowhere and confronted Stephen, his father. Freddy had thrown him out but what happened next? Had Freddy killed Dylan and buried him in the grounds, only to have the body resurface when the swimming pool was excavated? But, if Freddy had known the body was there, surely he would have stopped work on the pool? Was it possible that Iris had acted on her own? She's the oldest twin and always seems in charge. Besides, I'm a local and I'm an undertaker. I know all the village secrets. And I remember that Iris's teenage boyfriend, of whom Stephen had so strongly disapproved, was none other than Arthur, the gravedigger.

True to family form, Iris had extended the barn when she moved in. I looked back, through the rain, at the new wing, built of black weatherboard to match the original. What was under the foundations? Was it May Longstaff, her body removed so no-one could prove that she was no relation to Iris and Freddy, who would one day inherit everything? As I drove away from the Hall, the Tudor manor surrounded by smaller houses containing Longstaff offspring, I had to accept that I might never solve the mystery. I was due to retire in a few years and I had a sudden urge to get away from the village and all its memories. Starsky and Hutch had both died last year, within months of each other. My parents were long gone. Even the pub was a carvery now. I would sell the business and use the proceeds to travel. I might even go to Australia.

Let the dead bury the dead, as it says in the bible. I do like a nice scripture reading.

The Spirit Tree by Greg Herren

#

8. The problem of the crime must be solved by strictly naturalistic means. Such methods for learning the truth as slate-writing, ouija-boards, mind-reading, spiritualistic séances, crystal-gazing, and the like, are taboo. A reader has a chance when matching his wits with a rationalistic detective, but if he must compete with the world of spirits and go chasing about the fourth dimension of metaphysics, he is defeated ab initio.

"Turn right on Simmons Road and in a half mile, your destination will be on the right."

Tom Forrester slowed his official State Bureau of Investigation SUV and glanced in the rearview mirror. Nothing behind him but blacktop state highway back to the S-curve he'd just negotiated. He flipped on the turn signal and made the turn onto a back road. It stretched out before him, a narrow expanse of red dirt and gravel down to the bottom of a hollow and climbing back up the other side. He was getting a headache and wished again he'd asked for someone to come with him. He'd never been to Corinth County before, hadn't even driven through it. Yes, it was in his district, but it was remote. At least an hour to the nearest interstate. Outsiders had to want to come to Corinth County to get there.

It amazed him that there were still these random remote counties all over the deep South, seemingly untouched by the outside world.

But the county seat, for all its population of about three thousand, had a Walmart and a McDonald's, and almost every house or trailer he'd seen from the road had a satellite dish either in the yard or affixed to the building. Was anything truly remote anymore?

The road wasn't wide enough for two cars, so he hoped he didn't meet anyone coming from the other direction. A cloud of red dust followed closely behind the vehicle. At the bottom of the hollow there was a small stream flowing through corrugated iron beneath the pitiful road. And he noticed a rusty barbed wire fence running along the front of the pine forest on the left side, caught a glimpse of a rusted tin roof surrounded by overgrowth.

It looked…familiar.

Weird. Must be déjà vu. I've never been here before. But these foothill counties look the same in north Alabama. Probably some place I remember from being a kid.

He reached the top of the hill and saw a steadier decline to another hollow, much wider and more pronounced than the previous one. There was also a break in the pine forest up ahead on the right, and there was a tired old metal mailbox mounted on a rusted tin stand.

"Your destination is up ahead on the right", the soothing voice played out from the speakers.

He slowed again, the cloud of red dust behind him catching up and blanketing the car as it slowed. He managed to turn, almost hitting the mailbox. He braked again, bringing the car to a stop after slipping forward a bit in the dirt.

This—this also looked familiar.

Tom couldn't shake the feeling he'd seen this all before, had made this trip before, but he knew that wasn't possible. He'd never even heard of Corinth County before being assigned to this region. Alabama was divided into seven regions, and his field office for the State Bureau of Investigation in Tuscaloosa had a big map of the territory in the reception area. He'd never been called out here before. There had been a big ATF operation here a couple of years earlier—busting up a crystal meth lab and ring—but there had long been rumors around the office about corruption in the county. But nothing was ever tied to the sheriff or his office, and you can't bring charges on rumors and innuendoes.

# # #

You have arrived, the calm voice said through his speakers.

The driveway, or road, or whatever it was he'd turned on was narrow and needed leveling. The pine forest and underbrush crowded in on both sides, the branches overhead blocking the sun. The road ended in a small clearing with an old house off to the left, so close to the forest, the house looked like a growth on the ends of the branches—

The pain split through his head so suddenly he slammed on his brakes again. He opened the caddy between the seats and shook out two Advils, which he dry-swallowed.

The house—he knew the house.

He shook his head. *What is wrong with you, Tom? You've never been here before.*

The house needed to be painted and looked…well, tired. It was an old house, the kind built before the war in rural Alabama…and it was the exact same kind of house his great-grandmother had lived in on Sand Mountain. That, he realized with a bit of relief, was where the déjà vu had come from. Her house had been in the woods, too, the same four-room structure. Two bedrooms on the left, living room and kitchen on the right, porches in front and back. Gramma Opal Harrison had enclosed her back porch and turned it into a laundry room/bathroom. He wondered if this house's owner had done the same. Green paint had faded to a sickly, paler shade. Old, worn out–looking air conditioners leaned out of windows, dripping water into angry orange puddles of mud. A slanting roof that peaked in the center had rain gutters that looked like they'd fly off in the next big wind. The aluminum posts supporting the porch roof speckled with orange. A huge lilac bush exploding into purple blooms near the right back corner, and a small shed that housed the water pump stood at attention next to it, the tiled roof covered in dead blossoms.

There were two county sheriff cars parked alongside an ancient navy-blue Oldsmobile Delta Royale 88, resting on cinder blocks instead of tires. No license plate, and the back window was spider-webbed with cracks.

He parked behind one of the brown country cars. He got out of his car just as a gentle breeze made the branches whisper, and he noticed a whistling sound, coming faintly from the other side of the house.

What on earth?

The breeze faded away, and so did the whistling.

He couldn't shake the feeling the whistling was important. He shook his head. *What is wrong with you, Tom?*

He walked over the gravel to the two cement front steps and paused as something flashed to his left out of the corner of his eyes. He glanced over and noticed a small pine tree, cut and shaped like a triangular Christmas tree—but every branch had a glass bottle of some type slipped over its tip. Brown, clear, yellow, blue, and red glass sparkled when the sun's rays caught them.

A spirit tree.

He smiled to himself. He hadn't seen one since Gramma Opal died. She'd had one, too, up there on Sand Mountain near the Georgia and Tennessee state lines, where the devout handled snakes and drank poison to show they had the spirit of the Lord in them. She'd told him the spirit tree kept spirits out of the house, the clinking of the glass in the wind would draw them and they would get trapped in one of the bottles. Was that it? He scratched his head. It was something like that, something his grandmother and mother had scoffed at, shaking their head about the old- timers and the old ways in the back country and weren't they glad they'd gotten out of the hills?

This is why people think she's a witch, he heard his mother saying.

There were voices inside—they must not have heard him drive up— and the whistling sound from his left again.

The breeze had taken one of the lower branches, bending it almost to the porch floor. [It was an ancient Dr. Pepper bottle, with green-tinted glass, the old logo, and the white clockface with 10, 2 and 4 written on it. It whistled…

…and the sound of footsteps heading to the front door inside snapped him out of his reverie.

Even though it was only mid-May it was hot and humid as August already. He wiped sweat off his forehead as a man came out of the screen door. "You SBI?" he drawled. He was tall, wearing a tan cowboy hat that matched his uniform, and that long ugly brown tie all Alabama sheriffs and deputies seemed to wear. He was also whipcord thin, but wiry and strong. Veins bulged on his tanned forearms. His hair was cropped close to the skull and was shock-white. Freckles spotted his face above the thin lips and sharp pointed chin that almost looked like a can opener blade.

"Sheriff Bill Hackworth," the sheriff said, breaking the spell by putting out his big, calloused hand to shake Tom's. "Glad you could make it."

"Special Agent Tom Forrester," he said, smiling courteously. "What have we got here, Sheriff?" He stepped across the wooden porch, and the soft wood gave a little.

The window unit [in the window] was ticking and the ceiling fan revolved, too tired to make a breeze. The tin roof was a dead giveaway that the house was at least standing when Japan surrendered. It smelled musty in here, dank, like mildew and rotting paper. This room looked just like hers. There was a fireplace on the outer wall. A faded framed family photo was mounted on the bricks above. A big screen television between the front window and the fireplace. A ratty old couch, a tilted coffee table whose surface was scarred with cigarette burns and scratches, a reclining chair that was missing the footrest. The linoleum floor was yellowed and curling up in places where it met the wall. The bedroom door was closed.

"We found the body in here," Sheriff Hackworth stepped through the door to the kitchen. The body was already gone—

--the old woman had been sitting there at the table, drinking a tall sweating glass of iced tea—

He swallowed, shaking his head and blinking his eyes. There was a tape outline on the floor where the body had fallen, tacky drying blood in a pool around where the head would have landed. There was blood spatter all over the cabinets and the counter behind her, and specs of what must have been bone and brain scattered. He swallowed again, trying to keep the bile down. There was a buzzing in his head. Everything looked so—so—*familiar*—but how?

Hackworth was looking at him, an odd look on his face. "You all right, Special Agent?"

Tom nodded, but he was anything but. That buzzing in his head—the pounding of his heart in his ears—

In the right cabinet above the sink was where she kept her coffee and lard.

"You sure you're all right?" Sheriff Hackworth asked again. "I got some men checking the woods around the place, see if they can find anything."

"I'm fine," Tom said, but he wasn't. He wanted to open those cabinet doors, to see if it was where the dead woman kept her lard and coffee. It must have been where Mama Opal had kept hers, that's all it was. "Who was she?"

"Darla Tucker," Sheriff Hackworth replied. "Did you hear about that big drug bust here in the county a few years back? That were kin of hers. But far as I know, Darla didn't have anything to do with none of that mess. Her kids are all grown and moved away. Up North or Atlanta. They been notified."

Tom walked around the tape outline, avoiding the pool of blood, looking for the slightest thing that didn't belong on the kitchen floor. "Did you find anything out of the ordinary?"

Hackworth scratched his head. "No. And it just doesn't make sense." He swallowed. "Who would do that to Mrs. Tucker? She didn't harm no one, and she didn't have anything worth stealing. Why shoot her like that?"

"Any idea of time of death?"

"It'd been a while," Hackworth replied. "The blood was also tacky, and she was cold. Had to wait for the coroner—over in Winfield. We don't have a coroner in Corinth County, so we use Winfield or Carbon Hill." He scratched his chin. "Had to have been last night sometime. She went to bed early—"

"How do you know?"

"Well, Tom, I don't know if you know it or not but Corinth County's not exactly the big city," Hackworth shook his head. "Everybody knows everybody down here, and knows pretty much everything about everyone. Everybody knew Miss Darla was in bed every night by ten. So, if she was awake and in her kitchen it had to be before ten." He tilted his head. "Maybe not scientific, and sure, she might have stayed up for some reason, but I'd bet on my mother's grave it was before ten."

"Who found her?" Tom leaned over to look at something that had fallen into a slight crack between the floorboards, not far from where the head outline was. He knelt down, grabbed a pencil out of his shirt, and hooked it, lifting it up in the air. It was an earring, a small gold hoop with a small diamond—if it was real—dangling on a tiny gold chain. "Was her ear damaged?" Tom stood back up, his hamstrings complaining.

"Her face—"

"Never mind." He slid the earring into the small evidence bag Hackworth opened for the purpose. Tom wiped sweat off his forehead. "Who found her? The call came in about six-thirty this morning. Who was coming by here at that hour of the morning?"

"We got a tip." Hackworth's face was slick with sweat, and Tom could feel the dampness in his own armpits as a teardrop of sweat ran down the center of his spine. "About five in the morning. Some of the deputies on night duty came out to check on her. Found the all the lights in the house on, the front door wide open, and Darla—like *that*." He shuddered. "Be glad you didn't get here before they took the body out. I'll see that in my nightmares."

Curious, Tom looked back at Hackworth's face. He was younger than most sheriffs, sure, but still in his mid-thirties. How long had he been sheriff? Just because the SBI rarely got called out to Corinth County didn't mean there were no murders or felonies going on in the county. The SBI got called in when something was off, when it was more than the county cops could handle. Hackworth had to have seen gunshot victims before. Why did this one bother him so much? What had the gunshot done to her face?

Something…something here wasn't right.

But what?

"I need some air," Tom said finally. It was stifling inside—the windows in the kitchen were closed. That also didn't make sense. "Was the air conditioner on when you got here?"

Hackworth licked his lips and followed him back out onto the front porch again. Tom sat down on the porch swing. A cool breeze caressed him and felt marvelous. He looked over to where the sheriff cars were parked. If the killer had parked in the gravel, the tracks had been ruined when the deputies had pulled in. But still…if they'd gotten a tip that she was dead, wouldn't they have thought about that?

He'd worked with any number of sheriffs offices before. Some were…well, sheriff's departments in Alabama were always a mixed bag.

They were elected, for one thing, which led to all kinds of corruption and abuse. Some were professionals, other seemed like something out of *The Dukes of Hazzard*. Corinth County, with its slightly more than five thousand population, fell into the Boss Hogg camp. Hadn't the previous sheriff here gotten arrested in that big drug bust? And they'd missed the earring in their examination of the crime scene. They'd ruined any tire tracks from the killer's vehicle—this place was way too remote for someone to have gotten here on foot or bicycle. What else had they missed, had they ruined?

Was it incompetence... or something worse?

I should have brought someone with me and taken over the case, he cursed himself. It was exhausting, wasn't it? Bad decisions. He'd been making them ever since Press moved out and left him after four years together. *Get a hold of yourself.*

It was probably too late for this investigation already. The crime scene was probably compromised, who knew if the chain of evidence was done properly, and whoever had shot the old woman was probably hundreds of miles away by now. The Advil wasn't working. The pounding in his left temple made him grit his teeth a bit until it passed. *Maybe I should take two more...*

Another breeze came along, and behind him the bottles on the tree clinked again. He turned his head and watched as wind took hold of the branch with the Dr Pepper bottle again, bending it down as it whistled—

And he was sitting at that table in the kitchen, drinking a sweating glass of sweet tea. The window unit was blowing directly on him, bringing up goose flesh like creepy white freckles. Someone was coming. It was dark outside, and he'd heard the car pull up, didn't need to look to see. He'd known this was coming, nothing to do but face it. He was too old—

"Agent Forrester?"

Startled, he whirled back around. The whistling had stopped, the glass bottles stopped clinking together. A lance of pain seemed to shoot through his forehead into his brain, and he put his hand out to balance against the side of the house.

"Are you okay?" Sheriff Hackworth asked, his eyebrows raised. "You don't look so hot."

"Headache," Tom replied. "Hopefully the Advil will kick in."

"Why don't we have a seat, and I can fill you in on what we know." The sheriff gestured to two rusty metal porch chairs, the kind with the steel rods so they rocked.

Tom scribbled notes as the sheriff spoke in his low baritone. Darla Tucker: survived two husbands, and had a worthless son with each. She was kin to the Tucker drug family through her second husband but hadn't been involved with their operations. She'd inherited this land from her father—her branch of the family had owned the whole hollow at one point, but she was the only one left. Her oldest son was serving time, and the younger one had run off up north after he turned eighteen. He'd been a troublemaker, and would have been a headache for the sheriff's department had he not gone—he'd already been arrested several times before he turned eighteen. No, he wouldn't have come back and killed his mother. He'd been gone too long, why wait till now? The land wasn't worth killing her over. She'd been found that morning at about five when Travis Overton saw her lights were on when he was heading to Carbon Hill to go to work. He checked in on her now and then, so he did again, and he found her. He'd called it in and waited until a deputy arrived, who'd taken his statement and sent him on to work. Might have been a robbery—although she didn't have anything worth taking—or it might have been some kind of roving sex pervert, which he hoped to God it was not.

When he felt the breeze on his arms he stopped writing, stopped listening to what the sheriff was saying and looked back over his shoulder.

The Dr Pepper branch was bending down again, almost like it was reaching for him.

"You said the land's not worth anything?" Tom interrupted the torrent of words.

"Well, there's always some money in the timber—you know, having the loggers come out and clear the forest out some." The sheriff scratched his head again. "But I can't imagine it being worth killing her over."

The whistling started again.

He looked up from the table to see the man standing in the kitchen doorway. He knew the face, it was a man in a deputy's uniform and the face belonged to Deputy Andy Stoddard, and he raised the rifle and pointed it into his face and—

Pain flashed through his head again and he winced from the pain.

And he knew he was right.

Darla Tucker had been killed by a deputy.

He didn't know why, though.

And he didn't know how he could prove it yet.

The breeze blew again, and the Dr Pepper branch bent down again, only this time the bottle slid off the end of the branch, shattering on the porch.

They both started, Sheriff Hackworth swearing and jumping to his feet, Tom gasping, startled.

"I'll clean up this mess," he said, heading back inside the house, the screen door slamming behind him. "Stupid old superstitions."

On the porch, Tom got up. He knew he was right.

He heard Mama Opal's voice again. "The bottles will catch a spirit, keep them from getting in the house."

He bent down to pick up a piece of glass. It was the clock face, broken cleanly on every side like a talisman of some sort.

He knew he was right.

Getting evidence that would stand up in court would be a different story.

Maybe the Dr Pepper had caught Darla's spirit. Maybe her spirit had been talking to him, trying to let him know what happened to her.

Tom smiled. The headache was gone now. And somehow, he knew he'd find the proof.

He remembered something else Mama Opal had said. His mother had been teasing her about the old mountain ways.

"You go ahead and laugh, little girl," the old woman said. "But there's always been strange things up in the mountains, things no one can explain."

He looked back at the spirit tree.

The breeze blew again, and the branches of the trees and the bushes rustled, making whispering noises.

And Tom knew Darla was gone.

Better Together by
Delia Pitts

#

9. There must be but one detective—that is, but one protagonist of deduction—one deus ex machine. To bring the minds of three or four, or sometimes a gang of detectives to bear on a problem is not only to disperse the interest and break the direct thread of logic, but to take an unfair advantage of the reader, who, at the outset, pits his mind against that of the detective and proceeds to do mental battle. If there is more than one detective the reader doesn't know who his co-deductor is. It's like making the reader run a race with a relay team.

Arriving at the old Harlem YMCA after nine at night, I pushed through the twin glass doors and into the yellow light of the reception area. The sharp talons of gusty March clawed my neck as I shoved the doors shut. The lobby was empty, but I could hear cheers and shouts echoing in the distance. My muddy sneakers added to the thousands of shoe prints embossed in the gray-flecked linoleum tiles. When I lowered the wool scarf from my face, the stench of liniment and sweaty leather swabbed my nose. I approached the reception desk to ask a Black man there for directions. *My mother was in here, but where?* I was a grown man, at least passing for one, so, of course, that's not how I'd put the question.

The dun-colored skeleton behind the Formica countertop rattled to life and greeted me like a long-lost cousin. "Welcome! How can I help you?"

The man's badge read T. HADLEY. He'd been dozing, but his reedy voice piped a cheery salute. Despite his sunken eyes and yellow picket-fence teeth, the receptionist was as chatty as a kindergarten teacher. "It's late, so there's not as much activity to see at this hour. But you're more than welcome to check out the place."

He peered at his cell phone, hoisting it close to his nose. Then he hacked the nap-time loogies from his throat and launched into hype mode before I sputtered a word. "If you come back tomorrow during regular business hours you can meet with someone from our recreation staff to sign you up for membership. This your first time here at the Y, Mister…?"

"Roland." No need to give him my last name. My mother was neighborhood-famous. If I said our shared name this skeleton would recognize me as the child of the local private detective Fabrice Peters. "I'm meeting a, um, friend. Maybe at the pool."

Friend was a casual way to bracket our complicated relationship. My mother ran the security company, F.J. Peters, Investigations. The firm was named after its founder, her late husband, Franklin Peters. My father died four years ago, when I was sixteen, leaving behind a struggling enterprise and a wounded family. Fabrice and I were still stitching together the pieces.

Like a twitchy cheerleader, Hadley the manager led me on a roundabout journey through the building. We wandered past the basketball court, locker rooms, and a tiny snack bar served by four vending machines. A weight room stacked with barbells against the back wall was next to a door marked Office. Though the hour was late, teams of Black boys thundered around the court, a crowd of parents bouncing on the riser benches. A burly Black man pumped iron in the weight room and two giggling kids — Latino boy, African American girl — in giant satin shorts and hoodies held hands in front of the vending machines. I wondered how bags of Fritos were romantic, but Romeo and Juliet seemed glad to escape their families' smothering supervision for the evening. Their giggles over a shared cell phone tickled the walls of the tiny alcove.

Three Black women in leggings and T-shirts propped their feet on chairs in the lounge. Beads of sweat at their hairlines, plastic water bottles in hand, and pastel-colored mats rolled up on the floor suggested they'd just finished a yoga class. They were puffing hard, but their chatter never faltered as they powered through a week's worth of gossip.

# # #

Hadley had skipped the pool, so after eight minutes of this tour, I asked directly. Three more minutes for my guide to shuffle me to a regulation-size Olympic facility. Fabrice was in the lap pool, alone.

Hadley eyed her, then turned his lantern gaze on me. "Is Ms. Peters your friend? Is she expecting you, Mr. Roland? She didn't mention anything when she arrived."

I shrugged, eyes wide to convey she was a mystery to me. Inside, I was certain why she never mentioned me. *Well, she wouldn't, would she?* My mother was embarrassed by me. By my gangling arms and pigeon toes. By the way my shoulders jutted like rake handles beyond the collar of my track suit jackets. By the fact that my brown skin and hazel eyes were daily reminders of the man who'd abandoned us by dying. Was Fabrice sad to be widowed? Ashamed, stymied, angry? She never shared with me. Never tried to comfort or calm. Bottle up and push on was her style. So, I stewed alone. Until I managed the sadness by refusing to go to college. Dumb move, but withdrawal felt like a way to punish the world, myself, and my mother in one stupid swoop.

Hadley repeated, "Ms. Peters is expecting you?" Flinging his arms wide, Hadley inhaled the chlorine fumes as if the pool were surrounded by meadows of sweet hay. Dark eyes narrow, he glared at me. *Appreciate this rarefied air and privileged setting, or else.* I sniffed; his flush of anger subsided. I guess I made adults furious, just by existing.

I remembered how spitting mad my mother was when I voiced my determination to become a member of the Peters Security team. I wanted to be a full partner in the detective firm. Not the junior filing clerk or errand boy. As a concession, she'd given me an office next to the broom closet and business cards with INVESTIGATOR under my name. I sat in training sessions with the other operatives in our firm and handled minor cases of insurance fraud or missing jewelry. But Fabrice Peters shifted the more serious cases away from me. No files on missing persons or divorces crossed my desk. I was good for beefing up security at neighborhood events. And for driving. Lots of driving. Like tonight.

I stared until Hadley's cheesy grin withered. Through gritted teeth, I said, "I'm here to pick up Ms. Peters." I straightened to my six-foot-one and arched my chest to look like more than one hundred and sixty pounds. If I was going to play my mother's chauffeur, I'd be the tough-nosed SOB kind.

Raising a thin finger, Hadley pointed toward a flight of stairs. "You can wait up there for Ms. Peters to finish."

When Hadley disappeared, I climbed to a balcony overlooking the pool. I perched on a rickety metal folding chair as Fabrice sliced through the water, her red suit, dark shoulders, and white swim cap bobbing in graceful rhythm. No waves, no chops, barely a ripple disturbed the surface as she glided along.

Seeing my mother like that, calm and competent, fired something in me. I wanted to have it out with her. I'd pushed before, gotten nowhere. Now I determined to try again. I watched Fabrice pull her slim figure from the glassy pool.

To intercept her before she reached the locker room, I descended the balcony steps two at a time. But she had a head start and was through the swinging doors before I hit them. The corridor leading from the pool was tiled in sickly green with black trimming the walls at shoulder height. By the time I got there, the hall was empty.

I shouldered the door to the women's locker room. The space was empty, the shower enclosure abandoned and silent. Fabrice was already dressed when I rounded the corner to the third row of lockers. Her black jeans were belted in place and the yellow T-shirt was damp across the back where she hadn't dried off carefully. Her hair hung like a black mop and her mouth was turned down. She was sitting in front of an open locker, staring at the purple socks in her hand. With her bare face and brown smooth skin, she looked beautiful, but sour as a nun who'd lost her ruler.

"Roland." Not a greeting, an accusation. Fabrice answered my question before I posed it. "I saw you enter the pool room with Hadley." Her brown eyes stabbed me. "Get out of here." She jerked her chin toward the door. "I'll meet you in the lobby."

I had grappled with my approach to this ask for several weeks and faltered on at least five occasions. I couldn't come up with a better angle than the most direct one. So I took my shot now: "I want to be your partner in this operation. Not some two-bit sidekick." I stumbled over adding "Mom," but the term would weaken my ask, so I skipped it.

She gasped. "I decide when you're ready for promotion. If ever." The voice was muffled and shaky, like she was still underwater. She stuck her fists into the arms of her black wool overcoat. When they emerged, her fingers were still clenched. Mad, confused, horrified? I couldn't read her tight face.

"That all you got?" My shout echoed off the tile walls. "Not good enough. Not anymore."

She raised her eyes, bleak and red around the rims. The words came at me like a machine gun volley. "What do you want from me?"

I stretched my hands toward her, palms up. As I took a step, my throat tightened. "A say in this outfit. Not equals, okay. But I'm Dad's legacy, too. You owe me a chance to prove my worth."

"I'm not talking about this." She spat the words, looking to wound. "I gave you life. I don't owe you another goddamn thing!"

"You're right. You don't owe me a thing. I'm not your partner. You can toss me out of the office anytime." Bitter and true. But I hated the taste of the next words on my tongue even more. "But you can't erase my last name. Like it or not, I'm a Peters, too. I'm your child."

Fabrice lunged, and with surprise on her side, she shoved me against the lockers. Long fingers clamped, she slapped me hard. The thwack echoed through the locker room. "Boy, don't you ever speak to me like that. Never."

I gulped, bobbling a reply. I never got it out.

A gunshot blast thumped through the humid air. We turned in the direction of the sound, straining to catch its source through the thick walls. A shriek clarified the direction of the danger. We ran for the door.

We pounded down the hall, panting through the damp chlorine-laden air. In the main corridor of the building, a crowd rustled in front of the office. Two of the three women from the yoga class bounced on tiptoes. The vending machine lovers laced fingers and leaned forward for a better view. Basketball parents, coaches, and kids made up the rest of the crowd. Everyone waved cell phones like torches.

I pushed through the clutch of people, their hum vibrating like a bee swarm ready to attack. At the front of the crowd, I found Hadley, the building manager.

"It's locked. I can't open it." Hadley screeched, pink popping around his pupils. "The shot came from inside. But the door won't budge." Another tug on the doorknob, then he rattled its brass collar. "Mr. Roland. You gotta help." Fingernails clawed the dented knob. "Together we can break down the door."

We retreated two paces, lowered our shoulders, and ran at the door. No joy. Like linemen squaring against the opposing squad, we surged forward. Rebuffed. On our third assault, the wood frame cracked, then buckled.

I rushed over the threshold after Hadley. Behind us, my mother gripped the door frame as knob and brass assembly clattered to the floor. Wobbling in a crazy arc, a screw from the damaged door plate landed at the ear of the body stretched on the carpet. A single gunshot wound tattooed the dead woman's forehead.

She was dressed for a casual day in the office: chocolate brown slacks, a green tunic with orange-and-yellow leaves scattered across it. Her skin was brown, too, but now pigeon-feather gray stole across her throat and chest. Her black hair was ironed into a smooth cap, a neat row of bangs above her open eyes. The strands beside her right ear were scorched by the bullet hole.

"Look at this, Roland!" Hadley held a small pistol in his fist. Its nose wobbled as he thrust it toward my face. Sweat dripped from his side-burns onto his jaw. High emotion cast a brick-red tint over the beige of his throat.

Fabrice's voice sliced, drawing the man's attention. "Lower the weapon, Hadley. Put it back where you found it. Don't touch anything." She stepped forward, pointing at the dead woman's head.

He did as she ordered, placing the gun near the woman's right hand. As the weapon dropped from his fingers, he blubbered a name. "Carlina, Carlina."

I knelt to touch a finger behind the woman's ear. The skin was damp and still. Her head lolled to the right; for an instant, her jaw seemed to move. I jerked my hand, erasing the weird impression of life restored. My first dead body. After my father's. But when I found him, he'd looked peaceful, asleep in his bed following the massive stroke. This Carlina was different. She was young, maybe my age? Pretty, a might-have-been girlfriend? Life flew from her soft body only minutes ago. Her skin was still warm with the injustice of this end. As my cheeks heated, I lowered my chin so my scarf would hide the hard swallow.

Fabrice turned from me to the crowd in the corridor. She pointed at one of the basketball coaches, her command sharp: "Call 911. Now." He yelped in surprise but obeyed.

Police hustled into the Y six minutes after the first alert.

They were fast, but the crowd scattered like hot oil across a griddle. Parents grabbed sons by the backs of their necks and dragged them from the building. The two coaches remained, clutching their whistles as if they wanted to signal time-out from this calamity. Romeo and Juliet clung to each other, gazing at the mangled office door. Then they shuffled to the lounge to join Hadley, the yoga ladies, and the weightlifter who were also caught in the dragnet; Fabrice and I joined them, waiting for our turns under the police spotlight. I was glad for the chance to share our eyewitness reports. I hoped to have a chance to prove my professional worth to my mother.

# # #

Two by two, like Noah's waterlogged animals, witnesses marched from the lounge into an equipment closet the cops converted to an interrogation room.

First to go were Hadley and the weightlifter, who told us to remember his name was Alton Bush. Light-skinned and brawny, Alton begged us to record his presence in case he vanished while in police custody. The young lovers sprawled on a stiff couch, holding hands. Maybe fifteen years old. His hair captured in neat cornrows, hers in gigantic Afro puffs. The kid released his girlfriend's fingers to raise a cell phone and directed it at the departing weightlifter as requested. As he grimaced for the camera, the two lady yoga enthusiasts grabbed prime seats at a square table in the middle of the room. The basketball coaches leaned against the far wall, necks bent, foreheads together as if conferring about a referee's missed call.

Fabrice and I stood in a corner, shoulders touching, arms crossed. Drops from her hair sprinkled on my sleeve as she tilted toward me. Was she shivering? Had the same froth of fright, revulsion, curiosity, and excitement coursing through my body hit her, too? I knew this wasn't her first dead body. Her stories of unexplained deaths and murder cases filled downtime around our agency office. She'd always seemed so casual describing such incidents, maybe deploying banter to shield me or disguise her own emotions. Now attention tightened her lips and flashed keen in her eyes.

The police might have their official plan of action, but Fabrice seized the opportunity to ask her own questions. A detective, always on the case. My first instinct was to retreat, but my mother never took a backseat when she could grab the steering wheel.

"Did you hear anything? Before the shot went off?" Fabrice threw this general inquiry at the middle of the lounge.

Eyes dancing, the yoga lady in purple rushed to answer. "I heard something." She nodded as if reassuring herself. "Yeah, like raised voices in the next room."

"A fight?" Ramrod straight, my mother stepped toward the two women at the center table.

"Not that much heat. More like an argument or a spat." Eyes scrunched with skepticism. "My name's Caresse McCoy, by the way. What's yours?"

"Fabrice. And he's Roland." At the tip of her chin, I nodded like a pull-toy. I exhaled, grateful she skipped our last name, while consigning me to second-banana status.

Not to be outdone by her friend, the second yoga lady piped up. "Leeta Blunt here. We were talking pretty loud ourselves." She smoothed a green stripe on her black leggings. The lime color matched her sneakers. "So, you gotta figure the noise coming from the office was sharp and high-pitched. Or we wouldn't have noticed it in the first place."

"When did it start, the argument?"

The two women looked at each other for confirmation of shared impressions. Twin nods, then Caresse spoke: "About twenty minutes after Janet left."

"Who's Janet?"

"She's our friend. Janet Marvins. The one that got us into this fricking yoga class in the first place." Leeta spread her hands, palms up, as if their relationships were obvious. "When the session finished, the three of us hung around for a few minutes, catching our breath and what not." I'd seen the three women gossiping as they wiped off yoga sweat during my tour with Hadley.

Caresse chuckled and flapped her fingers before her still-raspberry face. "We were fagged out, girl. Beat like rugs in spring cleaning."

The grinning friends panted to show their exhaustion. Then Leeta drew the tip of her towel across her throat to illustrate mopping up after the yoga class.

A new voice joined the conversation. "And one of you came in to get drinks from the vending machine." Fizzy as the soda pop she'd been sucking. "I saw you." Afro-puff Juliet dropped her boyfriend's hand to point at the yoga ladies.

Caresse threw a scowl at the teenagers but extended the story. "True. I drew short straw, so I got diet Cokes for us both."

My mother jumped on Caresse's casual observation. "Both? You mean, by the time you went to get drinks, your friend Janet had gone?"

"Yeah, she said she wanted to head home early tonight 'cause she has a heavy shift at the hospital tomorrow. She works as a data entry tech at Harlem Hospital. She stood up when I did. And by the time I got back with the Cokes, she was gone."

Caresse shrugged and reached for the paper cup. When she'd drained the dregs of the soda and crunched the ice, she smacked her lips in regret. Leeta rolled her eyes in embarrassment at her friend's crude sounds.

As the sharing warmed, Fabrice moved to the center table, as did the teen girl, who introduced herself as Tamyra Crooks. Sitting, she announced her boyfriend's name was Von Alvarez. He didn't seem happy with being abandoned by Tamyra and dropped his chin to his chest in a sulk. From my spot on the periphery, the four women looked like a bid whist party. The only missing features were rosy cocktails with cherries on toothpicks.

Discretion was my best policy: between the cops and Fabrice's urgency, my role was limited. I pulled a vinyl-upholstered chair a few feet from the wall and sat down, stretching my legs, settling in for a long night's investigation. With wisdom beyond his years, Von Alvarez followed my lead.

As if this was girls' night out, not a murder investigation, Fabrice smiled to soften her persistence. "Did you hear anything? Could you make out any words?"

"Nah, it was just muffled rumbling." Leeta's eyes dimmed as she recalled that charged moment. "Then it got real quiet in there. I remember, because your voice sounded loud again, Caresse. We'd been shouting over the noise. Then, we didn't need to holler no more."

Her friend remembered too. "Real quiet. Too quiet. Then *blam*! A shot goes off." She clapped her hands. Everyone jumped. Everyone except my mother, whose frown seared me. If I'd scored a few points with her when I helped break into the murder room, I'd lost them all now. In our hidden argument, I needed to recoup my losses to prove I could be an investigator, despite my nerves.

"How did you know it was a gunshot?" Fabrice's formal precision stumped the others. The three women looked at her as if a rhino tusk sprouted from the middle of her forehead.

Leeta stated the obvious. "You live here, don't you? You know what a gunshot sounds like. No mistaking it. Only fools on TV think it's a firecracker or a car backfire." Neighborhood trauma didn't require fancy words or deep analysis. Hurt, big or small, was the unavoidable thread woven into our everyday lives. Our detective agency's business was built on easing those daily heartaches. The local pain too often overlooked by the police.

Tamyra eyed her boyfriend, who moved behind her, placing his hands on her shoulders. "It was a gun," she said. "No doubt about it. The sound was loud, flat, a dry pop. Nothing like it in the world."

Von asked the obvious question. "Did you see who got shot? We were at the back of the crowd. Couldn't get a look into the office." He rotated his head to include the entire room. "Who was it got shot?"

One of the basketball coaches stepped from the corner shadow. "I saw. It was Carlina Rivera. She's the office assistant. Been here longer than me, five years at least."

The coach wiped a stubby hand across his face, flicking tears from his nose. He said his name was Juan Harris. "Nice lady. Good to everybody. Helped with registering kids for after- school programs, setting up our tournaments."

The other coach took up the story. "I've only been here two seasons, but Carlina was the best. She had smarts and more patience than anyone I'd ever seen. Angry parents, unruly volunteers, scared kids without a ride home. Carlina took care of them all."

Harris shook his head, pulling at the black knots on the nape of his neck. "Look how smooth she operated enrollment for the summer programs this week? All that cash, not one receipt lost. No one jumped the line, no one complained. Everyone got the classes they wanted. She registered all those people. Without backup. Never seen anything like it."

"Carlina was a gem. No doubt about it." New voice, soothing as warm honey. The speaker was a short white man with a bald head and open face. Though his words conveyed sadness, his expression held onto the smile he must have perfected for his work. "I'm Dennis Stevens, Executive Director."

He moved around the room shaking hands with me and the kid, Von Alvarez. Stevens slung arms across the shoulders of both coaches, pressing his head to theirs in commiseration. Then he approached the ladies' table with more handshakes.

Fabrice gripped his fingers longer than necessary, forcing him to pause. "Is that your office, Mr. Stevens? Do you share it with Carlina?" Though a sweet smile played over her mouth, my mother's eyes stabbed.

"Yes, I do. Did." He gulped. "We're cramped here, so we make do. But Carlina was such an excellent colleague, it was a pleasure and a privilege to work next to her." Formulaic, as though he'd rehearsed the phrases. I figured a version of this tribute would be on the Y's website by tomorrow noon.

As he spoke, I scanned Carlina Rivera's social media posts on my phone. Lots of pictures of her out with girlfriends: a bar, a party, a coffee shop. Shots of her around the Y. With kids, with her boss, Mr. Stevens, with Hadley and the trim young coaches. Carlina was always smiling, eyes glinting, even when captured behind her desk in the office.

Frowns skipped between Fabrice's eyebrows. "Did you see if anything was missing, Mr. Stevens? Or anything moved out of place?"

"Only a quick look before the police told me to wait in here." He pulled a handkerchief from his back pocket and dragged it over his pink forehead. The cloth dipped over his eyes, a gesture that brought a quick glare from Fabrice.

I lifted my phone, showing the director its surface. "This picture of Carlina at her desk. What's she doing here?"

My mother frowned at my intervention, but Stevens answered immediately. "That's from yesterday. She's toting up the intake from our summer enrollment drive."

"And what's this box?" I flexed my fingers to enlarge the photo. I'd only been a few minutes in the office. How had the desk looked? Carlina's gray face swam and bobbed. Torn blotter framed in green leather. Four, maybe five ballpoint pens. Carlina's slack jaw shivered under my finger. Stack of manila folders. Desktop computer on the left edge. No metal box.

Stevens peered at the phone. "That's the cash box. She's got it on top of her desk, you know, to fill it."

Fabrice took up my lead. "I didn't see that box on the desk just now. Was anything missing from the office, Mr. Stevens?"

Head swiveling, the director grimaced. "I noticed one thing missing and one thing moved, Miss...?" He hadn't challenged my right to pose questions, but he couldn't take the grilling from a woman.

Professionalism salted her growl. "Fabrice Peters." When recognition swept across the director's face, she cut him short. "What did you see?" Clipped, no nonsense. She wanted no blabbing about her being the famous detective. Fabrice on the case for real. But she hoped to keep her identity under wraps as long as possible. I scanned the six others for rustles of insight. Nothing. Our double detective identities seemed safe.

Stevens said, "That lock box was moved from its drawer in the file cabinet. As soon as I got into the office, I checked for it. Gone. And..." He hesitated as though the next was too awful to say out loud.

I tried a deeper register to shake his hesitation. "And what, Mr. Stevens?"

"My gun. I keep a gun in my desk drawer. Sometimes I'm here late into the night and keeping a firearm gives a sense of safety."

"And the gun was missing?" My line of questions was getting us somewhere. I rubbed my nose, then chin, to smother the perking smile.

"No, not missing. It was there, on the floor." Stevens looked down, eyes foggy. "Next to poor Carlina. She shot herself with it. With my — my gun." He choked on the last words and staggered onto the tattered sofa.

As the director mumbled, a draped gurney rolled past the open door of the lounge, wheels whining. We watched in silence as medics bundled Carlina Rivera's slight body down the corridor. They wrestled with the double glass entrance doors, then pushed the cart into the night. Two basketball coaches, a pair of yoga practitioners, teen lovers, two detectives, and a distraught executive director. Strangers caught in a small room confronted with enormous tragedy.

In the distraction of the ghastly moment, the cops switched their captives, taking the teenagers and returning Hadley, the manager, and Alton Bush, the husky weightlifter.

#

"That was the most shocking fifteen minutes I've ever spent in my life." Alton's high-pitched squawk blew through the gloomy lounge.

Scorn inflected Caresse's response. "If getting asked a few questions by the po-po is the worst that's ever happened to you, honey, you ain't lived yet!" Her bitter laugh provoked smiles from her yoga gal pal, Leeta.

Fabrice took the opening. "What did they ask you, Alton?"

"Where I was? What I heard, what I saw? Did I know that poor wretched lady? Did I know any of the rest of you all?"

Leeta cackled. "Doesn't sound so tough to me. You need to lift a few more weights, muscle man." She wasn't letting Alton off the hook.

But Hadley intervened to save his interrogation partner. "It may not sound rough to you when Alton rattles the questions like that. But when you're in the middle of it, that's a different story. I assure you, it was *horrific*." A shudder enveloped his whole body.

Fabrice adopted a soothing tone, bland and phony. "Did the cops tell you anything new?" The others exhaled, welcoming her gentle-seeming intervention. My mother was good at this.

Lines on Hadley's brow relaxed. "They told us Carlina died from one bullet to the head. We already knew she'd shot herself, so I guess that wasn't anything new."

The heavy frown and pursed lips Alton Bush cast into the room suggested he found Hadley's discussion of the dead woman indelicate. *Suicide.* Had the police confirmed this interpretation of the evidence so soon after the event? Would they share their conclusion with two witnesses, even if they were positive it was a suicide? Fabrice's eyes narrowed; she drew a hand over her face, sealing in the questions, letting Hadley continue his account. She was the lead investigator, so I kept quiet, too.

"And they said the room had been locked from the inside. Which made the fact that poor Carlina took her own life so much sadder." Hadley sobbed into the elbow of his shirt. Caresse jumped at [to] a box of Kleenex on a side table. She handed a fistful of crushed tissues to the manager and patted him on the back.

After wiping his nose, Hadley continued through hiccups. "I told the police how Mr. Roland and I battered down the door and rushed in to find Carlina's poor dead body." Basset-hound eyes he cast toward me dribbled tears.

"Did the police confirm the door was locked?" I interrupted the sobbing. "Could they tell from the splinters and the door jamb?" I wanted to add, *Or did they accept your word for it, Hadley?* But I held my tongue. Fabrice looked at me with raised eyebrows. Was her glance warm? Progress was small, but I'd take it where I found it.

"Yes, they agreed the door was locked." Hadley's strident voice cracked with fervor. "I suppose they'll ask you to confirm the same thing, Mr. Roland. But we both saw how it was."

I measured my vague words. "Sure thing, Hadley. What you said."

Not the gushing endorsement Hadley wanted. His dark eyes slanted left. Objection stormed to his lips.

Before we could clash, Alton Bush took up the story. "I told them how I'd heard the shot. *Blat!* Then, after I returned my weights to the rack, I looked out into the corridor."

Fabrice led him. "Did you see anything?"

"Nothing, except Mr. Hadley struggling with the door."

"Was Hadley coming out of the office? Or trying to get in?"

Hadley interrupted with an epic harrumph. "What are you insinuating, Ms. Peters? How could I come out of the office? I couldn't get in it. It was locked."

"Of course, Hadley, that's right. I got confused." Fabrice's smile was demure, milky plain. Her eyes hard as granite. As she spoke, I rose from my chair and edged around the room toward the door. I stepped astride a rolled-up pink yoga mat on the floor, careful to keep my sneakers from touching it.

Silent until this point, the director David Stevens spoke from his depressed cushion on the couch. "Hadley, did the police ask you about the missing lock box?"

"No, they didn't mention that." The manager held out both palms.

"Yeah, they did. Don't you remember?" Alton Bush muscled into the middle of the recollection.

Hadley sucked his lower lip until it disappeared into his mouth.

Bush clambered on, "They asked us if we knew what had been in the top drawer of the file cabinet. You said it might have been a folder of newspaper clippings. Or a metal box. Or a pile of applications for the summer youth baseball league. You weren't sure. That's what you said." Bush jutted his jaw, convinced of the rightness of his memory.

"I suppose your mind is clearer than mine." Hadley sounded resigned to his fuzzy-brained condition. "I won't argue with you." Maybe he thought a stroll around the room would clear his head. He walked counterclockwise to my movements, aiming toward my position as he traveled.

Juan Harris, the basketball coach, asked the question Director Stevens refrained from posing. "Did you see the weapon?"

Hadley and Bush spoke at once: "Yes." Two pairs of eyes connected like magnets.

When the weightlifter snapped his mouth shut, Hadley expanded his account. "I told them I'd seen it on the floor next to Carlina's little hand. Remember I showed it to you, Mr. Roland?"

"I remember." I also recalled the smear of fingerprints Hadley's grab had produced on the weapon's handle.

Fabrice shot the next question through tight-pressed lips. "Was that your gun, Mr. Stevens?"

After a long pause, Stevens straightened on the couch. I bent to hear his whisper. "The gun's mine. Like I said, I kept it in my desk drawer. We'd had a few robberies on the block these past months. A couple of kids waving pistols stuck up the barbershop on the corner just last week. I brought my personal weapon from home, just in case." He sighed, the weight of the uncertain neighborhood on his shoulders. "We keep a large amount of cash on hand. You can never be too safe in these streets."

I looked at my mother. This was her case. Or maybe, just maybe, it was *ours* now. She nodded, no smile, no eye shift. Just the slight tilt only an attentive son could catch. The stakes shifted then, our focus tightened. Her high sign gave me the go-ahead. I might be number two in this show, but I had a role. I asked, "How much cash did you have in the office tonight, Mr. Stevens?"

"We just finished enrolling for our summer session. Over nine hundred people signed up in the past three days. Kids and adults both. Our biggest year yet." Pride stiffened the director's voice, the bright tenor ringing across the room. Death or no death, his program was an administrative success. "Some pay the full fee up front. The rest make a twenty-dollar deposit to hold their place. We had more than twenty thousand dollars in that lock box today."

Alton Bush blew a sharp whistle. I was impressed, too, but held my breath. A cool twenty thou was nothing to sneeze at. If I'd known, maybe I'd have robbed the Y, too. Fabrice's eyebrows disappeared under the damp curls on her brow.

A sob escaped Stevens's reddened lips. Was the director crying for the money, his dead assistant, or the stain on the reputation of his recreation program? When he continued, Stevens clarified his priorities. "The lock box was gone." He fluttered his fingers in the empty air. "All that cash gone. Just gone."

One more "gone" would've sent me leaping onto the sofa to punch his twisted mouth. Instead, I concentrated my fury: "Besides you, Mr. Stevens, who else knew about the gun in your desk?"

Confusion spun his eyes in their sockets. Maybe guns replaced those dollars, flying like gnats in front of his eyes.

"I — I don't know." Spit dribbled to the corner of his mouth. "Of course, Carlina knew about it because I showed her. Hadley, of course. And he might have mentioned it to the janitor, too. And Mia, the cleaning lady must have seen it. She sees everything."

Fabrice didn't care about the service crew. "That right, Hadley? Did you know the gun was in Director Stevens's desk?"

Hadley's hedging turned sloppy. "I guess I did, now you mention it." His eyes bulged and sweat beaded along his low hairline. He started to raise a finger to flick away the drops, instead lacing his hands together at his belt. "Mia did mention it to me, come to think about it."

At that moment, a young Black officer entered the lounge. Undersized, he didn't fill the shoulders of his navy uniform. Sincerity shone from his handsome brown face as he crooked a skinny finger at the yoga ladies, Leeta and Caresse. Giggling, they stood in unison, like a beached synchronized swim team. As the women minced across the floor, they turned their heads from side to side making sure we appreciated their graceful moves.

When the pair reached the door, Leeta paused. A hand on the door frame, she looked back at us and whined, objecting to this premature exit from the stage. "But I want to hear how the story ends. Caresse can go first, Officer. I'll wait."

The cop was built like a reed, but the wool uniform disguised his toughness. He pinched Leeta's elbow and pulled her through the door. She tossed one last question before she disappeared: "What're you doing with Janet's yoga mat, Mr. Roland? Why you standing over it like that?"

My ankles flinched when she called out my awkward pose. But I stiffened my legs to protect the evidence I'd identified.

Hadley lunged past my knee, his outstretched hand aimed at the pink mat. I grabbed his wrist, squeezing until bone slid against cartilage. He squealed, then wrenched. When I freed his hand, he cradled it against his chest. The lower lids of his eyes sagged with unshed tears as he shuffled backwards.

I stared at Hadley but raised my voice. "Nobody touches the mat until the police dust it for fingerprints."

In the commotion, the skinny cop lost his grip on his charges and both women jumped into the room. Her eyes shining with excitement, Caresse pointed at me, then toward the roll between my feet. "Why's Janet's mat still in here anyway? She took it with her when she left."

Rising from the table, Fabrice fired questions at the yoga classmates. "When did your friend leave? How do you know this is her mat?"

Caresse, eager to claim some spotlight, popped: "Janet took off right before I came back with the drinks. Maybe twenty minutes before the shooting started."

Not to be outshone, Leeta puffed her chest. "And I know that's her exercise mat because she tied it up with a yellow string. Said she liked the way the yellow and pink looked together. Matched the yellow stripe on her yoga pants, she said. What I want to know is why's it still here? Janet took the mat with her, I'm sure of that. Right, Caresse?"

"Sure did. That mat must've pulled a magic carpet trick and flown back here. It should be at home with Janet."

Fabrice approached me; I stepped aside. She seized the mat by the yellow string, holding it toward the young cop, whose mouth gaped like a tunnel. "Officer, this mat is evidence. Secure it now before anyone else touches it."

Smart man, he did as instructed. "Yes, ma'am. You got it." His hand twitched for a salute, but he suppressed the gesture at the last moment.

Creases popped around Fabrice's mouth. The harsh sound of that "ma'am" pinched, but she stifled objections. Unaware of his blunder, the junior officer rushed on, his button eyes sweeping the lounge. "Someone fill me in. How's this mat evidence? What's the story here?"

I shifted onto my heels, bowing my head in Fabrice's direction. A tiny gesture, only for her. She caught it, understood me, and took a deep breath. The flutter of her yellow T-shirt was slight when she rolled her shoulders. A fighter flexing before the match's final round. Our joint conclusion was hers to unpack.

"Here's the structure of this case, Officer. You've got theft and murder combined. The second to cover up the first. You don't need to look beyond this room for your murderer, although the thief is long gone."

Mumbles rose toward clamor, hums slithered into hisses. The crowd belonged to Fabrice, as witnesses, suspects, or both.

The kid cop knew his role in the drama. "Explain, Missus…?"

"Peters. Fabrice Peters. I'm a licensed private investigator."

The cop's eyes goggled with delight. "Hey, I know you. That detective agency, right? But I thought F.J. Peters was a man."

I coughed to interrupt my mother's explosion. She was in charge here, no need to discipline the poor clod.

Clearing her throat, Fabrice squared her shoulders. Her voice rang across the room like a pastor from the pulpit. "Here's how it went down this evening. The robbery was planned long in advance. As Director Stevens told us, the three days of registration for the Y's summer session ended today. So, a large sum of cash was in that office tonight." She swung her head toward the sofa where the director cowered against its arm. "You planned to take the money to the bank tomorrow, right, Mr. Stevens?"

He spurted agreement. "Yes, I certainly did." His hands clutched, fingertips rubbing as if petting the cold cash.

Fabrice pulled her eyes from his grasping. "That bank run set the timeline for the strike. The theft of the payload had to be this evening. The plotters needed access to the office. And they needed information about the location of the lock box and where to find the key to open it. Only a few people had that information: Mr. Stevens, his assistant, Carlina Rivera, and the building manager, Tom Hadley."

A flicker dented my mother's right eyelid. Doubt, slender, but nagging. How could she be certain Hadley knew about the lock box? What about the cleaning crew and the support staff? Fabrice was guessing. I knew it and admired her boldness. Her instinct guiding her over the rough patch, she plunged on, "When Stevens went home for the day, Carlina left shortly after as she usually did. Right, Hadley?"

"Yes, she left like always, at six-thirty." He stared bullets at Fabrice, whose smile snaked over her lips. Hadley didn't deny her claim. She'd won the concession she needed to close the case.

Fabrice turned to the young cop, who nodded for her to continue. Her voice strutted with rhythmic punctuation to underline her command position. "But Carlina came back. With fatal consequences. She'd left something in her office, maybe her cell phone, maybe gloves, maybe a subway token. Whatever it was, she returned to the office to retrieve it. And that's when Carlina confronted the robber."

Caresse's screech interrupted Fabrice's smooth delivery. "Who's the dang robber, woman? Don't drag it out like this!"

Fabrice's smile folded into a smirk. She'd inherited a flair for the tease and taunt from her storyteller father who'd run a strip joint when she was young. "Your friend Janet Marvins is the thief."

Caresse gasped, eyebrows crumpling in confusion. As the audience rumbled, I slid fingers over my mouth to plug a grin.

Fabrice continued before objections flew. "When she left you and Leeta, she didn't go home. Instead, she entered the office, opened the file cabinet, grabbed the lock box, and hid it inside something. Was she carrying a satchel or a gym bag?"

Leeta slapped a hand against her thigh. "She had that ratty pink sweatshirt. I wondered why she brought that old thing, smelly and full of holes like it was."

Fabrice nodded in satisfaction at Leeta's report. "Janet wrapped the lock box in her funky sweatshirt and stowed it under her arm. Ready to walk out of the Y and make a clean getaway. But Carlina Rivera came back. And confronted her. Carlina knew where Stevens kept his gun. She pulled it from the desk. Pointed it in Janet's face. The women argued. Then fought." My mother raised both fists to mimic the struggle. Upper cut right, jab left. "Janet knocked the gun to the floor. At that moment a new player entered the room."

Fabrice stopped talking, a smile skittering across her mouth. She swallowed, then cleared her throat, driving the suspense to the breaking point. She was having fun and so was I.

The others, not so much. Leeta screeched, spewing frustration felt by everyone in the room. "You gonna just hang like that? You evil woman!"

Fabrice's eyes raked the assembly, pausing a second on each anxious face. Until she settled her gimlet gaze on the only one who mattered.

"The new player was Hadley, the building manager. He knew where the money box was held. He was the one who left the office open so his accomplice, Janet Marvins, could enter to steal the cool twenty thou. He waited at his station in the entrance hall, guarding against interference. The robbery was going just as planned. But when Hadley heard the women arguing, he ran into the office. He picked up the gun from the floor and fired a bullet into Carlina's head, killing her instantly."

The audience gasped, air frozen in eight throats. Eyes rigid, hands clenched, lips skinned from dry teeth. No one moved. Except Hadley. One crab-step toward the door. Then a second. I moved behind Hadley. Muscle to keep the peace as Fabrice finished her account.

"Janet ran; cool head, colder heart. Taking the cash box with her. No way she went home." An accusing glance at the wall clock above the sofa. "She's probably past Exit 8 on the Jersey Turnpike by now."

Coach Harris found his voice for a high-pitched denial. "No, can't be like that, lady."

Not defending Hadley so much as challenging the basic geometry and physics of the crime scene Fabrice had described. He stood from his chair and stretched his arms wide.

"You got it wrong," Harris quarreled. "The office door was locked. From the inside. Carlina was dead inside a locked room. How could this Janet woman have escaped through a solid door?" He wriggled his hands in the air. "How could Hadley have shot Carlina and then passed like a ghost through the door, leaving it locked from the inside? It just doesn't add up."

Fabrice's smile was beautiful. Like ones she'd wrapped around me in our happy years before my father died. "Ah, but it does. Once you realize the door wasn't locked at all."

I'd been itching to spill the discovery for some time. But seeing her do it was perfect. Warmth cascaded from my chest to my knees. The open mouths, flared nostrils, pumping chests, and bugging eyes of the others in the lounge were priceless. Most precious of all was the deepening flush on Fabrice's cheeks. She glanced my way, smiles only for me.

Hand aloft, a professor instructing the freshman class, Fabrice continued. "Only Hadley claimed the room was locked. Remember, he told my son, Roland, the door was locked." Gulps and hisses greeted her revelation of my status. Pleasure thumped in my throat, but I nodded and kept quiet.

"Then he enlisted Roland's help to bust it down. When they shattered the door frame, they broke the handle, lock, and hinges, destroying the evidence that the lock had already been unfastened. Just as Hadley hoped. When they got inside, Hadley picked up the gun and showed it to Roland. With that move, he placed his fingerprints on the weapon in full view of a witness. Like that, he established a neat excuse for his fingerprints being on the gun."

That was my prompt. I'd sounded like a chump, blinded by panic in those first frantic moments after the crime. Sure, I'd blundered at the opening. But now I could redeem myself in the last act.

"That's the stunt Hadley tried to pull again with Janet's yoga mat," I said. "He saw she'd dropped it in the office during the fight with Carlina. He picked it up and brought it back to the lounge, leaving it here as if Janet had never removed it. But his fingerprints were on it. He wanted to take a second swipe at touching it, in our presence, so there'd be an excuse for his fingerprints again. But I blocked him."

Fabrice beamed at me, upper and lower teeth showing. My stomach skipped at the sight and the back of my neck warmed. I popped my lips, ready to expand on my exploits. The others might have been watching us. Or they might have been exploring a coral reef. I didn't know, didn't care. I'd made my mother proud. Proved I was ready to step into the front ranks of our detective agency. Justified adding my name to the main door.

Hadley lunged for the exit. The puny cop looked like a pushover and this was the murderer's best chance for freedom. He hadn't counted on the combined muscle power of the yoga ladies. In a synchronized swoosh, Leeta and Caresse swung beautiful roundhouse blows from the right and left side. Their twin punches clobbered both Hadley's ears at once. Hadley slumped in a heap. Groans trailed from his rubbery lips as the cop fastened cufflinks on his wrists. I lugged Hadley to his feet and frog-marched him to the hall, my mother striding behind me. When she touched a hand to my shoulder, her clasp was gentle.

# # #

An hour later, Fabrice and I walked from the YMCA, arms linked, the shoulder of her black coat bumping against my chest as the wind picked up along the boulevard.

"Thanks for your help in there, Roland." She disarmed me with a wink. "And for your non-help."

"Non-help? That sounds bad."

"I noticed you holding off. You got to the finish line when I did. I appreciate you let me take the lead."

I shook my head. "It was your investigation, Detective." I still stumbled over calling her Mom. Maybe next month. Or next year. "I was the clumsy Watson to your Holmes tonight." I leaned to kiss the damp coils on top of her head. "Or maybe I was Robin to your Batman. Your choice." I chuckled; she harrumphed.

I'd forgotten our locker room conversation in the bustle of the successful conclusion of the murder case. But Fabrice hadn't.

Eyelashes fluttering, she shook her head. "I'm sorry, Roland. For doubting you. For snapping. For all of it." She spread her fingers, then clasped them around my bicep. The corners of her eyes were heavy with tears. She looked sad but relieved.

"Hey, already forgotten. Partner," I said.

Not true. But that was the better choice, the right word for us now. Words done for the night, I hugged my mother to my chest. Arms entwined, we crossed the intersection and passed an all-night laundromat. We ambled to the far corner, heading home.

There were no quick answers ahead for us, no easy path. We'd work the cases, Fabrice and Roland together. A week, a month, a season, as long as necessary. It didn't matter. The thing was to work the future together.

The Upper Window by Erica Ruth Neubauer

#

10. The culprit must turn out to be a person who has played a more or less prominent part in the story—that is, a person with whom the reader is familiar and in whom he takes an interest. For a writer to fasten the crime, in the final chapter, on a stranger or person who has played a wholly unimportant part in the tale, is to confess to his inability to match wits with the reader.

London, 1930

Her employer's voice was loud, impossible to miss, really.

"Can you connect me with Dorothy Sayers? She's staying at your hotel." He paused. "Thank you."

Bridget was dusting on the landing above him, still attending to her work, but definitely listening. She knew that if Mrs. Jorgensen found her eavesdropping, she'd likely be dismissed, so she kept an eye out for the old battleax of a housekeeper.

"Mrs. Sayers, I'm Freddie Montgomery, I'm sure you've heard of me." He paused. "No? How unusual. Well, at any rate, you may have heard of the recent murder of my wife. By her own brother. He shot her twice right through the eyes." Another pause. "Yes, dreadful stuff."

It *was* dreadful stuff, and Bridget was only back at work this week after the murder. She kept her duster moving but frowned. Why on earth would Mr. Montgomery be phoning a mystery novelist about his wife's murder?

"I was wondering if you'd like to come take a look at the place," Freddie said.

At this suggestion, Bridget's duster stopped altogether and she had to physically stop herself from going to the stairs and peering down at Freddie, who was using the phone on the landing at the bottom of the winding stairs. It was a grand house, this one, and Bridget was lucky to have landed a position here, despite being "poor Irish trash."

Mrs. Jorgensen's words, not hers. Or even Mr. Montgomery's, for that matter.

"You're certain I can't convince you to come by? I would love to explain exactly how old Tommy did the deed." Freddie's voice dropped, conspiratorial. "Had the shellshock after the war. Never was the same, which is why he did it."

Bridget got her feather duster going again, glancing around her to make sure Mrs. Jorgensen wasn't about to pounce on her, catch her in dereliction of duty. The woman moved like a ghost through the halls; if Bridget hadn't actually touched her arm once, she might believe Mrs. Jorgensen was a spirit herself.

A heavy frown still furrowed Bridget's brow. She'd liked Mrs. Montgomery, a doctor who worked in the local hospitals, helping women give birth. Bridget didn't even know women could *be* doctors, and she hadn't known what to expect of Mrs. M when she interviewed here, but she'd been a kind lady. Bridget shuddered, thinking about what had happened to her.

But her brother Tommy had been kind, too. He'd been addicted to the laudanum, Bridget had seen it in his room more than once. And he'd jumped at the smallest noises, but he'd been awfully kind to the staff. He'd even given her a sweet last Christmas, a wrapped piece of licorice. Bridget had a hard time believing that Tommy could have shot and killed his own sister.

"Bridget," Mrs. Jorgensen's voice was loud in her ear, and Bridget jumped. How had she gotten here? "If you're finished here, I need you to do Mr. Montgomery's office, next."

Bridget nodded obediently, unsurprised at the directive. "I have to run an errand for Mr. Montgomery, but I will be back in exactly one hour," Mrs. Jorgensen continued. "I best not find that you've shirked your duties while I'm gone. No lazing about, you understand?"

Bridget stifled the urge to salute, instead nodding her head and doing her best to appear earnest. This was a perfect opportunity to do a little snooping, as long as she could get all the dusting done first. Mrs. Jorgensen would check her work, but Bridget had always been fast, faster than the average housemaid. It gave her a chance to peek at her pulps, do a little reading between assignments. And snooping is exactly what one of the heroes of her pulp magazines would do when confronted with a suspicious murder.

At least, Bridget thought it was suspicious. The police had come and looked around, and then done nothing else. They were convinced Tommy was the one who killed his sister, locked himself in the bathroom, and then shot himself. But the only person who'd been home had been Mr. Montgomery—the staff had been out that night, it being their evening off. If you were going to kill a person, that was the night to do it, but something about it all didn't seem right to Bridget.

She hurried to Mr. Montgomery's office, dusting the bookshelves, his desk and all the other bits of furniture in record time. She was nearly finished when she heard Jack behind her. "The old lady is away, and you're actually working?"

Bridget whirled on Jack, the stable hand who seemed to be dogging her every step, trying to chat her up every time Mrs. Jorgensen's back was turned. He was handsome enough, but there was something about Jack that Bridget didn't trust. Of course, her mother had drilled in her head not to trust *any* man.

"I'm busy, Jack," Bridget said, hoping that would be enough to get him to leave. She wanted to do a quick search of Mr. Montgomery's desk, see if there was anything interesting there.

But Jack was not easily dissuaded, creeping close to Bridget, much too close for her comfort. "What are you looking for?"

Her mouth twisted, but answered before she could think better of it. "I don't think Tommy killed Mrs. Montgomery." Bridget fully expected Jack to tell her she was being stupid, so she was surprised when she looked up from Mr. Montgomery's desktop and saw Jack looking speculative.

"I think you might be right," Jack said slowly. "But who else would have killed them both? Mr. Montgomery? Is that why you're looking at his desk?"

Bridget thought it was actually a reasonable question. "No, not necessarily. But maybe there's something here...." She trailed off. If it wasn't Mr. Montgomery, there wasn't likely to be something here. But who else? The other folks who lived and worked here were Mr. Montgomery's valet, Mrs. Montgomery's lady's maid, the housekeeper, the butler, and the two of them. It didn't seem likely to have been anyone else on that list, did it?

Bridget abandoned the desk and headed to the hallway, Jack hot on her heels. "Where are you going now?" Jack asked.

Again, Bridget didn't answer, but she rarely did when Jack pestered her, which did not dissuade him from flirting with her, as she hoped it would. She went up the servants' stairs, and down the hall toward the bathroom where Tommy was found, cautiously checking for Mrs. Jorgensen or Mr. Banks, the grouchy butler. Seeing that she—and Jack— were alone, she ducked into the bathroom. Hands on hips she looked around the small room. Was it possible that someone killed Tommy and got out? The door was locked from the inside when the police arrived, which was a neat trick. It was impossible to do that and escape, wasn't it?

Bridget got on her knees and looked around the floor, finding nothing but some dust behind the tub—she was surprised Mrs. Jorgensen hadn't found it and made her tidy it away, frankly. But there was nothing else—even the blood had been carefully scrubbed away, although not by her, so Bridget wasn't sure who had done it.

Then she glanced around the upper reaches of the bathroom. There was a window to the outside, but since they were on the second floor, it would be hard to get out that way, wouldn't it? Bridget pushed open the window and leaned out, examining the side of the brick house. She felt Jack beside her as he joined her in looking out. "I don't know if someone could have climbed down. And they would have had to close this window from the outside—not sure that's possible."

Bridget was disappointed, but she thought he was right. She closed the window behind them, and looked at the bathroom from this angle. There was another window, this one high up, and small, not much more than a rectangle cut into the wall near the ceiling. "What about there?" she asked, pointing to it. "Could someone have gotten out through there?"

Jack looked at it, walked to the wall and jumped, reaching the bottom sill with his hands. By gripping the bottom ledge, and bracing his feet against the wall, he was able to pull himself up nearly to the window. With another grunt, he dropped back down.

"I think it's possible." They both gazed at the boot marks he'd left on the wall, and Bridget grimaced. She'd have to wipe those off before Mrs. Jorgensen got home or she'd be in serious trouble.

"If someone were in socks, and was really strong," Bridget said thoughtfully, "they might have been able to pull themselves up and out the window, with the door still locked from the inside." The person would have to be a man, both for the strength to do it and because it didn't look like a woman's hips would slide through the window unless they were quite narrow. And no one on the staff was *that* slim. Not even Bridget. Cook's meals, even for the staff, were quite good. If she were dismissed, Bridget would dearly miss the food here.

Bridget did thank Jack for his help, and then shooed him away, running down the stairs to fetch a bucket and a rag. She was able to wipe away the prints made by Jack's boots on the wall just before Mrs. Jorgensen returned.

"What's that for?" Mrs. Jorgensen demanded when she found Bridget returning the bucket to the closet where she'd found it.

"I found a spot upstairs that had some dirt, and thought it needed cleaning," Bridget answered. It wasn't even a lie, not really.

Mrs. Jorgensen frowned at her for a long moment, then gave her instructions to dust the upstairs sitting room next. Bridget curtsied and hurried away, glad to have gotten away with that excuse, and as much snooping as she had.

#

Bridget lay in her narrow bed that night, exhausted, as she was every night, but for once, her mind wouldn't stop puzzling over what had actually happened the night Mrs. Montgomery and Tommy had died. When Bridget finally did fall asleep, she had unsettling dreams that she was the one who'd been killed in the bathroom instead of Tommy, so her eyes were bleary the next morning. She rushed through her morning chores, and slumped over her oatmeal at the servants' table.

Jack bumped her arm. "Didn't sleep well?"

She looked at him for a beat, then shook her head. "Bad dreams," she whispered.

"What's that? What are you two whispering about?" Mrs. Jorgensen demanded.

Bridget was too tired to come up with a good excuse this morning, and now everyone's eyes were focused on her as her face flushed red.

"Just telling Bridget she best eat all her porridge or I will," Jack said easily. Bridget flashed him a grateful smile once Mrs. Jorgensen looked satisfied and went back to her own meal.

Bridget assisted Mrs. Jorgensen with serving Mr. Montgomery his own breakfast—he slept much later than his employees, but that was the right of the wealthy. The children were back at boarding school, so it was an easy task to clean up afterwards. Once they were finished, Bridget waited for further instructions. Mrs. Jorgensen set down the cups she was carrying and huffed. "I have entirely too much to attend to today, so I need you to clean Mr. Tommy's room and turn it back into a plain old guest room." She gave her a sharp look. "Can you handle that, Bridget? It's a great deal of responsibility that I'm trusting you with." The housekeeper sniffed. "I would do it myself, but as I said I cannot, and we'll need it soon. Mr. Montgomery is expecting company."

Bridget wanted to remind Mrs. Jorgensen that were quite a few other guest rooms in the house, although Tommy had stayed in the nicest one. But she didn't argue, she just curtsied and promised to do a thorough job.

She hoped she'd done a good job of hiding her excitement. This was actually the best news that Bridget had had in some time, at least since her half day when she'd found a whole pound note on the ground. By cleaning Tommy's room, she had a reason to inspect all of his things as she put them away—perhaps she would find something that the murderer had left behind. Or even something that would point her to who the murderer was.

Bridget grabbed her supplies from the cupboard and hurried up the servants' stairs at the back of the mansion. She didn't need to be cautious today, since she was instructed to be there, but she was still [cautious]. Bridget got nervous upstairs when she was by herself. It was probably because of her mam's stories growing up about haints, spirits, and banshees heard in the night. But both Tommy and Mrs. Montgomery had been kind souls, and Bridget couldn't imagine they would be horrible ghosts, even if their souls *were* trapped here.

Tommy's guest room had a battered suitcase still open on the bed, and the door to the wardrobe was ajar. There was a smattering of things strewn on the dresser—a comb, cufflinks, and a pair of glasses, but nothing too far out of the ordinary. Except for the tube and hypodermic needle. Those were sitting on the bedside table, but there were no vials of laudanum as she expected. She'd come in here to stoke the fireplace and clean out the ash plenty of times while Tommy was staying here, and there had always been one or two vials of what he referred to as his "medicine." So where had that gone? Could the police have taken it?

Bridget got to work clearing everything up, thinking the entire time. It was strange that those vials were gone, and hadn't she overheard Mr. Montgomery say that they'd taken away the bodies—*shudder*—and the gun, but that was all?

She went to the wardrobe and gathered up the few things hanging there—a tweed suit, and some button-down shirts of fine linen. She carefully folded the items, even though Tommy was dead, and put them in the suitcase. But on a hunch, she took them back out, and poked through everything else that was still in the suitcase. She didn't expect to find anything of interest—maybe a bottle of cologne, but she was surprised when her fingers hit hard metal. She gingerly grasped whatever the item was and pulled it free from the soiled clothing, then dropped it in fright when she realized she was holding a revolver.

Glancing around behind her to make certain no one had seen either her snooping or the gun, Bridget covered it back up. It looked like a service revolver, not that Bridget knew much about such things. But her uncle had once shown her one, and this looked similar.

Bridget finished up her work, relieved to close up the suitcase. She changed the bedding on the four-poster bed, which was strenuous work by herself, stripping the sheets and pillow cases, getting the fresh ones on nice and tight. There was a trickle of sweat on her brow when she finished and she swiped at it before doing [finishing] the rest of the room. She wasn't sure what to do with Tommy's suitcase, so she carried it downstairs along with her bucket of cleaning supplies. She put the bucket back in the cupboard, then looked down at the suitcase. Perhaps it would be best to put it in Mrs. Jorgensen's office, a tiny room off the servants' dining area, next to the butler's office.

Bridget left the suitcase there, even though Mrs. Jorgensen was nowhere to be seen, then walked slowly down the hall, nearly running into Jack who was coming in from the opposite direction.

"You're thinking hard about something," Jack said.

Bridget frowned. Both because she usually frowned at Jack's clumsy attempts to make conversation and because she couldn't stop thinking about that revolver. "Jack, do you know if the police took the gun that Tommy used?"

Jack nodded. "I saw them myself."

Bridget's eyebrows, dark red like her hair, shot up. "You were here? I thought all the staff was gone that night."

Jack flushed, and gave a little shrug. "We were supposed to be out, but I stayed in the stable. You know Honey, the big mare? She wasn't feeling well so I stayed with her. To make sure it wasn't colic."

Bridget didn't know what to make of that. Should she believe Jack? It was plausible, but then again…

Her mind twisted away from Jack and back to the gun. Wouldn't Tommy have used his own weapon if he was going to kill his sister and then himself? If his revolver was safe in his bedroom, what gun had he used? Or rather, who had done the shooting using someone else's gun?

Jack answered her, which surprised Bridget and she realized she must have been muttering out loud.

"If that gun wasn't Mr. Tommy's," Jack said thoughtfully, "could it have been Mr. Montgomery's?"

Jack and Bridget locked eyes for a long moment. Had their jovial employer killed his wife and brother-in-law? Jack had further news that seemed to seal the deal. "You know the company that's coming?" When Bridget shook her head, Jack continued. "It's a Miss Amelia. A young woman." Jack gave her a knowing look, but Bridget didn't understand what that meant. "Mr. Montgomery was fooling around behind his wife's back, is what that means. He already has a single lady coming to stay."

Bridget felt her mouth fall open, but they were both interrupted by Mrs. Jorgensen. "What are you two doing here instead of working?"

This time Bridget was ready. "I left Mr. Tommy's suitcase in your office, ma'am. I didn't know what else to do with it."

Mrs. Jorgensen didn't look convinced enough, and Jack nodded. "It's true, ma'am. I was telling her she'd done the right thing."

The housekeeper's eyes were narrowed at the two, and she pushed between them, opening the door to her office and looking inside. "Very well. Jack, return to the stables. And Bridget, I want you to take this thing and drop it at the charity shop on the high street. They can have Mr. Tommy's things."

Bridget's eyes opened wide, since she'd never been given an outside task before, but she quickly agreed. Once she had her coat on and stood on the sidewalk, she thought about Tommy's revolver. The police would need that, wouldn't they, if Bridget was able to prove someone other than Tommy had killed Mrs. Montgomery? Not to mention, she shouldn't drop a revolver at a charity shop. Bridget glanced back at the house, and noticed a twitch of the curtains, up near Mr. Montgomery's room. That was strange—was Mr. Montgomery watching her? She couldn't help the thought that maybe he had killed his wife, especially since a new lady friend was coming to stay.

Nervous that she was being watched, Bridget walked two blocks, then two more, before doubling back. That should be enough time to make sure whoever saw her thought she was well and truly gone. She made her way to the stable, avoiding the house. She didn't want to open this suitcase on the street where she could be seen, especially since someone might be watching her. No, she would hide the revolver in the stables; maybe Jack would know where she could stow it.

Bridget snuck in through the side door, the sweet smell of hay tickling her nose. She sneezed and heard "Bless you" called from a stall at the end of the row on the right-hand side. On the left was a room full of saddles and other supplies, then storage for hay and oats. "Jack?" Bridget called. "I need your help."

There was no answer, and Bridget frowned. That was strange. Hadn't he just blessed her sneeze? Bridget set the suitcase down, cracked it open, and reached inside, easily pulling out the revolver since she instinctively knew it would have slipped to the bottom. She then tucked it into her coat pocket, quietly shut the suitcase, and left it as she walked to the end of the row. The horses had been let out into the small paddock behind the stable—this grand house had quite a lot of space, enough for a garden with space left over for the horses to enjoy. Mrs. Montgomery had been awfully fond of the horses—she spent a lot of her time away from the hospital here in the stables, brushing the beasts, and taking them out for rides.

"Jack?" Bridget called again. She came to the last stall, fully expecting to find Jack mucking it out, but instead he was huddled in the corner, a gag in his mouth and his arms tied behind him. He was looking at her wild-eyed, glancing to the corner behind her several times. Her blood froze when she heard a voice behind her.

"Oh, Bridget, you stupid, stupid girl," James Billingham said. It was Mr. Montgomery's valet. He was dressed impeccably, and had a pitchfork in his hands. "You couldn't leave well enough alone, could you? Had to poke your nose into things, when the police had it all sorted out."

Bridget watched James carefully, backing up until her back hit the wall next to Jack. "What do you mean?"

James laughed. "Don't be coy with me, girl. I saw you two in the bathroom, snooping. It was only a matter of time before you learned our plan and how we did it."

"*Our* plan?" Bridget asked. Maybe if she could keep him talking, someone would come find them.

"You don't think I did this alone, do you?" James took a few menacing steps toward her. "Where do you think I got the revolver?"

Maybe James didn't know about Tommy's revolver then. "Who helped you? And why would you kill them?" She could only assume that was the case since he was now threatening to kill her and Jack. The revolver in her pocket felt heavy. Could James tell it was there?

The valet ignored the first part of her question. "Because they were going to cut off my access to Tommy's medicine," James said with a shrug. Bridget had never really noticed before, but James did have a sallow, somewhat sweaty appearance. His eyes were glossy[, too]. It looked as though the valet was addicted to laudanum, too. "Mrs. Montgomery was going to get her brother off the stuff, and she found my stash, threatened to report me." James shrugged. "I'm not going to prison."

This seemed like an extreme reaction. So did killing the two of them, which was clearly what James intended, as he was still slowly advancing toward Bridget, working up to it, probably. "We won't tell anyone," Bridget said hurriedly. "There's no need to hurt us."

James chuckled. "The only way I can be sure is if you're dead." He aimed the tines toward her stomach and looked ready to make his move. Before he could rush forward, Bridget dropped to her knees, reached into her coat pocket and pulled out the revolver, then brought it up and squeezed off a shot. It went wild, but stopped James in his tracks. Bridget wasn't done, however. She shut one eye and aimed for James's leg, hitting him square in the thigh. He screamed and went down hard, grabbing at where she'd hit him. Blood was gushing freely, turning Bridget's stomach. She covered her mouth, then turned to Jack. He was staring at her with wide eyes. She gave a small smile, then hurried over to untie him. Once she got his hands free, he pulled the gag out of his mouth.

"You shot him!" Jack said.

Bridget nodded. "He was going to kill us."

"How did you learn to shoot?"

"My uncle taught me." Bridget had put the revolver on the ground, but she picked it up and was once again aiming at the valet.

Jack looked at her for a long moment, clearly trying to decide what to do. "I'll go get Mr. Montgomery," he finally said.

"Grand," Bridget said, the revolver neatly aimed at the writhing valet.

The police came and took James away, likely to the hospital to have his gunshot tended to before they took him to prison to be tried for murder. In the valet's room a constable found the bottles of laudanum that James had swiped from Tommy's room, plus a number of empty ones. Apparently, he'd been stealing it from Tommy for quite some time.

"I'm quite impressed with you, young Bridget," Mr. Montgomery said. "You solved my wife's murder, and cleared poor Tommy's name. We'll have to keep you on to protect all of us." This was said with a grin and a handful of notes pulled from Mr. Montgomery's billfold, more than she'd ever seen before in her life. Bridget considered turning it down, but accepted the money, vowing to give some to Jack, since he'd helped her. She might even let Jack take her out on their next half day.

But she also vowed to keep a close eye on Mr. Montgomery. As the police had taken James away, he'd been screaming that their boss had made him do it. Mr. Montgomery had laughed it off, the ravings of a drug-addled mind he'd said, but Bridget wasn't convinced.

She'd be wary of her employer. Just in case.

The Tell-Tale Thumb
by Tom Mead

# # #

11. Servants—such as butlers, footmen, valets, game-keepers, cooks, and the like—must not be chosen by the author as the culprit. This is begging a noble question. It is a too easy solution. It is unsatisfactory, and makes the reader feel that his time has been wasted. The culprit must be a decidedly worth-while person—one that wouldn't ordinarily come under suspicion; for if the crime was the sordid work of a menial, the author would have had no business to embalm it in book-form.

Saturday, August 5th 1939

The discovery made by Miss Lucy Raymond when she pried open the heavy oaken lid of the window seat that morning sent ripples of horror and disquiet through the heretofore placid environs of Titherton Mews. What she found was a body; a man's body to be exact, and quite dead. Her shriek rent the morning air and brought the other servants of that strange house scuttling to her aid.

"Whatever's the matter, girl?" demanded the cook, Mrs. Gray, with something akin to madness in her eyes.

"It's Mr. Eddowes," stammered the young housemaid. "He's in the window seat."

"Nonsense," scoffed the cook. But the parlour maid, Beth Sands, who was eighteen months older than Lucy and therefore considered herself somewhat of a mother hen, went and hugged her sobbing sister-in-arms, stealing a glance into the aforementioned window seat as she went.

"It's all right," Beth said, gently ushering Lucy away from the dreadful sight. "Someone had better tell the master."

The hullabaloo reached feverish new heights when a middle-aged man appeared in the doorway, looking irritable. It was Percy Eddowes, the valet in question.

Lucy shrieked and Beth clung to her. Mrs. Gray's right eyelid began to twitch wildly. The body was not Eddowes after all, though it was a reasonable enough misidentification, since the corpse wore the morning coat, wing-collar shirt, and pinstripe trousers of a butler or personal valet, and his face was turned away from the observers, and masked by shadow.

"Good Lord," said Eddowes, his rage stilled by the sight of the corpse. For it was not a servant at all who lay in that infamous window seat, but the master of the house, Mr. Hugh Westerby.

# # #

Inspector George Flint of Scotland Yard arrived to find a house in disarray. It was still comparatively early--nine-fifteen on a Saturday morning—and the previous night's revelries hung heavy on him. He'd overindulged on celebratory milk stout at the news of his eldest daughter's engagement, and was currently ruing his own lack of restraint with each blink in the blazing daylight. He was so distracted that he'd left his pipe at home that morning, and now found himself fidgeting as he paced up and down the drawing room. His pipe was an essential component of his investigative process; even unlit, he found the act of chewing on its stem helped to stimulate his occasionally sluggish deductive motors. Without it, he was utterly at sea.

Lucy Raymond was still in shock, so Mrs. Gray and Beth were looking after her in the kitchen. Flint opted for a "softly-softly" approach, which was not his habitual mode.

"Tea," he said, "that's the best thing for shock. Make us some, would you, Mrs. Gray?"

The cook gave him a disapproving look and then started bustling about. "The tea," she mumbled agitatedly, "where's the blasted tea?"

The clattering of tins and crockery sent waves of agony through Flint's skull. He tried not to let it show, but he wished she would hurry up and find the stuff.

"There was a full tin just yesterday...."

"All right," Flint said, "forget the tea. Lucy, why don't you just try telling me what happened this morning?"

Drying her eyes and sniffling stoically, Lucy began. "I was tidying the rooms before the master came down. Just like every other morning. And I opened the window seat and..."

"Slow down. Did you notice anything unusual in any of the other rooms?"

She shook her head. "I didn't go in the kitchen, though. Mrs. Gray was in there getting the breakfast things ready."

At this point, Mrs. Gray stepped in. "I got here at half-seven and went straight to the kitchen. Beth came down to collect the tea things for Mr. Westerby at around eight."

"I left the tray outside the master's door as usual," Beth explained quickly.

"And now the tea's gone walkabout...." Mrs. Gray persisted tiresomely.

Ignoring her, Flint continued to focus on Beth. "And did *you* notice anything out-of-the-ordinary first thing?"

Beth shook her head. "Lucy and I came downstairs at the same time. Neither of us spotted anything. Did we, Luce?"

Lucy shook her head emphatically.

The death of young Hugh Westerby was a matter of some note; his ubiquity in the society pages had given him a bloated sense of his own importance and--unfortunately--his importance in the eyes of the newspaper-buying public. A swift resolution to the matter would be advantageous to all--at least that's what Flint's superiors thought. They were even content for him to withdraw (briefly) from his investigation into the activities of the "Belgravia Burglar" who was proving so elusive, and possessed a worrying knack for cracking the safes of London's best and brightest.

It took Flint a little while to fathom the precise sequence of events here in the mews. First thing that morning, Miss Raymond, who had only been in the household since July, came into the drawing room to tidy up. Mr. Westerby had been up late the previous evening, and had left the room in a mess. In the act of tidying, she happened to open the window seat and discovered the body.

There was some nonsensical chatter about a chap named Eddowes, who turned out to be Westerby's valet. The dead man's attire had caused him to be mistaken for his manservant--an easy enough error, Flint supposed. Particularly for a housemaid who knew neither of the men particularly well. But on closer inspection, there were marked differences between them. The late Hugh Westerby was a foot taller than Eddowes, for one thing--though of course this was difficult to discern from the dead man's recumbent position, with his knees buckled inside the window seat. Eddowes was in the midst of drawing a bath for his master at the moment the grisly discovery was made; that is why he had not heard the housemaid's scream. It is also why he did not come running at the same time as the rest of the household--leading to that case of mistaken identity.

Now that the identity was established, though, the questions kept on coming. One of Hugh Westerby's most distinctive features had been his pencil moustache, which gave him such a caddish appearance. The corpse, however, was clean-shaven. Flint heard himself asking the ridiculous question: "Had Mr. Westerby expressed any intention of shaving his moustache?" There was much shaking of heads.

But the identification was sound nonetheless: Hugh Westerby had one truly inimitable feature: he himself referred to it as a "backwards thumb"; the thumb of his right hand had a warped, misshapen appearance after a childhood injury. It would bend outwards but not in.

Aside from the strange get-up, the abiding questions in Flint's mind were these:

First, how had Hugh Westerby died? And second, how had he come to occupy the window seat?

"You said Mr. Westerby was up late last night," he said to Lucy Raymond. "What was he doing?"

"I'm sure I don't know," she answered demurely. "He sent us to bed at nine. Only Mr. Eddowes was on hand to serve the drinks."

Moving on to Eddowes, Flint enquired, "What was your master up to last night?"

"I'm afraid I cannot say, sir," answered the valet, his immaculate composure restored. "It was a standing engagement of his. Once a fortnight he wanted the place to himself so he might entertain a guest."

"Who?"

Eddowes looked embarrassed. "I don't know, sir."

"And was it Mr. Westerby's custom to don fancy dress for the occasion?"

"I'm sure I wouldn't know, sir."

"The clothes—they're very similar to yours. Could he perhaps have borrowed them without your knowledge?"

"If you'll forgive me, sir, I should say not. The master and I do not measure the same. The clothes he is wearing are clearly tailored to fit."

Flint made a note of the fact. "So you don't know where they came from, or whether he'd worn them before?"

"No, sir. My only instructions on these occasions were to venture down to the wine cellar to retrieve a certain vintage, and to lay out a pair of crystal wineglasses. After that, my services were no longer required that evening."

"So you went to bed?"

"I did not, sir. I ventured out to the pictures."

"How was he dressed the last time you saw him?"

"Quite normally, sir. Smoking jacket, slippers…"

Flint nodded. Then, as an afterthought, he asked, "And what did you see at the pictures?"

"A double bill, sir. A pair of gangster pictures featuring Messrs James Cagney and George Raft."

"Where?"

"The Bijou, sir. Only a ten-minute ride on the Underground. Which is fortunate, for I left the house without my latchkey, and had to come scurrying back for it. I almost missed the start of the first feature."

"What time was that?"

"The feature?"

"No—your brief return to the house."

Eddowes looked nonplussed. "Only a few minutes after I had left."

"Did you see your master then?"

"No. My key was in the hall. I simply collected it and headed out once more."

"Did you go to the pictures alone?"

"Yes, sir. But no doubt the usherette will remember me."

"Oh, I'm sure. Presumably you are a regular?"

Eddowes nodded[, looking mildly embarrassed]. "I'm something of a cinema aficionado." Eddowes said this with mild embarrassment.

Mrs. Gray, the cook, did not "live in," and had returned home after the last of the dinner things were tidied away.

"I was gone by eight. The last time I saw Mr. Westerby he was alive and well."

The other maid, Beth, shared the attic bedroom with Lucy, so the two girls were able to supply each other's alibis. But Beth had a little more to say about these bimonthly engagements. "It started around three months ago, I'd say. I can't speak for Lucy, but I was under the impression Mr. Westerby had got himself a... lady friend."

"What gave you that idea?"

"Oh..." Suddenly she was coy. "This and that."

"Come along now."

"Well... I did happen, just the once, to catch a glimpse of a lady in the hall."

"Oh yes? Spying, were you?"

"I was not!" protested Beth.

"When did this happen then?"

"Last month. I happened to glance down from the landing just as Mr. Westerby was escorting her through to the drawing room."

"And what did she look like?"

Beth reached for the word. "Elegant."

"Would you recognise her if you saw her again?"

"I doubt it. Sorry, Inspector. The light in the hall is awfully dim."

Flint asked Lucy about the woman as well, but she had seen no strangers in the mews whatsoever. She stated this with the utmost certainty.

And so the evidence gleaned from the morning's interviews was disappointingly incomplete.

The only established facts were these: at some point during the evening, Hugh Westerby had changed from his regular evening attire into a costume resembling that of a valet. He had then promptly died, and his earthly remains been conveyed to the window seat by person or persons unknown. The whole thing was decidedly murky.

Murkier still was the report from the police surgeon, which came through later that Saturday. Like Flint, the surgeon had overindulged the previous evening, and was still suffering the aftereffects. But the results were intractable. Westerby's death was a natural one. There was no evidence of external violence, and the only toxins in his system were alcohol and nicotine. His servants confirmed he had been both a drinker and a heavy smoker—several packs a day. His physician, meanwhile, confirmed that he had a weak heart. He might have died at any time, and now, inevitably, he had.

No foul play at all! If anything, this merely compounded the bizarre nature of the circumstances. If Hugh Westerby had not been murdered, how had his corpse come to occupy the window seat? Why was he in that curious get-up? And who was his mysterious guest? Had she (Flint assumed it was a she) somehow hauled the dead man over to the window all by herself? What a strange thing to do.

Flint passed a hot and unsatisfactory day without his pipe, canvassing the other residents of the mews to ascertain whether any eyewitnesses had glimpsed the mysterious visitor for whom a second wineglass had been supplied. Predictably, no one had. The neighbours were all considerably older and more respectable than Hugh Westerby, and professed themselves scandalised at both the nature of his life *and* his death.

But with the revelation that Westerby's death was not the result of murder at all, Flint's business in Titherton Mews was more or less concluded. At the end of his working day, he returned home feeling as dissatisfied as only a detective thwarted by circumstance might [may] be. His wife, Julia, tried to cajole him with further news of his daughter's engagement: plans for the wedding ceremony and the like. And whilst he endeavoured to put on a show of eager interest, his thoughts were occupied by the body in the window seat, and the window itself, with its view out onto the cloistered mews.

Days passed and he returned to other matters. The Belgravia Burglar, who had been making a nuisance of himself since May, showed no signs of relinquishing his grip on the headlines. The papers had even begun likening him to a Raffles or Lupin, which Flint's superiors were keen to circumvent. Once the public starts siding with the criminal, can the descent into anarchy be far behind?

Through all this nonsense, though, Flint could not quite bring himself to forget the strange death of Hugh Westerby. Nor could he fully disabuse himself of the idea that there might be some connection—no matter how vague—between the two cases. Titherton Mews was only a short walk from Belgravia, after all.

#

The following Friday, Flint ventured out to Putney, and to a low-ceilinged Elizabethan public house called The Black Pig. In the cosy, fire-lit snug with its glowering deer's head on the wall and its moth-eaten furniture, he found his old friend and long-standing associate, Joseph Spector. As usual, Spector occupied the most comfortable arm-chair beside the fireplace, with a small glass of disgusting green liquid on a little table at his side. The glass contained absinthe; Spector was the only person Flint knew who could stomach the stuff. This was by no means all that was unusual about Spector's character, though. He was a retired magician who had previously trod the boards of the music hall stage. But that was in another life, and now he enjoyed a reason-ably peaceful retirement, only occasionally disturbed by his encounters with Scotland Yard. Spector's fascination with the bizarre, the baroque, the grotesque, as well as his knack for unravelling peculiar mysteries, had led to his recruitment on an ad hoc basis whenever the Yard had need of his services. Over the years, he and George Flint had forged an effective partnership.

Flint had not planned to mention Hugh Westerby--at least, he had not done so consciously. But the puzzle in Titherton Mews had bur-rowed so deeply into his unconscious that it was perhaps inevitable for it to resurface in his conversation with Spector. And when Spector hap-pened to mention something about a fancy dress ball, Flint could not help himself.

"Have you heard about the dead man that was found in fancy dress gear last Saturday?"

"Of course," answered Spector. "Hugh Westerby. The details are scant but remarkable. Dressed up as a butler, wasn't he? And concealed in a cupboard?"

"A window seat," Flint corrected.

"That's it. Not a mark on the body, isn't that so? And yet the press are adamant that it's murder."

"Well, the press are getting ahead of themselves, as usual. It's not murder. Just ordinary heart failure. And since there was no foul play involved, Scotland Yard doesn't have any particular interest in the matter."

"Well, *I* am not Scotland Yard," said Spector, "and I am very interested. So, please: tell me everything. Every detail!"

Flint regaled Spector with what little he knew of Westerby. It was mainly a matter of reciting certain salacious society pieces about the young man's exploits.

As he spoke, Spector took a sip of his absinthe. Then he steepled his long, spindly fingers, and seemed to lose himself in thought.

When Flint had finished his story, Spector said, "And what of the rest of the household? Was Westerby married?"

"No. A gay bachelor."

"Presumably there were servants?"

"Yes; a valet, Eddowes. Two housemaids, Beth and Lucy. And a cook, Mrs. Gray. But the suspect—if there *is* a suspect—seems to be the mystery lady who came calling on Westerby once a fortnight. Their assignations were carefully planned and regular as clockwork. He always made sure the servants were out of the way, but one of the maids caught a glimpse of an 'elegant lady.' Nobody has a clue who she might be."

Spector's eyebrows slid skyward. "Really? Not one of them? Well. Let that pass for now. Here's a more pressing concern: no doubt you've already made the connection between Westerby and the Belgravia Burglar?"

Flint nearly leapt out of his seat. "What connection?"

"Well, Titherton Mews isn't far from Belgravia, is it? And Westerby was a wealthy young man. It makes one wonder how much longer it would have been before he found himself in the sights of the notorious Burglar. Surely you've thought of that."

"I'm not saying I haven't. But if there's anything besides coincidence at play here, I don't see how it can be proved."

"Yes," sighed Spector, "I tend to forget how beholden you Scotland Yard men are to proof. It's inconvenient. But I think you'll agree there are... concordances. The Burglar strikes wealthy homes. Westerby was very wealthy, and I imagine he was acquainted with several of the victims. Perhaps he had even visited their homes for parties and the like. There's also the matter of his disguise."

Spector had chosen the word carefully. The costume and clean-shaven face bespoke more than a mere masquerade; they indicated outright impersonation of a deliberate, premeditated variety. There was another telling detail which had come to light only after the body was moved: a false moustache secreted in a jacket pocket. Thus, this disguise was even more calculated than had first been thought; Hugh Westerby's moustache was shaved off in advance, and the one he had sported during his last days alive was procured from a joke shop.

Who, then, had he been endeavouring to impersonate? Westerby and Eddowes looked nothing alike. The real valet was portly, balding, and imperious. And yet, the uniform had been made to measure. The clothes themselves carried the labels of a commonly used supplier, and a quick telephone call revealed that they had been ordered anonymously, with the measurements supplied by post.

"Why impersonate a valet?" asked Spector rhetorically. "There's the possibility, of course, that the Belgravia Burglar and Hugh Westerby were one and the same...."

"I had thought of that, Spector, believe it or not. Westerby was rich, but he was also a chancer with a highly dubious reputation. I certainly wouldn't put it past him to spend his evening swilling cocktails with his high society friends, only to come creeping back in the dead of night to steal their silverware."

"And yet," Spector countered, "you seem to have ruled it out."

"I have, and for good reason. The Burglar is a safecracker. You may not know safecrackers, Spector, but I do—it's a delicate art. Rather like conjuring, I suppose. You need dexterity. Absolute control. Westerby couldn't have done it because of his thumb."

"His thumb?"

"He had what he called a 'backwards thumb.' It was warped ever since childhood. But it meant he couldn't physically have committed that sort of crime. He wasn't capable."

"Well," Spector offered with a smile, "the spirit may have been willing, though the flesh was weak."

"Meaning what?"

"Meaning that if I were you I'd take a closer look at exactly *when* Hugh Westerby scheduled these mysterious rendezvous of his. Fortnightly, you said. Did they correspond with the activities of the Burglar?"

Flint took the pipe from his pocket and began to chew on it pensively. For once, he was ahead of Spector. "I've checked," he said, "and you're right. Those nights that Westerby wanted the house to himself coincide exactly with the Belgravia burglaries. But it couldn't be him."

"Someone in the household, then?"

Flint thought about this. "Not the valet. I checked at the Bijou Cinema, and it seems Eddowes is courting one of the usherettes. He goes there whenever he has a free evening. And not Mrs. Gray, the cook. She has a home and family of her own. She doesn't live in the mews."

"The housemaids, then?"

"They've given each other alibis. It would be impossible for one to sneak out without the other noticing."

"And you take them at their word? Well, in that case," said Spector, "you are left with only one course of enquiry: the phantom visitor."

"It's a dead end. I can't seem to find a lead on it. Nobody's saying a word."

Spector shrugged. "In that case," he said, "your only recourse is to wait."

# # #

As it transpired, Flint did not have to wait long. The following morning his sergeant, Jerome Hook, received a call from the Belgravia home of Lord Rosemont to report an unusual crime. Overhearing Hook's end of the telephone conversation, Flint was already getting into his overcoat. But it was not, as he had expected, another outing for the Burglar. It was an altogether stranger incident.

That morning, at precisely nine o'clock, one of Lord Rosemont's housemaids had gone up to his bedroom with a tray of tea things, as his lordship had requested the previous evening. He and Lady Rosemont were planning to sleep in, he had said. Poised to knock on the door, the maid waited for the large antique grandfather clock further down the corridor to chime. When the anticipated chime did not come, the maid glanced in the clock's direction. Something was wrong, though she could not immediately identify quite what it was. She approached the clock, still clutching the tray, and that's when she spotted that the elaborately woven rug leading up to it was rumpled—a pronounced anomaly. Then she heard the sound of muted chimes, as though the clock's innards were choked with some sort of debris. Standing at eight feet in height, its face glared down impassively at the small frame of the maid. She reached out for the little handle in its trunk, gave it a twist and pull. The door came open, and out tumbled the strange object which had cluttered the clock's innards. It was the body of Lord Rosemont, quite dead, and dressed—ridiculously—in the clothes of a valet.

By the time Flint reached the house, Lady Rosemont was fully apprised of the situation—a picture of composure. Flint disliked her on sight. She answered all his questions in the grudging, clipped tones of one who is compelled against their will to consort with the lower orders. But there was one word which sprang to mind when he saw her. *Elegant.*

She had gone to bed early the previous evening, she informed him, and had little idea of what her husband had been up to during his final hours on earth. She was aware of Hugh Westerby's demise—wasn't everyone?—but she had met him only once, and that was quite a while ago. Back in the spring, she supposed. She did not believe her husband had known him either. As for the Burglar, several of her dearest friends and neighbours had fallen victim to his outrages, though the Rosemonts themselves were mercifully unmolested. She seemed disinclined to assist the investigation further, and Flint left her alone soon after that.

Before leaving, he spoke to the housemaid who had discovered the body. He could not help recalling the similar interview with Lucy Raymond in Titherton Mews. This particular domestic, though, was made of stronger stuff. Her name was Bridget, and she was both older and wiser than Lucy. She had no illusions about the lives of the Rosemonts.

"This is not a happy household," she said delicately. "It hasn't been for a long time."

"The Rosemonts don't get on?"

"If they ever did. Now his lordship's dead, I doubt the mistress will hang around too long. I reckon she'll head somewhere warm, like the south of France. Somewhere she can find servants who'll work for a pittance."

"You won't miss this place, then?"

"None of us will. I shall probably go and stay with my sister for a while. Locke—he's the gardener—has got plenty of other irons in the fire. And Nicholls will settle down with that fiancée of his, Lizzie—"

"Nicholls is the valet?"

"Yes. But he's not here. He went up to Lancashire on Wednesday because of a family bereavement. He won't be back for another couple of days."

"Tell me this, Bridget," Flint said confidentially, "is your mistress in the habit of... leaving the house at night? Secret rendezvous, anything like that?"

Bridget's eyes were wide but she shook her head.

"Did she ever mention anything about Hugh Westerby? Or Titherton Mews?"

Again, a shake of the head.

Flint nodded ruminatively. "All right. Thank you."

He left the house, thinking about the troubling new direction in which the investigation was leading him. Features of the Westerby incident which had seemed circumstantial (the valet get-up, the window seat) were now part of an established pattern. The warped rituals of a homicidal maniac. And then there was the question of Lady Rosemont.

# # #

Flint, who really ought to have been spending his evenings at home, instead returned to The Black Pig. Spector was in his usual armchair in the snug, with his usual glass of absinthe on the table at his side. "Ah!"

he said when he glimpsed Flint. "Just in time. You find me on the cusp of an important revelation."

"You must have seen the newspapers? About Lord Rosemont?"

"I'm afraid so," said Spector, with a melancholy shake of the head. "Alas, I had anticipated something like this. Singular deaths tend to inspire imitators. But what interests me more are the *differences* between this death and that of Hugh Westerby. Perhaps you can fill in the gaps?"

Flint did. He explained that the body had been found not in a window seat but propped upright in a grandfather clock. That it had been dressed as a valet, but that the clothes were ill-fitting and obviously buttoned in haste. In fact, it appeared that the dead man had been re-dressed post mortem. And last of all, the cause of death. Whereas Hugh Westerby's demise had been a natural one, Lord Rosemont's was assuredly not. He had been killed by cyanide poisoning—the air around the body was choked with the scent of bitter almonds.

Throughout Flint's description, Spector nodded thoughtfully, gazing into the fire. "So, it *was* murder," he finally said, more to himself than to Flint. "Rather strange, don't you think, that the most curious elements of Hugh Westerby's demise were all of his own doing, whereas in the case of Lord Rosemont they were the product of some other malign intelligence?"

"Not sure I follow."

"What I mean is that Hugh Westerby himself was responsible for the costume and window seat in which he was found. His death is an apparently natural one—again, ultimately his own doing. In the case of Lord Rosemont, the costume was put on after death—hence the hasty, uneven buttoning—and the corpse was dragged over to the clock—hence the rumpled rug which first caught the maid's eye. And the cyanide poisoning is without doubt the result of foul play."

"Wait a moment, wait a moment," said Flint, getting flustered. "You've lost me there. How do you know Westerby got himself into the window seat?"

"Oh, please, Flint," said Spector with a little chuckle. "I worked *that* out as soon as you mentioned the telling detail of Eddowes's latch-key. The valet hastened back to the house to fetch his key. Westerby must have glimpsed him from the drawing room window, though of course *he* didn't know about the key. Rather than risk being caught in that strange costume—which he would have been unable to explain—Hugh Westerby concealed himself in the window seat and waited for Eddowes to leave again. While he was in there, though, his heart gave out. Perhaps it was the exertion of lifting the rather heavy wooden lid that finished him off."

"Yes," said Flint, "I suppose that fits. It could have happened that way. He was just unlucky that night. But it still doesn't tell us exactly what he was up to. And it makes the Rosemont business even stranger."

"I disagree," answered Spector. "In fact, I think it explains exactly what happened at the Rosemont residence. You see, you and I know Westerby's death was the result of natural causes. But you forget, Flint, that the *papers* reported it as murder. Therefore, if someone had been looking for a method to rid the world of Lord Rosemont, they might easily have struck upon the idea of copying the methods of a deranged murderer who was—apparently—still at large. Hence the contrived method; the choice of costume, concealment of the corpse—all designed to mirror the death of Hugh Westerby."

"In that case," Flint began, "the murderer is most probably…"

He looked at Spector, who shrugged. "*Cherchez la femme.*"

"Lady Rosemont?" said Flint, posing it as a question.

"You suspect her?"

"Oh, from the moment I laid eyes on her. She has motive enough, like any other wife. And I can't get away from the idea she may have been the woman who was seeing Hugh Westerby."

"Why do you say that?"

"I don't know. Just a feeling."

"What about the rest of the Rosemont household?"

"Only servants. A few maids, kitchen staff…"

"And a valet?" asked Spector, twitching an eyebrow.

"Yes: Nicholls. But he wasn't around when Rosemont died. He's been given a few days off because of a family bereavement."

"Convenient. The clothes Rosemont was dressed in, did they belong to him?"

"It seems so. I had a look round the valet's quarters in his absence, and the lock on his wardrobe had been tampered with."

"Which Lady Rosemont might easily have done," Spector observed.

"The problem is that I can't find anything—I mean *anything*—connecting Lady Rosemont to Hugh Westerby. The maid at Titherton Mews can't identify her. Westerby visited the Rosemonts once, several months ago, but that was for a cocktail party with some fifty other people. There's nothing to indicate he was a regular visitor, or even that he exchanged more than a couple of words with Lady Rosemont."

"Remember," Spector said sagely, "*she* is the one who's tried to manufacture a connection between the deaths. She has disguised her common-or-garden domestic homicide as something *outré*. Whether or not she was Mr. Westerby's lady is immaterial. And there's nothing to suggest she might be the Belgravia Burglar. But she *is* a killer, pure and simple."

# # #

Within the week, Flint was back at Lady Rosemont's home with an arrest warrant. It transpired that an insurance policy on the life of Lord Rosemont bore a double indemnity clause in the event of his death by murder—and thus, the motive was established. Lady Rosemont needed her husband to be murdered, but she had wanted to rule herself out as a suspect by copying the methods of a killer who was still at large. Unfortunately for her, that killer did not really exist.

Lady Rosemont went quietly, though Flint sensed she was saving her histrionics for the trial. He watched her step into the Black Maria with positively regal grace. She did not look at him once, even as the doors swung shut.

Bridget, the cynical housemaid of the Rosemonts who had furnished Flint with such wonderful gossip, stood beside him to watch her mistress go. He could positively feel the morbid delight rippling through her, but she did not let it show in her face or manner. Instead, she turned to him and said, "Well, sir, would you care to come in for some tea?"

Flint, who was parched, said that he would.

Leading the way back into the house, Bridget went on, "By the way, Inspector, Mr. Nicholls is back from Lancashire this morning."

"Mr. Nicholls?"

"The late Lord Rosemont's valet, sir. Would you like to speak to him?"

Flint wasn't all that keen, but he supposed he'd better. When this Nicholls appeared, though, the sight of him gave Flint the shock of his life.

"How do you do, sir?" said Nicholls solemnly. "May I be of some assistance?"

The face of Nicholls was the face of the late Hugh Westerby. The two men were doubles.

# # #

"Well, well," said a gleeful Joseph Spector, before taking a celebratory sip of absinthe, "I believe that settles the matter."

"It's a turn-up, all right," said Flint, who was still reeling from the discovery. "Do you really think it answers anything, though?"

"Of course! We finally have an explanation for Hugh Westerby's curious costume and—crucially—the shaving of his moustache. He was impersonating Rosemont's valet! This is the last piece of the puzzle. It answers everything."

"Then please," enjoined Flint, "for heaven's sake put me out of my misery. What does it mean? Hugh Westerby *was* the burglar after all?"

"Now we're getting somewhere. He was the burglar, all right; not in deed, but in thought. He was the mastermind. He laid out the plans, supplied the blueprints—but that thumb of his prevented him from carrying out the burglaries himself. He needed a surrogate who could follow his instructions to the letter. And his role in the scheme was to supply an alibi: on the nights in question, he would travel to the Rosemont residence and take the place of the *real* burglar: Nicholls the valet."

"So *Nicholls* is the Belgravia Burglar?"

"Think about it, Flint. You say Nicholls had an alibi for every single burglary, supplied by his employers and colleagues. Of course he did! That's because, on the nights in question, *Westerby took his place*. Westerby made sure to keep his own servants out of the way by inventing a phantom caller and demanding privacy. But really, he was using those evenings to switch places with Nicholls, who, in turn, would head out to commit one of his notorious thefts. Presumably another theft was planned for the night Westerby died, though it did not come to pass.

"Of course, Westerby worked hard to enhance the natural resemblance between the two men. No doubt he studied the valet's mannerisms, too, and covered the tell-tale thumb with gloves. He had visited the Rosemonts only once, in the spring, and presumably that was when he first encountered Nicholls. Don't forget, Westerby was in a perfect position to assess the security weaknesses of his various high society friends--he was a regular visitor to all of their homes (with the notable exception of the Rosemonts; he couldn't run the risk of anyone in the household spotting his likeness to Nicholls). So you see, *that's* how they did it: Westerby's inside knowledge *and* false alibi enabled Nicholls to commit each burglary without once coming under suspicion. Together, the two men added up to one perfect criminal."

"But the Rosemonts *must* have been able to tell the difference...." Flint protested.

"Why? It has been established time and time again that those who employ servants see only the *uniform*. And they don't engage in lengthy conversations with their staff."

Spector concluded cheerfully, "Anyway, that's how they did it. Buy us another drink, would you, Flint?"

Flint got obediently to his feet, and was turning toward the bar when Spector said idly, "Of course, there's still the question of who *really* murdered Hugh Westerby...."

Flint paused. "What? It was cardiac arrest. He had a weak heart-

-everyone knew it. Lifting the window seat lid finished him off. There was no poison in his bloodstream."

Spector was smiling that thin smile of his. "That's not quite true, is it? There was no *excess* poison in his bloodstream. In other words, nothing that resembled a fatal dose. But there were traces of poison; both alcohol and nicotine."

"He was a drinker and a heavy smoker," Flint replied with a shrug. "Everybody knows that."

"Yes," said Spector amiably, "everybody knows that. So anybody may have taken advantage of it. Extracting pure nicotine from ordinary pipe tobacco is easy enough; simply a matter of boiling it in water. It takes over five hundred milligrams of the stuff to kill a grown man. Naturally it would leave traces—*if* administered in a single dose. But an accumulation over time would be just as deadly, especially if he was also taking the stuff regularly by his own volition. It was a subtle murder—the man was poisoned while he was also in the process of poisoning himself."

"How do you know?"

"I don't!" said Spector gleefully. "But you know me, Flint. In cases of suspicious death, I always err on the side of murder."

"Presumably you're thinking of Mrs. Gray?"

"No. I am *not* thinking of Mrs. Gray, for one very clear reason. She drew your attention to the missing tea the morning Westerby's body was discovered. The nicotine used to poison Westerby was likely administered in the tea—it would be invisible amid the leaves. All the same, the killer was wise to get rid of it."

"So it could be either of the housemaids, or else Eddowes the valet."

"We can rule out Lucy, who had been in the household only a few weeks—the poisoning would have taken longer than that."

"Then it's Eddowes. Or…"

Spector gave Flint a pointed look. "Beth."

"The other housemaid? Why on earth should *she* poison her master?"

"You seem to have forgotten, Flint, that she and she alone claimed to have seen the lady friend of Hugh Westerby's. The lady friend whom she was conveniently unable to identify—because the woman did not exist. Such a strange lie to tell! *Unless* it was in Beth's interest for you to think there was another suspect…"

"But…" Flint said forlornly, "I never suspected Beth for a second."

Smiling, Spector said, "She wasn't to know that. And besides, she has a connection to the Belgravia Burglar as well. You mentioned that Nicholls the valet has a fiancée—do you recall her name?"

At length, Flint flipped through the pages of his notebook. "Lizzie," he supplied.

"Lizzie. Short for Elizabeth. Another name derived from Elizabeth is, of course…"

Flint smacked his forehead in frustration. How had he missed it? "Beth."

Spector nodded. "It will be simple enough to find out whether 'Beth' and 'Lizzie' are the same young woman. But if they *are*, then the question arises as to why the housemaid went by one name with her fiancé and another at her place of work. Most likely she wanted to keep her engagement a secret from Westerby. Why might she do that, do you think?"

"You reckon she knew about the scheme Westerby and Nicholls had going?"

"Not quite. She *did* know that Hugh Westerby wanted the house to himself on certain evenings, ostensibly so he could meet a romantic partner. And she also knew her fiancé was 'otherwise engaged' on the nights in question. Don't you think it would be natural for her to do a bit of spying one evening, to try and catch a glimpse of the phantom lady? And imagine her horror when she caught a glimpse one night of *her own fiancé* sneaking into Titherton Mews."

"So she thought…"

Spector nodded. "She thought she was caught in a love triangle, and that her employer was also her rival for Nicholls's affections. Of course she couldn't bring herself to confront Westerby about it, nor even to bring up the matter with Nicholls. Likely her pride wouldn't allow for that. She thought the two men were making a fool of her—so she decided to remedy the situation in her own way, and to protect Nicholls by supplying an encounter with a non-existent *female* visitor."

Flint began pacing up and down. "How in the hell am I going to prove all that--?"

"You're not," said Spector simply. "Flint, I would never have told you all this if I thought you had a chance of actually *convicting* the housemaid. She has been wonderfully clever. A truly admirable effort."

"That left a man dead…"

"Oh, Flint. Anyone ingenious enough to commit a truly untraceable murder is worth a hundred Hugh Westerbys. And you have caught Lady Rosemont, isn't that enough?"

Flint began to bluster, but Spector just grinned. By the firelight there was a shade of malice in the creases of his aged face. "Besides," he said, "there's a circuitous irony to the thing. Nicholls is the Belgravia Burglar, and Beth Sands is the Titherton Mews Poisoner. Nicholls committed his crimes out of love—to provide for his bride-to-be. Meanwhile the bride-to-be committed *her* crime out of love, too—a possessive, obsessive love. She killed Westerby to ensure Nicholls would never leave her. But in fact, she ensured the opposite. He'll go to prison, and she won't. If *she* hadn't killed Westerby, *you* never would have caught your burglar. A pleasingly symmetrical punishment, don't you think?"

Unpremeditated Art
by Marcia Talley

#

12. There must be but one culprit, no matter how many murders are committed. The culprit may, of course, have a minor helper or co-plotter; but the entire onus must rest on one pair of shoulders: the entire indignation of the reader must be permitted to concentrate on a single black nature.

It was a six-hour drive from Los Angeles to San Francisco, and another hour slog through rush hour traffic to the hotel in North Beach. Certain that they hadn't been followed, Frank Knowles slept soundly.

The first time he awoke – to the hollering of some late-night clubbers carousing in the street outside the window -- it was still dark. He turned over, refolded his pillow so his head rested at a more comfortable angle against the arm of the sofa and went back to sleep. The second time his eyelids snapped open, the morning sun was already slanting through the plantation shutters, casting corrugated shadows that warred with the black-and-white plaid of the carpet. He lay there for a long time, watching Susan sleep.

It'd been more than a decade since they'd shared a room.

Forty-eight hours earlier, he'd answered his doorbell and found her standing on his doorstep, stylish heels planted firmly on the mat that said Go Away. Susan. His ex. Looking as beautiful as the day they were married. Before he fucked it all up.

"Hey, you," she said.

"Hey, yourself." He massaged the sleep out of his eyes, half convinced that when he removed his fingers she would have disappeared.

He blinked, but Susan was still there, solid and smiling and smelling deliciously of lavender and lilac and saying, "May I come in?"

Frank shrugged, stepping aside as she strolled into his living room, suddenly embarrassingly shabby and small. "Coffee?" he asked. "I was just putting some on."

She raised a bag, holding it by its brown, string-like handles. "Got some. Starbucks. One for you, too, if you want it. Two-percent, three sugars, right?"

She'd remembered.

Frank took the coffee, thanked her, then pointed to the love seat, glad that he'd picked up his dirty laundry the night before. "So, to what do I owe … ?" He managed a smile. "That sounds lame, doesn't it?"

Her blue eyes flashed. "Yeah. So let me put you out of your misery."

"Meaning?"

"I think we have something in common."

Frank sipped his coffee silently, waiting for Susan to continue.

"A certain invitation."

He nodded. "Go on."

"She was innocent, you know. Christine Turner."

Frank laughed out loud. "That's ironic. Didn't you say I was obsessed? That I should be locked up in a rubber room, along with my goddamn briefcase and a gallon of Jim Beam?"

"Well, yeah. But I hear you cleaned up your act."

Frank simply stared.

"And since Calvin Patterson's invitation came," she continued, "I've had time to think."

Frank raised an eyebrow. "So, you got one, too?"

"Not me, exactly. Stu."

"So, what does Stu say?" Frank asked, although he didn't give a shit what Stu Ballad, his former partner at the LAPD, thought about anything.

"We don't see eye to eye on the grand opening." She sipped at her coffee, considering him over the rim of the paper cup. "Why the Dijkstra Museum agreed to name a sculpture garden after the woman who confessed to murdering one of its former directors is beyond me."

Frank rubbed his thumb and two forefingers together. "When you're the CEO of a multi-billion-dollar health care conglomerate and you decide to donate a sculpture garden, you can name it after your daughter, or anyone, I suppose, even your cat, Chairman Meow."

Susan giggled. "I once named a cat Cindy Clawford."

"That'd work, too," Frank said.

"Anyway, Stu says we're too busy. That I should send flowers."

"So, you're not going?"

Susan grinned, ice-blue eyes twinkling. "*Stu's* not going. I was hoping you were."

#

Two days later, as they sped up US 101 through Salinas and Gilroy, while Frank was still pondering the imponderables of Susan, but not really caring as long as she was beside him again, she'd said, "You staying at the Four Seasons, Frank?"

"You're kidding, right?" He cast her a sideways glance. "One night at the Four Seasons costs more than I make in a week."

"You checked?"

"You always had champagne tastes, Susie." He reached out to pat her knee like he would have in the old days, but drew his hand back in time. "Of course, I checked."

"It's the thought that counts, Frank." She rested her head against the headrest, adjusted her sunglasses. "So, where are you staying?"

"The Tuscan Inn at Fisherman's Wharf."

"Never heard of it."

"It's a Best Western. Hundred and eighty-nine dollars a night."

Susan groaned.

"Free wine and Italian beer in the lobby between five and six."

"Italian beer?" Susan snorted. "Well, that makes all the difference, doesn't it?"

# # #

When they finally found it, The Tuscan Inn at Mason near North Point looked more like a radiator than anything that had ever originated in Tuscany; a building as far removed from the Norwegian granite, rare imported woods, and modern art of the Four Seasons as a hotel could possibly be. Frank dropped his ex-wife out front, then drove his aging Volvo into a public parking garage next to the Safeway and Walgreens. All day, twenty-four bucks.

"They're fully booked," Susan pouted when he joined her in the lobby, dragging his bag, the silver, hard-sided wheelie that went every-where with him these days. "Internet World Expo," she explained. "But there's room at the Super 8 at Lombard and Divisadero." She grinned, her face luminous in the soft lobby lighting. "Not exactly walking dis-tance to the museum, though, is it?"

Frank stared, trying to interpret her expression, to see through that perfect façade, to read what was going on in her head. He'd never been particularly good at reading Susan's mind.

"You have a reservation, right?" she asked.

Frank nodded stupidly.

"And there's two beds?"

"I suppose so."

"Then it's settled."

Not two beds, as it turned out, but a double and a sofa plush enough to sleep on, if you had to. Since bundling boards were out of fashion, Frank figured he'd have to.

In return, Susan paid for dinner, enjoyed on the premises at Café Pescatore, where brick-oven-baked pizzas were served on proper white tablecloths, and copper pots and sailboat models dangled from the ceiling. Talking. Laughing. Like old times. Surprised it didn't take booze to grease the wheels.

In bed by eleven. Susan curled up on the double, auburn hair spread out on the pillow, smudges of blue under her eyes, a bolster at her back and the duvet tucked under her chin. Frank claimed the sofa and the remote control, and fell asleep in the middle of *MasterChef*, Susan's choice.

# # #

Six a.m. now, and she'd hardly moved. Frank got up and used the bathroom, rinsed the taste of last night's Thirsty Bear root beer out of his mouth, then quietly fetched his briefcase. He closed and locked the bathroom door, then perched on the toilet seat, balancing the briefcase on his knees. He eased open the catch, soundlessly, and began pawing through the contents, as familiar to him now as the deepening lines on his face when he studied himself in the mirror every morning.

A newspaper clipping, yellow with age, detailing Christine's trip to Mexico, where she told friends she knew Scott would never be coming home. Stupid-ass thing to say, Frank thought, like that crazy nurse in Maryland who'd offed her husband with succinylcholine chloride—on Valentine's Day no less—after describing to colleagues exactly how she'd do it.

Black-and-whites of the Turner children, Olivia and Noah. The same dark hair and inquisitive eyes as their mother, but where Christine's hair had been long, Olivia's was cropped and curly, almost the same length as her older brother's.

Frank did the math. Noah had been fifteen the night Christine died, and Olivia, thirteen. They'd be twenty-five and twenty-three today. He wondered if they'd show up at the opening. If he'd recognize them. Private boarding school could change a kid, and not always for the better.

Scott Turner's autopsy report, eighteen pages long, with diagrams, circles, and arrows. Crime scene photos, a dozen or more. A transcript of the trial where Detective Frank Knowles had testified for over two hours, his evidence putting Christine squarely in the frame.

Frank lined the clippings up on the rim of the bathtub, as if after all these years he'd see something new. Move this one to the right, that one to the left, and a new pattern would emerge, one that would prove Christine's innocence.

But it always came back to this.

He slid an issue of *Vanity Fair* out of its protective plastic sleeve, puzzled as always why they'd put Angelina Jolie on the cover of an issue containing the interview that had shocked the world. Where Christine Turner had confessed to that hot-shot investigative reporter. From the Central California Women's facility, wearing a blue-and-white long-sleeved prison T-shirt, Christine'd told the world how she did it. How she murdered her husband.

They'd fought over his extramarital affairs (many). She'd stormed out, but returned to the museum later, to apologize, she said, to seek a reconciliation, if only for the sake of the children.

Scott Turner had laughed, called her a stupid slut.

Slut! That was a joke. If anyone was a slut ... "What's the word for a male slut?" Christine asked the young journalist.

He hadn't answered.

Somewhere in the exchange of insults, Christine snapped. Grabbed the first thing that came to hand, she claimed, and clobbered him with it, a Paul Stankard glass-domed paperweight Scott kept on his desk. He collapsed on a rare Ladik prayer rug (circa 1792) and when he didn't get up, Christine panicked. Dragged her husband, rug and all, into a nearby gallery and hid his body in the *Eiserne Jungfrau*, an ancient iron maiden stolen during the Nazi regime which the museum was repatriating to Germany.

"And the paperweight?" the reporter had inquired.

She'd tossed it into the depths of San Francisco Bay.

Frank closed his eyes, sighed, rested his head against the cool bathroom tiles. Was it his fault he'd been in Belize with Susan, trying to save his marriage when the magazine hit the stands? Should he blame himself for not reading it sooner? He'd bought a copy at an LAX newsstand, but by the time he got around to reading the article, it was too late. Christine Turner had been found dead in her jail cell. She'd twisted a plastic trash bag into a noose and hanged herself from a sprinkler head in the ceiling.

Yet Christine had no more murdered her husband with a paperweight than Lee Harvey Oswald had the help of half a dozen marksmen on the grassy knoll. Frank knew the cops had recovered the weapon on day one—a hand-carved Hawaiian war club that had been displayed on the credenza in Turner's office, bits of his skin, hair, and blood all over it, fingerprints wiped clean.

Cause of death? Blunt force trauma. But they held back details about the murder weapon itself, information only the killer would know. It was a decision made at the highest level.

Then the war club had disappeared from the evidence room, skin, hair, blood and all. If there hadn't been enough evidence to convict, heads would have rolled, but they had witnesses, the lack of an alibi, Christine's tight-lipped silence, and her fingerprints all over the iron maiden.

A paperweight. Jesus Christ. Christine had to be covering for somebody, but who?

Frank put everything neatly away and closed the briefcase. He shaved, eased into the same shirt and trousers he'd worn the day before, then gently shook Susan by the shoulder.

"It's nine o'clock. You getting up any time soon?"

Susan moaned and pulled the duvet over her head. "Go away."

"I'm going down for breakfast. Want to join me?

The duvet shrugged.

"I take that as a no."

"I'll be down later." Muffled.

Frank settled into a tapestry chair near the fireplace with a cup of Italian roast coffee from the buffet and a complimentary copy of *USA Today*. He had read through the Life section and had started on Sports when Susan finally made her appearance, looking surprisingly fresh and bright, her hair still damp from the shower. She laid a hand on Frank's shoulder.

"I'm going shopping."

"For what?"

Susan straightened, extended her arms. "I can't wear *this* to the opening, now can I?"

In Frank's opinion, Susan looked spectacular. How she'd managed to sausage her extraordinary body into that white, scoop-necked sweater and lime green skirt, he never knew, but would have paid a thousand dollars just to watch. He raised an eyebrow. "I guess not. Where are you going?"

Susan shrugged. "Neiman's? Saks? Anyone who's anyone has a shop in Union Square. Dior? Armani?" She aimed a thousand-watt smile in his direction. "I'm sure I'll find something suitable."

Frank laughed out loud, glad that Stu was responsible for paying Susan's credit card bills these days and not him. "At that rate, you'll never make the opening. Five o'clock. Be there or be square."

Lord, did he always act like such a dope?

Susan grinned. "I'm a power shopper, remember?" She executed a delicate about-face, considering the height of her heels, waved, and was gone.

Frank downed a second cup of coffee, then left the hotel, walking down North Point to the Embarcadero. He turned left and wandered up to Grant near Pier 39, to the Dijkstra Museum, and the scene of the crime. The Dijkstra, a modern structure of glass and chrome, had a spectacular roof that swept upward like the wing of an airplane. Unusually quiet for this time of day, Frank thought. The back of his neck prickled, but he shook off the feeling he was being followed and walked on.

A few blocks later he had a proper breakfast at The Buena Vista -- a Mexican omelet and a Café Bustelo – then returned to the hotel to make a few calls about a bank security detail someone wanted him to organize.

He was sitting on the sofa grazing the channels, when his cell phone chirped. He didn't recognize the caller ID, so he kept on surfing. Bravo, Nature, Discovery, HGTV -- then the phone began chirping again.

"Shit." Frank pressed the talk button. "Hey."

"Knowles?"

"Yeah."

"This is Dick Barton."

Crap, Frank thought. Dick I-Never-Met-a-Snitch-I-Didn't-Believe-Barton. He sighed. "What can I do for you, Barton?"

"I hear you're in town."

"What gave you that idea?" Remembering the prickly feeling.

"Coming to the opening gala for Christine, right?"

"Busted."

"I'm at the museum with Astrid Haugen, and she's got a problem. We could use your expertise."

"What kind of problem?"

Dick's breathing was ragged, like a smoker who'd run for the phone. "There's been sort of a break-in."

"What do you mean, 'sort of'?"

"It's hard to explain."

Frank swung his feet to the floor and sat up, the remote in one hand, the cell phone in the other. As Dick filled him in, he switched absentmindedly from HGTV to the Style network where some butt-ugly chick was getting a makeover. "If you've got a break-in, why don't you call the cops?"

"I *am* a cop."

"The locals, I mean, asshole."

"Astrid doesn't want the publicity."

Frank checked his watch. Two p.m. Three hours to figure out whatever was bugging that high-strung director before guests started arriving at the museum. "Why me, Barton?"

"I hear you've never quite dropped the Christine Turner case."

"This better be worth it, man."

#

Frank dressed in his dark blue suit, left a note for Susan, and for the second time that day, headed to the museum. Now a catering van blocked a side entrance and worker bees were shuttling carts and trays from the van into the museum through a service door.

He found Dick waiting for him outside the main entrance, slouched against the white marble wall, wearing a tux, smoking a cigarette, and looking dangerously sober. When he noticed Frank approaching, Dick stooped, snubbed the cigarette out on the concrete steps, and tossed the butt into the shrubbery. He extended his hand, and when Frank took it, he covered it with his own. "Hey, Frank. Long time no see." He jerked his head towards the door. "Astrid's waiting in her office."

Frank followed Dick Barton across the polished marble of the spacious lobby, hung with colorful Calder mobiles. From the central dome, a Medusa-like chandelier depended, an enormous orange-and-yellow-glass creation by Chihuly that looked like a creature beamed down from the *Starship Enterprise*.

The men found Astrid sitting behind her desk, a cell phone pressed to her ear. She raised a just-a-minute finger. "How the fuck should I know, Alex? You were Chief Curator at the time. I thought you might remember something about this artist ..." Astrid pawed through several printouts on her desk. "... this Skye, Skye Whatshername. Ah, here it is. Lawrence." She paused for a moment, listening. "Well, if you don't, you don't. See you at the opening then?"

Astrid slammed the phone down on one of the printouts. "Senile old fool." Then turned a worried face to Frank. "We've got a situation here, Mr. Knowles. Dick tells me that it might have something to do with a case you've been working on."

"Please, call me Frank."

Astrid managed a smile that didn't extend to her eyes. "Frank, then."

She was dressed in an all-purpose black dress, accessorized with a double strand of Barbara Bush pearls and matching eardrops that bounced against her neck as she rose from her chair and walked around to the front of the desk.

Frank's eyes migrated from Astrid's ears to her shoulders to her hips – my God, the hips – as she led them next door into a walnut-paneled conference room where a vast expanse of glass overlooked San Francisco Bay. A painting approximately twelve by eighteen inches leaned against a bookcase, yellow lilies in a green glass jar by some French impressionist, unless Frank missed his guess.

Frank was just thinking that a conference room was an unusual place to store a priceless work of art when Astrid pointed to it. "When I came in today, this was just sitting there."

"So?"

"It's our Matisse," she said, as if that explained everything.

Frank whistled.

"Well, it doesn't belong *here*," Astrid drawled. She picked up her handbag, as if thieves might still be in the building, and said, "Follow me."

She led them down a short corridor, through a locked door and into a dimly lit gallery. Astrid flipped a switch, flooding a far alcove with light. "What do you make of *that*?" she snapped.

To Frank's untrained eye, the painting decorating the alcove was a semi-interesting swirl of cool whites—alabaster, cream, ivory, froth—with icy blue undertones, like a Sherwin-Williams swatch bundle. Feeling that a comment was expected, he said, "Nice."

Astrid rolled her eyes. "It's called *Snowbound*. Competent enough for a street art festival, but certainly not for *us*."

Frank leaned closer, squinted. Something was snowbound under all that white, an old-fashioned steam engine, maybe? He glanced over to Dick whose brow was as furrowed with puzzlement as his own. "Someone broke into the museum and *left* something? Shit. Was anything taken?"

Astrid shook her head. "Nothing. We checked. They just substituted *Snowbound* for the Matisse. It's by a local artist named Skye Lawrence."

Frank chewed his lower lip. The name rang a distant bell. Lawrence, yeah. Pretty girl, if superannuated hippies rang your chimes. One of Scott Turner's many conquests. Frank would bet his pension on it. He'd have to check his notes.

"Why the fuck they do that?" Frank asked, thinking about all the trouble someone had taken to defeat the Dijkstra's security system, evade the guards.

"Take a closer look."

Frank approached the painting, noticing a 3 x 5 card taped to the wall, hand-lettered in neat block capitals: GENESIS 3:7

"Help me out here. Been a long time since Sunday School."

" 'And their eyes were opened and they knew,' " she quoted. "I had to look it up."

"What the hell's that supposed to mean?"

Astrid folded her arms across her chest. "That's what I was hoping you'd tell *me*, Detective."

Frank shrugged. "What about your security systems? You got alarms here, right? Cameras?"

Astrid's face flushed. "It's embarrassing, really. But when the caterers plugged in their mobile kitchen this morning, it blew the grid. We have a backup generator, of course, but it took a good five minutes to get it up and running. Whoever switched the paintings must have done it then."

"Guards?"

"The one in this gallery went to check on the emergency lighting. Trust me, some heads are going to roll over this. I just hope it won't be mine."

#

With the Matisse hanging back in its accustomed place and Lawrence's *Snowbound* consigned to a corner of Astrid Haugen's office while she waited police instructions on what to do with it, Frank rode the elevator down to Level B and followed engraved signs that directed visitors to the Christine Turner Sculpture Garden.

Although it was only four forty-five, Susan had arrived ahead of him. Her shopping spree had produced a neon-yellow, long-sleeved sheath with a winged collar that extended so far past her shoulders she could probably achieve lift-off in a stiff breeze. Susan motioned to him from an open bar where she seemed to be waiting for—yes, he guessed correctly—a glass of white wine. Chardonnay, if memory served. "Later," he mouthed, then wandered to the opposite end of the garden where Calvin Patterson had corralled Faith Jeffers, the lead reporter from the *Chronicle* who had exhaustively covered his daughter's case. A scaffolding of steel resembling an emaciated cat and painted purple loomed over their conversation. A Giacometti (he later learned).

Christine's mother, Claudia, dressed in a navy-blue pants suit, leaned on a walker to her husband's right, listening intently. She'd arranged a colorful scarf around her shoulders —Hermès, if his time married to Susan was any guide—and secured it there with a bejeweled leopard brooch. Frank scanned the garden for Christine's kids and finally spotted them among a group of other young twenty-somethings clustered around a long table groaning with hot and cold hors d'oeuvres. For the centerpiece, the caterer had sculptured a gondola out of a block of ice and loaded it to the gunwales with shrimp.

Olivia turned, and his heart lurched. She was the image of her mother, whose gilt-framed portrait stood on an easel to the right of the podium. Olivia dredged a shrimp through the cocktail sauce and conveyed it to her mouth, a risky maneuver for someone dressed head to toe in white. The only splash of color was the designer pumps she teetered on, lipstick red and pocked with rivets.

Noah, looking *très GQ* and casual in a sports jacket and open-collar shirt, hovered at his sister's elbow, punctuating whatever he was telling his friends with a wave of a chicken kabob. Astrid Haugen, meanwhile, worked the crowd, smiling broadly, shaking hands.

Still clueless about the painting, Frank decided to keep his distance from the museum director and headed for the bar where he ordered a club soda with lime.

Dick Barton found him there. "Scotch rocks," he told the bartender. Turning to Frank, he stirred his drink with his pinky finger and asked, "So, what's the deal with the painting?"

"Inside job," Frank offered. "Just a guess."

The two men stood on the verge of a lawn, recently laid, that swept down to the water's edge. Faint outlines remained where sod had been unrolled along serpentine paths that wound from one modern sculpture to another, terminating at a gazebo overlooking San Francisco Bay. The gazebo had been designed by Kengo Kuma, its roof like a Japanese paper lantern, tipped back at a jaunty angle. Picture-perfect for weddings, Frank mused, if a panoramic view that included Alcatraz didn't bother you.

Dick leaned against the leg of a towering Calder labeled *Grenouille Rouge* and groused about the 49ers, who were having such a rotten season that they'd fired both their head coach and general manager. The LA Rams weren't doing much better, Frank observed, with their worst (1-7!) at home performance since 2009. By the time they'd finishing rehashing the 2016 NFL season, their glasses were empty and they'd arrived back where they'd started, opposite a dozen female figures, grouped on a chessboard, looking sad. Dick left to fetch a refill, while Frank, genuinely curious, leaned over to read the plaque next to the sculpture: TITLE: ARE YOU OKAY? ARTIST: BLOSSOM O'SHEA. MEDIA: WIRE. POLYMER CLAY. *Shoot me now*, he thought.

When he straightened, he saw Susan chugging toward him, pushing through the crowd like Moses parting the Red Sea. "Frank, come with me. You need to hear this." She executed a rapid about-face. He had to hustle to follow as she headed back into the building, moving so quickly that he didn't even have time to register surprise when she straight-armed her way through the door of a women's restroom, held the door open, and motioned for him to follow her inside.

He'd never been in a women's restroom, not even in all the years he'd been a police officer, and it felt pervy to be doing so now. A row of toilet stalls stretched out to his left with an equal number of sinks immediately opposite. He wasn't naïve enough to expect urinals, but was surprised to find a sofa flanked by two armchairs, upholstered in green vinyl, tucked into an alcove to the right of the swinging door. Olivia was perched on the edge of the sofa, a wad of toilet paper pressed to her eyes, weeping.

"Sit," Susan instructed, pointing to one of the chairs.

Ignoring the order, Frank remained standing, the ceramic tiles cool against his back.

"Olivia has something to tell you," Susan continued.

Olivia chewed on her lower lip while Susan rummaged inside a utility closet, located an orange CLOSED FOR CLEANING tent sign, and propped it open just outside the restroom door.

"Hello, Olivia," Frank said once Susan rejoined him. "I'm Frank Knowles. We met years ago."

Olivia shrugged, shook her head, obviously not remembering.

"Sorry," Frank said. "I used to be a police officer. If it's any comfort to you at all, I've never believed that your mother killed your father."

Olivia looked up at him with red-rimmed eyes. "I know she didn't, because I did," she sobbed, followed by a fresh flood of tears.

Frank took a deep breath, let it out slowly. Ten years of doubt, and there it was. "You? Wanna tell me why?"

"Dad caught me in bed with my boyfriend," she whimpered. "When he found out Danny was seventeen, he went ballistic. Threatened to send me to boarding school."

"But you were only thirteen," Frank said reasonably. He and Susan didn't have children, but if he'd caught some seventeen-year-old punk humping his daughter, the kid would have been cooling his heels in a jail cell, shopping for a dentist.

"Yeah, I get that *now*, but still . . ." Olivia looked up. "To Le Rosey, for Christ's sake. It's in fucking Switzerland."

"So, how . . ."

"How did I do it, you mean?"

Frank nodded in silent encouragement.

"Grabbed this crazy club thing Dad had on his desk and bashed him over the head with it."

Bingo, Frank thought. *The Hawaiian war club.*

Frank was formulating his next question when someone began pounding on the restroom door. "Olivia? Are you in there?"

"So much for signs," Susan muttered.

"It's Noah," Olivia sniffed. "Just ignore him."

The pounding continued. "Olivia? Are you okay? I know you're in there!" The door flew open and Noah blustered in.

Olivia considered her brother calmly. "Go away, Noah. I've just told them that I murdered Daddy."

Noah froze, then turned to face Frank, not seeming a bit surprised to be having a conversation with another man in a women's restroom. He folded his arms across his chest. Resolute. "No, she didn't, because I did."

"Shut up, Noah."

"No, I won't shut up, Olivia. It's time for the truth."

"Sit," Frank instructed, feeling strangely peeved. After Noah plopped down on the sofa next to his sister, Frank identified himself and said, "I think we all could use a little truth about now. So, what's *your* story?"

Noah leaned forward, rested his hands on his knees. "I was a sophomore at Los Gatos that year, but I got picked for the varsity football team. We were favored to win the NorCal regional championships, but Dad was being a total asshole about it. Wouldn't sign the waiver allowing me to play. Said playing football causes brain damage. I dunno, man, I just lost it. Dad kept this Hawaiian war club hanging on the wall in his office. . . ." He paused, swallowed hard.

Frank shivered, recalling Turner's autopsy report. If Noah were telling the truth, the kid had given his old man a major case of brain damage.

"Then what happened?" Frank asked.

Olivia answered for both of them. "Mom came back."

"Yeah," Noah agreed. "Earlier, she and Dad had got into a fight about, about . . ." His eyes flicked toward his sister. "Anyway, Mom threw a paperweight at him, then she came back to apologize. When she found us there, she . . . "

"… helped us wrap Dad up in the rug and stuff him into the iron maiden," Olivia continued. "Mom wiped the club clean, too."

"And ordered us to keep our mouths shut," Noah concluded.

Frank stared at the siblings, heartbeat pounding in his ears. The silence following Noah's confession lengthened, until it was punctuated by the flush of a toilet. Frank glared at Susan—*Didn't you?*—and Susan glared back—*Was it my job to check?*—when a woman emerged from one of the toilet stalls, crossed over to a sink and calmly began washing her hands. She wore a hand-painted linen tunic over gauzy harem pants. Feathered dream-catchers dangled from her earlobes. Skye Lawrence. Ten years older, ash-blond hair a bit grayer but still abundant and artfully arranged in a Gibson Girl topknot.

"But, he wasn't dead," Skye called out, reaching for the paper towel dispenser.

Who next? Frank thought. *Astrid Haugen? The security guard? The goddamn butler?* The room was getting crowded with suspects.

"So, why were *you* there?" Frank asked, his patience wearing thin.

"To talk to him about the baby, Detective." Skye crumpled the paper towel and tossed it into a trash receptacle.

So, she recognized him, too. "What baby?" Frank blurted and kicked himself immediately for being so dense.

"Do I have to draw you a picture?" She smiled. "The bastard wanted me to get rid of it. Promised he'd leave Christine and marry me if I did, but I knew he was lying. Scott promised me so many things over the three years we were an item—marriage, exotic vacations, my paintings hanging on the walls of the Dijkstra Museum—but there was always some piss-poor excuse for why it didn't happen."

The Dijkstra. *Now we're getting down to it*, Frank thought. "*Snowbound*," he said.

A shy smile. "That's mine."

"So how . . .?"

"Did I get around security? Pure dumb luck, actually. The Dijkstra's mounting a juried show this June called *There Is No Planet B.*" She drew quote marks in the air with her fingers. "It's themed to climate change. Artists submitted photos and *Snowbound* made the first cut. I was supposed to deliver my painting to the curatorial department this morning, but I never made it that far. Shortly after I passed through security and got my pass, all the lights went out. I knew my way around, so . . ." She shrugged, grinned. "I couldn't resist."

Skye wandered over to the sofa and motioned for Olivia to scoot over. Frank waited until the artist had relaxed into the cushions before asking, "Okay, can we get back to the day of the murder?"

Skye's pale cheeks flushed. "Yes, well, I decided to give Scott an ultimatum—his wife or me and the baby—but when I showed up, he wasn't in his office. I was about to leave, when I thought I heard moaning coming from the gallery next door, so I decided to investigate. I found Scott all slumped over in that old iron maiden, blood all over the place. I should have called nine-one-one, but I didn't, did I?" She frowned, looking puzzled. "I was so pissed off at him that I just closed the door and waited for him to die.

"That wasn't happening fast enough, though," she continued after a moment. "He kept on moaning, so I fetched a pillow from the sofa in his office and ..." She shrugged. "I know I should be, but I'm not sorry." She leaned forward. "That baby's ten years old now, Mr. Knowles. Charlie's the joy of my life."

Noah, Olivia, and Skye sat shoulder to shoulder on the sofa, studying him silently, as solid and immutable as the See No Evil–Hear No Evil–Speak No Evil monkeys carved on the wall of the Toshogu shrine in Nikko, Japan.

Still, something niggled at him. "About the painting, Skye, I get it, but what's the story with the Bible verse?"

Olivia and Noel exchanged quick glances.

" 'And their eyes were opened and they knew,' " Frank quoted for Susan's benefit.

"I'll give you a hint, Detective," Skye said. "The painting represents the *Orient Express*, snowbound in the Croatian mountains somewhere between Vinkovci and Brod."

"Ah." Frank flashed to the movie version of the Agatha Christie classic, not the one starring Kenneth Branagh and his preposterous mustache, but the all-star version he'd seen back when he and Susan began dating, with Albert Finney in the role of Hercule Poirot. "Where every passenger on the train had a motive to kill the odious Mr. Ratchett and they all . . ." He risked a glance in Susan's direction, then back to his bullheaded lineup.

Eeny, meeny, miny ... Oh, for fuck's sake.

"I gotta think," he said.

Back out in the sculpture garden, while he waited in line at the bar, Frank pictured the half-empty bottle of Valium in his medicine cabinet at home. Wishing he'd brought it with him. Feeling grateful for the warmth of the setting sun against his cheek.

"Sir? Sir?" The bartender centered a glass of club soda on a cocktail napkin and pushed it toward him.

"Uh, thanks," Frank said. He picked up the glass and sipped slowly, making it last.

It seemed like the program was finally getting started. The string quartet wrapped up a tinkly piece by Mozart and lowered their bows. At the podium, Calvin Patterson leaned into the microphone, cleared his throat. "Good evening, everyone. Thank you for coming."

Lined up on a row of gold-painted chairs behind him—ankles crossed, hands neatly folded, ready for the photo op—sat his wife with the mayor, the archbishop, the new president of the Board of Supervisors, a U.S. congresswoman whose name Frank could never remember, and two empty chairs. A nervous chuckle. "Noah? Olivia? Anyone seen my grandchildren?"

Her breath, suddenly warm against his ear. "Frank? You okay?"

Frank grunted. 'Don't step too close, Susie. That collar could put an eye out.'

Susan laughed. "That's the idea."

After a moment, he said, "Feel like blowing this pop stand? Going somewhere for dinner?"

Susan looped her arm through his.

His heart lurched. *Danger, danger!*

Frank turned his head, smiled down at his ex-partner's wife, ignoring the warning. He hardly ever agreed with Stu about anything, but this time, he'd make an exception. As Stu had grumped a million times, "Chill out, Knowles. Christine confessed. Slam dunk. Case closed."

Susan smiled back. "Fog Harbor Fish House?"

Frank deposited his empty glass on a nearby service tray. "Sounds like a plan."

Guilted Lily by Leigh Perry

#

13. Secret societies, camorras, mafias, et al., have no place in a detective story. Here the author gets into adventure fiction and secret-service romance. A fascinating and truly beautiful murder is irremediably spoiled by any such wholesale culpability. To be sure, the murderer in a detective novel should be given a sporting chance, but it is going too far to grant him a secret society (with its ubiquitous havens, mass protection, etc.) to fall back on. No high-class, self-respecting murderer would want such odds in his jousting-bout with the police.

Everyone in the private dining room of Goldenrod Court watched as I read the contract.

"Well?" Barton asked.

"It looks straightforward, and I'm not seeing any obvious red flags," I said, "but as I told you, this isn't my area of expertise."

Barton's brother-in-law Victor scoffed. "Lawyers won't go to the bathroom without a waiver. No offense."

I glared at him. "Barton asked for my opinion, which I am providing as a friend. He is free to accept it or not."

"Pay him no mind, Cassandra," Barton said. "I do want to know what you think."

"All right," I said. "I believe the contract covers all the issues you were concerned about. When the proposed updated film of *Gilded Lily* gets a distributor—"

"*If* it gets a distributor," Victor said.

I ignored him. "Upon the film obtaining a distributor, you will begin collecting five percent of all monies earned."

"Gross, right, Uncle Barton? I've read about Hollywood accounting." Victor's son Russell made air quotes as he said *accounting*.

I pointed out the pertinent clause. "It specifies gross, including ticket prices and all subsidiaries: merchandise, soundtrack, and so on."

"And producer credit?" Barton said. "Rights to see the filming? Invites to the premiere?"

I nodded. "Executive producer credit, up to three set visits at dates to be designated later—"

"If we have to come back to Goldenrod Court, try to avoid hurricane season," Russell said, as if the storm outside were the hotel's fault.

Adele said, "It's too soon to say if we'll be able to film here on the island."

Barton waved it off. "Preserving the story and picking the right actress to play Lily are more important."

"Absolutely!"

I went on. "Up to three set visits, and a minimum of ten invitations to the premiere."

"Then let's do this," Barton said. "Signing at the *Gilded Lily* Gala can only bring good luck."

I handed him the papers, but added, "Honestly, you really should consult somebody in the entertainment industry. Surely a few days won't matter."

"Yes, they will," Adele's assistant, Keely, said. "If we don't get the money to secure the rights right away, Netflix is going to swoop in!"

Though it looked as if it pained her, Adele said, "No, Cassandra is right. It's perfectly reasonable for Barton to find an entertainment lawyer to review the contract. If Netflix bags the rights in the meantime… Well, there are other properties."

"Not like *Gilded Lily,*" Barton said, "and Netflix isn't getting their hands on it. Who has a pen?"

Bowing to the inevitable, I handed him my Montblanc. Barton initialed where I showed him, signed both copies, and passed everything to Adele for more initialing and signing.

Barton returning my pen. "Thank you, Cassandra. One of those invitations to the premiere has your name on it. It's the least we can do to thank you for your help." Barton folded his copy of the contract and put it into the inside pocket of the blazer hung on the back of his chair. "Iris will take care of the payment."

Victor threw up his hands in disgust. "Unbelievable!"

Since he would soon be her ex-husband, Iris ignored him. "Bank transfer or check?"

Adele said, "A transfer would be easiest. Keely, give Ms. Belaney the account information."

Ever efficient, Keely already had it printed out.

Iris said, "My laptop's in my room—I'll go take care of it."

"First, let's drink to the project." Barton snapped his fingers in the direction of a waiter. "We need champagne!"

You couldn't fault the service. In mere moments, the waiter and Lou, the events manager, delivered a magnum of an expensive vintage and a tray of champagne flutes. Barton insisted on popping the cork himself, which made a mess and wasted carbonation, but it did set a festive tone.

Once Lou served everyone, Barton said, "To the new *Gilded Lily!*" We all clinked and drank.

Then Adele said, "To our new partnership!" More clinking and drinking.

There were toasts to both the book and movie versions of *Gilded Lily*, Goldenrod Court, the Gala, the actress who'd originally portrayed Lily, the singer who'd dubbed Lily's singing, the director, costume designers... Barton's command of trivia was unparalleled.

I heard Victor tell his son, "The man doesn't remember the names of half the executives in his own family's business, but he knows who catered the damned movie."

Outside the hotel, the storm roared, with rattling windows putting paid to the prediction that Hurricane Sophie would move out to sea. So it shouldn't have been a surprise when the power blinked out, leaving the dining room in darkness.

There were gasps but Lou calmly announced, "It's fine—the generator will kick in shortly." When it did so, perhaps two minutes later, it was an excuse for another toast.

When I saw Barton make a face and put his glass down, I figured the celebration was ending. Instead he invited Adele to dance as he hummed the love song from *Gilded Lily*. Frank took my hand so we could join in, and Russell took Keely's, but Iris rejected Victor's request. Despite that, it was a magical moment. At least it was until Barton stumbled and knocked Adele against the dinner table.

The dancing stopped as he retched, then collapsed onto the floor in a seizure. Iris knelt beside him while Russell yelled for somebody to do something. There was a bluish tint to Barton's lips and fingers, and after a few choked breaths, he went limp.

Lou ran out, and a moment later, returned with a woman I assumed was the hotel nurse, who started working on Barton. Since Victor and Russell were useless, I said, "Iris, let's give the nurse some room." As I leaned over to take her arm, I smelled something unexpected.

I got Iris seated, and should have said something soothing, but I was distracted by a quartet of disturbing thoughts.

One: Barton wasn't responding to the treatment. Two: I'd caught the scent of bitter almonds when there were no almonds present. Three: the only other thing I knew of that smelled like almonds was cyanide. Which led to four: Barton had been poisoned.

The nurse eventually stopped trying to revive him, wiped her brow, and shook her head. Iris, realizing what that meant, started sobbing.

I nearly cried along with her.

The con job had been going so well, and we'd nearly gotten our hands on that lovely, lovely money. But now the job was as dead as the man on the floor.

Before I could decide what to do about the cyanide, the nurse spoke to Iris. "I'm so sorry. I did everything I could."

"Was it his heart?" Iris said, sniffling. "Our father had a bad heart."

"His symptoms didn't present like a heart attack," she said carefully. "Did he have any allergies? Perhaps a nut allergy?"

"No, why?"

"While treating him, I smelled almonds, which is a fairly common allergy."

Lou said, "I smelled it, too."

Iris stared at them. "We were drinking champagne. Where would he have gotten almonds?"

Victor blurted, "Are you talking about cyanide? Are you saying Barton was poisoned?"

That's when things went to hell. Iris gasped, but couldn't make herself speak. Russell and Victor ordered Lou to call the authorities, but it turned out that the police couldn't get to the island until the weather calmed. Adele and Keely stayed as far from the rest of us as possible, and Frank looked as if he wanted to take notes for a book. Other hotel guests who'd gotten wind of the disturbance clustered around the door, but security kept them out of the room.

Finally Lou had the nurse escort Iris to her suite, with Russell accompanying them. Once they'd gone, he enlisted hefty staff members to take Barton's body away, presumably to store him somewhere chilled.

Frank handed Barton's blazer to Lou. "This was missed in the confusion."

"I'll take it to his sister. If any of you need anything tonight, please call the desk."

That sounded like a suggestion for us to retire. Victor made a beeline for the bar, where he was instantly surrounded by a flock of the curious, while the rest of us headed for the elevator.

Once the door slid closed, I said, "I don't want to be alone right now. Would anyone be willing to keep me company?"

They all were, and soon Frank, Adele, Keely, and I were raiding the minibar in my suite.

Of course, their names weren't really Frank, Adele, or Keely, any more than mine was Cassandra, but it's easier to stick with cover names during a job. My colleagues also weren't an author, a movie producer, or an overworked assistant, and I most certainly wasn't a lawyer. What we were was a crew of grifters who'd come to the *Gilded Lily* Gala to make a big score, only to have it slip away.

"Was it really murder?" Frank said. "Not a heart attack or a stroke or—"

"I smelled the cyanide," I said. "It was murder."

"Well, it's nothing to do with us. I say we get off this island right away."

"In the middle of the night? During a hurricane?" Keely asked.

"Then we leave on the first available boat," Frank persisted.

"That wouldn't arouse suspicion at all, would it?" I said. "And what about the con?"

"It's scorched," Keely said, the *duh* unspoken but clearly implied.

"My point is, how well will our cover stories hold up once the police start investigating?"

"Our covers are solid," she said indignantly. One of her cousins had provided our IDs and set up the websites and other online trails to make us look legitimate.

"Still, we can't keep our covers up forever, not with homicide detectives sniffing around."

Frank sniffed. "Have you ever seen me break character?"

"Never, but we've never been on a job that took more than a month. A murder investigation could go on much longer. What if they take fingerprints?"

"You're right," Frank conceded. "So what do we do?"

"The only logical choice is for us to solve the murder before the police arrive."

Grasping the brilliance of my conclusion, the others immediately agreed. And if you believe that, I could con you in my sleep. In actuality, they looked at me as if I were insane.

I said, "Think about it. We're expert observers, and we've thoroughly researched our mark. Or rather, the victim. Plus, we know that none of us is the killer, which drastically cuts down the suspect pool."

I didn't say that I'd considered the possibility that one of them had poisoned Barton, but had exonerated them. While one can never completely trust another grifter, not only had I worked with all of them before, but Barton died before the money was transferred to our account. No grifter would have committed murder before collecting the cash.

Though still doubtful, they accepted that playing detective was our best option, and we started by going over everything that had happened since the con began.

#

The previous afternoon
The waters of Narragansett Bay were choppy, thanks to Hurricane Sophie hugging tightly to the coast, and the ferry rocked even while docked. The crewman greeting passengers at the gangplank warned me that the deck was off-limits during the short trip to Goldenrod Court, instead directing me to the lounge. That suited me fine. It's hard to portray an urbane lawyer while trying to keep from falling overboard.

A handful of people was already there, including a man in his mid-sixties with a patrician nose, a button-down striped shirt, and impeccably tailored slacks. That was Barton Dreier, our mark.

He was examining one of the photos hung on the bulkhead. After accepting a glass of white wine, I sat at an empty table near a picture he hadn't reached, and took a tiny sip. While I sometimes act tipsy on a job, it's dangerous to actually overindulge. Then I pulled a battered paperback out of my briefcase to look at, hoping Barton would come my way.

Across the room, Adele and Keely were on their phones, evidently reading and sending important texts. Adele's sweater looked casual, but it was cashmere and her loafers were Gucci. Keely was all in black: skinny jeans, long-sleeved T-shirt, and boots. The only pop of color was her unnaturally vivid orange hair.

Frank, professorial in a tweed jacket, was in a corner typing on a laptop. Despite looking oblivious to the rest of us, I knew he was as attentive as I was.

Finally Barton reached my table, and I got lucky. The ferry started moving and he lost his footing, hip-checked my table, and spilled my nearly full glass of wine onto my book.

"Oh dear," I said, wiping with a minuscule cocktail napkin.

"Damn!" Barton said, then called out, "Somebody get a towel!"

"I'm on it, Uncle Barton." A dark-haired young man with a less sharply defined version of Barton's nose trotted past.

"I am so sorry," Barton said.

"It's fine," I said, trying for a mix of annoyance and civility. My book was soaked through, and I intentionally turned it over so he could see the cover.

"It's *Gilded Lily*!" he said, horrified.

Russell returned with a waiter and a handful of towels, but though they did their best to pat the book dry, I said, "It's a lost cause. Maybe we can give it a burial at sea."

The waiter carried away the soggy mess.

"Of course I'll pay to replace it," Barton said. "Russell, go get my checkbook."

"Don't bother. It was just a used copy I bought to read this weekend. The good copies are safe at home."

"More than one copy? You must be a fan."

"Aren't we all?"

"Not me," said Russell. "I'm only here for the scenery."

"This generation doesn't appreciate films like *Gilded Lily*," Barton said. "They want superheroes and chase scenes."

"Surely Goldenrod Court wouldn't be hosting a *Gilded Lily* Gala if there weren't interest." I nodded toward Keely. "There's a young person."

"She's working," Russell said. "She and her boss work in the movie business."

"Of course you already checked," his uncle said.

He shrugged. "Call if you spill any more drinks, Uncle Barton." Then he went back to sit with a woman I recognized as Iris Dreier Belaney, Russell's mother and Barton's younger sister.

The boat swayed alarmingly, giving me an excuse to say, "Would you like to sit down?"

"I think I should." He offered a hand. "I'm Barton Dreier."

"Cassandra Chadwick." I paused to think. "Dreier... Dreier Mining?"

"One and the same," he said deprecatingly, which would have been more convincing if he hadn't followed it up by snapping his fingers at a waiter. I've played server roles, and I detest being snapped at.

If the real waiter felt the same, he hid it well. "What can I get you?"

"Scotch, single malt. And for you?"

"Another white wine, please," I said, reminding Barton what happened to my first glass. A little guilt can help build rapport, motivating a mark to charm me so I won't have to work so hard at charming him. "I'm really looking forward to seeing Goldenrod Court in person. It looks so beautiful in the movie."

Barton said, "That photo above you shows the hotel during the filming of *Gilded Lily*."

I took a closer look. "Wouldn't it have been wonderful to have been there to see it happen? Or maybe watching the process would have tarnished the glamour."

"Not at all. Some of the most turbulent sets I've been on resulted in the best movies. Chaos helps form the art."

"I thought you were in mining, not filmmaking."

"I know people in the industry, which gives me access."

In other words, he'd used money and connections to barge onto to a number of movie sets, which I knew thanks to meticulous prep work. There's surprisingly little privacy for the obscenely wealthy.

"Your nephew said they were movie people," I said, looking at Adele and Keely. "Do you know them?"

"They do look familiar," he lied.

I'd hoped he'd suggest chatting with them, but when he didn't, I retreated into small talk. First Barton feigned interest in my cover story of being a commercial real estate lawyer. Not that I wanted interest— I needed to be a lawyer for the con, but preferred a specialty where no one would ask for advice or anecdotes. Then he enthusiastically humble-bragged about his business, travels, and amazing life.

Barton wasn't the least interesting mark I'd ever spent time with, but he was in the bottom ten. Since looking fascinated is exhausting, I was relieved when Frank stopped on his way back from the bar to peer out of the porthole next to our table.

"Can't see the hotel yet," he said. "Back in the days before light pollution, people could see the glow of Goldenrod Court from Newport. Some sources say they could hear music during the parties, too, but I haven't confirmed that."

At our baffled expressions, he said, "Sorry, I'm footnoting again. Occupational hazard. I'm writing a history of Goldenrod Court."

"I'm afraid all I know about it is that *Gilded Lily* was filmed there," I said.

"That's the best-known story, of course, but—" He looked at an empty chair. "May I?"

I glanced at Barton to make sure he didn't object. "Please do. This is Barton Dreier, and I'm Cassandra Chadwick."

"Frank Shepard. As I was saying, the story of the movie will fill up a good chunk of the book. In fact, my agent thinks I should consider a follow-up volume just about the movie, since period pieces are so hot."

"Are they?" Barton said.

"Oh yeah. HBO's show *The Gilded Age* and the Netflix series *Bridgerton* are both big hits." He took a swallow of beer. "Not that I'm an expert in media books—I specialize in histories of great houses—but I stumbled across some fascinating information about *Gilded Lily*. It turns out that—" He leaned forward as if to tell us something particularly juicy, but before he could finish the sentence, Keely came over.

"Excuse me, are you Frank Shepard, the author? And your agent is Elizabeth Kin?"

"Yes." He looked surprised but flattered, as would most authors of obscure histories.

"Would you be willing to talk to my boss? Your agent spoke to her agent and, well, maybe you should hear it from Adele. Adele LaPlante."

"Sure. If you two would excuse me?" He followed Keely to Adele, who appeared very happy to meet him.

"I know it's none of my business," I said, "but I'm dying to know what they're talking about. What did she say her boss's name was? Adele something?"

"LaPlante, I think."

I pulled out my phone, happy that there was a signal, and tapped my way to a web page. "Here we go. Adele LaPlante. She's a movie producer."

"May I see that?" I handed him my phone so he could read Adele's bio and credits. It was all fictitious, of course, but it looked convincing, even to the slightly outdated photo of Adele.

"I didn't know producers had agents," I said, which gave Barton a chance to share filmmaking lore in which I had zero interest. I was about to excuse myself to go to the ladies' room to splash cold water on my face when I finally saw our destination through the porthole.

Even through the rain, Goldenrod Court was breathtaking.

Depending on which travel site you believed, the ludicrously wealthy Jenson family had either wanted privacy or intended to upstage the Vanderbilts, Morgans, and other prominent families who cavorted in Newport, Rhode Island during the Gilded Age. So rather than put their French-inspired chateau alongside the other "summer cottages" on Millionaire's Row, they'd bought their own island. After the Jensons died out, the mansion was transformed into a luxury hotel, which was later made famous when it was used as the setting for the Hollywood musical extravaganza *Gilded Lily*.

Barton was known to worship the movie, and when we learned that he'd be attending an anniversary *Gilded Lily* Gala at Goldenrod Court, we'd designed our con accordingly.

I hadn't been entirely sold on the location because of limited exit strategies from an island, but once I saw the place, I was glad I'd been outvoted.

When we docked a few minutes later, hotel staff were waiting with umbrellas to escort us to the entrance. It didn't help much with the wind-driven rain, but it was a nice touch. Lou Jelinek, a tall, lean man with a warm smile, introduced himself as the events manager before distributing keys and welcome packets for the festivities. "There's an opening reception in the Lily Lounge in an hour," he told us.

That gave me time to inspect my suite, change into a flowing pant-suit, and freshen my makeup. Being a grifter is much more exciting than having a real job, and I do love the beginning of a con, when everything is going according to plan and the payoff feels like a sure thing. I couldn't wait to get down to business, which meant attending the reception.

When I found the Lily Lounge, there were so few people there that I thought I'd gone to the wrong room or had misheard the time. Seeing Lou serving drinks, I asked, "Am I early?"

"Right on time. Ms. Chadwick, isn't it?"

"What a memory! Though I suppose it's not being tested too much tonight. I was expecting a bigger showing."

He chuckled. "So were my bosses. When I pitched the idea of a *Gilded Lily* Gala, I warned them it might take a few years to build up attendance, but the numbers were looking good until the hurricane scrambled travel plans. More guests were scheduled for tomorrow, but it looks as if we won't be able to send the ferry out. Some of our employees are home dealing with flooding, which is why I'm tending bar."

"What a shame," I said, sympathetic for both him and for myself. A big showing would have helped persuade Barton that *Gilded Lily* was ripe for a remake. "May I have a club soda with lime?" It's not my favorite drink, but it masquerades nicely as a cocktail.

Before Lou could finish pouring my drink, a burly man with bushy hair and a wrinkled suit pushed past me and said, "Get me a bourbon."

"I'll be with you in just a minute," Lou said mildly.

I looked dismissively at the lout, and once I had my drink, went to scout the room. Adele and Keely came in, followed closely by Frank, and they started conferring earnestly near the bar. Normally being close to the source of alcohol would have been ideal, but Barton was a finger-snapper and would never get his own drink. So I raised an eyebrow at Adele and nodded at a table at the spot where the movie hero had first spotted the heroine. I felt sure Barton would go straight there.

They switched tables, barely beating out a trio of middle-aged women in *Gilded Lily* T-shirts, and I stationed myself nearby. Just when I'd decided that Barton was skipping the reception, Iris, Russell, and he arrived. As predicted, Russell veered off toward the bar while Barton and Iris headed for the center of the room.

I timed my intersection with them perfectly. "Hello again."

"Hello. Iris, this is Cassandra Chadwick. We met on the ferry. Cassandra, this is my sister Iris Belaney."

"A pleasure to meet you, Iris. Barton, you'll know this. Isn't that where Lily met Gregor in the movie?"

"Yes, it is." He frowned at the trio at the table, no doubt wondering how to get rid of them.

"That's Frank and the movie people," I said, waving at them. When

Frank waved back, I took it as an invitation. "May we share your table?" I said, including Barton and Iris.

"Please do," Frank said. After introductions, he said, "Adele and I were just discussing how the logistics of filming here were handled."

"I've done some reading about that," Barton said, which didn't surprise me, and let loose a flood of technical details while Frank and Adele listened attentively.

Since I didn't have to fake interest, I leaned toward Iris. "This is all going over my head."

"Same here," Iris said. "I watch movies to relax—I don't study them."

"But you are a *Gilded Lily* fan?"

"It's a good movie, but there are plenty of good movies. I only came to the Gala because I needed some time away."

"Is work keeping you busy?"

"That and—"

"There you are!" said the pushy man from the bar, who must have gulped his bourbon.

"Victor! What are you doing here?"

"I wanted to spend time with my lovely wife." He moved in for a kiss.

At least he tried to. Iris put up a hand to hold him off. "Why? Is your mistress busy?"

Shame on me for not recognizing him. I'd seen photos of Iris's husband, but since they were in the midst of a noisy divorce, I hadn't expected him to show up. Evidently, neither had Iris.

"Is this your doing?" Iris asked Russell, who'd brought drinks.

"No. I mean, I told Dad we'd be here, but I didn't know he was going to join us."

"He's not joining us."

There was a flash of anger in Victor's eyes, but he pushed it back. "I know I owe you an apology, Iris. Hell, I owe you all the apologies. That's why I'm here, to start working things out. Can we talk?"

Iris deliberately turned her back on him. "Barton, I've suddenly got a dreadful headache. I think I'll go back to my room and order room service." She exited with dignity.

When Victor started to follow, Russell grabbed his arm and said, "Not now, Dad," and dragged him out of the room.

"I've apparently lost my dinner companions," Barton said, sounding more irritated than concerned for his sister.

"Why don't we all dine together?" I suggested. With the reception ending, Keely scooted to the dining room to reserve a table and the rest of us followed at a more sedate pace.

From then on, the con went beautifully. After a few veiled hints from Frank at dinner, Adele told us in confidence that Frank's agent had told her agent that Frank had learned that film rights for *Gilded Lily* had lapsed. Moreover, Frank had been in contact with a great-niece of the book's author, who just happened to control those rights. Adele was looking to break into bigger projects, so she'd come to Goldenrod Court in pursuit of a deal.

Barton fretted that a new version would add "sex scenes, revealing gowns, and rock and roll music," but Adele assured him that her vision was a prestige film respectful of the original movie, while taking full advantage of the Gilded Age setting. She cited *Pride & Prejudice* and other movies Barton had expressed admiration for in interviews.

When Adele shyly revealed that movies like *Gilded Lily* were what drew her to filmmaking, so producing a remake would be a dream come true, I worried that she was overplaying her hand, but Barton lapped it up. By the time we called it a night, he was already dreaming of hobnobbing with movie stars.

The next day went just as well. In between screenings of *Gilded Lily*, a documentary about making the movie, and tours of the hotel, Adele and Frank staged conversations and phone calls, which I made sure Barton was in place to witness.

As I'd anticipated, he'd noticed the low attendance of the Gala and wondered if there was enough of an audience for a profitable remake, but we were prepared. Overnight, Keely enlisted her cousin in fabricating an active online fan community, complete with a popular podcaster who posted *Gilded Lily* content. She presented this all to Adele when Barton was nearby.

Adele started faux negotiations with the imaginary rights holder, and texted imaginary backers, becoming more and more frantic throughout the day. Keely confided that online rumors of Netflix looking to acquire the rights had her boss sweating.

That evening, Adele was morose because her backers couldn't come up with the cash as quickly as she needed. Netflix was probably going to win by a hair, and when Frank predicted that they'd sex up the show, Barton declared that he wanted in on the deal.

I'd been concerned that Iris would try to stop Barton from investing, and maybe she would have had her husband not been there. But when Victor proclaimed that the idea was a waste of money, she decided she was all for it.

Adele and Barton spent most of the next day negotiating the contract. It was moot, since nobody was going to make the movie, but he might have been suspicious if she'd given him everything he wanted.

Once terms were settled, Adele reserved a private room for a celebratory dinner, even inviting Victor, whom Iris endured for her son's sake. At the last minute, Barton decided he wanted legal advice, which I was on hand to provide. Minutes after the contract was signed, our mark was dead.

# # #

Which brought us back to the post-murder discussion in my suite. I said, "So, what's the consensus? Who killed Barton?"

"How quickly does cyanide kill somebody?" Frank asked.

Keely consulted the Internet via her phone. "It depends on the dosage, but generally, within minutes."

"So it was someone in the dining room," he said, as if it were an insightful deduction. "They must have put the cyanide in Barton's glass during the power outage."

Unless we posit a secret society of assassins sneaking in during those two minutes, I thought.

"That gives us Iris, Russell, Victor, and the serving staff." Assuming a pose from a job in which he'd played a detective, Frank said, "I deduce that it was Iris. She's fiscally conservative, and no movie is a safe investment. She only went along with the idea to spite Victor, but once she realized how much money was involved, she wanted to stop it."

Adele rolled her eyes. "She plainly loved her brother, and she's rich. She wouldn't have killed him for that amount of money. I think it was Victor."

"Why?" I asked.

"Barton supported the divorce, which infuriated Victor, and if he comforted Iris while she was in mourning, she might be vulnerable enough to give him another chance."

Keely said, "I vote for Russell because he's a weasel. He told Victor they were going to be here just to cause trouble. Plus, he's in Barton's will. At least he thinks he is, because he told three different women at the bar that he was going to be rich one day."

"All reasonable," I said. "How do we decide which one it was? And prove it?"

That's where we stalled. After an hour of fruitless discussion and sniping, I said, "Why don't you all go back to your rooms and plot out how to approach your suspects? We can meet again after breakfast. Frank, will you scout out a secure location? I don't want you seen coming here again."

"Of course."

"What are you going to do?" Adele wanted to know.

"I've got an idea of my own," I said, and ushered them out so I could do some research and thinking in peace. Once I confirmed my theory, at least to my own satisfaction, I treated myself to chocolate from the minibar.

The next morning, we convened in the parlor Frank had found and blocked the door. To be polite, I let them tell me what they'd come up with first before presenting my solution, which was patently the correct one. Eventually they admitted I was right, and we made the best plan we could, given limited time and resources. The weather was clearing, and the police would likely be there by early afternoon.

Once we were ready, Adele went to find the mark—or rather, the killer. Once she texted me that he was in the lobby, I sent Keely there, and after a few minutes, followed.

Keely was slumped on one of the sofas, looking miserable. She'd picked a good spot. The killer was behind us, but close enough to hear.

"Are you doing all right after last night?" I said. "That was a terrible thing to see."

"I don't think I'll ever un-see it."

"Or un-hear it," I said with a sincere shudder.

"I really am sorry for Barton and his family, and I don't want to make this all about me, but..."

"But?"

"So coming here was my idea. I convinced Adele that *Gilded Lily* is ripe for a remake, and then..." She swallowed. "Then I talked her into signing a contract for the rights yesterday afternoon. Before Barton signed their contract."

"You're not serious. What if he hadn't signed?"

"I know, it was stupid, but I kept hearing rumors that Netflix was going to swoop in."

"But Barton's family will honor that contract, won't they?"

"Not a chance. Adele spoke to Iris and she said that even if she wanted to move forward—which she doesn't—there are all kinds of legalities involved now that Barton is dead. Besides, both copies of the contract conveniently went missing after the murder." Very conveniently. To avoid incriminating signatures being found, Adele had "lost" hers instantly and Frank had snuck Barton's copy out of his blazer. "She can't pull a new backer out of nowhere, which means defaulting on the rights deal. Then Netflix wins after all, and Adele goes back to searching for a project. Between the strike a while back and the wildfires in LA, a lot of people are looking for work. Including me, as of today."

"Adele fired you?"

Keely nodded. "She's letting me keep my plane ticket, but once we get back to LA, that's it. Maybe I can work at Starbucks."

I made sympathetic noises. "If it's any consolation, I may be applying for a barista job, too. I'm sure my firm will take a dim view of my being tangled up in a murder investigation."

"Aren't you a partner? Isn't that like tenure?"

"Even partners have to answer to the other partners, and I have my share of enemies. A few of the old guard weren't happy with a woman partner, and some were furious when I insisted we expel a partner for indiscretions with an associate."

"That sucks."

I waved it away. "I shouldn't whine. The firm can't push me out without buying me out, and that should be enough to tide me over for a while. I just don't know what I'll do next. Law firms aren't eager to hire women my age, even without the murder taint."

"I guess the staff here is at risk, too."

"If people are afraid to stay here, they probably will be. So many people are going to be affected."

"At least it'll work to Frank's advantage. He can write about the case."

"No, he's in trouble, too. The kinds of shops that stock histories of grand houses want to hear about old scandals, not current ones, and he may not be able to publish his history of Goldenrod Court. Switching to books about murder would mean starting over from scratch, and his agent doesn't even represent true crime."

"That's just great."

"Of course Iris, Russell, and Victor will have it the worst. The police always look at the family first."

"At least they can pay for high-powered lawyers." Keely lowered her voice to a stage whisper as audible as her regular voice. "You know, they could afford to manufacture evidence against somebody else just to get the cops off their backs."

"I wish I could say that sounded farfetched, but these things happen." I'd planned to stop there, gauging that that was enough guilt to pile onto the killer's conscience, but something else struck me. "I keep wondering why somebody would murder Barton."

Keely, being a pro, played along. "It's got to be money, right?"

"Maybe it was revenge. Barton was charming, but he had skeletons hidden in his closet."

"Hidden? He took advantage of his sister and used Russell as a gofer. If he treated his family that way, who knows how he treated employees and business associates?"

"And he was a finger-snapper." The line wasn't quite in character, but I really can't stand finger-snappers. "Of course everyone at his funeral will praise him and call him a humanitarian. Don't you think a vengeful killer would want the world to know the truth?"

"Not enough to spend the rest of their life in prison."

"Juries can be sympathetic about a tragic past and an understandable motive, especially when the killer turns himself in."

"Cassandra, there's nothing sympathetic about feeding someone cyanide."

"Temporary insanity, or he didn't realize how bad the effect would be, or he miscalculated the dose. I don't handle criminal cases, but I know arguments can be made. After all, not all killers are the same. Most care nothing about the repercussions of their crimes, but the rare few never intended to cause collateral damage." I looked away as if I were deep in thought, then shook myself. "I should go pack."

"Yeah. Me, too."

Neither of us looked in the direction of the killer as we left, which was the hardest part of the process.

I knew it was one of the best tales I'd ever spun, but in every con, there comes a moment where the mark has to choose to take the bait. All one can do is wait.

The only thing that kept me sane for the next few hours was Frank texting me. His room had a view of the pier, so he kept watch and let me know when a boatful of police arrived. An eternity later, he let me know that he'd just seen Lou being escorted aboard that boat, in handcuffs.

Only then did I head for the bar. I needed a drink, and I wasn't going to be taking tiny sips.

It took the rest of the day for the police to question everybody, even though they already had the killer in custody and were obviously just going through the motions.

The next morning, we four caught the ferry back to Newport, but then separated, sticking to the travel arrangements we'd made in advance, in case we were being watched. Frank caught a train to New York City, Adele and Keely flew to Los Angeles, and I drove to Hartford.

After a week of lying low, we met in a hotel suite in Boston that I'd booked under a different name. It wasn't as grand as Goldenrod Court, but it had multiple exits.

Once room service delivered dinner, Keely said, "I never would have suspected Lou. I liked him."

"I did, too," I admitted, "but then again, some of my favorite people are criminals."

"There's an enormous difference between grifting and murder," Frank said stiffly.

I shrugged. "Murder is just another kind of con. Once I realized that, I wondered how I would have set up Barton's murder, and where I'd have done the deed. That led to Lou."

They looked confused.

"Once you've got a mark," I said, "what's the next thing you need?"

"Access to the mark," Frank said.

"Right. That eliminated Iris and Russell. They had more access than they wanted and could have killed Barton anytime."

"What about Victor?" Adele asked. "With the estrangement, he'd need an excuse."

"If it had been an impulsive murder, I might have suspected him, but this killer was a planner. He obtained cyanide ahead of time and kept it handy for when an opportunity arose. Does that sound like Victor?"

She shook her head.

"That left Lou, a planner who only had access to Barton while he was at Goldenrod Court. In fact, I'd bet that he dreamt up the Gala purely to lure Barton to the island."

"Did he arrange the power outage, too?" Frank asked.

"Maybe, or it could have been luck. Either way, Lou knew exactly how long he'd have before the generator kicked in."

"And his motive?" Adele said.

"Given Barton's character, I speculated that he might not have cared much about the welfare of his employees or pollution caused by mining. So I checked into Lou's background and found out that he grew up in one of the towns where Dreier Mining operates. His older brother died in a mine accident, and his parents died of cancer, possibly linked to exposure to toxic chemicals in the water. Including cyanide."

"That I understand," Adele said, "but how did you know that you could guilt him into giving himself up?"

"Because of what Lou didn't do, which showed what he didn't want. He didn't sue because he didn't care about money, and he didn't shoot up an office, because he didn't want innocent people hurt. So I showed him that he had, in fact, hurt innocent people because so many would suffer from a prolonged investigation. Admittedly, we were only relatively innocent, but Lou didn't know that."

"I get that part, but then you went off-script," Keely said.

"I couldn't help myself from gilding the lily. We grifters offer marks something they want, even if they don't know they want it. Like Barton wanting to make a movie. In Lou's case, I helped him realize that he wanted to tell the world about Barton's sins. Then I conned him into believing that by going to the police, he could tell his story, and maybe make himself a hero in the process."

"It was kind of a stretch, don't you think?" Frank said.

"Not really. After all, every confession starts with a con."

The Dinosaur and the Maiden by Donna Andrews

#

14. The method of murder, and the means of detecting it, must be rational and scientific. That is to say, pseudo-science and purely imaginative and speculative devices are not to be tolerated in the roman policier. For instance, the murder of a victim by a newly found element—a super-radium, let us say—is not a legitimate problem. Nor may a rare and unknown drug, which has its existence only in the author's imagination, be administered. A detective-story writer must limit himself, toxicologically speaking, to the pharmacopoeia. Once an author soars into the realm of fantasy, in the Jules Verne manner, he is outside the bounds of detective fiction, cavorting in the uncharted reaches of adventure.

I nearly jumped out of my chair when someone knocked on my door. In the Before Times, I'd have been delighted to have a possible client show up, to interrupt the tedium of staring at the frosted glass window where the letters were flaking off, so it now said R.C. CASSIDY, PRIVATE INVES. Well, actually SEVNI ETAVIRP YDISSAC C.R. from my point of view.

There was a time when I'd have badgered my landlord to have it fixed, and eventually he'd have done it. But my landlord had been eaten by velociraptors three months ago, so we tenants were on our own. Those of us who remained uneaten.

Of course, the upside was that with my landlord gone, there was no one collecting rent. Our benevolent dinosaur overlords had not yet discovered the concept of landlords and tenants. And luckily my office was in sauropod territory. My house—the neat little bungalow I'd bought as a fixer-upper and spent so many hours improving—was in theropod turf. The carnivorous theropods tended to eat the human population of their territory. The sauropods, being herbivorous, considered us amusing pets, or sometimes cheap labor. So while there was no one collecting my mortgage payments either, I knew better than to go back to my house.

Another knock. I could see the shape of my visitor. Human sized. Generally human shaped. But some of the smaller dinosaurs were getting sneakier. Especially the velociraptors.

So I sidled over to the door and peered out through the frosted glass. The shape was probably human. I was considering opening the door when my tin foil helmet buzzed slightly, the way it did when it was fending off a telepathic intrusion.

No, not an actual tin foil helmet. I'd long ago upgraded to a fairly high-end Faraday helmet. The tin foil only did so much. Although I was hoarding the stuff, in case my helmet malfunctioned. The guy I'd bought it from got trampled by a rogue triceratops six weeks ago, so when this thing went, I'd have to fall back on the tin foil.

"If you're human, use your words," I shouted through the door.

A brief pause.

"A thousand pardons, gentle being." The voice was hoarse, hesitant, as if its owner was out of practice using it. "This unworthy servitor brings a message from its master, the mighty—" There followed a burst of untranslated Saurian, sounding like a mix of gargling and the sort of sinister crackling and buzzing you'd hear if a downed power line landed in a hornet's nest. If I had to write it, I'd probably render it as something like *Qfkjvvx*. The sound made me wince. Saurian anatomy wasn't designed to produce human speech, and the human brain couldn't easily assimilate Saurian thoughts.

"Wilt thou consent to parlay directly with the peerless one?" the voice asked.

"I'm fine with you translating," I said. No way I was going to take off my helmet and give some giant lizard direct access to my brain.

"The great and powerful Qfkjvvx wishes to employ you to ascertain the whereabouts of one of his human servitors and restore it to his presence," the voice said. "Your success in this venture will be rewarded with a princely supply of comestibles."

"Well, I'll be," I said to myself. "A client." And one who'd pay in food, the only currency that meant anything these days.

I decided maybe it was safe to let the human servitor in. He was a slender man of medium height, with a receding hairline. He could be anywhere from his thirties to his fifties. He looked as nervous about walking into my office as I felt about opening the door. With luck, I hid it better.

"So who does your boss want me to find?" I asked.

The servitor held out a rather battered photo. It showed a pretty young woman in a slinky dress standing in a spotlight with a microphone in her hand. A publicity still, no doubt, from the pre-saurian days. Actually, at first glance it looked like a relic from the 1920s—she wore a short, slinky drop-waisted dress and a sparkly headband with a feather sticking up. On the back of the photo someone had stuck on a label with her name—Aimee Loran—and the contact information for her booking agency.

What did the great and powerful Qfkjvvx want with this young woman, anyway?

"I'm not trying to pry into your boss's business," I said. "But if I had some idea why he's so keen to get this chick back, it might help me figure out where she's gone. Or who might have taken her."

And whether it was a good idea to find her in the first place. In the Before Times, I'd been approached more than once to find someone who was better off not being found. Wives escaping abusive husbands, mainly, along with the occasional sex worker fleeing her—or his—trafficker. Usually I'd refuse to take those cases. Occasionally, if my would-be client was insistent enough, I'd pretend to take them, help the victim escape instead, and then apologize for my lack of success and decline to charge anything for my services. Half the time, if I did a good enough job of looking as if I'd been trying, they'd insist on paying me anyway.

But a saurian looking to find a particular human—this was a new turn of events. I needed to know more. I wasn't sure I wanted to know why Qfkjvvx wanted to find this Aimee, but I figured I needed to find out. Was it a romantic attachment? A sexual one? Was the shapely Aimee a lizard's moll? Did lizards even have molls? Or had Qfkjvvx been fattening Aimee up to serve as the main course when he was hosting a carnivorous saurian?

"It emits sounds of a pleasing nature," the servitor said.

"Sounds?" I echoed. "What kind of sounds?"

"They range between 100 and 1000 hertz," the servitor said. "They emanate through the being's mouth from vibrations in its esophagus. The illustrious one finds these sounds conducive to entering his daily dormancy period."

"She sings him to sleep," I translated.

"Yes." The servitor nodded vigorously. "And its loss has made it very difficult for the splendiferous one to achieve proper rest."

Okay, that was at least a plausible reason for a saurian to be seeking a human. If I managed to locate Aimee, I could always check with her. See if her story matched up with the lizard's.

I took possession of the photograph and the servitor paid me a retainer in the form of a large cardboard box containing several dozen cans of food and about ten pounds of dried rice and lentils. I waited until he'd left to hide most of the food in my main cache. And before he left, I extracted the fact that the great and powerful Qfkjvvx was a triceratops. Useful. Not that I could tell one trike from another, but at least I knew what they looked like. If some stegosaurus thundered up to me and asked if I'd found his pet human, I'd know he was trying to pull a fast one.

And then I waited until dark before setting out to look for Aimee. Safer that way. While there were some species of dinosaurs with the kind of night vision and keen hearing needed to hunt at night, there were still a lot fewer of them. And even those were less likely to go out in cold weather, so I was glad to see the thermometer was continuing to drop. Even gladder when an icy rain began. A miserable night for a human to be out in, but at least the odds of getting eaten were about as low as possible.

I wrapped up warmly, packed a few useful tools—a camera, a flashlight, a pair of binoculars—and set out as soon as it was fully dark.

I started by dropping by what few human-oriented nightspots still existed downtown, in cellars or back rooms, hidden in much the same way I imagine speakeasies were during Prohibition. Small spaces, mostly, with small entrances, the better to keep out the larger predators. By now most of them had nothing on tap but whatever rotgut the owners could manage to distill. And no one I talked to had seen Aimee. Not surprising, since most of the bars didn't bother with entertainment these days. Maybe that was why Aimee had taken to serenading lizards for her supper.

I knew of a few joints that catered to the cold-blooded crowd. The first one was closed. I took the time to puzzle out the alien squiggles the saurians used for writing and deduced that the place was only open in the daytime. The second one was closed, with a sign that proclaimed the lizard equivalent of "closed due to inclement weather."

The third dive was open, though sparsely populated. A pair of horny-headed dinos only about three feet tall, sharing a trough of mixed green vegetation. A smallish brontosaurus basking under an array of heat lamps on the raised area that had once served as the nightclub's stage. Or did it still double as a stage on warmer nights?

I spoke to the half dozen human staff there—or tried to. None of them admitted knowing Aimee. They all claimed it had been several months since they'd featured any kind of entertainment other than the heat lamps.

"We had this kind of punk band that used to play here," one waiter said. "Then one night a couple of velociraptors snuck in and ate their drummer. I hear the rest of the band went north after that."

Went north. You never could be exactly sure what that meant. You heard rumors sometimes that there were bands of humans surviving—in fact, thriving—in northern climes. Greenland, Iceland, the Yukon, Alaska, Scandinavia, and Siberia. Places like that.

But you also heard a lot of people using "went north" as a polite way of saying "died." Or maybe even "got eaten." After all, it wasn't dark and cold in those places all the time. Didn't the dinosaurs show up in the summers? And wouldn't it be hard to survive in places like that without all the modern technology that was gradually getting lost as the people who knew how to run it were wiped out? What if I set out on a trek to the Northwest Territories only to find that the thriving human colonies were just someone's pipe dream? Everyone knew someone who had gone north, but none of them had ever been heard from again.

I gave up interrogating the waitstaff after a bit. But I noticed that one guy seemed particularly anxious at being questioned. So when I left the club I found a place to hide in the alley behind it—a place with a good view of the human-sized back door that I suspected served as the staff entrance.

It was close to dawn by the time another couple of humans arrived and went inside. After a little while, a staff member left. Followed by another. And then the anxious guy.

He was so keyed up that shadowing him was hard. Was this just how he usually looked when he was trying to make his way home without getting eaten? Or had my questions made him nervous? Even more nervous than usual? And the chase was getting to me as well—his route veered perilously close to theropod territory. It wouldn't matter how much food Qfkjvvx rewarded me with if I got eaten while trying to find his pet singer.

Anxious Guy finally scuttled into the cellar entrance of what had once been a cookie-cutter high-rise apartment building.

I found a good hiding place on the fire escape of the nearly identical building next door, separated from the building in which my target had taken refuge only by a narrow alley. I settled in to watch the entrance—and wait out the dangerous daylight hours.

Nothing much happened for the longest time. The occasional saurian passed by—mostly herbivores. At one point a pterodactyl seemed to have spotted me—or maybe they hunted by smell. Fortunately for me its wingspan was too wide for the narrow alley, so after soaring overhead for half an hour or so it gave up and flew off.

Twice, humans emerged from the door and crept carefully down the alley. Three times humans crept down the alley and slipped inside.

It was dusk when I finally spotted her—a slender human figure whose hooded coat didn't quite conceal a bulky homemade Faraday helmet, timidly emerging from the building. While she paused in the entrance, looking nervously up and down the alley, I got the binoculars on her. It was Aimee.

She turned and headed for the far end of the alley. As soon as her back was to me, I began my swift but quiet descent from the fire escape.

She wasn't hard to follow. She did a decent job of finding cover, hiding behind Dumpsters, wrecked vehicles, and piles of rubble. But she spent too much time working up her nerve whenever she had to move from one hiding place to another across open space. If a carnivore has spotted you—or worse, gotten your scent—the last thing you want to do is hang around someplace until it has time to catch up with you.

I caught up with her while she was crouching behind a particularly smelly Dumpster.

"Aimee Loran?" I said it quietly, but she still jumped and had to stifle a shriek.

"Who are you?" She kept her voice low. "And why are you looking for me?"

"Qfkjvvx hired me to find you," I said. "The lizard who likes your singing."

She groaned and closed her eyes.

Just then we heard a commotion down the block. Three dilophosauruses were fleeing down the street, with a pair of enormous brontosauruses in hot pursuit. Nice to see that herbivores were still defending their borders.

Aimee moaned softly and froze. How had this chick survived so long on the streets?

"Follow me," I ordered—but I had to grab her and drag her to get her in motion. I had a bolthole nearby, and I half led, half dragged her there.

My bolthole was in the basement of a partly ruined brownstone. Scavengers, both human and reptilian, had long ago emptied the ground floor deli of its contents. But there had never been anything either edible or valuable in the basement. It had been a sort of catch-all shop for magic supplies. The walls were still hung with dried herbs, amulets, crystals, and other paraphernalia. The atmosphere always struck me as more voodoo than New Age. Maybe that was one reason people—and lizards—seemed to avoid the place. Maybe all that stuff really worked.

"So Qfkjvvx claims he wants you back so you can sing him to sleep," I said. "But before I tell him I've found you, I'd like to hear your side of the story."

"I thought I had it made," she said. "Thought I'd found a big, tough armored herbivore to protect me. Keep me safe from the T. rexes."

She sounded bitter. And a little hoarse.

"But he doesn't understand that I'm not a machine," she said. "I can't sing for ten or twelve hours straight, night after night. I'm afraid

I've already damaged my voice. And once I lose that, what's to keep him from trading me to one of his carnivorous friends?"

I nodded.

"So you'd rather not be found," I said.

"Please," she said. "Just tell him you can't find me."

"I can keep looking for a while," I said. "But not indefinitely. I don't suppose you have a place where you could lie low until I can convince him you're nowhere to be found?"

"I could probably hole up with a friend for a week or so," she said.

Her tone said that she knew that wasn't nearly long enough. Hell, a year might not be long enough. Dinosaurs, especially the big, slow herbivores, were stubborn and patient.

"I was trying to save up enough supplies to head north," she said. "I have friends who made the trek a couple of months ago. I turned down the chance to go with them. It was just after I'd gotten the lullaby gig—before I realized it was more of a trap than a safe haven. They sent word that I was welcome to join them, but I'm not sure I'll ever manage to get the supplies I'd need. Or the nerve."

She gave a humorless laugh at that last bit.

"You're actually in communication with people who made it north?" I asked.

"In communication?" she echoed. "That would be an exaggeration. But I did get a message that they'd made it."

"Interesting," I said.

"But I can kiss that idea good-bye if you're planning to turn me in," she said. "He'll make sure I never get another chance to escape. Please—just let me go. If you—"

"Shut up a minute," I said. "I need to think."

She shut up. I pulled out her publicity photo and studied it.

"I don't suppose you still have that thing," I said, pointing to the headband.

"I probably have it, back at my place." I could tell she thought it was a stupid question.

"Then I have a plan," I said. "Looks like you and I are heading north."

It took a while, my plan. For several weeks I had to string along Qfkjvvx's servitor while pretending to scour the city for Aimee. I ventured more and more into theropod turf, until finally I found what I needed.

The next time the servitor showed up in my office, I put on a long face.

"I have bad news," I said.

He turned pale. I gathered that even if Qfkjvvx wasn't a carnivore, he didn't react well to bad news.

I hauled out a heavy gray plastic tote and opened it up to reveal a jumble of bones. Some of the longer bones were broken, but most were still intact, and if you looked close you could see bits of sinew and other indigestible bits still attached. Also bits of excrement.

And tangled with the vertebrae were the remnants of that sparkly, feathered headband. A few of the rhinestones had fallen out and twinkled among the bones.

"She made the mistake of running into theropod territory," I said. "I tried to catch up with her, but one of them got her. T. rex, I think. I went back later and scouted around until I found this."

"The illustrious one will be most displeased," the servitor said.

"Tell him I'm sorry," I said. "I tried. I really did."

He nodded gloomily. I wondered if he'd actually tell Qfkjvvx that Aimee was dead, or if he'd try to cover it up. Keep making pilgrimages to my office every day or two so he could pretend I was still on the case.

I also wondered if Qfkjvvx would try to take his disappointment out on me. You never knew—so I didn't plan to stick around to find out. As soon as the servitor was on his way back to Qfkjvvx's lair, Aimee and I were taking off for parts north.

Wish us luck.

The Devil and Zephyr Devlin by Gigi Pandian

#

15. The truth of the problem must at all times be apparent—provided the reader is shrewd enough to see it. By this I mean that if the reader, after learning the explanation for the crime, should reread the book, he would see that the solution had, in a sense, been staring him in the face—that all the clues really pointed to the culprit—and that, if he had been as clever as the detective, he could have solved the mystery himself without going on to the final chapter. That the clever reader does often thus solve the problem goes without saying. And one of my basic theories of detective fiction is that, if a detective story is fairly and legitimately constructed, it is impossible to keep the solution from all readers. There will inevitably be a certain number of them just as shrewd as the author; and if the author has shown the proper sportsmanship and honesty in his statement and projection of the crime and its clues, these perspicacious readers will be able, by analysis, elimination and logic, to put their finger on the culprit as soon as the detective does. And herein lies the zest of the game. Herein we have an explanation for the fact that readers who would spurn the ordinary "popular" novel will read detective stories unblushingly.

One Year Ago

Sanjay Rai didn't *hate* Zephyr Devlin. Not exactly.

No, who was he kidding? Sanjay hated him.

That didn't mean he couldn't appreciate Devlin's performance, as he watched the stage from the back row of the theater. Devlin had perfected an old-school style of days gone by, when magicians pretended to conjure devils and demons.

Performing under the stage name The Hindi Houdini, Sanjay brought elements of classic magic into his shows as well, such as wearing a tuxedo and his signature bowler hat on stage, but his own specialty was escape acts, just like Houdini. One of which he'd be performing that night— if the performance proceeded as scheduled.

Sanjay squirmed in his seat. Why had that disquieting thought popped into his mind? Of course they'd be performing that night. And yet...

Something was simmering beneath the surface at the theater. He'd sens
it since arriving. He rubbed his tired eyes and shook off the feeling. F
was exhausted from a pre-dawn flight. That was all.

Devlin stood dead center on the stage and pulled a small, crimsc
book from the breast pocket of his Victorian tailcoat. Wisps of smo]
emerged from the pages as he opened the cover.

"What did you say, Beelzebub?" Devlin spoke to the wisp of smo]
hovering above his shoulder. His accent while performing was ind
terminate, as if from a fictional far-off land. He stroked his goatee ar
nodded, as if in response to a voice only he could hear, then threw f
head back and laughed. "You *are* a naughty devil, aren't you? Yes, I su
pose I could do that before I disappear and join you."

Even in this empty theater, Devlin didn't break character. This w
only a rehearsal for the short set in which both stage magicians would I
performing at a charity show that night. Sanjay twirled his black bowl
hat in his hands without shifting his gaze from the stage.

Devlin darted across the stage in what looked like carefully chore
graphed steps. Nobody besides a fellow performer would have notice
but Sanjay always learned something from Devlin. Or rather, from h
shows. It was best to be the opposite of Zephyr Devlin in the rest
one's life.

Devlin's tailcoat swayed as he climbed higher and higher via hidd
notches on the side of a spirit cabinet made of antique wood, the so
prop on the otherwise empty stage. As Devlin stepped onto the top
the cabinet, he froze.

So did Sanjay. Comedy magicians often made it look as if they ha
made a mistake before a grand revelation that makes the audience bo
laugh and gasp with wonder. But Devlin wasn't that kind of performe

"What are you doing?" Devlin shouted. He swung his arms throu;
the air in front of him. "No!"

With a violent motion, Devlin jerked backward. No, that wasi
exactly what Sanjay saw. Someone had *pushed* Devlin. Shoved hir
Hard. The only problem with what Sanjay was witnessing? *There w
nobody else on stage.* The person who'd given Devlin a shove was *invisib.*

Unable to steady himself, Devlin tumbled over the back of the cabin
to the stage, at least eight feet below. A thud sounded a moment late

From stage left came a scream. Amethyst. A talented magician in h
own right, she'd started her career as a sideshow performer who swa
lowed swords and regurgitated coins before becoming Zephyr Devlir
assistant, and after one last show with Devlin today, she'd be headli
ing her own show.

"Who screamed?" The new voice came from behind Sanjay. It was Mary, the operations manager of the theater and the only other person in the theater with the three magicians. She must've been in the front of house, probably the box office where she'd been when he arrived.

Sanjay ran down the aisle, Mary right behind him. Skipping the stairs along the left and right sides of the stage, he leapt onto center stage and reached Devlin behind the cabinet only a moment after Amethyst. Unlike Devlin, she wasn't yet dressed for the show in her purple costume, but instead wore a white sundress. Her long black hair was pulled into a bun on the top of her head, held in place with hair clips shaped like butterfly wings.

"What the devil happened?" Mary called. She hadn't caught up to the others yet. She was old enough to have retired ages ago, but this theater was her life. Sanjay guessed it was the twenty-pound utility belt she wore around her waist rather than her age slowing her down.

"Are you hurt?" Amethyst knelt at Devlin's side as he groaned and sat up.

"Do I look all right to you?" he snapped. "Someone pushed me!"

Yeah, he was fine.

Sanjay ran past Devlin to the dark corner of the stage and slipped through the gap in the back curtains.

Nobody.

He jogged back to the others and yanked open the cabinet doors, including the hidden compartment. Again, empty. While Amethyst and Mary helped Devlin up, Sanjay kept looking for the assailant. Not a soul could be found in the wings, the catwalk, or the dressing room. And he hadn't heard the back door open.

"No broken bones," Mary declared.

"You'll need your backup costume, though." Amethyst wriggled her finger through a rip in his tailcoat.

"You won't find him, Houdini," Devlin snarled as Sanjay climbed to the top of the spirit cabinet.

Sanjay hopped down. "You know who pushed you?"

"Of course I do." He spat out the words. Angry. No, furious. But a second later, it was as if a switch had flipped. The anger faded and another emotion took over. *Fear.*

"Nobody," Devlin stammered. "Nobody pushed me."

"What just happened, then?" Sanjay asked. It was only the three of them in the theater. The rest of the crew and staff would arrive a little later that afternoon. Yet someone—or some*thing*—had clearly been on the stage with Devlin. He glanced up at the lights. Could something have been dropped from above? A weighted sandbag, perhaps? But how would it have been invisible?

"I—I slipped." Devlin rubbed his elbow. "What are you all staring at? I'm fine."

Whatever had happened, it was most certainly not a simple slip, and Devlin was far from fine. A trickle of blood escaped from the side of his mouth.

Amethyst caught it, too. "You're more injured than you're letting on. We should—"

"Flowers," Devlin stammered, hurrying off stage towards a bouquet of flowers that had been delivered right as Sanjay had arrived, an expression of thanks from the charity for headlining that night's benefit show. "Been neglecting these flowers. I should put them in some water." He hurried out of sight, toward the dressing room.

"What was that about?" Amethyst asked Sanjay.

"No idea."

"Performers," Mary muttered.

Ten minutes later, Devlin still hadn't emerged.

Sanjay knocked on the dressing room door. "Devlin?" He tried the handle. *Locked.* "Come on, Devlin."

The door opened a crack. "Houdini. Good." Devlin's hair was wild, but not quite as wild as his eyes. "Nobody else is with you?" He looked past Sanjay, then pulled him inside before slamming and locking the dressing room door.

"What the hell is—?"

"*Shh!* He'll hear." Devlin pressed his ear to the door, looking more maniacal every moment. Sanjay wasn't so sure he liked being locked inside this small room with Zephyr Devlin.

"*He?*" Sanjay thought Amethyst and Mary were the only ones there with them. "Who exactly will hear?"

"You've got to help me, Houdini."

Sanjay hated to ask, but his curiosity was piqued. "Help with *what?*"

Devlin's gaze darted around the room erratically. "Did you hear that?"

Sanjay stood in silence for a few seconds, listening. Footsteps. "I expect it's Amethyst practicing on stage."

"If only that were true." Devlin, his whole body shaking, collapsed onto the floor. "He's back to collect."

"Who?"

"It was foolish of me to think this charity show would make the angels look out for me and keep the Devil at bay."

"The Devil? C'mon, Devlin. You don't have to stay in character back-stage. You slipped on stage. It happens to the best of us."

"Not to me. Not since…"

Sanjay didn't like Zephyr, nor did he respect him. Why was he humoring him? He turned toward the door.

"Wait! It's just so difficult to say out loud." Devlin closed his eyes and took two deep breaths. When he opened his eyes, he was calm. No, not quite calm. Resigned. "Ten years ago today, I made a deal that helped me get where I am today. A staggeringly awful deal, it turns out."

"You signed a bad contract?"

Devlin barked out a humorless laugh. "You could say that. Ten years ago, I sold my soul to the Devil."

Sanjay waited for a laugh that didn't come. "Good story. You should use it in your show."

"I wish I was joking. We're so foolish as young men, aren't we? Ten years… it sounded like such a long time…." Devlin stood and brushed invisible lint from his torn tailcoat. He met Sanjay's gaze with a defiant stare. "I know you don't like me. Normally I wouldn't care. But now… I need your help. I don't think he'll come to collect if I'm with someone else. At least I hope not…. Since we're both performing tonight, don't let me out of your sight, okay?"

"To protect you from *the Devil*." Sanjay thought of himself as a good guy. A patient one. But this? "I'm hungry, Devlin. I had a long flight. I'm leaving to get some food."

"Wait! Let me tell you what happened. Then you'll understand."

"Two minutes." Sanjay flipped his bowler hat onto his head. "You have two minutes."

"You know how long it takes to make it in this career. Surely you understand the temptation…. Ten years ago, I had already been doing gigs for years. I was frustrated after being heckled at a particularly humil-iating show at a frat house. God, how I hate frat houses. But they have money. For a starving performer, the paycheck was too good to refuse. But the drunken audience was out of control. I wandered around that college down around midnight, getting mind-numbingly drunk, even though I had a flight to catch before dawn the next day to yet another show that was sure to drain my will to live."

The words were rushing out of him now. He wasn't looking at San-jay, but at an insignificant spot on the wall as he conjured the memory.

"I came to an empty intersection. That's when I remembered that story about being able to summon the Devil at a crossroads—the idea that you could sell your soul to him to achieve success. I was drunk enough that I stood there in that empty intersection and laughed as I called for the Devil. Though I was alone, I heard a noise. But of course it was only my imagination—or so I thought. The Devil didn't show himself, so I pricked the tip of my finger and crisscrossed my finger through the night sky, signing my name in the air—with my blood."

Devlin lifted his index finger, then pulled back as if recoiling from an electric shock.

"I was already beginning to hone my act with devils appearing at my shoulder, so it was a drunken joke. I thought nothing of it, even as my career began to take off. A producer was in the audience of one of my shows that very week. One thing led to another from there."

"That," said Sanjay, "was already more than two minutes."

"You don't believe me?" Devlin whispered.

"I believe you'd been working hard for years by that time. As much as I hate to say it, you're good. You were bound to find success. And to make enemies. One of whom is messing with you."

"You don't understand. That night, I sold my soul to the Devil."

"I'm hungry, Devlin."

Devlin stepped between Sanjay and the dressing room door. "It was ten years ago *today*." He paused. "And last night, I had the most frightening dream I've had in my entire life."

"Well?" Sanjay prompted.

Devlin tugged at his collar. A trickle of sweat ran down his forehead. "I was at a party. In a grand ballroom. It looked a bit like one I performed at for a private event a few years ago. Only this time, it wasn't people in the room. It was red…"

"Devils?"

"Don't mock me, Houdini! Yes. The ballroom was stiflingly hot, with flames crackling in every nook and cranny, and everyone there was a demon. I didn't just slip on that stage just now. I can see it in your eyes that you believe at least that much. We're magicians. Someone who doesn't like me could have done something to that cabinet to make me lose my balance. Sure. But *how could they induce that dream*?"

"Your subconscious—"

"When I left the hotel this morning, I was nearly hit by a car when crossing the road. Dozens of people saw it, including Mary. That wasn't someone simply *messing* with me, as you speculated. And that accident on stage… Were you watching my act when an invisible hand pushed me?"

Sanjay twirled his bowler hat in his hands and studied Devlin's face. Did Devlin believe what he was saying? "Maybe."

"*I knew it.* I knew you were watching to steal my methods."

Sanjay reached for the door handle. "Why do you have to make it so hard to help you? I'm out."

"Please," Devlin pleaded, holding the door shut. "I'm sorry. Truly. I know you're not trying to steal my act. You have your own. And it's good. Old habits, you know? But I'm a changed man."

Sanjay would have been moved by the desperation in Devlin's wild eyes if he hadn't known the man. "You're seeking *redemption*. That's why you let Amethyst out of her contract today. A good deed to get out of your contract with the Devil."

"That may have occurred to me...."

"You should have let Amethyst out of her contract ages ago when she asked. Not just today, to ease your guilty conscience."

Devlin narrowed his eyes. "She should have thought more carefully about her contract. Just like I should have mine."

"A lot of people you've worked with dislike you, Devlin. But you're right. Trying to hit you with a car and shoving you off a high cabinet are more than pranks. I'll keep an eye out, okay? Come on. You can tag along to lunch. You're buying."

Devlin grinned. "In spite of what I've said about you before, you're not such a bad lot, Houdini."

Sanjay didn't ask what Devlin had said about him. It was better not to know. The two men walked out of the dressing room and toward the stage.

"What's that sound?" Sanjay whispered as the edge of the stage came into view. The white stage lights were no longer white—but blood red. Underneath the eerie lighting, Amethyst pushed a wheeled box into place. A faint squeaking noise accompanied the movement, but those wheels shouldn't have made noise. When she stopped, it became clear that the sound wasn't coming from Amethyst's actions on the stage, but from above them. He expected to see Mary on the catwalk, the tools in her tool belt making the sound, but she wasn't there. Nobody was. Not unless they were invisible.

"A squeaking," Devlin whispered. He gripped Sanjay's arm. "Where? Where is he?"

"It's the *lights*." Sanjay shook off Devlin's grip. A heavy stage light swayed precariously from high above. He rushed forward, hoping he'd be in time.

"Look out!" Sanjay called. Only a few more seconds to reach her. Only a few more steps—

The lighting gave a final groan before crashing to the stage below. A scream.

Then silence.

Sanjay hadn't reached Amethyst in time.

She lay beneath the twisted metal and glass, unmoving.

"It was meant to be me," Zephyr kept repeating, as if in a trance, as an emergency crew carefully extracted Amethyst's broken, yet living, body. "I'm living my life right from now on. I promise. I'll keep the angels on my side. I won't give the Devil any opportunity to collect my soul."

Sanjay had been surprised many times in his career as a stage illusionist. He did not, however, believe that Devlin would surprise him by changing his tune. Nor did he believe a supernatural Devil was responsible. And yet… there was something devilish about the attack. Something Sanjay knew would haunt him until he figured it out.

# # #

One year later: Today

Zephyr Devlin had not, in fact, lived virtuously for the last 365 days.

His second virtuous act of the past year was taking place today, performing at a charity fundraiser on this fateful anniversary.

Amethyst had survived the terrible accident, but the fallen lights had crushed her right arm and hand. She'd recovered enough to live a relatively normal life, but not to be the standout sleight-of-hand magician she had been poised to become. Or even to be a magician's assistant as she'd been before. Devlin's first virtuous act of the year had been offering Amethyst a stable job as his stagehand, including paying her during her recovery before she was able to work again.

Sanjay was certain it wasn't the Devil who tried to kill Devlin and got Amethyst by mistake, as were the authorities. Someone human had indeed been trying to kill, or at least injure, Zephyr Devlin. The theater wasn't at fault for the light falling. It was a deliberate act of sabotage. Attempted murder. The police hadn't found the culprit, so Devlin had hired more private security for tonight's event. Just in case whoever tried to kill him last year tried again.

"This isn't funny, Houdini." Devlin thrust a note into Sanjay's hand. The following words were written in block letters with blood red ink:

You escaped before.

This time, you will suffer.

This time, you will drown in the ocean.

"Drown in the ocean?" Sanjay repeated. "I'd recommend you not go to the beach."

"He's messing with my head!" Devlin screamed. His next words were a whisper. "I nearly drowned in the ocean when I was a child. I lost consciousness. I think I was technically dead. That's the reason I won't perform any water stunts like you do. Don't you see? *He knows.*"

They stood in the same theater dressing room they'd been in the previous year for a similar conversation. The accommodations had deteriorated over the past twelve months. Mary would be retiring shortly, and it looked like the theater would be closing down with her. Their surroundings were a sad excuse for a dressing room. A solitary chair in front of the vanity. Half of the light bulbs that encircled the mirror were burnt out. A lopsided clothing rack held a dozen bent hangers. The bright spot was a bouquet of wilted red roses in a vase on a bookshelf with a few books and a large candy dish that looked left over from Halloween. The candy dish was disappointingly empty. Sanjay remembered similar flowers from the previous year, but even the flowers had been nicer then.

"Shouldn't you tell your security guard about the threatening note?"

"Cobra is only muscle. Not brains."

"That's what you get for hiring someone who calls himself Cobra."

"I didn't take you for being so judgmental."

"You're the one who said—" Sanjay stopped himself. If Devlin could so easily make Sanjay want to strangle him, it was hard to believe only one person was trying to kill him.

"Cobra won't leave my side. He's got another man he's working with who's less conspicuous, who'll see if anything else is—" Devlin jumped at the sound of a knock on the dressing room door.

"I brought coffee," Amethyst called through the door.

Devlin looked at Sanjay with pleading in his eyes. "Coffee. That's liquid."

"Even the Devil can't drown you in a cup of coffee."

"The Devil might be working through her. Or Mary. Look what she's let happen to the theater? You can't leave me alone with them. Or with anyone."

"But you trust *me*?" Sanjay blinked at his desperate frenemy.

"You've solved a bunch of mysteries. I can't think of anyone else to trust right now."

"Fine," Sanjay agreed. "But may I suggest after tonight, you both show this note to the police and follow through on living a life of generosity? Doing the right thing for Amethyst and doing one charity gig every year doesn't absolve you."

"Just get me through tonight."

Another knock sounded on the door. "You okay, Mr. Devlin?" a deep voice asked.

Sanjay nodded and opened the door.

Cobra stood in the doorway with his massive arms crossed. Behind him, Amethyst held a takeaway coffee-cup holder in her good hand. "You'll look into that creepy guy I saw at the box office?" she was saying to Cobra.

He gave a curt nod, and Amethyst stepped into the dressing room. Cobra closed the door.

Sanjay had visited Amethyst in the hospital several times, but he hadn't seen her since. Today, she was a completely different woman than the one he'd known before the accident. Her sprightly, graceful movements that had always reminded him of a butterfly were now timid and halting. Her wings had been clipped. The light has gone out of her.

"I got you extra whipped cream on your mocha, Devlin," she said. "The other two drinks are frothy cappuccinos for me and Sanjay."

Devlin stared at the cup like it was poisoned. Which he probably thought it was. Sanjay took one of the cappuccinos and Amethyst handed Devlin his mocha.

"I've given up sugar," Devlin sputtered.

"Since when?" She scowled at him.

"Switch with me, then." Sanjay swapped their drinks.

Devlin watched Amethyst's face carefully. Was he looking to see her reaction to switching the supposedly poisoned cup?

"This is ridiculous," Sanjay muttered. He took a sip of the mocha. Devlin didn't try to stop him. Which, if Devlin was truly worried about the mocha being poisoned, showed the true nature of Zephyr Devlin's character.

"It's all right?" Devlin asked.

"A bit sweet for my taste—hey!"

"Thanks for the taste test." Devlin swapped their drinks back and took a gulp of the mocha.

Though he didn't appreciate being used as a king's taster, Sanjay was far happier with the cappuccino.

Amethyst pressed a hand to her throat. "I think...I think need some air." She coughed, took a step forward, then stumbled. Devlin caught her.

"Careful, my dear." He, too, began to choke.

Sanjay stared at Amethyst. Were those horns emerging from her temples? No, he couldn't really be seeing that, could he? Amethyst wasn't the Devil. She wasn't... Oh no... Sanjay felt the room swaying underneath his feet.

They'd been drugged.

"Call for help," Sanjay croaked. At least that's what he meant to say. He wasn't entirely sure the words escaped his lips. Or if he'd made a sound at all before he hit the ground.

# # #

When Sanjay woke up, the room was no longer spinning or swaying, but he felt like vomiting. Was that the sound of the ocean he'd heard right as he was waking up? And what was that sulfurous smell? *Brimstone?* Not brimstone. Stale coffee. Devlin's coffee cup lay askew on the linoleum floor next to Sanjay, its light brown contents forming a heart shape on the tan linoleum. Sanjay's paper coffee cup had overturned and spilt onto the floor as well. The shape looked like a butterfly. Or perhaps a hummingbird. *Focus, Sanjay.*

He shook himself. Bad idea. A wave of nausea passed over him. A small plastic trash can rested under the vanity, and although it was only a few feet away, it looked like miles. Gingerly, he pushed himself onto his knees.

Devlin and Amethyst both lay still on the floor next to him. Devlin lay on his back, one arm outstretched and his neck turned to one side. His eyes were open. *Unblinking.*

Sanjay felt for a pulse, but couldn't find one. Oh, God… Had the Devil had really gotten him?

"Amethyst?" he whispered.

No response. His hands trembled as he moved to Amethyst's still body and felt for a pulse. This time, he found one.

Sanjay gave himself a few moments to breathe with relief, then realized he needed to act. He fumbled for his phone to call 9-1-1, but before he could do so, banging sounded at the door. "Come in!" he croaked.

"We've been trying," Cobra called through the door. "It's bolted from the inside. You weren't answering. I knew nobody got past me to get inside, but it's been so long I was about to call the police."

Sanjay tugged on the door, but Cobra was right. It was still bolted from the inside. His drugged reflexes were slow, and it took him two attempts to unlatch it. "Call for help," he wheezed, then passed out again.

Sanjay woke up to the sharp prick of a needle in his arm. Opening his eyes, he discovered he was in a hospital bed.

He hated hospitals.

His eyes focused on a nurse. "Is he dead?"

A nurse with kind eyes met his gaze. "Let me get the doctor."

"Is he dead?"

"I'll see if the detective is still here. But first, you need the doctor."

As soon as the nurse left the room, Sanjay swung his legs over the edge of the bed. He was relieved to find he was still wearing his trousers, though his white dress shirt had been replaced with a gown that allowed an IV to be attached to his arm. Why did they make these gowns so scratchy? He grabbed the IV pole and poked his head out the door. The nurse disappeared around the corner. He scooted down the hallway in his socks.

He found Amethyst sitting up in a bed that looked much like his own. Her face was pale, her hair was tangled, and a few minor scratches crisscrossed her fingers. She smiled when she saw Sanjay. "I'm glad you're okay."

"Devlin?" Sanjay asked.

Her face fell. She shook her head.

"The coffee," said Sanjay "Our coffee was poisoned."

Amethyst shook her head again. "The detective told me Devlin didn't die of poison. All three of us were drugged, but it was nothing serious. Just a knockout drug. That's not how he died."

"How—" Sanjay began, but he had a terrible feeling he already knew the answer.

"Devlin *drowned.*"

"Locked inside that dressing room with us?" Sanjay murmured.

"I saw a weird guy around the theater earlier," Amethyst said. "I told the detective about him. Cobra knew about him, too."

"But Cobra was outside the door the whole time," Sanjay murmured. He willed the tickle of an idea in the back of his foggy mind to show itself. He closed his eyes and gripped the IV stand more tightly.

"Cobra went to check on the stalker," Amethyst said. "The creepy guy must have gotten inside our dressing room when Cobra was gone."

Sanjay shook his head. "No. Cobra's job involved not leaving Devlin's side. He was working with someone else, though, so that's who would have checked on a problem patron. I'm sure they'll confirm that."

"Oh… I didn't realize… God, that means it really was impossible for anyone to get inside and drown Devlin. You don't think—" She pulled a thin blanket tightly around herself. "Could it really have been the Devil?"

"The coffee," Sanjay said. An idea was forming in his mind. No… it couldn't be. Could there have been enough coffee in their cups to drown Devlin? Surely that wasn't possible. And yet there was something in Amethyst's eyes. A hardness that hadn't been there before as she spoke of the Devil.

"I wonder if there was enough coffee to drown Devlin if he was unconscious," Sanjay said, his eyes locked on Amethyst's, seeing what she'd make of the veiled accusation. He doubted it was possible, especially since their drinks were mostly foam and whipped cream.

As she held his gaze, he was again struck by the fact that she wasn't the same woman he'd known before the accident. Her spirit. Her very being. It had died when her dreams were crushed by the stage light. The accident that wasn't an accident.

A flash of emotion widened her eyes. "Oh, didn't I say? The detective said salt water from the ocean killed Devlin. Just like the Devil said he'd do to him. The detective found the threatening letter as well."

Sanjay glanced over his shoulder. The door was open, but the two of them were alone. "Where's the detective you mentioned?"

"She left. You were unconscious for such a long time."

Grasping the IV pole, Sanjay took a step back until he was nearly in the doorway. He looked over his shoulder again. "It was you," he said. "You killed him."

"Why would I do that? Without Devlin, I don't have anyone else who'll hire me."

"Sometimes revenge is worth it."

Her eyes blazed.

"I'm sorry," Sanjay whispered. "I'm sorry he did that to you."

"I don't know what you're talking about." Amethyst's voice barely shook. She was a performer, after all. But the rage simmered under her words.

"Last year," said Sanjay, "when we all thought someone was trying to hurt Devlin, he made it up. All of it. *That's* how the culprit was invisible on the stage when he fell."

"Why would he do that?" Amethyst spat out. "No, I don't care. I need rest. You should go."

"Devlin was the one who rigged the lights to fall last year," Sanjay said. "That's what must have happened. He made them fall—on you. He couldn't bear the thought you becoming more famous than he was. And you surely would have. So he clipped your wings instead."

"That's an interesting theory. But how could I have killed him? If you're sure Cobra was still posted at the door, then only the Devil himself could bring the ocean to our little dressing room." Amethyst blinked innocently at Sanjay. "You're the one who said nobody got past Cobra. It's impossible. Unless you're saying I summoned the Devil to do my bidding."

She was right. It was impossible.

He closed his eyes and thought back on what he'd seen in that dressing room. It was sparse. No sink. No drain. A dressing table with a mirror, an empty clothing rack, and a shelf that held a few books, an empty candy dish, and a bouquet of flowers.

"The flowers," said Sanjay, his eyes popping open. "Wilted roses in a vase. They wilted so quickly because you put salt water into the vase of roses delivered to Devlin from an anonymous fan. That's why they were already drooping. The empty candy bowl in our dressing room was huge. Big enough to drown an unconscious person."

For the first time, Amethyst's smile faltered. She quickly recovered. "I don't remember seeing any water—salt or otherwise, in the room. You're imagining things. If I drowned him there, not all the water would be in his lungs. Where did the supposed water go?"

"You drank it."

Her eyes flashed with anger. "People can't safely drink ocean water."

"But magicians who know how to regurgitate can. Which you used to do. I heard the sound of water right as I was waking up. Did you drink the salt water right as I was starting to stir, then throw it up right after witnesses found us? We were drugged, so it would have been natural for you to say you felt sick and run to the restroom."

Amethyst balled her hand into a tight fist. The one that hadn't been crushed by the stage light exactly one year before. In Sanjay's current state, he was relatively certain she could knock him out simply by breathing on him. As soon as she moved, Sanjay took one more step backward to the door.

"Detective," he said to the empty hallway outside the room, "I don't know if it's possible to test that she swallowed salt water she then threw up, but I bet you'll find those scratches on Amethyst's hands came from the thorns on the roses."

"No—!" Amethyst shouted, but instead of leaping off the bed and calling Sanjay's bluff, she collapsed onto the pillows. There was no more fight left in her.

"You really thought revenge was the answer?" Sanjay asked softly.

"Of course I wanted revenge! You were right. I realized a while ago that it was Devlin who dropped that light on me last year. It was never meant for him. A stage magician with impeccable timing would also know how to make it look as if he was almost hit by a car. All that talk of the Devil was an act. He couldn't stand the idea of me outshining him. I had one more year in my contract with him, but I was already doing my own shows on the side and getting better press than he was. He only let me out of my contract that day because he was going to make sure I'd never be able to perform again."

"You knew his secret about nearly drowning when he was a boy. You knew how to frighten him today."

he nodded. "He had to tell me so I'd understand why he refused to do certain types of illusions. After what he did to me, I wanted to make him suffer before I killed him. I would have been more famous than he was if he hadn't done this to me. Instead, I had to make my own deal with the Devil. I suppose I'll still be famous. Just for a different reason. I'm the devil who killed Zephyr Devlin."

Dalliances by Art Taylor

#

16. A detective novel should contain no long descriptive passages, no literary dallying with side-issues, no subtly worked-out character analyses, no "atmospheric" preoccupations. Such matters have no vital place in a record of crime and deduction. They hold up the action, and introduce issues irrelevant to the main purpose, which is to state a problem, analyze it, and bring it to a successful conclusion. To be sure, there must be a sufficient descriptiveness and character delineation to give the novel verisimilitude; but when an author of a detective story has reached that literary point where he has created a gripping sense of reality and enlisted the reader's interest and sympathy in the characters and the problem, he has gone as far in the purely "literary" technique as is legitimate and compatible with the needs of a criminal-problem document. A detective story is a grim business, and the reader goes to it, not for literary furbelows and style and beautiful descriptions and the projection of moods, but for mental stimulation and intellectual activity—just as he goes to a ball game or to a crossword puzzle. Lectures between innings at the Polo Grounds on the beauties of nature would scarcely enhance the interest in the struggle between two contesting baseball nines, and dissertations on etymology and orthography interspersed in the definitions of a crossword puzzle would tend only to irritate the solver bent on making the words interlock correctly.

Inspector Beckett Blackwood knew the proper approach to solving an investigation.

Examine the scene of the crime, the position of the body, the fingerprints or the lack of them, the forensic evidence in all directions.

Interview the witnesses, hear their words, read their body language.

Sift these clues, weight them proportionally, appreciate fully the ones that emerged as important, discount prudently the ones that didn't.

Chart motives, opportunities, and means. Build timelines.

Find patterns. Examine contradictions.

Bring to light the lies.

Shine that light on the truth.

Beckett knew all this, but with his latest case, his focus kept wandering astray.

Still intent on discovering who murdered Aidan Blunt and bringing justice to one of the two women who'd likely killed him, Beckett increasingly found himself struggling to apprehend something deeper and more urgent about attraction, desire, and the mystery of love.

# # #

Beckett hadn't even known about the women at first, not while he and Chase were following through the initial steps of the investigation—the routine, that formula.

They'd hurried to the hotel after the call that a maid had discovered a body mid-morning. They'd interviewed the maid and the manager on duty. They'd learned the name that the deceased had registered under—Aidan Blunt—and the fact that he had not called the front desk, had not ordered room service, had not in fact been seen or heard from by anyone on staff since checking in a few minutes after three p.m. the previous afternoon. The hotel, disappointingly, had no security cameras on the deceased's floor or in the lobby.

They'd surveyed the crime scene—a slickly contemporary junior suite—and assessed the disturbing state of the corpse. The deceased, wearing an untucked button-down and a pair of jeans over bare feet, was slumped face-forward against the partial wall between a small seating area and the bedroom, as if he had been moving from one space to the other but had veered off-course and died en route. (Something about the shape of the dead man's face, the graying of the sideburns, the crow's feet reminded Beckett with brief unease of his father, his father as he had seen him when he was younger. Then he recognized that the dead man was, of course, closer to his own age now, and he felt some fresh layer of empathy with the shock imprinted in those eyes, still startlingly wide open. He reached into his pocket, pulled out his notebook and pen, his finger brushing the frayed edge of a business card lingering uncomfortably there.)

They'd left it to the medical examiner to inspect more closely the body and the wineglass on the floor and the smear of red wine splashed against the wall.

Except for the death and its evidence, the room had seemed largely unused—the man's suitcase unopened, the bed still crisply made. A single hand towel had been unfolded on the basin, and several items sat on the coffee table: an iPhone, an open bottle of wine, and a corkscrew, the cork still skewered. The man's shoes had been tucked loosely underneath the table, as if casually kicked off.

The bottle had earned most of Beckett's attention. The label carried a single word—INTRINSIC—above the image of a dark-haired woman. Her arms were raised above her head, as if she were dancing or twirling or in some brand of ecstasy. Her hair whipped across her face. Her dress was an unfurling of red ribbons.

Beckett lifted the bottle, sniffed tentatively at it, sloshed it gently, and then peered inside.

"What do you know about wine?" he asked Chase.

Chase glanced toward the body. "Enough to know I wouldn't pour a glass of that myself, Inspector."

"We'll run a tox screen, of course," the medical examiner said without looking up. "The bottle, the glass, the . . ." He gestured vaguely—at the corpse or the stain or both.

The death had occurred late afternoon or early evening of the previous day, the coroner speculated, promising a more precise timeline later, and he handed over the wallet from the dead man's pocket. The identification confirmed that Aidan Blunt had given his actual name at check-in. His own business card—embossed, a small stack in a silver case—provided his place of work, an investment firm downtown. Beckett copied down the information.

And so the formula had continued to progress: Interviews with two of the firm's partners, the expected responses of shock and sadness and disbelief, several protestations that he'd been a good man and that no one would've wished him any harm, the discovery that he had no next-of-kin—parents deceased, no wife or ex-wife, no children, no siblings.

But a single bit of important information had presented itself—courtesy of the deceased's administrative assistant, whose desktop calendar was synced with her employer's phone.

"Mr. Blunt's schedule shows an appointment with Gabrielle at three-thirty p.m. and with Marissa at four," the assistant had said, a thirty-something blonde in a herringbone blazer. "Except for the hotel reservation, this was all Mr. Blunt had planned for the balance of the afternoon and evening."

"Do you know these women? The deceased's relationship with them? The nature of these appointments?"

The woman's face had been, as Beckett thought about it later, a perfect mix of candor and circumspection. Her blue eyes met Beckett's straight on, without blinking. "I'm certain it would be better to ask them."

"And do you have their contact information?"

Candor and circumspection *and* efficiency—her lips curving into a thin smile. "Of course."

#

"Which is the greater asset in an administrative assistant," Beckett asked Chase as they headed for their car, "organization or discretion?"

"Attractiveness, sir," Chase said, not a moment's hesitation. "And I'll bet this Gabrielle and Marissa are some tasty snacks, too. "

Snacks? Beckett thought, but he chose not to embarrass himself. "What do you think the deceased's plans were with them?"

Chase stopped short, and Beckett almost lost his balance as he pivoted to face him. From Chase's bewildered expression—head cocked, eyes narrowed—Beckett knew he'd stumbled into embarrassment anyway.

"Hotel, wine, women? Respectfully, sir, you're old, but you're not *that* old, are you?"

# # #

So… sex then? Beckett thought. Sex, of course? Because that "of course" was implied in Chase's reaction, his incredulous tone.

But no—Beckett wavered in this idea—I am not so old, that's not the point.

The point was: even if sex were at the core of the case, there were so many possibilities and permutations for assembling all the participants together in a coherent manner.

A crime scene, a murder mystery specifically, was a tale with a blank in the middle of it (this was something Beckett had said often), a hole that needed to be filled with the *who*, the *how*, and the *why* for the narrative to be complete—and that last aspect of *why*, the motive, was often the key piece that brought the entire story to completion.

But if hotel, wine, and women added up to sex ("sex, of course" Beckett wrote in his notebook) as a central motive of the deceased's late afternoon plans, was sex also somehow central to the motive behind the crime, too? And then what about the connection between the two halves of that question? This next thought built on another of Beckett's beliefs about a murder investigation: It wasn't solely the motives of the killer but the motives of the victim that helped fill the blanks in the story, the interplay and intersection of the two, the clash between the different desires of the players involved.

Player, Beckett thought, and he lingered over the word. Beckett had considered the word as an actor in some drama, but it was also (and this next would've been Chase's version, Beckett knew) a man pursuing many women indiscriminately, perhaps indiscreetly as well, without any significant attachment. Was the deceased a player in that way, too, simply looking to satisfy his lusts, or was he sincerely in love? Or what was the balance between lust and love? Were they two sides of a coin, distinct but attached? Or ends of a spectrum, with shades of emphasis between the extremes?

More to the case at hand, was it love or lust that primarily defined the deceased's relationship with the women? And love or lust to the same degree with each? From the opposite perspective—what were the women seeking from him, and in what balance in each of their cases? And given only a half-hour difference between the meeting times, did either woman know about the other?

Perhaps the deceased had planned to break up with one of the women to pursue the other—declaring his own ultimate preference. Perhaps he was partial to both, trying to reach some decision, *forcing* a decision by calling them together. But how might the women have reacted to either of these possibilities?

Love triangles had often, too often, been part of the complex emotional geometry of Beckett's murder investigations. He wrote the word *Geometry* as well, and then a list of emotions. Jealousy and envy. Pride, humiliation, and resentment. Insecurity and shame and fear. Embarrassment, outrage, helplessness, despair, anger… The list rolled on. Despite what Chase may have thought about Beckett's naïveté, Beckett had ceased to be surprised by the range of . . . interests that people had, the myriad preferences and passions and proclivities. (He hesitated to add *perversions*—recognizing each to their own, not wanting to judge.)

In short: anything could be happening in the story unfolding before them, and with such range, it was perhaps inappropriate to speculate too far ahead of the facts. But Beckett's mind played forward nonetheless—and backward, too, to his own life, his mother and father (the resemblance he couldn't shake) and what had seemed to him once (once) the ideal of relationships—his father reading his paper, sipping a martini on the rocks, while his mother moved here and there through the kitchen, cabinet to table to stove—and then thinking of his own wife, the stability and steadiness of his own marriage, its own routine of orderliness and ordinariness.

Notes thickened on the pages. The business card in his pocket sat heavier.

#

Beckett returned to the hotel and commandeered a meeting room: small conference table, a half-dozen chairs around it, a whiteboard he wasn't sure whether he would use. Chase had contacted Gabrielle and Marissa and scheduled their interviews a half-hour apart, an echo with the deceased's own schedule that Beckett only recognized later.

Gabrielle Riley was the first interrogation and ultimately proved to be the older of the two women—early- to mid-forties perhaps. Her features were sharp-edged—short hair, narrowing eyes, high cheekbones, a slim nose—and her lips pressed themselves regularly into a tight smirk, the lipstick purplish-black. She wore earth tones (ivory linen top, coffee-colored trousers), minimal jewelry (silver hoops at her ears, a slim silver choker, nothing on her wrists or fingers), and a mix of maturity, confidence, and world-weariness.

"Given that I'm obviously a suspect," she said, "shouldn't you be interrogating me at the police station?" She'd carried herself into the room with coolness and confidence, settled into the seat at the head of the table like a CEO ready to deliver directives to her team. There was no hint of loss or grief.

"My boss is quirky," Chase said, taking his own seat. He'd led her in from the lobby. "Like those detectives on TV. No offense, sir."

Beckett waved his hand. "Being adjacent to the scene of the crime is both practical and convenient."

"Perhaps less convenient for some than others." Gabrielle offered an empty smile. "And less pleasant."

"My apologies," Beckett said, realizing his own tone belied any sincerity. "But I appreciate you accommodating us so swiftly. We have only a few questions." He poised his pen over his notebook.

Gabrielle gave the briefest of nods.

"How long had you known the deceased?"

Gabrielle leaned back in her chair. "The deceased and I began our relationship two years ago. We met at a charity ball and saw one another more frequently after that."

"Your job?"

"I own a real estate agency. Brokerage, management, investments. My firm was a sponsor for the ball."

"And when you say you and the deceased saw one another more frequently, that was social, business, perhaps both?"

"I oversee my own investments," she said. "Purely social."

"And by social"—he looked up—"you mean romantic?"

Gabrielle met Beckett's gaze, tightened her jaw. "By social, I mean sexual."

Beckett glanced at Chase, who raised an eyebrow—a hint of triumph in the younger man's expression.

"Would you say, then"—Beckett returned to his notebook—"*not* romantic?"

She sighed, more impatience than wistfulness. "The deceased and I had much in common. We were both professional, both serious about our work and our lives, both driven. Strong personalities, no nonsense."

"Nonsense?"

"I try to be very clear about what I want—and what I don't. Planning, determination, lines in the sand. The deceased seemed to feel the same way."

Beckett laid down his pen. "You are perhaps mocking me?" he asked. "Using the word *deceased*?"

"It's appropriate," she said. "He's dead, isn't he? But he was already dead to me—the moment I walked out of that hotel room."

"Figuratively, you mean?"

She laughed lightly. "I'm not offering a confession, no. He was very much still alive at that point."

"Reassuring to hear," Beckett said. "Can you tell me the nature of your appointment yesterday?"

"The deceased—*Aidan*—had a proposal for me," she said. "Again, social, not business. But the terms were unacceptable."

"As you said, you're clear about what you want."

"Exactly."

"And what were these unacceptable terms?"

Gabrielle stretched out the fingers of her right hand, closed them into a light fist.

"He told me, with a mischievous look in his eye, that he was seeing someone else, and that he'd invited both of us to the hotel. She would be arriving later. He said he'd invited me first, because I was more . . . *sophisticated* is one of the words he used. *Experienced. Enlightened.*"

"The other woman was younger."

"Yes"—hesitation—"though he was intelligent enough not to phrase it like that. She would take more convincing, that's what he said, and he felt sure I could help with that. A new beginning for all of us, that was how he envisioned it. He'd bought a special bottle of wine—a toast to the future."

"He was proposing a relationship? Or merely"—Beckett searched for the word—"an encounter?"

"He was so focused on what he wanted in the moment—excited, anticipatory—I don't believe he was thinking clearly beyond that, whatever he was *saying* about the future. You know how men get." She leveled her eyes at Beckett. "He did that thing with his hands I hate so much. Turning the wrists up, widening his fingers, like he was gesturing toward possibilities—but it's really a mark of inarticulation, of helplessness, inviting someone else to do the work of filling in the blanks."

"Whatever he was proposing, though—you weren't interested?"

"I don't share the stage. Or the bed. And so I left. He pleaded for me to stay, to keep an open mind—to at least *meet* her. *Marissa.*" The name seemed to carry a sour taste, the way she spit it out. "I saw her in the lobby when I left. Crinkly hair, sparkly sundress, a low-grade trifle. If *that's* what he wanted, I was *clearly* not the woman for him."

"You felt anger about his . . . preferences? His betrayal?"

"Angry enough to get revenge? That's the question, isn't it?" She gave a small snort—disgust, dismissal. "If I wanted revenge, murder wouldn't be the choice I'd make. It's too easy. I'd want . . . pain, suffering. Do you know what Thai women do to cheating husbands? The trend in Thailand, I mean? They remove the offending . . . member. Thai surgeons are specialists in handling reattachments. I read this recently. I'm . . . unclear whether I could do that myself, but it's certainly more my style. Let him *feel* the regrets. Let him live with that memory for the rest of his life without . . ."

"Without?"

"Me."

Chase shifted in his seat, and then again. Beckett turned his attention to the whiteboard, focused on the blankness, sorting through his notes in his mind.

"Did you ever feel love for the deceased?" he asked. "Or do you believe he loved you? Or is that nonsense, too?"

Gabrielle seemed to consider that. "Aidan went through the motions of love. He sent roses, gave gifts he"—Beckett could hear a pause, a stumble—"gifts he *thought* I'd like. But really it was about him, not me, not things I would've wanted, not my style. More evidence that he wasn't paying attention, didn't understand me. I kept some of them— only for when he was around, the way you put out the awful afghan your grandmother made you whenever she comes to visit. Otherwise, I passed them along to others on my staff, donated to Goodwill. I disposed of the rest of it last night." She twisted each of her wrists back and forth, as if brushing away dirt. "I'm not the sentimental type, clearly, no patience with *that* nonsense. So . . . no, I don't think what he felt for me was real love. And I felt little for him. None now."

Beckett could feel Chase watching him—some message being sent, some certainty the younger man must have been feeling, some clue he thought meant more than it did. Beckett turned the other way, stared again into the blankness of the whiteboard.

"Where did you go after leaving the hotel?" he finally asked.

"I went home, stayed by myself. No alibi." She shrugged. "But then I didn't know I would need one."

"And if you had killed him—"

"I would've arranged an alibi, yes. I'm a professional, as I said. I handle my own affairs, and I handle them well."

# # #

"Is it me or did the room warm up when she left?" Chase let out a long breath. "Ice princess—wow. No, scratch that. Ice *queen*. No doubt she could've killed him, never blinked an eye."

"She said she'd never loved him." Beckett didn't look up, kept writing in his notebook. "Wouldn't someone need to care in order to kill?"

"Maybe," said Chase. "Maybe a lot of other emotions could get you there, too. And that thing she said about Thai women, is that true? I need to Google that one."

Beckett did look up then. Already, Chase had pulled out his phone, was pecking at the screen.

"Or"—Chase winced—"maybe not."

"It's a dramatic story, at least," Beckett said. "And intentionally or not, a distracting one."

He returned to his notes.

What is it that a man wants? he'd written. *And a woman, too, of course?*

#

What is it that a man wants? And a woman too, equally germane?

Beckett corrected himself even as he thought it: What do *people* want from one another? But then he second-guessed himself again—because how *did* gender figure into the equation? Women from Venus, men from Mars? Or what varieties beyond such binaries, and how specific to the individual person?

Perhaps each person had an ideal partner somewhere in their minds, even if they couldn't articulate those characteristics clearly—or a type that they were attracted toward, drawn to unconsciously, inevitably, time after time. The unintentional draw was more likely—physical preferences more emphatic maybe in this regard. Tall, dark, and handsome—this was the cliché. And another: Gentlemen prefer blondes. But surely other men were drawn more strongly to brunettes or to redheads, or to bobs or braids or waves, or to a voluptuous figure or a slender frame, or . . .

Fun-sized, Chase had called the woman he'd last dated. *Just the way I like 'em.* Beckett hadn't pursued the conversation further. Each to his own.

And beyond the physical, an array of other characteristics. Intelligent or emotional in varying degrees. Strong or sarcastic or submissive. Traditionally feminine. Sporty and athletic. Elegant. Tomboyish. Prim and proper. Witty. Playful. Which combination of intrinsic qualities and external attributes, and more, constituted each person's particular ideal?

Beckett realized he was leaning in on men's preferences about women—stuck in his own gaze? And then that "and more" echoed, because of shared interests and hobbies and passions and—

Beckett stopped again. He was thinking of all this too simply, too straightforwardly—simple-mindedly really in so many directions. It was the word *shared* that brought him short this time.

Even on the question of interests and hobbies, what was behind the assumption about similar interests as the root of attractiveness? Why not find someone whose differences broadened your horizons? Beckett had known couples who thrived in both directions.

Another cliché: Opposites attract.

And the present-tenseness and bold simplicity of that cliché struck him as well—as if not simply universal but eternal, as if what holds true for attraction today will hold true tomorrow as well.

(More of Chase's words: I'm not looking for Miss Right, just Miss Right *Now*.)

Timing weighed heavily here—and the various, and potentially recursive, shifts in context, negotiation, evaluation, epiphany, decision. In short, tastes change, particularly as you work through the stages of your life, as you learn, as you grow. Sowing oats, ready to settle down, mid-life crisis . . . And why, oh *why* was his mind so mired suddenly in these clichés? But there was truth here—and a memory popping to mind: a woman Beckett had known in college, a conversation at reunion, the way she beamed at her new husband, tall and gangly with thick spectacles: "I was always attracted to the *jocks*," she said. "That first marriage—such a mistake. Then I met Glen, who's *nothing* like I ever wanted. But honestly, I couldn't be happier."

What sparked attraction at this moment? And this one? What satisfied short-term interests, and how was love sustained over the longer term? Were the qualities one looked for in a partner for a lifetime starkly different than those in a partner for the night? Were the two in conflict with one another? How did past experience impact future possibility? And what caused the roots of love to wither?

(Beckett did not believe in soulmates, but neither did he believe that choosing a life partner was merely a question of practical suitability. He'd seen firsthand the limitations of faith in both directions, and he knew that the sustainability of a relationship was built on communication, on compromise, on . . . Reflecting on his own youth, Beckett considered now how his own ideal leaned toward red hair, a flair for cooking, a grace and elegance that would've been a marked contrast to his own admitted awkwardness. His wife, though, was a dusky brunette who relied on canned foods and frozen entrées. She spent most of her afternoons binge-watching true crime TV—part of her own attraction to Beckett himself, as she explained it, their similar interests. They had been together for more than twenty years.)

What had drawn Aidan Gabrielle's way? Was her stylishness attractive? Was her aloofness a challenge? Was her prominence in their shared community a useful asset? And if so—if *all* that—what had drawn his attention elsewhere? A similar type? Entirely different?

As if on cue, there came a knock at the conference room door.

#

Chase went to answer it, but Marissa Brooks was already opening the door, shyly stepping in.

The contrast between the two women stood out from the start—both Marissa's hesitancy compared to Gabrielle's confidence but also their looks, carriage, manner, dress. Marissa was clearly younger than Gabrielle, fifteen to twenty years, Beckett guessed, and she exuded a sense of wholesomeness and innocence, eyes literally wide, dimples in her cheeks, lip gloss the color of strawberries—and a darker redness under puffy eyes, the hints of actual grief a stark contrast, too. Marissa's hair was a layer of short curls, curving around her ears. A white blouse draped off her shoulders, a pleated skirt hung barely mid-thigh, white crew socks accented black pumps, her handbag was too large for her.

("Young and perky," Chase said later. "That Aidan was a lucky bastard, wasn't he? Him smashing the both of them, yeah?" Beckett would find himself lingering over both words. Had Chase meant *perky* physically or more abstractedly? And didn't *smashing* mean *lovely, marvelous, sublime*? In Chase's phrasing, it sounded like a verb.)

"Should I sit, or . . . ?" Marissa's bracelets jangled as she gestured, and when Chase answered that anywhere was good, she moved toward a seat to the side of the table's head. Different from Gabrielle here as well, Beckett thought—her choice of seat, the trembling in her fingers as she pulled out the chair, her apprehensive glance his way. What had drawn Aidan toward her?

"I'm sorry for your loss," Beckett said.

"It's awful"—the words nearly under her breath. She didn't meet his eyes.

"You'd known the deceased for how long?"

"A year, a little less than a year," she said. "Aidan and I met at a gallery walk. An art co-op. I have a studio there." She shook her wrist lightly. "Jewelry designer."

"He came specifically to see your work?"

"Oh," she said. "No, it was a First Friday thing. Once a month, cheap wine in plastic glasses, cheese and crackers, and all the studios open. A friend of his dragged him there, and he wandered into my space. We started chatting. One thing led to another, and then . . ." Her face had begun to beam a little but then shifted and crumbled again. "I still can't believe . . ." She touched a corner of her eye.

Emotion, Beckett thought, perhaps that was simply the draw. Gabrielle had had a short supply.

"This was where the relationship began? That night?"

"No, not immediately. That 'one thing led to another' took longer. But he was . . . attentive, you know? Even from the start. The way he looked at me, the way he was admiring my work. There was . . . appreciation. I thought it was for my jewelry. He bought several pieces that night, some of the more expensive pieces. Honestly, I figured for his wife or girlfriend—*taken*, that's what I thought, kind of tamping down my own attraction. But then a couple weeks later, he called and asked me out."

"So you suspected from that beginning he might be seeing someone else?"

"No, that's not, that wasn't what I meant. I mean, I'd assumed, and then . . . I guess I'd assumed not. We'd never had the conversation. Exclusivity, you know. Not explicitly. Maybe I had . . . wondered? At first, yes. The way he was always busy. Sure, I knew there was the possibility that he was seeing someone else, but . . . He's also got a business, he's . . . I don't know. *Older.* Real job. *High-powered* job. But over time, as we got closer, I didn't *think* so?" Beckett could hear the question marks punctuating so many of her sentences. "Because it felt special. Between us."

She lifted her hand to her face again—and at first, Beckett thought it was to cover tears, but then he noticed how the light had shifted, the sun cutting through the window and across her eyes, glinting against her earrings, a pair of gold butterflies—more of her handiwork, Beckett assumed. He gestured to Chase to lower the blinds.

"You saw the deceased yesterday," he said. "Around what time?"

"Thank you," Marissa said to Chase, and then to Beckett. "At four. Aidan asked me to meet him at four."

"Did he tell you yesterday about the other woman in his life?"

Marissa blushed—redness suffusing her neck and the top of her chest. "Yes."

Beckett waited. Why would the deceased have told her this? Gabrielle was gone, out of the picture—at the moment, at least. Was he anticipating that she would reconsider? Laying groundwork to continue his plan? Many other follow-up questions he could've asked. What did the deceased say about the other woman? How did he characterize the two relationships? What was he searching for, what was he lacking? How did she see herself in this triangle? Did these questions matter?

He opted instead for the interrogator's trick—leave silence for her to fill.

"Aidan was"—she sighed—"upset when I got here. I could tell that something was wrong. I tried to comfort him, sat with him on the couch, rubbed his back— supportive, you know, encouraging him to open up. If you love someone . . ."

"You would call it love then?" Despite his plan to let her speak, he surprised himself, blurting out the question.

Marissa seemed taken aback, too, as if slapped by the word. And then, slowly, the tears did come, welling lightly at the corners of her eyes.

"I would. I think I would." She wiped them away. "I loved him, yes. But then to find out that what he felt for me was . . ."

"Yes?"

"He told me that he cared for both of us equally. He'd wanted me to meet her, he'd wanted … He told me he wanted both of us. In his life."

Chase rolled his eyes. ("In his bed," he'd tell Beckett later. "That's all he wanted.")

"How did this make you feel?"

"Surprised. Sad. Conflicted . . . because I loved him, like I said, and when someone you love wants something, you kind of want that for them, too, right? But . . . *this*. I mean, I wasn't sure. It was all so new. I told him . . . I told him I needed to think about it."

"And then you left?"

"He wanted me to stay, asked me to stay with him. He had a bottle of wine, he had the hotel room, obviously. A splurge. Room service, he said, and then time to talk it over more . . . To persuade me—pressure me, I guess. I'm not stupid. But I needed space. So yes, I left."

"What time was this?"

"Four-thirty, four-forty-five? A little later? I don't know . . . It was all so much, I wasn't—I wasn't watching the time."

"And this was the last you saw of the deceased?"

"Yes." She bit her lip, shook her head. "Aidan."

"What did you do after that?"

"Took a walk, called a friend and started to tell her about it, but *didn't*, because I knew what she'd say—and then whatever happened, she'd keep saying it. Even if you get over someone treating you . . . *badly*, your friends, they won't. Your family won't. But I kept thinking about it—considering. I called him back later, because . . . well, because I felt myself thinking, why not? Why not try it? I mean, I was open, if that's what he wanted, and if I didn't . . . If it didn't feel good, then . . ."

Beckett saw Chase mark his own notebook—*check the phone records*, he felt sure.

"You talked to him then, explained this."

"Call went to voicemail. And . . . I didn't leave a message. Because suddenly, well, jealousy, you know? I figured he wasn't answering it because he was with her, and then thinking that—*feeling* that—well, that told me that no, maybe I didn't want to do this, because *that* was the direction it would be going in, right? Wondering where you stood. So *clearly* I needed to think about it more, and then this morning . . . well, then you called."

"What time did you call him last night?"

"Seven-thirty? Eight?"

Beckett nodded. The man had been dead by then—but the question, of course, was whether Marissa had already known that?

Two timelines ran through his mind. First, the timeline of the previous evening—visits by two women, staggered assignations, intended to intersect, and then, if both women were to be believed, their departures, the latest around 4:45, and the deceased's death late afternoon or early evening. And then the larger timeline, the history of the relationships: Marissa with Aidan for about a year, and Gabrielle with him for twice that—a more established relationship to some degree, though not what Beckett would call long-term, not a marriage, not even living together. Still . . .

What expectations? What commitment? From any of the players, he meant—Aidan included. And did time together matter? Gabrielle, though a longer relationship, seemed (*seemed*) not to care, while Marissa seemed (or only seemed?) more invested emotionally. . . . The question he asked Chase echoed: Wouldn't someone need to care to kill? And then the insistent thought returned that the victim's motives were as important as the killer's—not only the women's sense of surprise, betrayal, anger, jealousy, all those rolling out, but the deceased's as well, seemingly hoping to keep both women in his life and instead seeing both walk out.

Beckett thought of the piece of paper in his pocket. Felt the futility of other questions he already knew the answer to.

"Thank you for your time," he told Marissa. He gestured to Chase to lead her out.

But, as she rose to leave, Beckett found himself asking one more anyway—a gratuitous question, he knew, even as he asked it: "I don't mean to be too . . . personal," he said, "but your earrings, the butterflies . . . You designed these yourself, too, yes? Not only the bracelets."

Marissa smiled. "Yes," she said. As if by reflex, she reached up to her ear to touch them. The butterflies' wings were rich mosaics of color, out-lined and striated by thin lines of gold. "I'm not sure they're very good. It's a new technique. New to me, I mean. A lot of time to put in, a lot of investment, materials." Another reddening across the top of her chest. Sudden self-consciousness. Pride brimming beneath the modesty? She lifted her shoulders, pulling her bag tighter against her—almost a hug, Beckett thought at first. "I invest a lot of myself in my work. A passion project. I . . . I have an Etsy shop, too."

"They're lovely," he said. "The earrings. You're a passionate woman, it seems—with your art, with people. It's"—he thought about Gabri-elle, her coldness, her control—"a breath of fresh air."

Yet another cliché, but as he said it, she seemed relieved, brighter.

# # #

"Look at you, Inspector," Chase said, returning to the conference room. " 'Your earrings are so *lovely* '"—mimicking Beckett's voice. "What would your wife say about you flirting with a cute young thing?"

"I wasn't flirting," Beckett said.

"So that's your type, huh? Young and perky"—and that was when the rest of Chase's words ran on, *perky* and *smashing* and Aidan being *a lucky bastard.*

And in the midst of parsing through those words, Beckett was reminded of how young Chase was—and of Marissa's youth too, her innocence and her emotional openness, and then of Gabrielle's coldness and of what might be at the root of it, some resilience that came with experience, maybe a mask for a hurt she didn't want to admit, and then he remembered the more visceral hurt: the horror on the dead man's face, the contortions of his body, the steep price of his pursuit of . . . what-ever he was after—and in the tumble of logic and emotion, Beckett felt himself on the edge of a growing melancholy, tipping toward sadness.

"Not so lucky," he told Chase. "No, I wouldn't say that."

# # #

Jealousy, embarrassment, outrage, humiliation, anger . . . That list ran again. But no, Beckett realized now, *love triangle* wouldn't be the right term. The geography was more jagged, the emotional terrain more treacherous. The landscape of infidelity and adultery—that was where this was venturing. The cheating spouse, the philandering partner, the wayward heart—someone being *unfaithful*, being *untrue*.

He weighed those words, too—and the more he did, the more for-eign and unclear they seemed. *Faith*—in what? The relationship? The person? And true to *whom*—or true to *what*? What truth?

Loyalty, he knew. *Trustworthiness and honesty*. Clarity, communication, confidence. The phone call Marissa claimed she made, her decision not to leave a voicemail, her suspicion that Aidan might be with Gabrielle. Gabrielle's own appraisal of Marissa in passing, her recognition that if *that* was what Aidan had wanted, then she wasn't the woman for him. These were evidence of the loss of faith, of the unraveling of trust. Each woman's conception of her future, her present, her*self*—splintered.

But it was another shift in truth and another form of bad faith Beckett found himself considering—because what was the difference between, the *conflict* between, being true to others and being true to yourself? And what worse bad faith than detaching oneself from what one wants, denying who one wants to be?

These were the questions that suddenly pressed more intensely against him, same as the corner of that business card cutting now at an odd angle against his thigh.

Infidelity suggested concealment, deception, deceit. But Aidan had—both stories agreed—told each woman about the other, proposing a future for the three of them. In the process (couldn't it be argued?) he had offered clarity and communication, taken a leap of faith, brought truth to light—and wasn't that an effort at being true to himself?

I am who I am? Or no, not essence, but existence—choice: The decisions I make assert who I want to be—which then establish the truth of who I am?

No doubt, no doubt (Beckett was not a fool), such truth to self would feel like betrayal of another—and this returned him to the heart of the case, the victim's motives, the killer's motives, the blank spot in the narrative where the stories came together. And wasn't it accurate that a man's confession to . . . to *indiscretion* (was that an appropriate word?) . . . that the deceased's confessions to each woman might be motivated by the pressure of living with a secret, by remorse and regret and mounting guilt, by a loathing for what he was hiding, a loathing of himself for hiding it, instead of by a proactive, progressive even, decision to reconcile one's desires and one's life? —which, importantly, seemed a negation of self-determination.

How does someone keep faith with others while also being true to self?

And was the look on the dead man's face surprise at his killer's actions? Or shock about what he'd done to himself?

# # #

As he and Chase walked to the front desk. Beckett found his mind moving further and further back—not only through the key points of the interview, but into his own memories, both recent and distant, and toward the card still biting into his thigh. His thoughts moved forward, oo, through the next steps in the investigation—though he felt he already knew the direction things were going to go, at least for the case.

"The two women we interviewed," he said to the desk clerk. "Those were the ones you saw yesterday, correct?"

"Yes," he said—Lloyd, Beckett saw on the name badge. "They were both here yesterday. I didn't check the times, didn't know I'd need to know the times, but . . . They came today in the same order as yesterday—the older one first, and then I remember her in the lobby again about the time the younger one came through."

No new information there. Gabrielle had already confirmed seeing Marissa. "And then the older woman left?"

"No," he said. "That's why it stood out. Because of what happened between them."

"Wait, like they *talked?*" Chase leaned in, and Beckett felt his own surprise. "They *knew* one another?"

"No," the desk clerk said. "They didn't seem to know one another. But the first one, the older one, she'd already caught my eye, the way she was walking—she had this *stride* coming out of the elevator, beeline for the exit, *purpose*. But then after she passed the younger one, she almost came to a stop, and she looked over her shoulder, and then it was like the younger one had seen something, too, or could tell she was being looked at, and that younger one, she glanced back, only a quick one, but it seemed . . . significant . . . like she felt something. And then she kept walking. The older one, after a minute just standing there, she sat down, that big red chair"—he pointed—"and stayed for a while."

"For how long?" Beckett asked.

"I don't know. Ten or fifteen minutes? Not super long."

"And what was she doing for those ten to fifteen minutes?"

Lloyd shrugged. "Staring at the elevator. And then she left. And then the second girl, the young one, she came down and left, too."

"And how late were you here?"

"Till ten."

"Could either have returned at a later time?"

"I don't remember seeing them," he said. Then more firmly, "No, I don't think so."

#

"Someone left out a key bit of the story," Chase said after they'd stepped back to the conference room.

Beckett sighed. "You have her number?" And when Chase provided it, Beckett opened his phone, dialed, put it on speaker.

"I understand you remained in the hotel lobby after leaving the deceased's room," he said, when Gabrielle had answered. "After seeing the other woman's arrival."

There was a long pause—sound of movement over the speakerphone. "I didn't think anyone would've noticed that."

"Perhaps you cared for him more than you admitted to us?"

A dry laugh. "Not at all. It was . . . curiosity, I suppose. I was wondering what story he was giving her, if he was abandoning his plan since I'd already said no, whether she was going to stay."

"And you were considering what to do next? Possibly weighing whether to go, or return to the room yourself?"

"Why would I do that?" The voice was flat.

"Curiosity, as you said. Or maybe you were feeling your anger getting the better of you?" Beckett paused. "Or maybe you were reconsidering his proposal, thinking about going back up, raising your glass to toast new possibilities?" As he spoke, a new clue came to mind, one he'd recognized but hadn't fully realized.

Gabrielle gave a dry laugh. "I assure you, Inspector, no matter how the two of them might have been celebrating, my own glass would've stayed dry."

"I don't believe her," Chase said after they'd hung up. "I think she would've filled the glass up and then thrown it at him. Or no, no, she'd've smacked it against that coffee table and shoved the sharp ends in his face."

"So you see her as capable of violence?"

"That one? No doubt." He gave a low whistle. "You don't?"

"If I did," Beckett said, "we would've gone to her in person instead of calling now."

Chase shook his head. "The things you see. Either way, it's past five now, and all this talk of drinking has me ready for one myself. You up for a break, sir?"

# # #

Like a TV detective, Beckett thought as he settled into a table at the rear of the pub. Too often, he felt like a character in a show or a film or a book rather than himself—like he existed as a role in some rote genre rather than the real world, following his own prescribed formula.

Chase had spotted the pub earlier, about a block from the hotel—always on the lookout—and there was good business already: a few men at the bar—regulars, Beckett had the [that] feeling—a couple at a small bistro table, and a quartet of young women, university-aged, slightly older perhaps, in a booth, leaning in toward one another, laughing over their wineglasses.

Beckett had left the chair against the wall for Chase, knowing he would appreciate the view of the TV and of the foursome of women while he sipped the IPA that was his custom. But the gesture wasn't purely altruistic. Beckett generally preferred to face walls—an emptiness to project his thoughts on. But a span of mirror reflected the scene behind him, reflected Beckett's own face, and he found himself staring instead into the bubbles of the club soda Chase had brought him, the fizz and sparkle—memories frothing up, his childhood. There was the martini Beckett's father mixed each evening at five-thirty—no measurements, little attention at all really, except for the exactness of the hour. (Beckett could picture now the cavalier swirl and swish he'd admired as a child, the plop of the olive—a rite he'd hoped to master himself one day.) There was his mother through the archway to the kitchen, seasoning or stirring or basting—the whisper of her radio, a local station, classical music. Rarely at this hour did anyone speak.

One evening, though, Beckett's father had roused from his silence, cleared his throat, and offered a confession.

"Sometimes, son, the world seems out of sync—or at least my world, my place in it." The glass in his hand had tilted forward, a precarious angle, the contents threatening to spill. "All of it such a grind, and the timing's off, grit in the gears, no sense of . . ."

His father hadn't looked Beckett's way as he spoke, and Beckett hadn't looked at him either. Instead, he had been watching his mother at the stove, had seen her pause in her stirring, knew she'd begun to listen, too.

"The things you want, the things you need," his father went on. "Always just out of reach, and the same cycle rolls out over and over and . . ." A small breath. "Some days, it would be so easy to go away, disappear, remove myself—leave everything behind."

Beckett had wondered if "everything" included him, too, but he hadn't asked—hadn't said anything at all—even as his father turned to face him, stared hard at him. Resignation in his gaze? Desperation? Some tentative gesture toward a bonding moment? Even then, Beckett had known it was none of that. There was no pleading in his father's voice, no yearning for connection, little emotion at all. Simply cold clarity in his words, as crisp and cutting as the glint of gin in his glass.

The silence between them stretched. Slowly, his father had lifted the martini to his lips, taken another sip, resettled in his chair. Slowly, the spoon in his mother's hand had begun to stir once more.

Beckett stared down now at the club soda on the table, untouched. Across from him, Chase bobbed his head to some beat, music that Beckett must have tuned out. In the mirror, Beckett could see the couple he'd noticed before, and he wondered what they were talking about, what was their situation, first date, long married, getting along well or not, what their future held. The mirror was cracked slightly, the angle crooked. Beckett couldn't read the scene. He turned back to his club soda.

Soon after the night of his brief confession, Beckett's father vanished.

"He's gone"—these were his mother's only words on the subject, as flat as his father's had been, no matter how often Beckett had asked, even after he had discovered the truth of the disappearance. Though he'd imagined gruesome accidents, romanticized kidnappings and even suicide, and conjured up extravagant adventures—his father was an explorer, he was a CIA agent—Beckett had learned the truth from an older boy in the neighborhood, who'd told him, with a sneer, that his father had simply run off with one of his clients, a widow who'd inherited substantially after her husband's death, who wanted to live a little.

Beckett's mother had gradually settled into drink herself, and it had slowly changed her, broken her. Beneath the silences that became her custom, a blankness that he tried to solve, Beckett sometimes thought he could glimpse frustration and regret, then rage and resignation, ultimately some fundamental sense of futility that followed her finally to her grave. Other times, unable to stomach those glimpses, he had simply looked away.

Another cliché: You marry some version of your mother or father.

And another: The sins of the father are visited on the son.

At some point, Beckett had sworn abstinence from alcohol, vowed to avoid however possible the place his mother had found herself in, the place his father had brought her to—vowed never to follow his father's footsteps in any way. And yet in the evenings too often, he returned home and sat down with a club soda and the newspaper and settled into silence himself while his wife heated up something in the kitchen, a crime show droning along on the TV on the counter.

# # #

Beckett raised the club soda to his mouth, felt the bubbles bristle against his lips.

"I wonder," he began, and he waited as Chase dutifully came to attention. "I *keep* wondering about the question of motive, keep returning to the various motives here, and I question whether emphasis in another direction would be more useful."

"How so, sir?"

"Either of the women have motives, of course—the sting of betrayal at the heart of it. The worldly woman incensed that her lover has become entranced by a younger woman—bitter perhaps, despite her dismissal of emotion, and wanting, as she did admit, to have him suffer for it. And then there's the younger woman, feeling that she's building a relationship and suddenly discovering that it's not what she thought, recognizing her foolishness and naïveté. The two of them had become entangled in the web of"—he considered the next phrase—"the web of a greedy man's selfishness. Each—in her own way, at least initially—felt the need to exit the scene. But at least one of them had turned to revenge."

"Seems to sum it up."

"But consider"—and here Beckett recognized he was again choosing carefully his words—"we found only one glass used."

"The one he drank from," Chase said. "The one that one of his girlfriends must've poisoned."

"But perhaps only one of those statements is true." Beckett raised his hand, wagged his finger. "Both women have said they didn't poison him—"

"Which they would, of course."

"—and both have said they declined, at least initially, the deceased's suggestion of a new relationship."

"Though Marissa reconsidered later. Still waiting to hear on those phone records, but that's what she said."

"Yes." Beckett thought again of the girl, how young she seemed, how frail the jewelry he'd commented on. "I trust that she made the call, which leaves us with two options: she was sincere in her reconsideration, or she made the call knowing he was already dead—because his death, of course, came earlier, and that's the blank in this story that we have to fill in. What happened at the time of his death? Or, really, just before his death—again *if* both women are indeed telling the truth, which . . . which I would argue they may well be."

He was tempted to watch Chase's reaction but instead closed his eyes, watching the story unfold in his mind. "Imagine. First Gabrielle leaves him—not only dismissal but disgust. He has time before Marissa arrives—and a decision to make. Clearly, Gabrielle has removed—at least for the evening, more likely for good—his opportunity to pursue his plans for the three of them, and perhaps her resistance has made the decision for him about which woman he could pursue individually. In either case, it would make sense to abandon his original proposal, continue the evening with the second woman without sharing any of this with her. But he's still flustered when Marissa arrives, and he's still concentrating on his original plan, clearly committed to it enough that instead of hiding the reason for being upset, he chooses to share it with her as well—opening up to her, honesty about what he desires, about the plans he's built in his head—and then . . . Then he's rebuffed again, at least for the time being, possibly here, too, for good."

"Marissa said she told him she was still thinking about it," Chase said.

"Yes." Beckett kept his eyes closed. "But after Gabrielle, how much faith might he have in her coming back? In the immediate moment, he's alone, both women gone. The empty hotel room reminds him how his plans, his world, have been thrown out of sync. Here's the bottle of wine, mocking him— celebration turned consternation. He pours a glass and then another—half the bottle gone, only one wineglass used—but by the second pour, consternation has turned toward desperation, the things he wants, that he needs, suddenly out of reach. He is left to face himself and the sad place his choices have brought him. Perhaps"—Beckett opened his eyes—"perhaps desperation took an even darker turn."

"He poisoned *himself*?" Chase's expression didn't hide his skepticism. "A little extreme, isn't it? I've been shut down a time or two myself, never took it that hard."

"Indeed, an extreme decision—one he would have immediately regretted as the poison took effect. Then, as desperation turned in yet another direction, a more urgent one, he recognizes his own foolishness, he rises to rush to the bathroom, frantic to do something, to save himself, but . . ."

"It's too late."

Beckett returned to the blank wall in front of him, seeing again the position of the body and the stain on the wall and the dead man's expression. He thought again of his father's expression, the blankness he'd tried to decipher there, too, and of his mother's grief. He thought of Gabrielle's coldness and Marissa's warmth and the earrings he'd complimented her on, how Chase had accused him of flirting. He felt the card in his pocket, no longer poking him, hardly a physical presence at all, but a weight, nonetheless. He waited for Chase to respond.

"It's possible," Chase said, finally. "Guess love comes with a hard cost sometimes."

Beckett felt himself take a breath he hadn't known he'd been holding. Behind him, he heard suddenly the movement of people who'd filled the bar, he smelled the beer, the fried food, the interplay of colognes and perfume.

No, the narrative he was proposing didn't fit all the evidence, didn't fully fill in the blank at the story's core—Beckett recognized this too well—but it satisfied something on a deeper level, and there was a kind of justice there. Resolution was nearly in sight, at least for one part of the story, and he felt his weariness begin hesitantly to lift.

But at that moment, his phone rang, the call he'd been both anticipating and dreading— the medical examiner, a conversation that would determine Beckett's every next step.

"Time of death between four and six p.m.," the medical examiner reported. "Best I can do. And it was indeed poison, no surprise."

"Hydrocyanic acid," Beckett said.

"Good eye, Inspector. Yes, exactly. A quick death, but a brutal one."

"And I'm anticipating there was no acid in the wine bottle?"

"No."

"But hopefully in the glass."

"Hopefully?"

"I'm"—he stumbled over the correct word, chose a safer one— "anticipating again that I'm correct."

"Surprisingly, no, there too. Only in the body. Don't mean to complicate things further, but we deal with the facts we have."

"That is"—Beckett felt the weariness settling once more— "unfortunate."

# # #

Chase had been watching Beckett carefully throughout the call.

"Bad news?" he asked after Beckett hung up.

"For one of our suspects."

"So not suicide then?"

Beckett tipped his club soda at an angle—half of it left, leveled now against the rim of the glass. It was only afterward that he realized he'd echoed his father's precariously tilted martini.

"Honestly"—Beckett let out a reluctant sigh—"I never believed it was."

# # #

What did a man want? A woman?

Where did desires and motives cross and tangle?

Two weeks earlier, Chase had been off for the day, and Beckett had pursued a call outside of his normal duties: a late-afternoon break-in in a neighborhood conveniently on Beckett's drive home, possible burglary—"*possible*," the dispatcher stressed. "The woman seems a little fuzzy about whether anything's been stolen."

The house was a storybook cottage: red brick amidst lush landscaping, layered gables on one side and echoes of those gables in the slant of the roof on the other side, an arched doorway flanked by spiraling cypress trees.

Beckett parked on the curved driveway, knocked at the door. He expected the woman who answered to be distraught and distracted—even ditzy perhaps, given the dispatcher's account. But instead, she seemed calm and congenial. "Thank you for coming, so much fuss over . . . well, not nothing, I know, but . . ." She wore a simple black dress with a camel-hair sweater draped over her shoulders, the sleeves tied loosely at the front. Dimples framed her smile. Auburn hair curved around her cheeks. Her eyes were warm and inviting. Annabel was her name. "Please do come in."

The interior was as elegant as the exterior: plaster in various shades accented by wooden beams and panels, plushly upholstered chairs and couches, colorful vases, portraits and landscapes in oil and pastel. Not the scatteredness Beckett had anticipated. Instead, a sense of serenity in all directions.

"This is where it happened," Annabel said, ushering him into a kitchen so pristine it was like something out of a magazine—sparkling appliances, copper cookware, rows of cookbooks. The space was seem-ingly undisturbed: no broken glass, no rummaged drawers or cabinets. She pointed toward a back door that opened onto a brick patio. Through the window, teak furniture gleamed golden.

"The alarm went off," she explained. "A woman living alone, you know, I couldn't not have one. When I came downstairs, this door was ajar, almost as if the breeze had opened it, until . . ." She opened the door and pointed to the latch, scratches and dents. "I use the deadbolt at night, but only the twist on the handset during the day. I'll need to change my ways, I suppose. I have a locksmith coming this evening to replace the broken mechanism. He's planning to add a camera as well."

"Were you frightened?" Beckett asked, and Annabel seemed sur-prised by the question.

"I should have been, shouldn't I? I'm sure if there had indeed been a man standing here, tools of the trade in his hand . . . Certainly, that would have been a different story."

Beckett had his questions ready, another routine to run through: Had she seen anyone through the window? Had she stepped out into the yard? Had there been any other reports of break-ins in the area? Had she checked further to see what might be missing? A list of them. But he'd barely asked the first before she interrupted him.

"Would you care for some coffee while we talk? I usually have one this time of the afternoon."

Despite himself (and, he wondered later, what was it that drew him to make this decision?), he agreed.

She led him into the living room and served them coffee—dark and rich topped with the slightest froth of steamed milk. The small cup—

amber glass, double-walled—felt too delicate in his ungainly hand, but it had tasted heavenly.

No, she said, she hadn't seen anyone. No, it had always been a safe neighborhood. No, nothing missing that she'd seen. The alarm must have scared whoever it was away. She didn't know anyone who would mean her, personally, any harm.

Soon, the conversation had drifted into other directions. She'd asked about how he became involved in police work, what he enjoyed about it, what worried or frightened him, what he had originally dreamed of being when he grew up, what he pictured for his life ahead. And she'd shared things about herself, too, her husband's early death from cancer, her longtime love of interior design, how she'd started her own business with the life insurance money.

"I miss him," she said. "Terribly. He was my life. But I recognize that I've found myself in a new way, what I love to do, where I belong, in a manner I might not have . . . otherwise." She seemed to turn inward, a wry smile, a small nod of her head. "I'm being too personal. I'm sorry. Something about you has . . ."

A small table separated the armchairs where they sat, and she reached briefly across it toward him before pulling her hand back.

Reticence was, Beckett knew, one of his strengths as an investigator: a reserve which created a silence, another blank space, that witnesses and suspects often stepped in to fill, sometimes to their own detriment. Introversion may have also suggested solidity and steadiness, inviting confidence. And perhaps, he suspected, surprising himself with the thought, there was something appealing about it as well?

The doorbell rang. The locksmith had arrived.

Beckett thanked her for the coffee, rose to take his leave, but before she answered the door, she asked him to stay a moment while she escorted the locksmith to the kitchen.

Beckett's conversation with her had been pleasant but uneventful, unremarkable really, and yet when she walked to the back with the locksmith, he was stuck by an unexpected and irrational sense of loss, of the precipitance of loss, a wave of nostalgia for something he hadn't actually experienced or remembered, a compulsion to act, to do.

But to do what? And why? And how had these feeling assailed him so swiftly?

Was it physical attraction? The tilt of her lips, the curve of her cheekbones, the flow and tumble of her auburn hair.

Was it the steadiness of her eyes watching him, the warmth of that attention, her interest and engagement? That mix of delicacy and firmness, emotion and ambition—aspects of her he'd barely glimpsed but felt some urgency to explore more deeply?

Had he been taken in by the setting she'd created—elegant, comfortable, inviting? A scent of vanilla lingered somewhere—a candle? Her perfume?

He felt lured in, and he feared—inexplicably—the loss of this feeling.

Annabel returned. *She's lovely*, he thought, and he felt himself standing taller—then felt guilty for his thought, his posture.

"You seem . . . such a kind man," she said. "I hope I'm not being too forward when I say I . . . I wouldn't mind at all seeing you again, under different circumstances, of course."

Her hand did touch his this time, a charged encounter—literally a spark.

Static electricity, he told himself later. Her feet or his shuffling on the carpet. The dryness of the air. But in the moment, he had felt jolted off-balance, unmoored from himself, and it had taken him several seconds to realize she'd handed him a card: Annabel Eldridge, Interior Design. A printed email address, a phone number in blue ink. Her handwriting was lovely, too.

If he had indeed been a TV detective, what would she have been? Damsel in distress, drawing him into her troubles? Femme fatale, sultry and seductive? One archetype tipping toward the other?

But the invitation here seemed different. A promise, a possibility—an unexpected path opening forward. The road not taken? That would be too dramatic, but a reminder of other roads at least, of other possible lives.

Some curse of midlife, he considered, striving to be as observant of himself as he was of any case he was investigating. Some echo of his father, he feared—the world out of sync, his place in it, and the impulse to change, to escape. But those thoughts only came later, as he was trying to fill the blank spaces of Aidan Blunt's death.

"I'm afraid," Beckett told Annabel at the time, struggling to straighten himself again, "that I can't. Thank you, though"—he met her eyes— "for the coffee."

But he'd pocketed the card, and he'd carried it each day since. The number she'd written there, he knew it now by heart.

# # #

Beckett allowed Chase to handle the arrest, standing close in case Marissa put up resistance—but he anticipated she wouldn't, and she didn't. When she opened the door, she nodded, as if she knew why they were there. She stared at the ground as Chase read her rights, and then she held close the right to her silence.

"When did you know she'd done it?" Chase had asked on the drive to her apartment. "Before the forensics came back?"

"Yes," Beckett had said.

He'd expected one question from Chase, but got another: "So how'd you know?"

"The wineglasses were the first clue," Beckett said. "Only after we'd seen the deceased's calendar, however, not the first time in the hotel room."

"There was no poison on the wineglass, either of them, right?"

"The initial problem wasn't the presence or absence of poison. It was the number of glasses. If the deceased had planned to split the wine with two women, as we discovered later, there should have been three glasses. One was missing. Where had it gone? And had it been used? I felt that it must have been used, or else why was it not there, and if it had been used and taken, what was the killer trying to hide?"

"Hide the poison, hide the evidence."

"Which was a key mistake, of course. If the poison had been on the glass, that might've told one story—the narrative I sketched out for you earlier. But no poison on the glass, that meant that someone had killed him and tried—frantically, misguidedly—to cover up the crime."

"So Marissa had indeed drunk a glass of wine with him."

"Yes, she'd poisoned his glass, then replaced it with her own untainted one—a decision, ironically, providing proof that a crime had indeed been committed."

"But you said that was the first clue. Was timing the other one? Marissa the last to see him alive?"

"Unless Gabrielle had come back, of course—a possibility. But no, it was the jewelry. The butterfly earrings, Marissa's artistry. Her jewelry is created through electroplating, a process of layering metal upon metal—gold, silver, copper . . . an electrical current is involved, and a solution in which to submerge the jewelry. For gold-plating in specific, that solution contained hydrocyanic acid."

"Hydrocyanic?"

"Yes. Cyanide. And she had some with her—even during the interview, I believe. You remember her talking about new techniques, new materials, the investment in them . . . and the way she hugged her bag, the way she reddened as she said it."

"Means and opportunity," Chase said. "And motive, too, plenty of it."

"And perhaps a specific trigger as well. Marissa said that Aidan had bought much of her jewelry at the art walk the first time they met. Gabrielle made a comment about the gifts that the deceased had given her, how they weren't her style, how she'd disposed of the last of it yesterday. She twisted her wrists as she said it—showing off her bare hands, the fact that the bracelets were no longer there. But I wondered if she was wearing it yesterday when Marissa passed her in the lobby—the double-take that the clerk described, Marissa recognizing her creations on a woman who would soon be revealed as her rival. Another layer of betrayal."

"Salt in the wound," Chase said. "Insult to injury."

# # #

"And all such a shame," Chase said, still talking about it as they left the precinct. "Such a pretty girl, that Marissa. So much going for her, don't you think? And she throws it all away for . . . what? Not for him, really, but . . . well, *because* of him."

"For pride maybe," Beckett said. "For herself."

"Didn't help her in the long run."

"It's the worst of our choices perhaps," Beckett said, "that have the most telling consequences."

# # #

"Till tomorrow," Chase said, as they parted ways in the lot—another day ahead, other cases, same routine, rolling out endlessly.

Beckett sat in his car without starting it and stared through the window at the streetlights, the night sky, the moon above. In the slant of the windshield, he projected the drive ahead, the same turns as always, the same small stretches of traffic, and then the familiar four-square, the porch light burning, his wife waiting inside.

He pictured, too, the turn he could take along the way, the small detour toward the house he'd visited two weeks before, the break-in, Annabel.

Hesitantly, he pictured up the phone, dialed the number.

"I've been waiting for you to call."

"Time got away from me," he said. "A difficult case today."

"And did you fill in all the blanks?" She laughed. She knew him too well.

"Nearly all."

The line fell silent, some emptiness in the connection, and then his wife's voice again.

"I waited to put the Stouffer's on," she said. "Wanted us to have dinner together tonight, doesn't matter how late."

"Lasagna?" he asked.

"It's your favorite," she said, a little lilt in her voice. "And I saw one of those new non-alcoholic wines, too—something a little special. Thinking of you!"

Beckett stared again into the windshield. When the lights from a passing car caught the glass right, he thought he caught a glimpse of himself, dim and distant.

"Twenty-five minutes," he said. "I'll look forward to it."

"Me, too."

After he hung up, he dug awkwardly past the seat belt and into his pocket, retrieved the frayed business card. He looked at it one last time, then tore it into quarters, stuffed the pieces into the trash bag in his console.

He put the car in gear and began the drive he knew too well.

Home.

The Society Set by
Alan Orloff

#

17. A professional criminal must never be shouldered with the guilt of a crime in a detective story. Crimes by house-breakers and bandits are the province of the police department—not of authors and brilliant amateur detectives. Such crimes belong to the routine work of the Homicide Bureaus. A really fascinating crime is one committed by a pillar of a church, or a spinster noted for her charities.

My employer, the brilliant private investigator Burke Farrington IV, carefully set down his Bernardaud teacup and glared at me with a sour expression, one I'd long been accustomed to seeing. He perched regally in an Eames chair behind the walnut desk in his opulent study with the eight-foot ceilings, while I slouched in the corner, balancing on a rickety folding chair that could disintegrate any second. "Rollins, did you steep my Gyokuro for the precise two minutes and twenty-five seconds? Remember, I instructed you to reduce the time by six seconds after yesterday's fiasco."

Yesterday's fiasco had him drinking tea that had been steeped six seconds too long. *Heavens.* "Yes, I remembered. Two minutes, twenty-five seconds. On the button." I rose, knowing where this was headed.

"Well, you erred somewhere. Please try again. This tea is dreadful. Virtually unpotable." He gestured to the lady sitting across the desk from him. "Mrs. Lancaster deserves the best. For that matter, *all* of my clients deserve the best." He graced me with a smile that said I was an idiot.

I'd put up with him for the past nine years, just as I'd put up with his father, Farrington III, for fifteen years before that. Sometimes rudeness, condescension, and dismissiveness had to be tolerated in the name of genius. Besides, the pay was outstanding.

I crossed the room and placed their cups on a silver tray, then whisked it all away like a well-trained butler. "Sorry about that. I'll be right back with some fresh tea." I took no offense; the shabby treatment was part of the gig.

"Remember, two minutes and twenty-five seconds. And make sure the temperature of the water is correct, too. Precision is important." He flashed a smile at Mrs. Lancaster that reiterated I was an idiot. "We'll wait until you return before we get into the specifics of the case."

I knew he would, too. In addition to being Burke's tea maker, I was his note taker. He claimed he couldn't think and write at the same time, and I didn't doubt him for a minute. As he often admonished me, he needed to *concentrate*.

While they embarked on a journey of small talk, I left the room. I returned a few minutes later with fresh tea and served Burke and Mrs. Lancaster, careful not to spill a single drop.

"Thank you, Rollins. You may foul things up more than your share, but you're worth every penny I pay you, and then some."

"Yes, sir. Thank you, sir." I smiled and tried to look grateful, then took my place in the corner and picked up my pad of paper and a pen. I knew the drill. After years of working for Burke, I certainly knew the drill.

My boss cleared his throat. "Let's start at the beginning, Mrs. Lancaster. Tell me everything."

"Please, call me Edwina." Her voice was thin and reedy. She was eighty-five, if she was a day.

"Very well, Edwina. I'm all ears." Burke turned toward me and made a writing gesture in the air, as if I'd forgotten what I was there to do.

"I'm terribly distraught. You see, three valuable diamond necklaces are missing, and I'm afraid they've been stolen. Right out of the doll-house I use as my jewelry box in my bedroom. I'd been laid up for a week after spraining an ankle, and because my bedroom required me to climb a few stairs, I'd been set up to sleep in one of the guest rooms. I had no idea anything was amiss until I was dressing for the Willingham Charity Gala. When I went to put on one of the necklaces, it was gone!"

"Are you sure it was stolen?" Burke asked.

"Maisie—she's my housekeeper—and I searched all over. To no avail. Someone must have broken in and stolen the necklaces." She dabbed her eyes with a silk handkerchief. "I considered calling the police, of course, but..." She shrugged. "I'm not absolutely, positively, *definitively* sure that I didn't misplace them. So, I thought I'd hire you first. After all, you do have a well-known reputation as the 'PI of the Society Set.' I knew your father, I did. A fine man."

The description was apt. Burke came from a long line of Farringtons, PI, and their clientele consisted mostly of people who didn't have to work for a living. Farrington III himself used to say, "It is better to have clients who can afford to pay than those who cannot." And I couldn't quarrel with logic like that.

"Are you getting all this, Rollins?"

I scribbled something on the paper to make it look like I was. "Yes, sir. Society Set, sir."

"Very good," he said to me, but he'd already turned back to focus on Mrs. Lancaster. "A terrible thing, of course. I assume you are aware of my fee?"

She waved her hand. "Those necklaces are worth hundreds of thousands, but to me, they are priceless. They were gifts from my late husband, Huston, and I treasure them very much. I'll have my bank wire over your retainer. I trust you can get started immediately?"

"Of course, Edwina. We can get started this very instant. First order of business: we shall visit the scene of the crime. And do not fret. I'll have those necklaces back to you very, very soon. Of that, I am confident."

Burke was the most confident man I'd ever known, and, honestly, not without good reason. That's why I worked for him. I liked working for a winner. Even a condescending one.

And did I mention the lucrative compensation?

# # #

In addition to being Burke's tea maker and note taker, I was his driver, too. We arrived at the Lancaster Mansion about sixty seconds behind Mrs. Lancaster—and her driver—and we caught up to her on the porch.

The Lancaster Mansion was built with the profits of the Lancaster Land Development Trust, established 1814, which was started by the Lancaster Family from Lancaster, Pennsylvania. Their money was so old that it might have been made from papyrus.

Edwina was the last with any claim on the Lancaster fortune; a few members of the extended *extended* family existed but they had cut familial ties, not wishing to be tainted with the curse of greedy wealth. Their loss.

Maisie met us all at the front door and ushered us into the parlor, then began fussing over Mrs. Lancaster to make sure she wasn't too tired to answer some more questions.

"Actually, Edwina, I think we'd prefer to talk to Maisie alone," Burke said.

Maisie's eyes went wide, and she immediately glanced at Mrs. Lancaster.

"It's all right, Maisie. These gentlemen are here to get my necklaces back. Answer whatever questions they have, and please be frank. I'll be in the sitting room… well, sitting."

Mrs. Lancaster shuffled off.

"Have a seat, Maisie," Burke said. "This is Rollins, my assistant. He'll be taking notes."

Maisie took a seat on the brocade sofa, but she sat up on the edge, as if she'd need to pop off in a flash if Mrs. Lancaster returned suddenly.

"Wh…what questions do you have?" Maisie asked, voice wavering.

"No need to be nervous," Burke said. "I'd just like to get a sense of what you think might have happened."

"I don't know. One day, Mrs. L just said she was missing her neck-laces."

Burke nodded sagely. "And you looked all around for them, without any luck. So, let's assume they were stolen. Do you have any idea who might have done it? Anyone that wasn't usually here who might have had access to the jewelry? The necklaces were in her bedroom, correct?"

Burke could be charming when he wanted—when it served his pur-pose—and he was doing a damn good job of putting Maisie at ease. I wondered why he couldn't be nicer more often, to more people.

"Yes, in her bedroom. She'd been sleeping in the guest room for about a week prior—injured ankle—but I can't recall anyone here who shouldn't have been." Maisie looked up at the ceiling while she thought. "The family lawyer stopped by, Mr. Dunsworth. And there was her friend, Mrs. Quillen. Paulie, the handyman, changed out some doorknobs—nothing wrong with what was there, but Mrs. L wanted to freshen up the place, she said. That's it." Maisie brought her gaze down and faced Burke. "Do you think one of them stole the necklaces?"

"Do *you* think any of them stole the necklaces?"

Maisie bit her lip. "No. I mean, I don't think so. I don't *want* to think so. Mrs. L is the best woman I've ever worked for—twenty-two years now—and I sure hope that nobody thinks I had anything to do with this."

I'd been jotting down notes, but I stopped. Of course, the house-keeper had to be a suspect.

"Do you believe that people think you're involved?" Burke leaned forward, ever so slightly.

"It's only natural, I guess. But I would never do that. Never." Maisie sat back and crossed her arms across her chest.

I believed her, and I felt like I had a pretty good barometer when it came to ne'er-do-wells.

"Of course not." Burke rose. "Would you show us Mrs. Lancaster's bedroom?"

We traipsed upstairs to the alleged crime scene. An ordinary old-lady bedroom: frilly curtains, frilly bedcovers, frilly pillowcases covering about two dozen pillows. Pastels and paisley everywhere you looked. And a slightly musty smell hung in the air.

Burke went directly to the dollhouse on the dresser. "I assume the necklaces were here."

"That's right."

Obviously, the dollhouse had been customized. It stood about a foot and a half tall, with an extra-large front door that Burke now opened to gain access to the jewelry inside. Necklaces, bracelets, rings, earrings— Mrs. Lancaster had everything. And if I had to guess, none of it was costume. All precious stones and valuable gems. Worth a tidy sum, no question.

So why had the thief only taken the three necklaces and left everything else?

"There are some valuable pieces here. Do you know if Mrs. Lancaster ever considered some kind of more secure situation? A safe, perhaps? Video cameras? Security system?"

"Oh no. Mrs. L is very trusting. And there's always someone around. Me or someone else. Hard to get inside unless you are invited."

Burke closed the dollhouse door abruptly. "I've seen enough here. Rollins, get a few pictures and meet me downstairs. We've got more people to talk to and time's a-wasting, so chop-chop. Maisie, would you mind escorting Rollins down when he's finished?"

In addition to being Burke's tea maker, note taker, and driver, I was also his photographer.

#

As soon as we set foot in Stannis Dunsworth's office, I knew that he and Burke were brothers from different mothers. The furnishings were all high end, and the exquisite Persian rug probably cost more than my last three cars combined. Everything was in its place, just so, and there was a scent in the air so fresh that it had to be out of a can. Nothing in nature smelled so sweet.

Dunsworth and Burke sat side-by-side on a supple leather couch, while I slumped in a wing chair that looked way more comfortable than it was. I had paper and pen at the ready.

"So, Farrington, what can I do for you?"

Burke disliked being called solely by his last name, so I was surprised that he didn't correct Dunsworth. Maybe the lawyer got some leeway by being of the same pretentious ilk. Was there a Pomposity Club they all belonged to? With a secret pompous handshake?

"I'm investigating the theft of Mrs. Lancaster's jewelry. She had three valuable necklaces stolen."

Dunsworth nodded gravely. "I heard about that. Pity. Edwina is a wonderful person. So generous."

"You visited her last week?"

"Yes. We had some estate business to go over. Why?"

"Someone had access to those necklaces."

Dunsworth's spine straightened. "You think I had some—"

"Oh, no. No. Of course not. I was just wondering if perhaps you saw something while you were there. A professional like yourself has different observations than the, well, hired help, no offense intended."

"Oh, I'm still the hired help. Just at a much, much higher hourly rate." Dunsworth chuckled.

Burke laughed, too, but I knew it was forced. Even if Dunsworth *had* said something actually funny, Burke didn't have much of a sense of humor.

"So, did you? See something out of the ordinary?"

"Let me think. We met in one of her guest rooms, and she didn't even get out of bed. I had some papers for her to sign, and we chit-chatted a bit, but I wasn't there for more than half an hour or so. I saw the housekeeper, of course, Maisie. But she's been with Edwina for so long that I'm sure she had nothing to do with it. And there was a handyman doing something or other, I believe. Edwina complained about him puttering about so long—I got the impression that it was taking him longer than expected to do whatever he was supposed to be doing."

"No one else?"

"If you're asking if I saw someone with a ski mask and a sack over one shoulder skulking around, the answer is no. Of course, I didn't go upstairs where the crime allegedly occurred. But..." Dunsworth lowered his voice, although I wasn't sure why. There was nobody else around except Burke and me. "Have you considered that maybe Edwina did something to the necklaces herself and just doesn't remember? Put them someplace else? Sold them? Gave them to a friend?"

"Is she having cognitive issues?" Burke asked.

He shrugged. "She's almost ninety. Isn't everybody by that age?"

"She seemed sharp to me."

Dunsworth shrugged again. "I suppose you're right. I just hate to think that someone burgled her home. I mean, she could have been hurt. Or worse."

I wondered how much of Dunsworth's concern was for Mrs. Lancaster's well-being, and how much was concern for his legal fees. I didn't have a high regard for lawyers.

"Yes, it's a good thing no one suffered any bodily harm." Burke stroked his chin, and it reminded me of an old British TV show where the private investigator always stroked his chin theatrically before he asked a piercing question. "Can you reveal anything of a more personal nature about Mrs. Lancaster that might lead me in the right direction? After all, you knew her quite well. As her attorney, you probably knew she kept quite a collection of jewelry right there in her mansion. I wonder who else knew of her stash?"

Dunsworth jerked upright and his features tightened. "Once again, I resent your insinuation. You honestly can't think that I had something to do with this, do you?"

"Not at all," Burke said calmly.

"I have an impeccable reputation, and I wouldn't risk that for anything." Dunsworth rose. "If we're done here, I have client business to tend to. Might I suggest that you spend your time and energy trying to find the actual thief?"

# # #

Nancy Quillen agreed to meet us at the Willingham Historical Society, where she volunteered as a docent. The society was—as you might expect—housed in an old building that had been restored to look like it had in the early 1700s, back when the town was founded.

To me, it looked like Nancy was as old as the weathered wooden floorboards.

"Thank you for meeting with us, Mrs. Quillen," Burke said.

"Mrs. Quillen is my mother. Please call me Nancy."

I started to laugh—Nancy's mother was still alive?—but quickly turned it into a cough. Both Nancy and Burke glared at me.

"Sorry about that. Something went down the wrong pipe." I held up my notepad. "I'll just take notes while you talk."

Burke nodded at me, and a moment later I was forgotten, just a hundred-seventy-pound fly on the wall.

"I'm here to ask you a few questions about your dear friend, Edwina Lancaster." One of Burke's eyebrows rose. "And her missing necklaces."

Nancy clutched her pearls—literally. Two strands of pearls hung around her neck, and her fingers worked them like they would a rosary. "Terrible. I know Edwina is heartbroken. Those pieces mean a lot to her. And to think some low-life took them. Right from under her nose!"

"Yes, terrible. Edwina wasn't able to pinpoint exactly when they were stolen, but it was around the time that you paid her a visit. Do you recall seeing anything out of the ordinary when you were there?"

"I've thought about that, at some length. And the answer is no. I even went into her bedroom to get her favorite comb, and I didn't see a thing out of place. Her dollhouse was closed tightly. Of course, Maisie does a wonderful job keeping everything neat and tidy over there. She's a treasure, that one."

"You went into her bedroom, and noticed her dollhouse was closed."

"That's right."

"Had you been in Edwina's bedroom before?"

Nancy pursed her lips, thinking. "No, I don't believe I had been. We usually visit down in the parlor, but with her injured ankle…"

"Then why did you specifically reference her dollhouse?"

"Why, that's where she keeps her jewelry."

"Did Edwina tell you that?"

"No, I don't believe so." Nancy seemed puzzled.

"If you've never been in her room before and the dollhouse door was closed, how did you know that she kept her jewelry there?"

Nancy's face shaded red. "Well, I, uh…" She took a deep breath. "I knew she kept her valuables in her room someplace, so I nosed about. I'd seen many of Edwina's pieces over the years, but I'd never seen them all in one place like that. Very impressive."

"Were the stolen necklaces there?" Burke asked.

"Yes, they were. All of them."

"So, I guess that means someone stole them *after* your visit, correct?"

Or during, I thought.

Nancy nodded, and her two pearl necklaces clicked together. "Yes, I suppose you're correct. You know, there was her handyman lurking about. I'd seen him around town, doing miscellaneous jobs." Her lips puckered. "He always seemed a bit…"

"A bit what, Nancy?"

"A bit *hard*, if you know what I mean."

"Hard?"

"You know, had a tough life. You can see it on their faces."

Burke let that pass, but I filed away her disdain for those beneath her.

"I'll be sure to talk to him, of course. Anything else you can think of that might help my investigation?" Burke asked.

"Not that I can think of. But if something comes to me, I'll let you know."

#

We met Paulie Winters at the Main Street Diner, a place where Burke often met those he interviewed, operating under the "if you feed them, they'll talk more" rule of thumb. The food was bad, but plentiful, and I knew for a fact that Burke himself wouldn't eat anything there except the rhubarb pie.

When he found out Burke was paying, Paulie ordered approximately half the menu, and he'd finally come up for air after polishing off two entire entrées. Burke cleared his throat. "Mind if we get started now? I've got some questions for you."

"Sure, sure." Paulie wiped his chin with an already-soiled napkin.

"I understand you were doing some work for Mrs. Lancaster. Changing out some hardware and fixtures, I believe."

"That's right. Doorknobs, cabinet pulls, switch plates, what-have-you. She wanted to give her home a bit of a facelift." He nodded to himself. "I've done a number of jobs for Mrs. Lancaster. Nice lady. Gives me a holiday bonus, too. I wish all of my clients were so thoughtful."

"When did you start working for her?"

He tapped his chin with a grimy finger. "Three years? Maybe four? I'm one of the go-to handymen in this town. I pride myself on my thoroughness and attention to detail."

"That's what I've heard. I wonder how you got your first job here." Burke paused, raised an eyebrow. "Considering…"

Paulie's brow furrowed. "Considering?"

"Considering your background."

Something flashed behind Paulie's eyes, and his entire demeanor darkened. I could see now what Mrs. Quillen meant by *hard*.

"What do you know about my background?" Wariness tinged his words.

"I'm an investigator. I do background checks on many of the people I encounter when I'm working on a case." Burke leaned in, lowered his voice. "I know about your record. Breaking and entering. Three counts. Your guilty verdicts. Your time upstate."

Paulie's mouth opened and closed. Twice. Then, "That was a long time ago. I made some foolish mistakes, and I paid for them. That's not who I am today." He glanced around. "My reputation matters. All the work I get is through word of mouth. If that got out, it would ruin me."

"You're aware that three necklaces were stolen from Mrs. Lancaster?"

"I didn't take them."

Burke turned toward me. "You're taking notes, aren't you, Rollins?"

I held up my pad. "Of course."

"Very well. Make sure you get down every word. Paulie here says that he didn't take the jewelry."

"Yes, sir." I knew that he liked to show his interviewees who was boss with this showy power play. He'd done it so many times that it no longer irked me.

Burke shifted his attention back to Paulie, whose face had turned pale. "Why did this job take so long? I understand you were there for the better part of a week."

"Because Mrs. Lancaster kept changing her mind. First, she wanted the brushed nickel, then she changed her mind and wanted the stainless, then the gold, then back to the nickel. I just try to keep my clients happy. I kept my head down, minded my own business. Like I always do. Handymen should be seen and not heard."

I knew that feeling.

"Why do you say that, about keeping your head down? Did something happen?" Burke asked.

Paulie considered Burke, his lips pressed together.

"Paulie, I'll find out eventually. And if you don't tell me, I'll think it's because there's something you're hiding."

"It's not like that. Clients don't want me telling their business. I mean, I'm in people's homes. I see stuff. Not bad stuff, but maybe stuff people don't want made public."

"What did you see at Mrs. Lancaster's?"

Paulie sighed. "Not what I saw, what I *heard*. An argument, between Mrs. Quillen and Mrs. Lancaster. I couldn't make out all the words, but Mrs. Lancaster was mad about something that Mrs. Quillen did. Said something to the effect of 'It'll be a cold day in hell before I let you do that to me.' Paraphrasing, of course."

"And you have no idea what she meant by that?"

"Like I said, I keep my head down. I get paid to change doorknobs, not to meddle in anyone else's affairs." Paulie shook his head. "Mind if I order some pie?"

"Please do," Burke said. "It's on me, of course."

"In that case, I think I want it à la mode."

# # #

"Rollins, this Gruyère is a few days past its prime." Burke held up his grilled cheese sandwich so I could see. "And you burned the toast."

In addition to being his tea maker, note taker, driver, and photographer, I was also his cook. The toast was ever-so-slightly darker than normal in one teeny-tiny corner. "Would you like me to remake it?"

He frowned. "Ah, forget it. I'm too hungry. But next time, could you take more care?" He took a couple of bites, made a face, then set the sandwich aside. "Let's review the case. Four people had the means and opportunity to steal Mrs. Lancaster's necklaces: the housekeeper Maisie, the lawyer Dunsworth, her friend Mrs. Quillen, and the handyman Paulie Winters. But who had motive?"

He gazed at me expectantly, but I knew better than to answer. This was Burke's show, all the way. Always was, always would be.

He nodded. "Although Maisie seemed happy in Mrs. Lancaster's employ, the temptation to cash out might have been too great. Dunsworth seemed like a man who enjoyed nice things, and by all accounts, those necklaces were very nice. In that same vein, Mrs. Quillen might have been the victim of envy, seeing Mrs. Lancaster at all the charity galas wearing that exquisite jewelry. Would she have stolen it to prevent her friend from being the belle of the ball? And let's not forget the way the handyman inhaled the food I'd treated him to. I believe he would have risked quite a lot to be able to retire in style and have all the pie he desired. Do you have anything to add?"

"Actually, I think you summed it up quite nicely." I tipped my head in acknowledgment and cut to the chase. "Do you know who did it?"

"I believe I do, Rollins." Burke winked at me. "I believe I do."

# # #

Burke, Mrs. Lancaster, and Stannis Dunsworth nestled in comfy chairs in Mrs. Lancaster's sitting room. I sat off to the side in my usual station, unnoticed, irrelevant. My preference, actually.

Burke kicked things off. "I believe I know who stole your necklaces, Edwina, but I have a few more questions." He turned to Dunsworth. "And I've asked your lawyer to join us because I have some legal issues regarding the theft I'd like to be clear about."

"I'm an estate attorney, not a criminal lawyer," Dunsworth said.

"These matters are not too complicated. I'm sure your legal expertise will be fine," Burke said. "Edwina, I interviewed the people who had access to your bedroom—and the necklaces—during the week you were laid up in the guest room. And I believe I know who did it."

Mrs. Lancaster's eyes had become misty. "I can't believe someone I know—someone I *trusted*—stole from me."

"There, there, Edwina. It'll be all right. Farrington here may be able to get your necklaces back to you." He turned to Burke. "Isn't that right?"

"You are correct. Now, as I said, I have a few questions."

Dunsworth nodded, *Go ahead.*

"Did you know where the necklaces were kept? Had you been in Mrs. Lancaster's bedroom?" Burke asked.

The lawyer thought for a moment. "Yes, once, a few months ago when we were working out some details about the necklaces for the updated will. In that crazy dollhouse. Told her she should put all her valuables in a safe, in fact. I'm sorry that—"

"Just a second," Mrs. Lancaster said, features contorted with confusion. "That dollhouse is new. A gift from Nancy, actually, for my eighty-seventh birthday. But back when I showed you the jewelry, I kept it in an ordinary wooden jewelry box." She skewered Dunsworth with an evil eye. "In fact, how did you even know that I *have* a dollhouse in my bedroom?"

Burke smiled, looking pleased with himself. "Yes, Dunsworth, how did you know that?"

Dunsworth all but *harrumph*ed. "Are you accusing me of something?"

"Yes. I'm accusing you of stealing Edwina's necklaces." Burke stood and began pacing, channeling a detective from an Agatha Christie novel. "If someone wanted to maximize the financial windfall from the theft, they would have stolen *all* the jewelry—earrings, bracelets, rings. Taken together, quite a treasure. So that leaves out Paulie and Maisie. And—"

"Maisie would never do such a thing. She's like a daughter to me." Mrs. Lancaster appeared on the brink of a waterworks.

"No, no, of course not," Burke said. "I only mentioned her so I could clear her name."

"This whole thing is ridiculous." Dunsworth stood. "I'm leav—"

"Please sit back down," Burke said.

"Yes, Stannis. *Sit down*," Mrs. Lancaster said, quite forcefully. "I pay your fees, by the way."

Dunsworth slowly lowered himself back into his seat.

"Although you had an argument with Mrs. Quillen, she freely admitted going into your bedroom and peeking into your dollhouse. I don't think she would have stated that if she had been guilty. So that leaves you, Dunsworth. Someone who likes nice things and doesn't mind stealing them. Someone who likes the thrill of the theft. Someone who likes to make a big splash."

"Preposterous. I'm an upstanding citizen of this town. I'm a church deacon, for chrissakes," Dunsworth sputtered.

"I run background checks on those I investigate. Imagine my surprise when I perused the results of yours. Upstanding citizen? Not when you were known as Stephen Daniels. With a record of theft and burglary and fraud a mile long. Why, you're just a common crook in a fancy suit."

Dunsworth looked as if he'd aged a decade in the past three minutes. "I'd like to call my lawyer."

Burke turned to me. "Rollins, don't you just love the smell of irony?"

# # #

The next day, Burke and I went over his monthly bills. I handed him the checks, one by one, and he signed them without giving them a second glance, as always. Some details, he just didn't have the patience for.

"Interesting case, hmm?" Burke said, still flying high from his success.

"Yes, sir. Once again, you cracked it." I handed him another check.

"Well, thank you." He signed it and handed it back. "And thank you for your help."

"You're welcome." I set another check down in front of him. "Here's the last one for this month."

He signed it with a flourish, passed it back. "I'm going to take a nap now. Please don't disturb me."

"Yes, sir."

Burke shuffled off to bed, and I glanced at the last check he'd signed. My paycheck. As usual, I'd added an extra zero to the amount.

You see, in addition to being his tea maker, note taker, driver, photographer, and cook, I was also his bookkeeper.

And, as the great man himself said, *I deserved every penny, and then some.*

Who was I to argue?

\

Anna's Story by
John M. Floyd

#

18. A crime in a detective story must never turn out to be an accident or
a suicide. To end an odyssey of sleuthing with such an anti-climax is to
play an unpardonable trick on the reader. If a book-buyer should demand
his two dollars back on the ground that the crime was a fake, any court
with a sense of justice would decide in his favor and add a stinging
reprimand to the author who thus hoodwinked a trusting and kind-
hearted reader.

On the afternoon of October 5, 1948, Luke Walker was sitting on
a bench beside the iron fence at Jackson Square, watching the artists
and the passersby. There were always passersby here, weekend or week-
day, rain or shine, warm or cold, and this autumn Tuesday was as hot
and steamy as mid-July. In south Louisiana, Mother Nature rarely consulted the calendar.

But a pleasant breeze was blowing off the river, and Walker closed
his eyes a moment, wondering where to take his sister Vinnie for supper tonight. Her bus would arrive at six, and he still had to tidy up his
apartment before she—

"Lucas Walker?" a voice said.

He looked up to see a young woman standing in front of him.

Walker rose to his feet, blinking. "That's me."

"I'm Anna Kelzo," she said. "With a Z." Her hair was red, her face
chalk-pale, her voice tired. "Your secretary told me where to find you."

"My secretary?"

"Said her name's Gladys. She was sitting in your desk chair, drinking coffee."

Walker sighed. Gladys Porter wasn't his secretary, she was the building's cleaning lady. And it probably wasn't coffee she had in her cup. He
reminded himself to start locking his desk.

"What can I do for you, Miss Kelzo?"

"Mrs.," she said. Then: "I understand you're a private detective?"

"Maybe I shouldn't be. I didn't detect your wedding ring."

That produced a tiny smile. She looked around. "Could we find some shade?"

Walker picked his hat up off the bench and escorted her back to his office on Chartres Street. It wasn't far, which was a good thing; Anna Kelzo looked worn out, and not just from the heat. When they arrived, his office door was open and Gladys was gone, probably along with the bourbon bottle he kept in his desk drawer. He and his visitor sat facing each other while his ceiling fan moved the humid air around.

"My husband Eddie's in jail," she said simply. "For something he didn't do."

Walker frowned, waiting.

She leaned forward, her knuckles white around her purse. "I need—*we* need—your help."

Walker felt his shoulders sag. *Why now?* he thought. Vinnie was on her way here from Natchez, at this moment, and he hadn't seen her since Christmas. *Come on down*, he'd written to her. *I'll take a few days off. We'll go to the zoo.*

Anna Kelzo kept looking at him. She had tears in her eyes.

"Mr. Walker?"

He let out a breath and nodded. "I'm listening."

#

Her story wasn't the kind Walker was used to hearing. According to Anna, a so-called literary agent here in town named Eason Weaver had charged her four hundred dollars over the past six months to edit and then market a number of her short mystery/romance stories to local and national magazines, and—

"So you're a writer," Walker interrupted.

Another hint of a smile. "Maybe I shouldn't be. None of the stories sold."

"But?"

"But when I demanded to see my manuscripts . . ." She paused. "Do you know anything about writing or publishing, Mr. Walker?"

"Very little," he said.

"Well, it turned out Weaver hadn't edited much of anything, which was part of what I'd paid him to do. And when I dug deeper, I found that my stories hadn't even been submitted anywhere." She sighed. "Since then, I've learned that agents aren't supposed to charge for submitting their clients' work. They're paid only later, as a percentage of what we earn—and most agents don't do editing, and certainly don't bill for it if they do."

Bottom line, Anna said, the whole operation was mostly a racket, unethical if not illegal, designed to fleece unpublished and unsuspecting writers like her, and legitimized only because Weaver did represent one bestselling author. When Anna eventually revealed all this to her husband, who'd always supported her literary efforts, he'd informed her that he would handle it.

Which he did, in his own way. Steelworker Eddie Kelzo had learned to box while in the Army, and shortly before five p.m. yesterday he'd paid a visit to Eason Weaver's office on the second floor of the Stenman Building, on Canal Street. Eddie found him alone there, and demanded he refund Anna's four hundred dollars. When Weaver refused, he received, in the next thirty seconds, a broken nose, a blackened eye, assorted bruises, and a threat that this would happen again if he didn't pay up. Eddie left the office without his wife's money but with at least some satisfaction. According to what he'd told Anna, Weaver's moans and curses as he lay on his back on his office floor followed Eddie all the way to the stairway, outside in the hall.

"The problem is," Anna added, "the story doesn't end there." Again, her eyes welled with tears. "Have you seen the afternoon paper?"

Walker hadn't, but it was right there on his desk. Apparently Gladys had fetched it for him during his absence—maybe she'd read it while sipping her "coffee." The headline immediately caught his eye: LITERARY AGENT MURDERED IN CANAL STREET OFFICE.

Which of course changed everything. As he scanned the article, Anna said, "He was alive when Eddie left him, Mr. Walker. Eddie beat him up, that's true—but that's all."

He looked up at her. "According to this, Weaver's throat was cut."

"I know," she said. "But not by my husband." What she didn't say was, *But who would believe that?*

Walker realized he was missing something. "How'd the police even know your husband was there, Mrs. Kelzo? Did he turn himself in, after hearing this Weaver guy was dead?"

"No." She pointed to the newspaper in his hand. "Keep reading. Near the end it says Mr. Weaver's partner, Gus Foley, discovered the body, and remembered seeing Eddie leave the building fifteen minutes earlier. The cops came to our house and arrested him last night."

Walker read it, and asked, without looking up, "How'd this Foley know Eddie's name?"

"Foley was nearby, the last couple visits I made to Mr. Weaver's office. Eddie had gone with me a few times, always waited for me on a bench in the hallway. Foley must've seen him one of those times, and remembered."

Walker met her gaze. "So Foley says he saw Eddie again, yesterday. Did Eddie see *him*?"

"He did, but realized it only later. Eddie told me he'd noticed an older man with a vaguely familiar face, entering the lobby from the street at the same time he was going out."

"And did Eddie admit, to the cops, that he went to Weaver's office?"

"How could he deny it? Foley'd seen him leaving the building. Besides, why shouldn't he admit he went there? He didn't kill anyone."

Walker let a few seconds pass, then said, "Did your husband say he saw anyone else, in the lobby?"

"Two people. A young woman minding the newsstand, and a shoeshine boy."

"How about anyone upstairs, in the hallway?"

"What would it matter?" she asked. "The police already know Eddie was there."

"It matters because you said he told you he could hear Weaver's voice, calling to him as he left the office. If anyone else heard that, it'd prove Eddie didn't kill him."

Anna nodded dazedly. "Yes. I see. But he said he saw no one else." Finally she asked, refocusing, "If you *are* going to help me—shouldn't you be asking Eddie these questions?"

"I plan to." Walker checked his watch. "He's probably been arraigned by now, which means a lawyer might need to accompany me, to question him."

Anna shook her head sadly. "I can't afford to hire a lawyer, Mr. Walker."

"Then one'll be appointed by the court. Don't worry."

After a pause, she looked again into his eyes. "What about you?"

Walker knew what she meant: *I can't afford you either.*

"We'll work it out," he said.

Solving her problem, though, would be a lot harder than working out a fee, Walker thought as he re-read the news piece after she'd left. The cops already had a suspect in custody who had admitted to assaulting the murder victim shortly before the body was found. In their minds, they had their killer. Why should they do any more investigating?

He found himself wishing Gladys had kept her mouth shut.

# # #

An hour later Walker found he had guessed right: Edward Kelzo had been booked and arraigned and was sitting in a cell at the city jail. His assigned lawyer, Robert Gilmore, was an acquaintance of Walker's from his days with NOPD, and happily arranged an interview with Eddie.

They were also allowed access to the medical report, which was interesting only because of the consistently shallow depth of the throat wound, suggesting an extremely short-bladed knife—and no such tool/weapon had been found on the suspect or at his residence. As for the questioning session, it turned up nothing Walker hadn't already known, except a strong sense that Eddie Kelzo was no killer. But how would he prove it?

It was past four o'clock when Walker left the jail. Hopeful or not, he figured he had time to at least make a start. He popped into a phone booth, found the number for Weaver's agency, dialed, and was surprised to hear someone pick up. It was Gus Foley, Weaver's associate. Walker introduced himself, asked if they might meet, and twenty minutes later was facing Foley across a cluttered desk that still bore Eason Weaver's nameplate.

"So you're in charge now?" Walker asked.

"I suppose," Foley said. An obese man with a white mustache and thinning hair, he seemed less than enthused by the idea, but sometimes it was hard to separate truth from acting. Foley had a right to be depressed, Walker thought: his colleague—and presumably his friend—had been murdered. On the other hand, Foley might be the murderer.

With all that in mind, Walker asked for his version of what happened.

"I already told the cops what I saw," Foley said. "Monday afternoon I returned to the office after running an errand and found Eason—Mr. Weaver—lying right here, in a pool of blood. His face was battered, and"—Foley swallowed hard—"his throat was slashed, ear to ear." He took a breath and shook his head. "Eason and I didn't always agree, but finding him that way—"

"I understand," Walker said. "What were some of your . . . disagreements?"

"I don't know, business matters, mostly. I'd heard there'd been some complaints, in the past. I'm officially a partner because Eason needed the money and I bought into the business, sort of rescued him, but I haven't done much. Only been here a few weeks."

"So, before you came—"

"Eason ran it alone. He always seemed short on cash even though he had one well-known writer, but I think Eason earned a bit from his own book."

"His own? What kind of book?"

"A seafaring novel, called *Pequod*. Based on *Moby-Dick*, same characters and such."

"Didn't Melville already write a sequel?"

"Beats me," Foley said. "I think Weaver's novel was more of an 'inspired by' thing."

"How about the dispute between Mr. Weaver and the wife of the suspect?" Walker asked him. "Know anything about all that?"

"No—that was before my time. When I saw her husband in the lobby the day of the murder, well, I recognized him from when they'd been here before, but I'd never spoken to him, him or his wife either." He ran a hand through his sparse hair. "Sad thing, all the way around."

"You said there'd been complaints. Who, exactly, complained?"

"Don't know. Like I said, I haven't been here long."

Walker had a sudden thought. "Did Weaver keep a list of clients?"

"Sure. Want to see 'em?" Foley heaved himself out of his chair and trudged into the other room. After a moment he returned with a single sheet of names. "Take it, I got two."

Walker looked it over. "This all there is?"

"That's it. We were never a big deal, here. And I expect our one big-name client'll probably bail out now that Eason's gone."

Walker pocketed the list, then asked, "Where does that leave you?"

"Will I stay on, you mean? No. I'll probably sell the agency. I'll come out okay."

Which was something to remember, Walker thought. Of the three crime factors—opportunity, means, and motive—Foley certainly had the first, and the second one, too, if he owned a small pocketknife. Now he had the third as well.

"When exactly was it," Walker asked, "that you saw Kelzo in the lobby?"

Foley scratched his double chin, squinting. "Let's see . . . I came in the Canal Street door same time he was leaving. I noticed he looked upset, frowning and all, but didn't dwell on it. That was right at five—I remember worrying that Ruby might lock up before I got back."

"Ruby?"

"Ruby Longtree, runs the magazine stand in the lobby. The building's owner pays her to open up every day at seven and lock up at five-thirty."

"Long hours," Walker said.

Foley shrugged. "Lotta folks get to work early and leave late. And Ruby's single."

Walker thought a moment. "Clear something up for me. You got back to the building at five o'clock—but the news report says you discovered the body at five-fifteen."

"That's true," Foley said. "I stopped to chat with Jake Wilson—he's the shoeshine kid, in the lobby—and he talked me into getting a shine. He usually works fast, but this time he took a little longer." He paused and added, "Not that it would've mattered. If this Kelzo fella was the killer, Eason was already dead."

Walker didn't reply. *If*, he thought.

Reading his mind, Foley said, "Are the police sure he's guilty?"

"Oh, they're sure," Walker answered.

He was beginning to wonder if they were right.

# # #

Walker was still thinking about that as he parked his '41 Buick at the Trailways Bus Depot on Tulane Avenue at a quarter to six.

He wandered into the station and was standing there, scanning the crowd, when a short blond woman marched up to him and wrapped him in a bear hug. Shocked, he disengaged and looked into the grinning face of his sister Lavinia. "You're early," she said. "Are you drunk?"

He laughed and hugged her himself. "Just surprised. What'd you do to your hair?"

"It's a wig. Joe Ethridge suggested it. Said it'd make me look like Lana Turner."

"Yeah, well, you tell Ethridge to watch his step."

"Ha! I'm sure he'll be terrified." She looked past his shoulder. "Where'd you park?"

Walker grabbed her bag and steered her outside into the heat. Three minutes later they were headed north on Sarasota, then east on Canal. He slowed the Buick a bit as they approached the Stenman Building, giving it another long look. When he'd left its lobby twenty minutes earlier, the young woman he'd seen at the newsstand was locking up. He planned to question both her and the shoeshine guy tomorrow, and as many of the building's other tenants as possible. And the agency's clients. The thought was daunting.

Vinnie, who never missed much, was watching his face. "You working a case?"

He grinned. "You better hope so. Otherwise I'll need to come live with you awhile."

"Come ahead. I got plenty of room." Which she did. Vinnie had a farm outside Natchez, where she'd lived since her husband died in the war. "What kind of case?" she asked.

He stopped at a traffic light directly beside the Stenman Building. With one arm resting on his open window, he pointed with the other [hand]. "Someone was murdered there."

Vinnie followed his gaze. "I didn't think private eyes investigated murders."

"Usually don't. But this time the police won't. They think they already have their man."

"Do they?"

"I'm not sure. I'm being paid to find out."

"Paid?"

"Well . . . hired."

She smiled and gave him a *You'll never change* look. "Tell me the details," she said.

"About the case?" He shook his head. "I'd rather not."

"Why?"

"Because the last time I got you involved, I almost got you killed. Remember?"

"I remember." She gave him another smile. "You almost got us both killed." Another silence. Walker studied the red light while Vinnie studied the building.

"Tell me," she said.

# # #

The next day, Wednesday, was spent doing grunt work. With the help of the phonebook, the newspaper archives at the city library, the few cops Walker still knew well enough to pester, and his curious sister—he was grateful she was here, though he doubted they'd be going to the zoo anytime soon—he tracked down most of the names on Gus Foley's client list and some of the occupants of nearby offices. Another resource turned out to be Ruby Longtree, the woman who ran the lobby newsstand. Not only was she pleasant and eager, she knew almost everyone in the building, and had a good memory for names and times.

"Yes, Mr. Kelzo came in that afternoon," Ruby told Walker and Vinnie, as she straightened magazines and opened half a dozen incoming boxes. "Around four forty-five. He looked upset, marched right past me and up the stairs. I'd met him a couple times, when he and his wife came here. She'd usually stop and buy a *Newsweek* or a *Good Housekeeping*."

"And you saw him leave again, that day?" Walker asked her.

"Yep. About fifteen minutes later." She paused, shook her head, nodded toward yesterday's paper. "Hard to believe he's a murderer."

Walker made no reply. When he then asked her if she'd also seen Gus Foley that afternoon [also], she said yes, he'd strolled in around five, the same time Mr. Kelzo left.

"Did he also go straight upstairs?" Vinnie asked. Vinnie was her normal dark-haired self today, for which Walker was thankful. He hated the blond wig, and had told her so.

"No, I think he stopped to get a shine first," Ruby answered, pointing across the lobby. "He does that sometimes." As Walker turned to look, she added, "Shoeshine boy's gone for two weeks, visiting kinfolks. Left town yesterday."

He then showed her Weaver's client list. "Recognize any of these names?"

"Two," she said, indicating the famous author and Anna Kelzo. "And this one." Her finger had stopped on the name R. BUCK STUBBS.

"Who's he?"

"She," Ruby said, grinning. "That's me."

Walked frowned. "What?"

"It's my pseudonym. You know, my pen name."

"You call yourself R. Buck Stubbs?"

"I did," she said, "when I was writing. The R's for Ruby, Buck because it sounds like a man, and Stubbs was my mama's maiden name."

Walker stared at her. "Don't tell me Eason Weaver was *your* agent."

"Yep. For a few months, years ago. Tried to sell some of my writing, though I doubt he tried very hard. I'm surprised he kept my name on his list." She made a face and said, "Weaver was a lazy, sneaky bastard. What didn't surprise me was that he also swindled the Kelzo lady. She told me all about that, some time ago."

"How about the other names?"

"I don't recognize any more. Again, though, some might be pseudonyms."

Walker let out a sigh. For every step forward, it seemed, he took two steps back. Ruby did have some encouraging news, though. An attorney on the third floor, Cecil Linwood, was rumored to have had recent business dealings with Weaver—and Linwood was a known associate of Carlos Marcello and the New Orleans mob.

That was the only promising piece of information gathered that day. Seated in Walker's small apartment after a long afternoon of canvassing other inhabitants of the Stenman building and then a late dinner at the newly opened Gumbo Shop on Saint Peter Street, he and his sister reviewed what little they knew.

Assuming Eddie Kelzo had not murdered Eason Weaver, their best and only suspects so far were Weaver's colleague, Gus Foley, and the as-yet-unquestioned mob lawyer Linwood. But they had no proof of anything, and no reasonable plan of how to find any. Besides which, neither Walker nor Vinnie truly believed Foley was the killer, and Walker had discovered this afternoon that Cecil Linwood was—like the shoeshine guy—out of town and wouldn't return soon. Vinnie suggested it might be time to admit to Anna Kelzo that the case was going nowhere.

"Not yet," Walker said. "Something'll turn up."

But it didn't, at least not the following day. Thursday was spent asking more questions and checking more details. Walker met again with Gus Foley, who seemed as gloomy as before but no less helpful. He provided names to go with the other pseudonyms, along with phone numbers since most lived elsewhere. Walker talked with the clients he could locate and phoned those he couldn't. Ruby Longtree still seemed willing to assist as well. But nothing panned out. The one good thing to happen was that Foley offered Walker an empty ground-floor storeroom as sort of an on-site headquarters. It had no phone but was accessible from the alley, so they could use it after hours. He even provided a key. Even so, Walker and Vinnie made little progress. Eddie Kelzo's case, a long shot to begin with, had become a lost cause, a fact that Walker reluctantly passed on to Anna. There were no clues, no leads, no hope.

Until Friday afternoon.

Walker was sitting alone in their little room in the alley across from a dress shop next door, sifting through mostly useless information, and Vinnie had walked back to Walker's office to search a file. He was re-reading a section of his notes when the answer hit him.

It had been there for two days, right in front of them. They just hadn't seen it.

# # #

At 4:35, shortly after the puzzle pieces had clicked into place in Luke Walker's head, he left the alley office, entered the Stenman Building, and made a long call from the pay phone across the lobby from the newsstand. After hanging up, he took a notepad and pencil from his pocket and scribbled a message.

Then he crossed the lobby and focused on Ruby Longtree.

"I need a favor," he said.

She nodded, wide-eyed.

"I can't seem to reach my sister right now, but she's supposed to meet me here in the lobby at five-fifteen. You'll still be here, right?"

"Yeah—I lock up at five-thirty."

He folded the note he'd written and handed it to her. "Give her this, okay? And thanks."

With that, Walker marched out of the building, car keys in hand.

For the first time in three days, he felt confident.

# # #

At ten minutes to seven, Luke Walker parked a block east of the Stenman Building, circled around to approach the building from the rear, and crouched in the alley thirty feet from the small room he and Vinnie had begun calling their command center. By that time, 6:55, the sun had been down half an hour and the alley was dark, its only real light the distant glow of a streetlamp at the far end. The room's door was closed, its light was off, and its single window revealed the outline of someone seated inside. Good, Walker thought.

At exactly seven o'clock he saw a shadowy figure move down the alley from Canal Street, kneel beneath the room's window, and rise slowly to peek inside. Then a handgun appeared, and fired five shots into the room. It didn't take long, but it was enough time to allow Walker to cross the alley and put his own pistol to the head of the shooter. "Drop it," he said.

The smoking gun, a small revolver, fell to the ground. Walker held his own weapon steady as he pulled Ruby Longtree to her feet and patted her down. Inside the dim office, whoever had been in the chair had fallen to the floor. Vinnie emerged then from a closet, switched the room light on, and opened the alley door.

"Find a phone," Walker said to her, as he cuffed Ruby's wrists. "Call the cops, if they're not already on the way." Vinnie nodded and hurried off.

Ruby's face was beet-red. "You're a private investigator—you can't arrest me."

"I can sure hold you till the police get here."

She seemed about to say more, then stopped, her chest heaving. At last she said, "What did I kill, just now? A dummy?"

"You're the dummy, Ruby." He looked at the bullet-shattered window and then back again. "What a damn stupid thing to do."

"What was stupid was talking to you at all, the other day." After a pause she met Walker's gaze and asked, "How'd you know?"

"I didn't for sure, till now. But I had a funny feeling, watching you slice open those boxes the day we met. The police report mentioned the consistent depth of the throat wound."

"The box cutter," Ruby said, breathing hard. "I knew I should've used a knife on him."

"Even so, I didn't give it much thought. Later, though, all that explaining you did, about how you chose your pseudonym—"

"You checked," she said.

"Why not? It wasn't hard. Turns out your mother's maiden name was Cox. Not Scruggs."

Ruby glared at him. She was caught and knew it, but still defiant. "You're lying to me," she said. "That's not enough to go on, to set up this kinda trap." She waved her cuffed hands to encompass the dark alley, the room, the broken window. "What are you not telling me?"

At that moment Vinnie returned, along with two uniformed cops. One of them took Walker aside while the other checked Ruby's handcuffs and searched her further. "What else did you know?" she shouted to Walker.

After a barrage of questions and explanations and examining of credentials, he and Vinnie stood alone, watching Ruby being led away up the alley toward Canal. In Vinnie's hand was the blond wig she'd taken from the head of the dress-store mannequin they had propped up in the chair, inside the dimly lit room. The wig was torn in several places by bullet holes.

"Couldn't you have gotten to her before she shot my new hairpiece?" Vinnie asked.

Walker smiled. "I never liked that thing anyhow."

Then she noticed the folded slip of paper in his hand. "That the note you gave her?"

"Yeah. It was in her pocket." He'd forgotten that Vinnie had only been told what to bring and do, in his phone call to her from the lobby. He watched her now as she read the words:

Vinnie – Found a witness. She saw Kelzo leave, heard Weaver moaning, saw real killer enter office. She'll come to our room in the alley tonight at 7. I'm gone to borrow voice-recording equipment, might get back late. Meet her there and lock the door. – Luke

"You sly dog," she said. In the distance, a siren wailed, and gradually faded. Then she looked up at him. "What exactly *was* it that you found?"

Walker rubbed his eyes. "I don't know everything myself yet, and won't until Ruby tells the police, but it was enough to make me pretty sure. Enough to try what we tried, anyway."

"So tell me."

He looked up at the strip of starry sky above the alley. It was full dark now.

"It goes back to all that reading Ma made us do, as kids," he said. "Remember I told you Gus Foley said Weaver published a book of his own? A novel called *Pequod*?"

"Yeah. Sort of a sequel to *Moby-Dick*, you said."

"And Ruby told us she was a writer, too, remember? Pen name, 'R. Buck Stubbs.'"

"Right. So?"

"Two of the main characters in Herman Melville's novel were the first mate and the second mate. Know what their names were?"

She stared at him, waiting.

"Starbuck and Stubb," he said.

Vinnie blinked. "You're kidding."

"Nope. What I think is, Weaver didn't write that seafaring novel of his. Ruby Longtree—R. Buck Stubbs—did. I think Weaver claimed it as his own, and if she kept no old drafts or other proof, she couldn't argue it. He cheated her like he cheated Anna, just a hundred times worse."

"And she hated him for it."

"Right. Probably for years. Then Anna and Eddie Kelzo come along, and Anna tells Ruby that Eddie's furious about what Weaver did to her. Then Ruby sees Eddie charge into the building Monday afternoon and storm back out again after a few minutes—"

"And figures he must've had a fight with Weaver," Vinnie said. "So Ruby quick goes upstairs and kills Weaver while Foley sits unaware in the lobby, getting his shoes shined."

Walker nodded. "She probably knew the shoeshine kid would be out of town afterward, in case anybody asked him if she was at her post at the time—which she wasn't. It's something I would've asked Foley about, if I had known to." He paused. "Again, I don't know the whole story. But based on what she was willing to do just now, to eliminate any possible witness . . ."

"But wait," Vinnie said. "You said Foley told you his shoeshine took a bit longer than usual—"

"Yeah. That was an accident. And lucky for Ruby." Walker paused. "Actually, Weaver's death might've also been an accident."

"What?"

"They later found a deadly gash on the back of his skull consistent with his having fallen and struck his head—and also found traces of blood and hair on a sharp corner of his desk. Besides that, there were two big pools—not just one—of blood on the floor."

"Meaning . . ."

"It's possible Weaver rose to his feet after Ruby's shallow slash of his throat and fell again. The severity of the head wound was such that it would've killed him instantly, so it didn't happen earlier, as a result of Eddie's beating—he was still alive when Ruby got there. Either way, Ruby's guilty. The judge'll have to decide *how* guilty."

Vinnie thought this over, smiled, and nodded. "Not bad, big brother." She took a breath. "So what now?"

"Now we call Anna, then go to the station and make our statements. And watch Eddie Kelzo go free."

"And tomorrow?"

Walker grinned. "Tomorrow we're going to the zoo."

Later On, We'll Conspire
by Michael Thomas Ford

#

19. The motives for all crimes in detective stories should be personal. International plottings and war politics belong in a different category of fiction—in secret-service tales, for instance. But a murder story must be kept gemütlich, so to speak. It must reflect the reader's everyday experiences, and give him a certain outlet for his own repressed desires and emotions.

"When do Julie and the kids arrive?" Ida asked, setting a plate of cookies on the table and then sitting down. The apron covering her dress was dusted with flour that matched her white hair, which she'd recently cut into a charming bob.

Clementine took a gingerbread reindeer, bit the head neatly off, and chewed. "Tuesday," she said. "And I haven't done a thing."

"Someone is particularly grinchy this year," Sukie remarked. She took a drag on the Pall Mall in her hand.

"Sukie, you haven't tried the cookies," said Ida, sounding hurt.

"Indeed, I have not," said Sukie, tapping the ash from her cigarette into the green Fiestaware ashtray that sat beside her coffee cup on the table. She looked at Clementine. "How do you feel?"

Clementine, a reindeer leg sticking out of her mouth, spit it into her hand. "Damn it!" she said. "Not again. Ida, what did you put in them this time?"

Ida waved a hand at her. "Nothing," she said. "They're just plain old gingerbread. Not a drop of poison in them."

"Are you sure?" said Clementine, clearing her throat. "Something is leaving a burning sensation."

"That's the clove," Ida assured her.

Sukie watched Clementine carefully for a long moment. Then, satisfied that her friend was not in danger of needing either resuscitation or an antidote, she picked up a gingerbread snowman and dunked it into her coffee.

"Although, if I *were* going to poison someone this time of year, there are a lot of options," Ida said cheerfully. "Mulled wine. Fruitcake. Eggnog. Not only would all those flavors help mask any chemical taste, but death could be blamed on any number of perfectly reasonable things. Allergies and whatnot. Did you know some people react to cinnamon the same way others react to bee stings?"

"It's the most wonderful time of the year," Sukie declared brightly.

"Insufferable," said Clementine. "I can't wait for it all to be over."

"Your poor grandchildren," Sukie said, shaking her head.

"My poor grandchildren are spoiled rotten," Clementine declared. "Just not by me. I think the UPS driver has been to the house every day since Thanksgiving, delivering everything Julie's bought them. It will take her a week to wrap it all."

"She's making up for the Christmases she never had," Ida said.

"I *tried*," Clementine said. "I was just never any good at it. Some women get the Christmas gene. I got the gene that makes you want to dissect human bodies to find out what killed them."

"And it's a good thing for us you did," said Ida. "All those years as a medical examiner have come in *very* handy. Now, shall we talk about the inquiry from Johan?"

The other two nodded. Apart from enjoying one another's company, this was why they had gathered in Ida's kitchen on a snowy December evening.

"A good murder is exactly what I need to put me in the holiday mood," Clementine said.

"You're positively Dickensian," said Sukie. "Don't be surprised when three spirits visit you in the night."

Ida shushed them. "I don't know how I feel about this one," she said.

"It's not like you to be squeamish," Clementine remarked. "Is it a child? You know we don't do anyone under eighteen. Even if they deserve it."

"It's not a child," Ida said. "It's a politician."

"Oh," Sukie said. "That's a problem."

"We've done politicians before," Clementine reminded her. "There was that mayor a few years back."

"That wasn't about politics," Sukie argued. "It was personal. All those little girls. We made an exception for him."

"Maybe this one is personal, too," said Clementine. "Who is it, Ida?"

Ida told them the name of the intended victim.

"I don't even know who that is," said Clementine. "What country is he from? And what is he, a king? A president? I have no idea."

"How can you be so smart and yet have no grasp whatsoever of world affairs?" Sukie asked.

"I'm a doctor, not a politician," Clementine retorted. "After all these years learning the million-and-one things that can go wrong with the human body, my brain is full. I can't hold another fact. Also, politics bores me. A bunch of man-children squalling for attention."

"He's a deputy prime minister," Ida said.

"Well then," Clementine said, waving her hand. "No one cares about them. I'm sure no one will even notice he's gone."

"He's a very *important* deputy prime minister," Ida informed her. "Particularly if the prime minister over him were to die. This one would take his place."

"Is the current prime minister in imminent danger?" Sukie asked. "Is he elderly? Infirm?"

"Not that I know of," Ida said. "But who knows? I'm thinking it's likely that someone might be planning on causing his early retirement," she said, "in order to put our target in his position."

"I take it that would be a bad thing?" Sukie said.

"Depending on your political leanings, yes," said Ida. "The current prime minister and the deputy prime minister couldn't be farther apart."

"And if they're both out of the picture?" Sukie asked.

"Then the second in line takes over," Ida answered. "She's much more in the mold of the current prime minister."

"It's starting to make sense," said Sukie. "Someone fears the prime minister is not going to be in his position much longer, either due to natural causes or a twist of fate, so they're hedging their bets and trying to ensure their preferred candidate gets the job when he vacates it."

"Exactly my thinking," Ida said. "There's also an important vote happening shortly after the new year. It could swing things in an entirely different direction. I think we're being asked to help one side gain an advantage."

"I find this whole idea appalling," Clementine said.

The other two looked at her. "You do?" said Sukie.

"Of course," Clementine snapped. "If someone is planning on eliminating the prime minister, that means we're being relegated to the B-team!"

The other two shook their heads.

"Don't tell me you wouldn't like to bag a prime minister," Clementine said, helping herself to another cookie.

"This isn't a hunting expedition," Ida said. "It's not like we're going to taxidermize the kill and mount the head over the fireplace."

"Can you imagine if we did?" said Clementine. "How fantastic would that be?"

"I think it's too risky," Sukie said. "The whole thing. A small-town mayor is one thing. This is international politics."

"The world is one small town now," said Clementine. "It's not like the Cold War days, where you had to sneak across enemy lines to assassinate someone, or parachute into Baklavaria or wherever in the dead of night to launch a covert war. For heaven's sake, a boy band breaking up has international consequences now. Julie said that when Kylie's favorite K-pop band broke up she wouldn't come out of her room for four days."

"That's not quite the same thing," said Ida.

"Isn't it, though?" Clementine argued. "My point is, the difference between domestic and international, the personal and the public, is smaller than it's ever been. Like all those crystal-licking New Age types like to say, we're all connected." She took another cookie. "Personally, I think it all started when that wall came down in Germany."

"You sound disappointed," Sukie remarked.

"Maybe just nostalgic," said Clementine. "You have to admit, James Bond was always more exciting than Jessica Fletcher."

"Not to me," said Ida. "I'm much more interested in the personal than the political. Spies and international intrigue and all that are for, what did you call them, Clem, man-children?"

"Maybe," Clementine conceded. "But the gadgets!"

"Ida is right," said Sukie. "The motives behind political hits are so crude. Power. Money. Keeping the rich rich. Personal vendettas are about the human—betrayal, jealousy, revenge. Betsy-Lou Neighbor is furious that after years of competing to be the best bakers in town, Maggie Housewife steals her recipe for cherry pie and wins the blue ribbon at the county fair, so she offs her. That's a much more satisfying story than eliminating a contender for the throne. There's a reason cozy mysteries fly off the shelves at my store."

"Speaking of such things," Ida said, "do you like the gingerbread? I'm thinking of putting them in my cookie boxes this year. I want them to be better than Katerina Lovejoy's gingerbread. She's always bragging about how she uses her great-great-great-grandmother's recipe. It's tiresome. She probably got it out of *Good Housekeeping*."

"They're very good," Sukie assured her.

"Just very good?" Ida said, sounding wounded. "Maybe I should put more black pepper in them."

"They're excellent," said Clementine. "If they *had* been poisoned, I would at least have died happy. But I'm curious. Why does Johan want us for this job? Can't they find someone more local to the prime minister runner-up to do it?"

"I was going to get to that part," Ida told her. "Once we decided if we were even interested. Are we?"

"Yes," Clementine said.

"Sukie?" Ida asked.

Sukie shrugged. "I admit it's an intriguing offer," she said. "I assume the terms are good?"

"Enough to pay for that little cabin on a lake you said you'd like to have for next summer," Ida said. "Maybe even the lake itself."

Sukie raised an eyebrow. "Tell me more."

"It just so happens the deputy prime minister is about to arrive on a tour of our fair land," Ida said. "A kind of Christmas goodwill thing. He's visiting places that have sizable communities of people who share his heritage. And one of those places is our very own charming city. After meeting with local business leaders, he's going to be attending a service at St. Joe's on the twenty-first. The Nativity pageant, as it happens. There's a social afterward."

"That doesn't feel coincidental," Clementine remarked. "I don't suppose Johan has connections to the deputy prime minister's schedule coordinator?"

"It wouldn't surprise me in the least," said Sukie. "Johan has connections to everybody."

"I treasure that autographed poster he sent me from Anna Netrebko's performance of *Manon Lescaut* at Salzburg," Clementine said.

"There will be a fairly small contingent accompanying him," Ida continued. "Staying at the Sugarplum B and B." She looked at Sukie. "That's where you come in."

"Another lucky coincidence?" Sukie asked.

"I might have suggested it to Johan as an option," Ida admitted. "Local color and all that."

"So, I'll be distracting Noel," said Sukie. Her on-again, off-again romance with the Sugarplum's widower owner was currently in the on-again category. "What's the rest of the plan?"

Ida told them. When she was finished, Clementine clapped enthusiastically. "There's a role for each of us. Just like in the old *Charlie's Angels* episodes."

"Poor Sabrina," said Sukie. "She never got to wear the booty shorts."

"We're agreed, then?" Ida said. "I can tell Johan we'll take the job?"

She and Clementine looked at Sukie. "Why not?" Sukie said, lighting another Pall Mall. "What are the holidays without a little murder?"

# # #

"Tummy, take Elphie and go join the angel choir," Clementine said, shooing her grandchildren in the direction of a gaggle of other youngsters.

"Those names," Ida said. "What was Julie thinking?"

"I just can't call them Tumnus and Elphaba," said Clementine. "But I suppose it's my fault for leaving her home alone with nothing but a stack of books for company during her formative years. Where did she go, anyway?"

"I sent her to the fellowship hall with the julekake," Ida said. She looked at her watch. "The deputy prime minister should be arriving any minute."

"But there's nothing—helpful in the julekake?" said Clementine.

Ida shook her head. "It's a diversion. Should, later on, anyone want to examine the food from the social for some reason, my julekake will be absolutely innocent." She held up the small gift bag she was carrying. A jolly Santa waved at them from the side. "This is the important thing."

"Do tell," Clementine said.

"Something to make the deputy prime minister a little sleepy," Ida said. "So that when he gets back to the Sugarplum, he'll be less of a problem for you."

"Very thoughtful," Clementine asked. "How are you going to get it into him?"

"Leave that to me," said Ida.

A commotion behind them made them turn around. Three people had entered the church: an older man with silver hair and beard flanked by a young man and a young woman, both blond, who could reasonably be assumed to be siblings given their similar appearance.

"The deputy prime minister has arrived," said Ida.

"And so it begins," added Clementine.

The political contingent was greeted by Pastor Karlsson, a gaggle of deacons, and assorted parishioners.

"They look like pigeons descending on bits of bread," Clementine said.

"Let's take the opportunity to find good seats," said Ida. "The pageant is sure to be horribly delightful, and I want a view."

She was not wrong. As soon as the flurry of excitement over the visiting dignitaries subsided, the church settled back into its usual pattern of subdued Lutheran celebration. Introductory remarks were made by Pastor Karlsson, the deputy prime minister was acknowledged, and then the pageant began. The lights were dimmed to almost nothing as the congregation sang "The People That in Darkness Sat" while candles placed strategically throughout the sanctuary were lit. Then the organist launched into "While Shepherds Watched Their Flocks by Night" and a group of children wearing their fathers' bathrobes walked out, herding even smaller children covered in cotton-ball-studded sheep costumes before them and assembling at the front of the church, singing badly but dutifully about the celestial revelation of the birth of the Savior.

Then it was the turn of the angel choir. "Hark! The Herald Angels Sing" was of course performed, Tummy and Elphie waved at their mother and grandmother and Ida, and all was tinseled halos and giggling while verses 8 through 14 from the second chapter of the book of Luke were recited dramatically by none other than the deputy prime minister himself in a surprise guest appearance as an angel of the Lord.

"He has a lovely voice," Clementine whispered to Ida. "I almost hate to kill him."

Ida shushed her, and Clementine was silent for the remainder of the pageant, which featured the usual cast of characters, including a passably realistic baby doll swaddled and lying in a manger while Mary and Joseph regarded him adoringly and the shepherds and angels grew restless. A rousing group performance of "Joy to the World, the Lord is Come" concluded the performance, after which Pastor Karlsson requested that parents wishing to take photographs of their children remain for a few minutes while everyone else repair to the fellowship hall for refreshments and conversation.

"We're on," Clementine said. "What do you need me to do?"

"Come with me," said Ida.

They left Julie to get shots of the children and walked down a passageway to the fellowship hall. There, tables were covered with holiday-themed baked goods of all kinds. Ida's julekake was one of half a dozen. It was surrounded by plates of cookies, trays of fudge, and punch bowls filled with festive beverages in garish colors.

Ida left Clementine standing by the tables and went into the kitchen attached to the hall. When she returned, she carried a tray filled with paper cups. Most were red, but three were green.

"When the deputy prime minister comes in, we're going to greet him and pass these out. Make sure he and his associates get green ones."

"What's in these?" Clementine asked, sniffing. "They smell wonderful."

"Glögg," said Ida. "Spiced wine. Loaded with sugar. Plus, a little something extra in the green ones."

"What if they don't want it?" Clementine asked.

"They will," Ida assured her. "Glögg is mandatory at Yule. It's hardwired into their psyches. Also, it's delightful. Gets you drunk *and* gives you a sugar rush."

"Now I want some," Clementine said.

"None for you," said Ida. "You still have work to do. We can celebrate after."

A cacophony of voices filled the room as the revelers poured in from the sanctuary. At the front of the group were the deputy prime minister and his assistants. Ida headed for him, followed by Clementine.

"Deputy Prime Minister," Ida said. "We're so glad you could join us tonight. May I suggest we toast the occasion with some glögg?"

The [deputy prime] minister's face lit up. "Glögg!" he said. "Of course!"

Ida deftly picked up a green cup and handed it to him. She handed two others to his assistants, then allowed the red cups to be taken by everyone else.

"*Skål!*" the deputy prime minister called out. *"God Jul!"*

"*Skål!*" the others echoed, lifting their cups.

Ida watched as the deputy prime minister drank.

"That's strong glögg," he said appreciatively.

All the better to mask the taste of the sedative, Ida thought as she smiled and nodded.

The dose wasn't strong enough to render anyone incapacitated. But combined with the effect of the glögg, it would put the deputy prime minister and his associates in a relaxed state that would make what came later easier. Well, easier for Clementine. To make this even more likely, Ida monitored their drinking and conveniently appeared with new cups from time to time.

On one of her trips to the kitchen, she encountered Katerina Lovejoy.

"I tried your julekake," Katerina said sweetly. "It's nice."

Ida knew what *nice* meant, and it wasn't nice. It meant *dry.* She also knew her julekake was anything but.

"Your springerle look lovely, Katerina," she said. "The feet are perfect. Did you use hartshorn?"

"Of course," Katerina said. "It's traditional. Along with the anise."

"I can never get mine as pure white as you do," said Ida.

"No one can," said Katerina. "You have to have a special touch."

"You must make sure the deputy prime minister tries them," said Ida. "I'm sure he'll love them."

"What a wonderful idea!" Katerina said. "Excuse me while I make him a plate."

She watched as her rival trotted off. Katerina's devotion to making traditional springerle was well known, mostly because she never stopped talking about it. The cookies were indeed tricky to make, as Ida had discovered, but not impossible. And the many different molds available for creating the intricate designs on the cookies' tops were the stuff of a baking collector's dreams. As Katerina was quick to tell anyone who would listen, her molds had been handed down over generations. She also liked to have an audience, and instead of baking in her own home, she used the church kitchen for much of her holiday baking.

"Are these supposed to be like rocks?" said Clementine. Coming to stand beside Ida, she held up one of Katerina's creations. It was a rectangular shape, with the image of an angel stamped into the snow-white dough. One corner had been bitten off.

"Yes," Ida said. "You're supposed to dunk them in coffee or cocoa or something to soften them."

"I almost broke a tooth," said Clementine. "And they taste like licorice. Why would anyone make these?"

"They're traditional," Ida said.

"So was sacrificing the king to the land to ensure a good harvest," said Clementine. "But they don't let us do that anymore. Someone should ban these."

"How is the [deputy prime] minister faring?" Ida asked.

"He seems to be in a good mood," said Clementine. "Yawning a bit. I think they'll be leaving soon."

"Good," said Ida. "Once they leave, you take Julie and the kids home. That will give our trio time to settle in. I'll stay here and be seen talking to people. We'll reconvene at my house when you and Sukie are done. I assume Julie bought the story about the three of us doing our annual gift exchange at Sukie's house later tonight?"

"She did," Clementine said. "With any luck, the kids will be in bed and asleep by the time I get home. If I have to sit through that goddamn *Peanuts* holiday special one more time, I might lose it. They watch it every night. Oh, can I get some of that glögg of yours for them?"

"Poor Julie," Ida said. "Did you have *any* Christmas traditions at all?"

"Presents," Clementine said. "But that was Charlie's job. I just showed up on Christmas morning."

"If I'd had a husband and children, I'd have done it all," Ida said. "The cats appreciate the tree, but it's not the same."

"If you'd had children, you probably wouldn't have had the career you did," Clementine reminded her. "It's difficult to be a mother *and* a chemical engineer."

"I sometimes wonder if the tradeoff was worth it," Ida said.

"No sense worrying about what might have been," Clementine told her. "You have a wonderful life."

"Looks like the deputy prime minister is leaving," said Ida. "He's saying his good-byes."

Indeed, the deputy prime minister was shaking hands with the men and accepting the occasional hug from the church ladies surrounding him. He looked decidedly tipsy, his assistants standing close by and looking a little woozy themselves. With a nod to Ida, Clementine made her exit ahead of them. She found Julie and the grandchildren and managed to get them out to the car with a minimum of fuss.

Once they were home, the kids went to change into their pajamas and Clementine excused herself to go over to Sukie's. "I won't be terribly long," she told Julie.

Alone in her car, Clementine turned on the stereo. The voice of Joan Sutherland filled the air, singing "*Il dolce suono*" from *Lucia di Lammermoor.* The mad scene was Clementine's favorite moment in all of opera, and she listened to it the way some athletes listened to rock songs to get themselves pumped up for a match. Although she'd told Ida that worrying about roads not taken was a waste of time, she did sometimes allow herself to fantasize about another life lived, one where she was on stage, performing the music that moved her so deeply.

She'd fallen in love with Sutherland's Lucia after listening to it through headphones while performing autopsies. It was easy to be swept up in the passion of the poor woman manipulated into marrying a man she didn't love, ultimately descending into madness and murder. It was opera, really, that led her to the work she did now. All those hours listening to the tragedies wrought by men (for the most part) against women had fueled in her a desire for revenge. Even after all these years she still enjoyed most the hits that involved eliminating someone who had used their power and influence without concern for the damage done.

She knew nothing about the deputy prime minister's personal life. He seemed like a jovial man, although she knew that a pleasant public personality often belied a cruel private life. Still, he seemed affable enough. That wouldn't prevent her from killing him, but it did seem a little unfair. He was just in somebody's way. She wondered, but only for a moment, if there was a partner of some kind who would mourn his passing.

She drove in the direction of the Sugarplum, stopping a short distance away and pulling into the Heavenly Slumber cemetery, which sat on the other side of a small wood from the property. Cutting the engine, she reached into the backseat for the pair of men's boots, size 12, that sat on the floor. Donning several pairs of thick socks, she slipped her feet inside the boots, opened the door, and stepped out into the snow.

The walk through the connecting wood to the B&B was not long, but Clementine hoped she had eaten up enough time for the deputy prime minister to settle into his room. When she drew close to the house, she texted Sukie with the prearranged code: ARE YOU WATCHING THIS HALLMARK CHRISTMAS MOVIE? ALYSSA MILANO PLAYS SANTA'S DAUGHTER!

Then she waited, standing outside the back door of the house. The snow-shrouded remnants of a small vegetable garden lingered nearby like the ghost of summer, and the air was filled with lightly falling flakes. It was a lovely night. Maybe, Clementine thought, she would at least *try* to watch the horrible *Peanuts* special with the kids when she got home.

A minute later, the lights inside went on, then Sukie opened the door. "Come on in," she said.

"Nice robe," Clementine remarked, going in and shutting the door behind her.

Sukie was wearing a man's terrycloth robe that had seen better days. The faded blue material was frayed, and there were holes at the elbows.

"Don't start with me," Sukie said. "I'm not in the mood. I had to do the thing I usually only do on his birthday, and it took forever."

"Which one of you was Santa and which one was the naughty elf?" Clementine cracked as she removed her boots.

"Take the keys," Sukie said, "and leave them on the counter when you go. I'll pick them up and have them back in Noel's pants pocket before he wakes up."

"And our guest of honor?" Clementine asked.

"I don't know," Sukie said. "They're all in their rooms, but whether they're sleeping or not, I can't say. So be careful."

"If I walk in on the deputy prime minister in his underpants, I'll just pretend to be another guest who wandered into the wrong room," Clementine said. "Or maybe I'll do the thing Noel likes. Do you think the deputy prime minister would enjoy it?"

"Go," Sukie said, pointing. "Room seven. Third floor. And use the back stairs."

"Just like a scullery maid," Clementine said. "Off about some illicit business."

She crept up the stairs, easily falling into a fantasy about being a woman entering a castle to get revenge on a lover who betrayed her. She was no longer Clementine; she was Anaïs, French, with a tréma, and a vendetta. She was there seeking justice against Marcel, dashing but heartless, who had stolen both her heart and her ruby necklace. Now, he would pay.

She moved stealthily, ascending to the third floor and the chamber where, hopefully, Marcel slept, unsuspecting. In her pocket she carried a vial of poison and a hypodermic needle with which to inject it.

When she reached the door to Room 7, she paused. She heard no signs of movement from behind it and so she slipped the key into the lock and turned it. There was the faintest of clicks, and the door opened. She peered inside, saw that it was dark, and felt a thrill ripple through her breast. It was time.

She entered the room, her stockinged feet silent as cat's paws. Moonlight filtered through the curtains and illuminated the bed on which Marcel lay, one hand dangling conveniently over the side, his fingertips almost brushing the carpet. The gentle rasp of his breathing filled the room. *Drunk,* Anaïs thought. *On wine bought with my rubies.*

She knelt beside the bed, uncapped the needle, and took her lover's wrist in her hand. Before she could press the needle into his flesh, he stirred. He mumbled words she could not understand. Then he turned his head, opened his eyes, and looked at her.

"Who are you?" he muttered.

"A dream," Clementine said, and slipped the needle in.

A moment later she was back on the stairs, then in the kitchen. She slipped her feet into the boots, left the keys on the counter, and went out into the winter night. She did not look back at the castle as she returned to the path through the wood. Her work was complete.

###

It was early afternoon of the next day before they could reconvene in Ida's kitchen to discuss the previous evening's events.

"The police were at the Sugarplum for most of the morning," Sukie said. "The general consensus is that the deputy prime minister had an unfortunate heart attack."

"Good old digoxin," Clementine said.

"However," Sukie continued, "they would like to test the food from last night's event at the church. Just in case."

"Let them," Clementine said. "They won't find anything."

"Well," said Ida.

"Well?" said Sukie. "Well, what?"

"They might find *something*," Ida said. "If they test Katerina's springerle. I made sure there were some left over. In fact, I saved them in a container that is very clearly marked with her name."

"What did you do?" said Sukie.

"Me?" Ida said. "Nothing. But Katerina might have put something in her springerle dough. I wouldn't know."

Clementine cackled. "You set her up," she said.

"It's her own fault, for leaving her molds in the church kitchen," Ida said. "I couldn't resist borrowing one."

Sukie shook her head. "You really shouldn't have."

"She's just so smug," said Ida. "She said my julekake was *nice.*"

"Rude," Sukie said. "I hope they put her away for a very long time. But you did break one of the cardinal rules. You let it become personal. And Johan is going to be upset if this gets turned into an international incident. Why would Katerina Lovejoy want to kill the deputy prime minister? What motive would she have?"

"She was trying to kill *me,*" Ida explained. "Jealousy over my superior baking skills. The deputy prime minister was a regrettable accident."

"You stole that idea from me!" Sukie exclaimed.

"Perhaps you *inspired* it," Ida admitted.

"Consider it my Christmas gift to you," said Sukie.

"That's very generous," Ida said. "I only got you a bottle of Shalimar."

"Are we really doing gifts?" asked Clementine. "I thought that was just something we told Julie." She stood up and pulled her coat on. "Damn it, now I have to go shopping."

"Sit down," Sukie told her. "Christmas isn't about gifts. It's about being with the people you love."

Clementine made a gagging noise. "You sound like that little thumb-sucker in the cartoon the kids love so much. Screw him and that ratty little tree. You're both getting Coach bags. Act surprised when you open them."

Sukie looked at Ida. "It's a wonder Julie isn't a homicidal maniac, isn't it?"

"Don't get my hopes up," said Clementine as she headed for the door. "I'll see you girls later. Don't kill anyone without me."

"We wouldn't dream of it," said Sukie.

When she was gone, Ida refilled her and Sukie's coffee cups. "Are you and Noel spending Christmas together?" she asked.

"I don't think I'm ready for that kind of commitment," said Sukie. "Besides, it will take him a while to get over finding a dead diplomat in his guest room. He thinks no one will want to stay there now."

"I think people are *more* likely to want to stay in a murder house," Ida said. "Oh, but I guess they don't know it's murder." She sighed. "I hate that our best work has to remain a secret. Anyway, you're always welcome to come here. I can make pancakes."

"Hopefully, not from Katerina Lovejoy's recipe."

"No," said Ida. "This one is all my own. I use pecans and brown sugar."

"That sounds wonderful," Sukie said. "And I'll need it after Christmas Eve. That's our busiest day at the bookstore. All those last-second shoppers. By the time we close, all I want to do is take my shoes off and stuff myself with sugar and booze. And speaking of presents, what did you ask Santa for this year?"

"After the deputy prime minister, I'm afraid I'm on the naughty list," said Ida. "He'll only bring me coal. For all the jollity, he's terribly judgmental. Honestly, it borders on child abuse, the way they live in fear of him."

"Maybe you should leave out some cookies and milk for him anyway," Sukie said. "Just to be on the safe side."

"Perhaps," Ida agreed. "But not milk. I think, perhaps, a cup of glögg."

Shabu and the Golden
Goose Murder Case
by Richie Narvaez

#

20. And (to give my Credo an even score of items) I herewith list a few of the devices which no self-respecting detective-story writer will now avail himself of. They have been employed too often, and are familiar to all true lovers of literary crime. To use them is a confession of the author's ineptitude and lack of originality.

— Determining the identity of the culprit by comparing the butt of a cigarette left at the scene of the crime with the brand smoked by a suspect.
— The bogus spiritualistic séance to frighten the culprit into giving himself away.
— Forged finger-prints.
— The dummy-figure alibi.
— The dog that does not bark and thereby reveals the fact that the intruder is familiar.
— The final pinning of the crime on a twin, or a relative who looks exactly like the suspected, but innocent, person.
— The hypodermic syringe and the knockout drops.
— The commission of the murder in a locked room after the police have actually broken in.
— The word-association test for guilt.
— The cipher, or code letter, which is eventually unravelled by the sleuth.

Another painfully beautiful day in San Diego, and I stood poolside, waiting for my boss, Shabu the killer whale, a.k.a. the world's greatest detective, to answer a question.

Completing another gentle circuit, she surfaced, looking at me intently with one very clear blue eye. Her "voice" came out of the speaker near the slideout, translated via AI into English: "Give me the bad news first, if you please, Angie."

"Finally! Well, what you expected has happened. Ocean Park

Management's new board of directors is not going to honor your old handshake—*flippershake*—deal."

"How much do they want?"

"They've reassessed your, ahem, value. They say you have nostalgia appeal. You know the money they make off Shabu T-shirts, flip-flops, and candy is insane."

"How much for my freedom, Angie?"

"The board says they won't let you go for any less than eighteen million dollars."

I knew what was coming. Shabu dove down—as deep as she could in that human-made tank—and stayed there, stewing. I took a seat on a diving board, water lapping at my feet, and waited. Orcas can hold their breath for fifteen minutes or so, and Shabu was one stubborn orca. She would stay down as long as cetaceously possible.

I was scrolling through one of several dating apps on my phone when, from underwater, Shabu said, "The cowards didn't have the nerve to tell me themselves."

It was that neutral AI voice, but I could hear anger and disappointment in it.

"Well, when they visited you, you did call them 'feebleminded, even for humans,' so . . ."

"An unfortunate slip. What, pray tell, is the current aggregate of my accounts?"

I was tempted to exaggerate. But she would sense it. And I was pretty sure she knew the answer already. "After the last case, you have three hundred and forty grand and thirty-two cents in assets."

"Closer and closer," she said. Then suddenly she breached and spun, gleaming in black and white. When she landed with a splash, she said, "So what is the good news, Angie?"

"I got invited to a party. A fancy one."

"While I am pleased that your social life is progressing, I wonder what this has to do with me?"

"Funny enough, the invite came from Annette Lagares. She's an old friend, haven't heard from her in years."

"Continue."

"Well, Annette married Gregg Lagares, from the big seventies–eighties family singing group Lagares. You know, 'Dancin' Dummy,' 'I'll Wash Your Back,' 'Playthings.'"

I knew that since Shabu was wirelessly connected to the Internet, she was already researching the group and its songs faster than I could tell her about them.

"Clamorous, saccharine-pop effluence, with interminable redundancy and inexorable verve."

"Yep, that's them."

"Internationally famous," she went on. "Composed of two sets of triplets. Seven number one hits. Mostly due to the star power of the youngest brother, Roberto. They were successful until his onstage behavior became increasingly bizarre. Such as not singing but instead performing slam poetry accompanied by a slidewhistle."

"Yep, he flushed his career down the toilet, and since he was, let us say, the golden goose of the group, that meant the rest of the family got flushed, too. Big but, however—with royalties and investments, they're still pretty rich. At least Roberto is. Through clever—some would say 'sneaky'—lawyering, he wound up owning everything."

"Does the occasion of this party have to do with rumors of a yet another reunion album and concert?"

"It doesn't say so on the invite, but that'd be my guess."

"And you believe something is amiss regarding this potentially lucrative business, and your old friend has invited you to the party in a surreptitious effort to hire me?"

It wasn't unusual for people to want to engage Shabu in a roundabout way—who wants to be seen hiring a four-ton orca to fix their problems?

"Yep. Annette and I were close, but that was a long time ago. And my name was in the papers last month because of the exploding teapot investigation we did."

"Yes, the Chamomile High Murder Case."

"She hasn't said so, but it makes sense."

"Indeed," said the killer whale. "It is good news."

# # #

Roberto Lagares lived in an impressive Queen Anne, probably built in the 1880s, over in Heritage County Park. I have a thing for impressive Victorian houses. Probably because I'll never own one. Its distinguished gray shingle roof and classic Corinthian columns seemed to clash with the pink, yellow, and green paint job—but the curved, windowless turret jutting above the porch brought it all together.

As I walked up the balustraded stairway, I made sure Shabu was with me, listening to everything through my mePhone.

Annette met me at the door with squeals and hugs. She looked the same, terrific in a rose-gold jumpsuit and her dark hair pulled to the side. But there was worry in her eyes.

She saw I wanted to ask, but she said, "Not yet. Drinks first. And let me introduce you around."

In the massive parlor, crowded with famous faces and lined in old movie posters, Annette introduced me first to Marsha, the oldest of the female triplets, who wore a kinda-sorta Civil War–era getup. "Welcome."

Next was Pedro, the bass player, who I'd had a crush on as a girl. Time had not been kind to him. He wore dark shades, an awful rug, and appeared to be drunk. "Have you seen Brittney? Where is Brittney?" he said, brushing past us.

Talking to some promoters were the youngest female triplets, Cyndy and Janet, one dressed in a pleather dominatrix outfit and the other in a headband and a diaphanous gown. In the kind of harmony they were known for on their albums, they said, "Welcome to our house," and went back to their conversation.

As we walked away, Annette whispered, "All the Lagares siblings live here. Since their attempts at solo careers dried up, they've had no choice but to live under Roberto's charity. Including me."

She pointed out her husband, Gregg, the oldest sibling, across the room, talking to servers. I noticed there was a monkey on his shoulder, smoking a cigarette.

"Um?" I asked.

"That's Maurice, his emotional support macaque. He's never without it." She gave me a knowing look. "*Never*. I used to dream about marrying an older, mature man. I just didn't count on his having a monkey."

At the set-up bar, she ordered us two lemon drop martinis.

"You remembered," I said.

"Sure enough."

In my earpiece, I heard Shabu: "And the golden goose?"

I said to Annette. "Hey, where is—?

"Roberto? Roberto doesn't *do* parties. He's upstairs, probably getting ready for his evening soak. It's where he spends most of his time."

"In the bath?"

"Actually, yes. But I hear your boss does the same."

"Funny! As a matter of fact, she and I are wondering—not that you wouldn't invite me anyway—but, perhaps, you invited me because you want to consult us about something?"

She giggled as if it were the craziest idea and then her eyes went serious. "Now that you mention it—" She gestured me for me to follow her outside to the porch. "You may have heard, Roberto's had this idea to record one last album and do a reunion tour—before they all get too old. Most of the family seemed to agree—I think they all want one last blast of cash so they can move out. Gregg certainly does. I mean, it is a nice house, but it does get cramped with all of us. Although of course there's been some grumbling about who will sing what, who gets a solo, et cetera.

"But then, as they started rehearsals, weird things started happening. Someone tried to break into the toy room. Electric feedback on a mic shocked Marsha. A car almost ran over Pedro . . . Anyway, it's given me a bad feeling, and when I saw your face in the paper—well, I'm sorry to be the kind of friend who only calls when she's in trouble, but will you and Shabu help?"

I heard the orca in my ear: "Inform her that we will take her case for—" Shabu stated a very hefty price.

When she heard it, Annette didn't blink. "Roberto can cover it—and Gregg handles the books, so."

For the next couple of hours, I circulated, eavesdropped—and learned nothing. In the meantime, I'd had too many lemon drops. The loo downstairs was occupado, so I decided to check out the upstairs. On the second floor, I saw a room filled with old toys—action figures, Rip-'Em-Sick-'Em robots, and in the middle of it all, an original version of GI Joan, all of them behind a locked glass door like some exhibit. Cute, if a little juvenile. The bathroom next to that room was also in use. Turning from it, I almost fell into a wheelchair someone had left in the hallway. "What the hell?" But then I saw, at the top of more stairs, like a beacon of hope to my bladder, a door open to a shiny bathroom. Next to the door, a stuffed parrot rested on a tall, wooden perch. As I gingerly ran toward it, the parrot proved to be real—and squawked like a siren. At that exact moment, Roberto Lagares appeared, looking older but still, well, gorgeous, wearing a seen-better-days hotel bathrobe. "What are you doing up here?" he yelled.

I had to yell, too, to be heard over the sound of the bird. "That bird sure is loud!"

"He only does that with strangers. Which you are."

"Yes, sorry! Sorry to intrude! But I really need the facilities!"

"That's my special private bathroom. No one else is allowed to use it."

"I won't be a minute!"

"You're cute, whoever you are. Okay, you may use my bathroom. But I'm timing you!"

"Thanks?" I said, closing the door.

The whole time the parrot squawked at the top of its tiny lungs.

The bathroom was spotless, smelled recently bleached, and was decorated like a spaceship. Stainless steel surfaces, a silver tub. Stars and planets on the walls. Light came from a saucer-shaped fixture descending from the pointed ceiling, and I saw now that there was a tiny window—the bathroom must be in the house's turret, and the window was situated below the rim of the witch's hat. When I emerged, Roberto—carrying the still-squawking parrot on its perch—immediately went in and locked the door.

I turned and saw the Lagares family looking at me from the landing.

"Is Roberto all right?" Janet said. "We heard Bubbles all the way from downstairs."

"Bubbles?"

"The parrot," Annette said. "World's best intruder alarm, and believe me, with all that's going on, he's very necessary. We're all on edge."

"Yeah, they just went into the bathroom," I said, and they all looked relieved.

Steering me downstairs, Annette whispered in my ear, "Roberto locks himself in there and always takes the bird in for a good steam."

"Curious," said Shabu in my other ear.

#

I was back downstairs for another lemon drop and something to eat. The hors d'oeuvres included sushi pizza, foot-high canapés, and, unexpectedly, tater tots. I guess the rich could show good taste.

I then found a quiet spot on the porch to consult with Shabu about what to do next.

"I would like you to remain overnight, if possible, to ascertain—"

Just then, as I was wondering if Shabu expected me to seduce someone, there was a scream—a series of them.

"That's Roberto!" I told Shabu. "I recognize that fifth octave."

I ran in the house. People rushed past me, but I was right on their heels, running upstairs.

When I got there, Gregg and Marsha were trying to open the door. From inside, Roberto yelled, "Help me! The zombies are here! Help! *Eee-heee!*"—then went abruptly silent. As Gregg was about to kick the door in, it opened—and Roberto stood there, naked, wet, pale, then collapsed in a heap.

Instantly, the hot room crowded with Lagares siblings. In the steamy haze, one of the sisters (Janet? Marsha?) screamed, "No! Not Roberto!" I elbowed my way to the door, took out my mePhone, began filming. As I moved closer, Bubbles of course went wild, screeched so loud I covered my ears—and immediately Shabu said: "Angie. I can't see." I clenched my teeth, aimed the camera lower, under the thick mist, had enough time to see Roberto on the black tile floor—no blood anywhere—but a notebook lay next to the body. Gregg knelt over him, yelling "His heart's not beating!" He began doing CPR, someone else yelled, "Open a window!" and someone else, "Can't reach it!" "Get off my foot—don't step on his hand!" Then: "Get Bubbles out! Get that woman out of here!" I asked, "Is he—?" But someone (Cyndy? Marsha?) was already leading me out, and Gregg passed carrying the parrot. He quickly returned sans parrot as I got to the end of the second-floor landing, and someone yelled, "He's gone. Roberto's dead!"

#

Downstairs, Shabu wanted to know everything. "Recount to me now, Angie, while your memories are fresh, all that you sensed in that room."

"Well, it was steamy, as expected. But there was a sweet smell the room didn't have before—his shampoo and soap maybe?"

"Go on."

"Roberto's lips were blue! Like he had been suffocating."

"Good. Who else was in the room?"

"Gregg. Marsha. Janet. Cyndy. Not Pedro—but here he is now."

Pedro stumbled near where I was standing. He looked dazed. "Have you seen Brittney?" he asked me.

I shook my head and he kept on stumbling. Had no one told him about his brother? If I told him, I wasn't sure it would register.

"And I used to make out with his headshot," I said.

"How tragic. Tell me: Where was Gregg's monkey—on his back?"

"Come to think of it, *no*. The monkey was missing!"

When Inspector Didi McCall of the SDPD inevitably arrived, she was not happy to see me. "I suppose you're doing footwork for Fudgie again."

"She's right here," I said, "on speaker."

"Good evening, Inspector," said Shabu. "It is always a pleasure to speak to you long distance."

"Just run down what you saw," said McCall. "I gotta gang of crazy rich people to interrogate, and frankly I'd rather be home watching my plastic plants collect dust."

"Shall I, Shabu?"

"Hey, now," said the inspector, "anything you tell the swimming tux you gotta tell me, or else it's concealing evidence."

Shabu piped up: "I shall disregard your atribilious nature for the sake of our mutual enlightenment. Angie will tell you what she witnessed, and perhaps you will consider showing us the notebook that was found along with the body." "In due time. First my guys gotta take a look at it."

I told the inspector all I had seen and found out. She didn't seem impressed.

"We'll wait for the autopsy to confirm, but it's obvious what we have here—another big star OD'ing in the bath. Everything's a remake nowadays."

# # #

Every morning, Shabu played with her *Sims*—she had created a baroque villa populated by Hemingway cats. It was her daily diversion, and to interrupt her while she did so was verboten.

I arrived after she was done. I said, "I feel bad we didn't get a look at the notebook. I've asked Annette, and she said she often saw Roberto carrying one. She assumed it contained ideas for new songs."

"No need to feel bad. You captured the opened pages on your camera. During my unihemispheric sleep last night, I was able to enhance the image."

A swoop sound on my phone told me I'd received a picture from Big Momma Splash (Shabu's profile name).

"Wow! Super high res! But what does it say?"

"I first believed it to be cacography, but I have concluded that it is a code. While the inspector is eager to write this death off as an overdose, there is clearly more afoot."

"Agreed."

"To make certain of this, I need you to go back to the Lagares residence and climb the roof—the turret roof, specifically."

"Say what now?"

A few hours later I was airborne—via crane. The mechanical kind. Annette had informed me it was how the trees were trimmed, the gutters cleaned. There was no other way to reach the turret.

So, after calling on the tree service company, I found myself halfway off the crane basket, looking at lovely roof tile. "I can't see the window from here," I told Shabu.

"Closer," she said.

"Oh, brother." I climbed cautiously onto the witch's hat, about fifteen meters above the ground. "I went to Scripps. I got a doctorate from Stanford. Look at me."

"Solving crime is akin to chess—except every move is more intricate, and the stakes are far higher."

"And gravity is a harsh mistress, Shabu." I could just see the tiny window around the bend. "There it is—but what am I looking for?"

"Clues."

"Duh, you kn—wait!" On the edge of the roof above the window were several cigarette butts, smoked down to brown-and-gold filters. I showed the orca.

"Those are Morley's brand cigarettes," she said. "Collect them and please return to the ground safely."

"Shall we tell the inspector about these?"

"In due time."

# # #

I was doing my best to keep up with my dance partner at the Onyx in the Gaslamp, when I stopped to catch my breath. I don't usually check my phone, but the music was giving me a headache. I must be getting old.

There were three messages from Shabu.

"Autopsy reveals two foreign chemical agents in Roberto Lagares's body."

"Conclusion is undisputable: murder."

Then: "Police's likeliest suspect is Gregg."

My dance partner came over and asked me if I wanted to do a body shot off his chest. I begged off. There was work to do.

I caught a ride to the precinct and waited while Gregg was being grilled. Afterward, I caught Inspector McCall in the hallway.

"So what gives?"

"Might as well," said McCall, with a shrug. "Gives me practice for the goddamn press conference. Roberto Lagares was killed with a combination of nitrous oxide, you know, knockout drops in some form, as well as ve-uh-vecu—I'll get it—vecuronium bromide, which caused paralysis and respiratory failure. Coroner found an injection site below the ribs on his left side. Gregg was right over the body. He had the best opportunity to do it."

"But he was doing CPR—and then he took out the parrot. When would he have had the chance?"

"Jesus. You make my head spin. Doesn't matter. We found a needle hidden in his nightstand, and he ain't no diabetic. Tests indicate the needle contained the bromide! My bet is we'll find his prints all over it."

"That sounds a bit too neat, doesn't it, Inspector?"

"You sound too much like your friend, Flailing Nemo."

# # #

The Lagares family lawyer got Gregg out on bail in less than a day.

The trial would be in a few months but would no doubt be delayed indefinitely.

Shabu asked me to call Annette and have her come to Ocean Park with her husband—and his monkey.

Shabu emerged onto the slideout to greet our guests. "I need to ask you—and your monkey—questions."

"Sure. Why not?" said Gregg. On his shoulder, the monkey lit up a cigarette.

I was about to tell the monkey it would stunt his growth, but I kept quiet.

"Where was your monkey when Roberto was found?" began Shabu.

"Maurice was in the kitchen, scarfing down tater tots," said Gregg. "Ask the kitchen staff."

I was confused. "I thought this monkey had to be with you at all times."

"Not when there are tater tots around. He can't resist them. But when he leaves me, I do get so awfully low."

"Are you medically trained?" asked Shabu.

"No."

"Is the monkey?"

"Not as far as I know. He was a circus entertainer. I had him shipped from Japan."

"Does he always smoke?" I asked.

"More when he's nervous."

"Listen, it's going to be a big part of the prosecutor's case. Butts were found outside the bathroom window. Whoever put the nitrous oxide in the room likely did it from there. And it will look like you trained your monkey to do it."

"True, Angie. However, please take a close look at Maurice's cigarette brand."

"Holy cow. He smokes Vicejoys—not Morley's. It wasn't him on the roof!"

# # #

A few days later, the inspector marched out to the pool. I expected the usual irascibility, but McCall was in a surprisingly friendly mood.

"We're in the doghouse, you and I," he said to the orca.

So that was why. She didn't mind being in trouble, as long as he could drag Shabu down with her.

"I got a fun visit this morning," the inspector said. "Cyndy Lagares came to my office, screaming and cursing. She thinks I'm dragging my heels and implied that you were dragging your tail."

"Investigations take time," said Shabu. "We cannot will evidence to appear."

"That's just it! You probably know that she's into a lot of . . . woo-woo."

"Please define 'woo-woo.'"

"I think the inspector means the paranormal, Shabu."

"The inspector does. Cyndy wants to hold a séance to contact her brother to find out who killed him."

"Great Triton! Such flummery cannot be tolerated."

Indeed, neither Shabu nor McCall had any intention of handing the investigation over to the uncertainties of a psychic. But I had an idea: Sharon Pizzarelli from the gift shop had some acting experience, and she had helped us before.

We had the Ocean Park conference room draped in black curtains. Sharon walked out, all five-feet-three of her. And that was in heels and a turban.

"Everyone," I said, "please welcome Delpha Tofana—"

"*Madame* Delpha," said Sharon.

I gave her a look to say, "Don't lose yourself in the part."

"*Madame* Delpha Tofana. She is a master of palmistry, astrology, numerology, and allied miscellany."

I hit the lights. Candles flickered on the table, casting shadows on the curtained walls. Eyes half-closed in concentration, Madame Delpha sat with her hands poised over a "crystal ball"—an old fishbowl turned upside down. Around the table, the remaining Lagares children, the inspector, and I sat holding hands. In a seat of her own, Shabu watched from a computer monitor.

"Tonight," Madame Delpha intoned, "we here seek the presence of a soul taken too soon. We ask for Roberto Lagares!"

There was a knock—from a carefully placed speaker. The Lagareses all gasped, and the inspector gave me a wink.

"Roberto?" Delpha's voice climbed. "Is it really you? We ask you to reveal yourself. Give us a sign!"

Another knock and more gasps.

"He says . . . 'I did not deserve this.' I wanted to go home. I was tired,'" she whispered. "He's here! He says he feels . . . heat . . . so much sand. Up ahead . . . a lonely road."

I looked at Shabu and Shabu looked at me. Our sham psychic was going off script.

"I am not feeling this," said Marsha.

"This is ridiculous," said Gregg.

But their sister Cyndy was loving it. "Blessed spirit, speak to us!"

"I see him—on the ground—a man in pain—covered in blood—and . . . tire tracks?"

Janet suddenly jumped out of her chair, screaming, "All right! I did it! I admit it!"

"You killed Roberto?" asked the inspector.

"No! But, but—in the nineties—it was either the Final Reunion Tour, or the Final Final Final Reunion Tour—whichever one was in Vegas, I ran over a man. I panicked! I kept on driving. I killed him!"

# # #

Later, I asked Sharon why she'd gone rogue. She said she'd read the lines we'd written for her, but in the moment she went into improv mode. She didn't know what came over her. We chalked it up to opening night jitters.

In the end, we did get a confession. Just not the one we were looking for.

We decided to interview each member of the family, everyone who had been in that bathroom, in more depth. All of them were still suspects, despite the too-on-the-nose evidence against Gregg and the wackiness at the séance.

First up was Gregg, who arrived with Annette and his monkey.

"Tell us," Shabu asked, "about the reunion tour. Were you in favor of it? Do you know anyone who was not?"

"I was iffy on the tour, to be honest," he said. "I think we're all a little long in the tooth and out of voice, sadly. I knew my siblings wanted to do it—they wanted to be in the spotlight again, not to mention the money. But I was afraid we'd all be embarrassed."

"Would any of them stand to gain something with you out of the way?"

"I guess all of them would—one less person to divide Roberto's fortune. Oh, also, I've already heard them talking about a 'Goodbye Roberto Reunion Tour,' and I would definitely oppose that."

"Hey! I have a question," I said. "Who is this Brittney that Pedro keeps asking about?"

"Some woman he knows, I guess. I don't know her." At that moment, his phone pinged. "Good news, honey," he said to his wife, "the Rip-'Em-Sick-'Em robots sold."

Annette turned to me. "Roberto put all the toys up for auction. Gregg is handling it now."

"Is that to help pay for the reunion tour?" I asked.

"Oh, no. I think Roberto had finally grown up. Well, a little."

Later, Cyndy glided in, wearing a black pleather bustier and black pleather capris. Ever since the faux séance, Shabu and I weren't her favorite beings.

Shabu asked her about the reunion tour, if she was eager for it to take place.

"I wanted the tour to happen," she said. "Marsha was the one who wouldn't do it unless she got a spotlight to sing from her solo LP *Forever Young*. Which, honestly, Roberto was right to nix. Her stuff is crap."

"Oh, I have a question," I said. "Who is this Brittney that Pedro keeps asking about?"

"Not a clue."

Marsha sailed in in a purple pseudo–Royal Navy uniform, including a purple tricorne hat.

"I was all for the tour," she said, "but it was Janet who didn't want to do it unless she got to perform her solo material. And, to be honest, Roberto was right to shut that down. Have you heard her one single? 'Bite Me, Spank Me, Love Me'? It's terrible!"

On Brittney: "Never heard of her."

Janet showed up in a sleeveless mesh top and micro-minishorts.

"I was eager for the tour, but Cyndy wouldn't go along unless she could perform her own tracks. Honestly, Roberto made the right call—her New Age music is so awful it makes my stomach hurt."

But when I asked about Brittney, she said something almost interesting: "Don't you have more important things to do?"

"There's no telling what small thing might lead to something important," I offered.

"Whatever it is I don't think it's any of my business and it's certainly none of yours."

We couldn't get a hold of Pedro, so the next day Shabu sent me out to interview him at the house. The other siblings were there and busy. Janet and Cyndy were talking to someone, and Marsha was in her office. None of the servants knew where Pedro was. I looked all around inside the house. No dice.

Finally, I went outside and walked around the lovely Queen Anne. That's when I found him. Face down, a knife in his back.

# # #

"It looks bad for Gregg," I told Shabu. "His prints were on the syringe—and now they're on the knife handle."

Shabu was raising her flukes above the water's surface and bringing them down with force to emphasize her words. "Someone. Wants. Gregg. Lagares. Out. Of. The. Way. Why?"

"With him gone the reunion album and concert will happen. But here's something maybe more interesting—Roberto's inheritance goes primarily to Gregg. All the siblings get plenty of money, but Gregg gets music rights, the trademarks, as well as the house and everything in it."

She turned, dove into the water, and then spyhopped. "What are the alibis of the remaining Lagares siblings—our remaining suspects?"

"Gregg and Annette were across town with the family lawyer. Marsha was in her office downstairs. Pedro was killed outside her window, as a matter of fact, but the curtains were drawn and she didn't see anything. Oh, and Janet and Cyndy were meeting with their manager, Kincaid Ruben, in the library. So everyone's alibi looks solid. You know what keeps bugging me—Pedro kept asking for Brittney, and no one seems to know or wants to admit to knowing who this Brittney is."

"I have had Fulvio working on that part of the case."

"What? Why didn't you tell me?"

Fulvio Pieker was a local PI that Shabu liked to call in to assist from time to time. Not the sharpest PI in the rack but always reliable.

"That's going to cut into our profits."

"Justice matters above all else. In the meantime, I have a mission for you."

As she said this, I simultaneously got a text from Big Momma Splash. It was the address for a place called Sherman's in the East Village. Below it read: "pw: Swordfish."

Shabu said, "Ask for Tony."

"Tony?"

"I would rather have Tony's help than that of the whole protective force of San Diego."

I knew better than to ask what she was talking about. I'd find out soon enough.

# # #

As I approached Sherman's, which had all the appearance of a regular local pub, the door opened and out walked a swan. Followed by a familiar-looking collie.

The door closed swiftly behind them, so I went up and knocked.

It was opened a moment later by a rather large male grizzly wearing a cheap cybernetic implant—a crude version of what Shabu was equipped with. He said, "Passwoid."

"Er—swordfish?"

The bear looked down at me. "I don't t'ink so."

"Listen, I'm here for Tony."

"Piss off."

He was about to shut the door when I said, "Shabu sent me!"

"Shabu? Come in," he said, then he pointed with his snout: "Tony. At da bar."

Sitting at the first booth I passed was a dog I recognized as Dan the Doberman, a TakTik star. One table over was a tabby who had been in a million TV commercials. The cat was playing cards with the spokes-llama for a laundry detergent. In fact, the place seemed to be filled with animal performers.

Tending the bar was a Pacific harbor seal—and a Dodgers fan, judging by the baseball cap he wore. It just hid his implant.

"Brave to wear that hat in this city," I said.

"'You can't choose who you love. Love chooses you,'" said Tony, quoting somebody, I couldn't remember who. Maybe a greeting card. Then he said, "Shabu told me you come. One you are looking for is at end of bar. Been away for a while. Just showed up again today."

I looked over and knew immediately why Shabu had sent me there.

# # #

Everyone was gathered around the pool. None of them looked particularly happy to be there.

"Sorry to bring you out here on such a spectacular day," I said.

Gregg wore purple pinstripes, Cyndy a cloak, Marsha a Royal Guard uniform, complete with a bearskin cap and sword, and Janet strategically placed body tape.

Shabu began: "The Lagares family was on the cusp of a yet another reunion tour and album that would profit everyone. Why then did someone want to eliminate the show's star? Why in his bathroom? Why did he scream? Why did his parrot not squawk? Who left cigarettes on the roof? All puzzling. And why kill Pedro Lagares as well? As clues were found, it became obvious that there were many red herrings."

"You thinking about the case or about lunch?" said the inspector.

Ignoring McCall, Shabu continued: "Let us consider the day of the party. Everyone in the family knew that Roberto would eschew the proceedings and spend the time locked in the bathroom with his bird. Knowing this was a perfect time and place to strike, the murderer devised a two-step plan.

"First, they needed Roberto to open the door. The problem was how to get him to do that and not set off his squawking parrot. Angie, if you please."

I whistled and out of the staff entrance walked a macaque—who looked exactly like Maurice.

Gregg turned to his own monkey. "You never told me you had a twin!"

Maurice shrugged.

"This is Robin," I said, "Maurice's identical twin!"

"Like many performance animals of his species," said the killer whale, "he was imported from Japan. Gregg's mention of importing Maurice from there gave me the idea to trace Maurice's relatives. Unlike his brother, Robin has not lucked upon steady employment. Angie found him a bar by the docks frequented by many animals in the same situation, out of work and willing to do anything. You'll note he's been equipped with a speaking device similar to mine."

I said, "Which means we can interview him."

Inspector McCall looked ready to implode. "Now I've seen everything!"

"Hold on, though," I said. "A macaque's brain is not like an orca's, so don't expect him to be as eloquent as Shabu."

"Thank you for your kind words, Angie. To simplify matters, I will first attempt to use word association to communicate with Robin. Let us begin."

The other monkey took out a hamburger from its bag.

"He must have stolen that from that concession stand," I said. "C'mon, guy, talk first, then burger."

I snatched the burger. If you've never gotten an angry look from a macaque, you should give it a try. It will freeze your spine.

Shabu began: "Roof."

"Hamburger," said the monkey.

"Window."

"Hamburger."

"Come on, Robin," I said.

"Hamburger."

"Angie," said Shabu, "give the monkey the hamburger."

I did so. The monkey nibbled on it slowly while giving me the wickedest stink eye. Of course, while it ate, its voice box could still answer.

"Perhaps we can try longer questions," said Shabu. "Did you kill Roberto Lagares?"

"No. Once killed human in Paris, stuffed body up chimney."

This interested the inspector, who immediately started taking notes.

Shabu continued. "But you were on the roof on the Lagares residence?"

"Yes."

"What were you doing there?"

"Climbed in. Over bath. Dropped bath bombs into tub."

"The bath bombs must have contained the nitrous oxide," said the inspector.

I said, "And the parrot remained silent because it knew Maurice—and mistook Robin for his twin!"

"In a large dose," said Shabu, "the released gas would make Roberto paranoid. This is why he saw zombies and why he wanted to escape the bathroom. It would also explain the sweet smell and his blue lips, the result of cyanosis. Now came the second part of the killer's plan. In Roberto's deluded state, he opened the door—and it was then that the vecuronium bromide was administered. In the chaos and the steam, almost anyone could have done it."

"Hold up!" said McCall. "I want to know who hired the monkey."

"Robin, can you tell us who among these humans met with you?"

"Female. Female had mask. Gave hamburgers, whiskey, box Morley's."

"What? And no bananas?" said the inspector. "This is a dead end."

"Angie, could you show our simian guest a picture of Pedro Lagares."

"Sure thing, boss." I did so.

"Robin, have you ever seen this human?"

"Was watching when woman-human hired."

"So, Pedro knew who the killer was," I said, "that's why he was killed."

"Exactly! Thank you, Robin. You may go."

"Wait a second." The inspector moved to cuff the monkey.

"Human law does not apply to our friend," said Shabu.

Robin saluted his brother, then made toward the concession stand.

"You still can't prove Gregg Lagares is not the killer," said McCall.

"Patience. Enter please, Fulvio."

Fulvio Pieker walked in, holding a large paper bag—and pushing the wheelchair I'd seen in the house.

"Fulvio, please show everyone what you obtained in the garbage bins outside the Lagares residence."

"Tape," Fulvio said, pulling a tangle mess of old cellophane out of the bag. "Wads of it, all with Gregg Lagares's fingerprints."

"These were the killer's attempts to transfer Gregg's prints to the syringe and to the knife."

Gregg and Annette sighed and embraced.

"The DA won't like that," said the inspector. "It ain't conclusive. So what's with the wheelchair?"

"From the beginning, the identity of Brittney has been a mystery, and has particularly fascinated Angie. Everyone in the family fully knew who she was, but they were ashamed of her existence."

At that moment, Shabu breached—and on her nose was balanced a figure I couldn't believe I was seeing. Neither did the inspector.

"Please meet Brittney," said the killer whale, as the surprised-looking figure landed with a splash in front of us.

"Oh geez, is that . . . is that a sex doll?"

"Indeed it is," said Shabu. "Found deflated and folded in the trash. The errant wheelchair intrigued me, and quick research informed me that wheelchairs are often used by owners of sex dolls to transport them, as part of the pretense of animation."

"That ain't right."

"Now, now, don't judge, inspector. So why was Pedro looking for it? It's not the kind of thing you or misplace. Someone must have taken it."

"The killer knew that Pedro was obsessed with the doll. Perhaps they used it as blackmail to keep him quiet. Or, more likely, they knew its loss would also keep his addled brain occupied and unable to draw conclusions on the day of the murder. It is also likely that the killer used the doll to lure Pedro to his death."

"How so?"

"All of the siblings had people with them—save one. Janet, could you please describe what you saw when you looked into your sister Marsha's office?"

"She was sitting at her desk. It was dark."

"Did you actually see her face?"

"Come to think of it, now, no, only her silhouette."

"As I suspected. The sex doll had been placed in the office to make everyone think Marsha was working at her desk. It was also near the window, which drew Pedro's attention—long enough for Marsha to kill him."

Marsha marched forward. "Are we going to believe a stupid whale—?"

"Stupid killer whale," I corrected.

"This is outrageous. I'm going to sue."

Annette spoke up then. "But why would she do all this just to sing a solo?"

"No, her motive was more childish than that," said Shabu. "As I noted at the start, it seemed that everyone was at least grudgingly willing to do the reunion. In that case, what other motive could there be besides stopping the concert? Angie, at the house you noted a room full of old toys."

With this, Marsha gasped.

""Siblings, even famous ones, are notorious for fighting over toys, especially ones close in age, as Roberto the youngest male triplet and Marsha the oldest female triplet were. Roberto hoarded the family's toys as part of an exhibit, but most especially the GI Joan. There was one that Marsha treasured, one that fits her military motif. She could not stand the idea of its being auctioned away before she possessed it. That is why she tried to break in and take it. When he died, Gregg was given charge of the toys. And if he were out of the picture, they'd go to Pedro. Another reason to kill him."

"And after him it'd go to the oldest of the triplets," said the inspector. "Marsha Lagares, you are under arrest."

"I hate whales! I hate them!" Marsha drew her toy sword and launched into the pool, flailing toward Shabu. But the detective/*killer* whale easily evaded her until we fished her out.

# # #

The case stayed in the news for weeks, and with it, fewer clients seemed shy about engaging a killer whale's help to solve their problems. We'd also received an obscenely healthy check from Gregg Lagares. Business—and finances—picked up.

"I've been meaning to ask you," I said to Shabu.

"About the notebook."

"Yes! Did you ever get to crack that code?"

"Indeed. The code was merely Latin-script alphabet written upside down and backward."

"So, was it a hidden batch of new songs or a tell-all autobiography?"

"One page contained a reverie about Roberto and Bubbles living together on a magical farm. The other page began with the sentence 'Marsha wants to kill me for that stupid soldier doll' and went on to elucidate in detail."

"I'll be damned! So that's how you broke the case?"

"It was merely circumstantial—but it helped lead the way."

"So it wasn't all big brain deduction?"

"Every little bit helps, Angie. Which brings to mind—let us review again the current aggregate of my accounts."

Double Crossing Van Dine

DOUBLE CROSSING VAN Dine is printed on 60-pound paper, and is designed by Jeffrey Marks using InDesign. The type is Garamond Pro. The cover is by Jackie Webber. The first edition was published in a per-fect-bound softcover edition and a clothbound edition accompanied by a separate pamphlet of" was printed by Impress Print. The book was published in August 2025 by Crippen & Landru Publishers.

Contributors

Publisher

Jeffrey Marks has been nominated for an Edgar (Mystery Writers of America), three Agathas (Malice Domestic), two Macavity awards (MRI), three Anthony awards (Bouchercon), and a Maxwell award (DWAA). He won the Anthony for his biography of Anthony Boucher. His short works have appeared in anthologies and *AHMM*. In his "spare time" he is the editor/publisher for Crippen & Landru. Marks writes from his home in Cincinnati, which he shares with his husband and three dogs.

Editors

Donna Andrews was born in Yorktown, Virginia and now lives in Reston, Virginia. *Birder, She Wrote* (August 2023) and *Let It Crow! Let It Crow! Let It Crow!* (October 2023) are the 33rd and 34th books in her Agatha-, Anthony-, and Lefty-winning Meg Langslow series. She is also the co-editor, with Barb Goffman and Marcia Talley, of ten—soon to be eleven—short story anthologies. She is a longtime member of MWA and Sisters in Crime and currently serves as MWA's Executive Vice President. Website: http://donnaandrews.com

Greg Herren is an award-winning author and editor from New Orleans. His next two novels, *Mississippi River Mischief* and *Death Drop* will be released in Fall 2023. He has published over forty novels and over fifty short stories, and has edited over twenty anthologies. He lives in New Orleans with his partner of twenty-eight years.

Art Taylor is the Edgar Award–winning author of two collections: *The Adventure of the Castle Thief and Other Expeditions and Indiscretions* and *The Boy Detective & the Summer of '74 and Other Tales of Suspense*, both published by Crippen & Landru. His debut book, *On the Road with Del & Louise: A Novel in Stories*, won the Agatha Award for Best First Novel, and his short fiction has also won the Agatha, Anthony, Derringer, and Macavity Awards. He is an associate professor of English and creative writing at George Mason University. Website: www.arttaylorwriter.com.

Introduction

Catriona McPherson (she/her) was born in Scotland and immigrated to the US in 2010. She writes: preposterous 1930s private-detective stories about a toff (book sixteen is *The Witching Hour*); realistic 1940s amateur-sleuth stories about an oik (book two is *The Edinburgh Murders*); and contemporary psycho-thriller standalones (the tenth is *Deep Beneath Us*). These are all set in Scotland with a lot of Scottish weather. But she also writes modern comic mysteries about a Scot-out-of-water in a "fictional" college town in sunny Northern California. The seventh of what was supposed to be a trilogy is *Scotzilla*, and books eight and nine are coming.

Catriona's nationally best-selling work has won multiple Agathas, Anthonys and Leftys and been shortlisted for an Edgar, three Mary Higgins Clark awards, and a UK dagger. She is a proud lifetime member and former national president of Sisters in Crime.

Toni L.P. Kelner, who also writes as Leigh Perry, recently celebrated her thirtieth anniversary as a mystery writer. She's published seventeen novels and one collection, and has co-edited seven anthologies. She won the Agatha Award for Best Short Story, and her short fiction has been nominated for the Anthony, the Macavity, and the Derringer. Reading stories on Reddit is one of her favorite ways to procrastinate, but darned if it didn't inspire this short story.

Contributors

J.C. Bernthal is based in Suffolk, England. He is an Edgar Award-nominated Agatha Christie scholar, and author of Agatha Christie: A Companion to the Mystery Fiction. In 2025, he won the Crime Writers' Association Short Story Dagger.

John M. Floyd is the author of more than a thousand short stories in publications like *AHMM, EQMM, Strand Magazine, Best American Mystery Stories*, and *Best Mystery Stories of the Year*. A former Air Force captain and IBM systems engineer, John is also an Edgar nominee, a Shamus Award winner, a six-time Derringer Award winner, and a recipient of the Edward D. Hoch Memorial Golden Derringer for lifetime achievement.

Michael Thomas Ford is the author of numerous books for both adults and young readers. His most recent novels are The Headless Doll and Every Star That Falls, and his short fiction appears in Weird Fiction Quarterly and the anthologies We Mostly Come Out at Night, Other Terrors, and White on White: A Literary Tribute to Bauhaus. He has been a finalist for the Shirley Jackson Award, the Bram Stoker Award, and the Ignyte Award, and is a five-time winner of the Lambda Literary Award. He lives in rural Ohio with his husband and dogs. Visit him at www.michaelthomasford.com.

Barb Goffman (www.barbgoffman.com) has been a finalist for major crime-fiction short story awards forty-eight times, and she's won the Agatha four times, the Macavity twice, and the Anthony, Derringer, and Ellery Queen Readers Award once each. Barb was the 2024 recipient of the Short Mystery Fiction Society's lifetime achievement award. She is an editor *of Black Cat Weekly* and works as a freelance editor too.

Elly Griffiths is the author of thirty-two crime novels including the bestselling Dr Ruth Galloway series, the Brighton Mysteries and The Frozen People. She won the 2020 Edgar Award for *The Stranger Diaries* and, in 2025, was given the Theakstons Old Peculier award for Outstanding Contribution to Crime Fiction.

Cheryl A. Head writes the award-winning, *Charlie Mack Motown Mysteries, set in Detroit.*
Time's Undoing, her 2023 historical fiction novel, unravels the mystery around the police murder of a young black man in Birmingham, Alabama's Jim Crow era. The book is based on her family's personal tragedy and was a finalist for the Los Angeles Times Book Prize, as well as the Agatha, Strand Book Critics, Macavity, Anthony, and Hurston Wright Legacy Awards.

Vaseem Khan writes two award-winning crime series set in India. In 2021, *Midnight at Malabar House,* the first in the *Malabar House* novels, set in 1950s Bombay, won the Crime Writers' Association Historical Dagger. His latest is *The Girl in Cell A*, a psychological thriller set in small-town America. Vaseem is also the author of the upcoming *Quantum of Menace*, the first in a series featuring Q from the James Bond franchise.

Edith Maxwell writes Agatha Award-nominated short crime fiction, with over thirty published in juried anthologies and magazines, and the Agatha Award- winning historical Quaker Midwife Mysteries. As Maddie Day she writes several popular and long-running cozy mystery series, plus the historical Dot and Amelia Mysteries. Maxwell/Day is a member of Mystery Writers of America and a proud lifetime member of Sisters in Crime. She lives north of Boston with her beau and their cat Martin, where she writes, cooks, gardens, and wastes time on Facebook. Find her at her web site and at Mystery Lovers' Kitchen.

Tom Mead is a Derbyshire mystery writer and aficionado of Golden Age Crime Fiction. His novels include DEATH AND THE CONJUROR, THE MURDER WHEEL, CABARET MACABRE and THE HOUSE AT DEVIL'S NECK, and he also recently published a collection of mystery stories, THE INDIAN ROPE TRICK (AND OTHER VIOLENT ENTERTAINMENTS). His books have been translated into twelve languages (and counting), nominated for various awards and named books of the year by The Guardian, The Telegraph, Publishers Weekly and Crimereads.

Richie Narvaez is the Agatha- and Anthony-winning author of the thriller *Hipster Death Rattle* and the YA whodunnit *Holly Hernandez and the Death of Disco,* as well as the collections *Roachkiller & Other Stories* and *Noiryorican.*

Erica Ruth Neubauer is the author of the Agatha Award-winning Jane Wunderly mystery series. She spent eleven years in the military, two years as a cop and one year as a high school English teacher before finding her way as a writer. She was also briefly a private investigator, because why not? Erica Ruth reviewed mysteries and crime fiction for several years at publications such as *Publishers Weekly*, the *Los Angeles Review of Books* and *Mystery Scene Magazine* and is a member of both Mystery Writers of America and Sisters in Crime. She is from Milwaukee, WI.

Alan Orloff has published thirteen novels and more than sixty short stories. His work has won an Anthony, an Agatha, a Derringer, and two Thriller Awards. He lives and writes in South Florida, where the examples of hijinks are endless.

Gigi Pandian is a *USA Today* bestselling author and locked-room mystery enthusiast who's been awarded Agatha, Anthony, Lefty, and Derringer awards, and been a finalist for the Edgar. Gigi writes the Accidental Alchemist mysteries (humorous mysteries with a touch of magic), the Jaya Jones Treasure Hunt mysteries (lighthearted adventures steeped in history), and the Secret Staircase mysteries (locked-room mysteries called "wildly entertaining" by the *New York Times*). She lives in Northern California with her husband and a gargoyle who watches over the backyard garden. Learn more and sign up for her email newsletter at www.gigipandian.com.

Leigh Perry, who also writes as Toni L.P. Kelner, has published seventeen novels and two collections, and has co-edited seven anthologies. She won the Agatha award for Best Short Story, and her short fiction has been nominated for the Anthony, the Macavity, and the Derringer. She wishes that Goldenrod Court, the setting for this story, really existed so she could go visit, but she'd be happy to skip the murder.

Delia Pitts (www.deliapitts.com) wo
rked as a journalist before earning a Ph.D. in African history from the University of Chicago. She is a former university administrator and U.S. diplomat. Her newest novel, featuring a Black woman private investigator, *Death of a Ex,* was published by Minotaur Books in 2025. Her mystery, *Trouble in Queenstown,* was nominated for a Shamus award. Delia has also published several acclaimed short stories, including, "The Killer," which was selected for inclusion in *Best American Mystery and Suspense 2021.* Delia is an active member of Sisters in Crime, Mystery Writers of America, and Crime Writers of Color.

Marcia Talley is past-president of Sisters in Crime, Inc. and served on the national board of Mystery Writers of America. She divides her time between Annapolis, MD and a quaint, Loyalist-style cottage on Elbow Cay in the Bahamas.

Elaine Viets has written 35 bestselling mysteries. She returns to her adopted home of Florida with her new humorous series, *Sex and Death on the Beach*.
Her other series include the hard-boiled Francesca Vierling newspaper mysteries, the traditional Dead-End Job, the cozy Josie Marcus Mystery Shopper mysteries, and the Angela Richman, Death Investigator mysteries.

Elaine's *Deal with the Devil and 13 Short Stories* was published by Crippen & Landru. Elaine was given the Lifetime Achievement Award at the Malice Domestic Mystery Conference. She's won the Agatha, Anthony and Lefty Awards and was shortlisted for the International Thriller Writers Award. www.elaineviets.com

Crippen & Landru, Publishers
P. O. Box 532057
Cincinnati, OH 45253
Web: www.Crippenlandru.com
E-mail: orders@crippenlandru.com

SINCE 1994, CRIPPEN & Landru has published more than 100
first editions of short-story collections by important detective
and mystery writers.

*This is the best edited, most attractively packaged line of mystery
books introduced in this decade. The books are equally valuable
to collectors and readers.* [Mystery Scene Magazine]

*The specialty publisher with the most star-studded list is Crip-
pen & Landru, which has produced short story collections by
some of the biggest names in contemporary crime fiction.* [Ellery
Queen's Mystery Magazine]

God bless Crippen & Landru. [The Strand Magazine]

*A monument in the making is appearing year by year from
Crippen & Landru, a small press devoted exclusively to publish-
ing the criminous short story.* [Alfred Hitchcock's Mystery
Magazine]

Previous Crippen & Landru Publications

OTHING IS IMPOSSIBLE: *Further Problems of Dr. Sam Hawthorne* by Edward D. Hoch. Full cloth in dust jacket, signed and numbered by the publisher, $45.00. Trade softcover, $19.00.

ALL BUT IMPOSSIBLE: *The Impossible Files of Dr. Sam Hawthorne* by Edward D. Hoch. Full cloth in dust jacket, signed and numbered by the publisher, $45.00. Trade softcover, $19.00.

CHALLENGE THE IMPOSSIBLE: *The Impossible Files of Dr. Sam Hawthorne* by Edward D. Hoch. Trade softcover, $19.00.

SWORDS, SANDALS AND *Sirens* by Marilyn Todd. Full cloth in dust jacket, signed and numbered by the author, $45.00. Trade softcover, $19.00.

HILDEGARDE WITHERS: FINAL *Riddles?* by Stuart Palmer with an introduction by Steven Saylor. Full cloth in dust jacket, $29.00. Trade softcover, $19.00

CONSTANT HEARSES AND *Other Revolutionary Mysteries* by Edward D. Hoch. Full cloth in dust jacket, signed and numbered by Brian Skupin, $45.00. Trade softcover, $19.00.

THE KINDLING SPARK: EARLY TALES OF MYSTERY, HORROR, AND ADVENTURE by John Dickson Carr with introduction by Dan Napolitano Trade softcover, $22.00.

THE ADVENTURES OF THE PUZZLE CLUB AND OTHER STORIES by Ellery Queen and Josh Pachter Full cloth in dust jacket, signed and numbered, $47.00. Trade softcover, $22.00.

THE ADVENTURE OF THE CASTLE THIEF AND OTHER EXPEDITIONS AND INDISCRETIONS By Art Taylor   Full cloth in dust jacket, signed and numbered, $47.00. Trade softcover, $22.00.

A QUESTIONABLE DEATH AND OTHER HISTORICAL QUAKER MIDWIFE MYSTERIES by Edith Maxwell. Full cloth in dust jacket, signed and numbered, $47.00. Trade softcover, $22.00.

THE KILLER EVERYONE KNEW AND OTHER CAPTAIN LEOPOLD STORIES By Edward D. Hoch with Introduction by Roland Lacourbe. Full cloth in dust jacket, signed and numbered, $47.00. Trade softcover, $22.00.

SCHOOL OF HARD KNOX Edited By Donna Andrews and Greg Herren and Art Taylor Full cloth in dust jacket, signed and numbered, $47.00. Trade softcover, $22.00.

THE SKELETON RIDES A HORSE AND OTHER STORIES By Toni LP Kelner Full cloth in dust jacket, signed and numbered, $47.00. Trade softcover, $22.00.

THE WILL O' THE WISP MYSTERY By Edward D. Hoch Introduced by Tom Mead Full cloth in dust jacket, signed and numbered, $47.00. Trade softcover, $22.00.

Subscriptions

Subscribers agree to purchase each forthcoming publication, either the Regular Series or the Lost Classics or (preferably) both. Collectors can thereby guarantee receiving limited editions, and readers won't miss any favorite stories.

Subscribers receive a discount of 20% off the list price (and the same discount on our backlist) and a specially commissioned short story by a major writer in a deluxe edition as a gift at the end of the year.

The point for us is that, since customers don't pick and choose which books they want, we have a guaranteed sale even before the book is published, and that allows us to be more imaginative in choosing short story collections to issue.

That's worth the 20% discount for us. Sign up now and start saving. Email us at orders@crippenlandru.com or visit our website at www.crippenlandru.com on our subscription page.